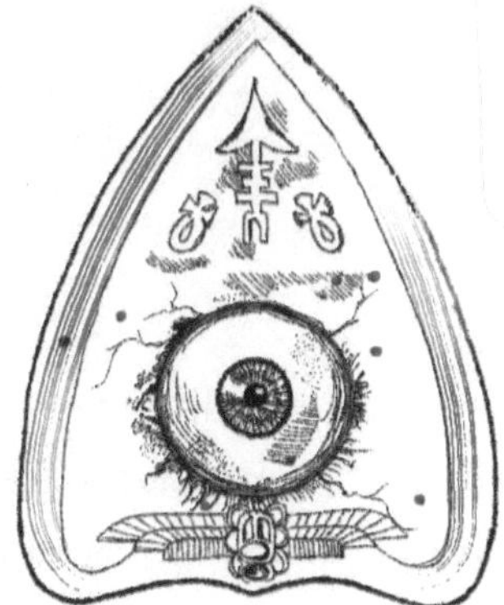

Hereafter Lies

Book I

R.I.P.

Elijah B. Wilder

BOOK I

R.I.P.

To Mel, for believing in me, and to all the stories
lost to oblivion for want of belief in them.

A perfect and passionless levelling was no more palatable an idea in the hereafter than it was on Earth. The desire to surpass caused a man like Reilly to build a tomb like the Pharaohs of ancient Egypt, to brood all his life about death, to live continually trying to find ways of preserving his property and status in the gray uncertainties ahead.

Immortality, Inc.
Robert Sheckley

Lord, what can the Harvest hope for, if not for the care of the Reaper Man?

Reaper Man
Terry Pratchett

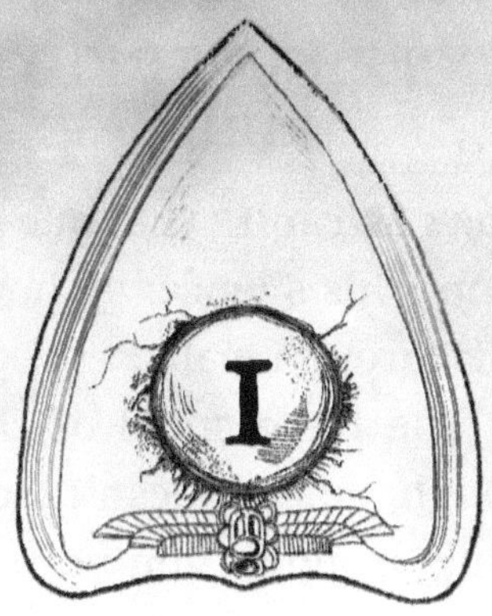

A man who makes no echo is less than alone, and his foot steps make no sound on the linoleum. There must be a hundred doors in these halls but none of them has what he needs. Not when he needs it.

He checks a door.

Nothing.

He checks another.

Nothing.

He checks another.

Overturned desks and scattered books are a hopeful sign, but nothing appears. He reaches the second-to-last door and runs through it, not sparing a glance for the source of his silent, beating-drum panic. Other footsteps now. He stares at the chalkboard and waits, willing this to be the one he needs. Options are running low.

In the end, it is what he needs, just when he needs it—as always. If only the news were better.

None of the broken pieces of chalk scattered on the floor move, but a looping, chalk line emerges on the board all the same, drawn from the dust around it. The footsteps get closer, the panic higher. His dry sob goes unheard as he reads what, deep down, he always already knew:

THEY'RE HUNTING YOU.
RUN.

But he can't. He *knows* he can't. That one brute fact is confirmed by the voice that interrupts his silence: "Where are you?"

If only he could walk through walls.

He closes his eyes. The fresh smell of chalk tells him another message is coming through, but he doesn't look. If it's telling him to keep going, keep running, begging him not to give up just yet—no. He can't see that.

He has given up.

"Are you there?"

What can he do in the face of the whole world? Not just one but *two*? Whatever the writing had told him in the past, whatever he'd been desperate and lonely enough to believe, it just wasn't true. He is alone, here at the end. He always already was.

The door opens.

A last glimmer of fight he didn't even know he had gives him just enough will to say, "*Memento mori—*"

"*Vale?*"

The voice sounded from the other side of a wall. And Agent Deja Vale, for all his talents, couldn't walk through walls.

"Vale," that voice repeated.

Deja jerked forward when the train turned. Chugging, rattling sounds suggested what eyes soon confirmed: No strange hallway, no cryptic chalkboard, no warnings disguised as promises that he didn't understand beyond the sense of betrayal. Just the mahogany benches and paneled walls of the Styx train. The compartment looked warm and inviting yet also very, very gray. The only interruption was the subtle green glow of the gaslight lamps swaying with a *creak...creak... creak...* overhead. Wren, Deja's old teammate, was staring at him from the seat opposite, face hidden by a white mask—gossamer thin but utterly concealing. Even so, the mask was no more effective at cloaking her tension than the large, black hood draped across her shoulders. Not from him.

The train turned again and shadows swelled within clouded windows behind her, bleeding into the blackness of her uniform jacket. Ten eight-inch iron nails strapped to the thick belt at her waist broke up that encroaching dark. They glinted green in the gaslight of the lanterns above them—just on their pointed tips polished by use. Wren counted them with light piano-taps of white-gloved fingers, probably not even aware she was doing it. Tether nails were purely functional, sure: but as a fashion statement, they'd be right at home at a Slipknot concert. No point saying so. Nobody else on this train even knew who that was.

Then again, he wasn't really sure why *he* knew who that was.

"You all right?" Wren asked. "You were pretty zoned out."

Deja gave her half of a smile before resting his head against the window once more, eyes barely open. "I'm fine," he said. "Why wouldn't I be?"

Wren huffed a laugh at that. "Why indeed."

"You, on the other hand," Deja said, "*you* worry me."

"Oh?"

"Oh, yeah." Deja's voice softened with arch sympathy. "And not just me"—Wren scoffed but Deja pressed onward—"people talk, you know. Hereafter's a small place. It's theoretically *infinite,* I guess, but you know what I mean: small-town vibes and all that."

"You know," Wren said, "half the time, I have *no idea what you're talking about?*"

Deja's right cheek hurt; it'd been that long since he'd smiled so much. It wasn't even that wide of a smile—and just on the one side too. Good gravy, that was a depressing fucking thought.

As if she could read said depressing fucking thought, Wren said quietly, "Just... take it easy." Deja's brows went up to say *Really?* and Wren's shoulders sank a bit. "You know what I mean. *Relatively* speaking." Deja opened his mouth and she headed him off, "Relative to the *situation,* Vale. Not relative to *you.*"

"Wren," Deja chided. "When in the history of my sterling, uneventful career have I ever done anything but take it easy?"

"So reassuring," Wren said, not at all reassured. Somehow, her sigh managed to sound even less reassured than her sarcasm had. "Rest up, Vale." Before Deja could protest that he had been doing just that before she'd woken him up (more or less), she added, "Consider it a personal favor. For old time's sake."

Deja gave her a small smile and an even smaller nod, and Wren relaxed—as well as she could, anyway. She was so short that slouching was out of the question with all those nails strapped to her waist. Wincing himself, Deja shifted in his own seat and took inventory of old pains. Abdomen still achy? Check. Eyes still feel like they're going to pop out of his skull like twitchy deckhands jumping ship? Check. He suppressed a grimace at the sudden stab in his right hand. It went as quickly as it came. Pain was a poor substitute for memory, but it was what he had. That, and the comfort of knowing the whispers drifting from the other end of the compartment were real, and that wasn't nothing in these trying times. He double-checked, just in case. Yup. Real agents whispering real whispers. Catty ones, too. Another stab in his palm. Seemed gratuitous at that point.

Wren was taking inventory herself. But now that she was done counting nails (consciously or not), she was counting people—sizing them up. They were all Omega agents, but they weren't exactly a team. Lear, Wren, and Deja were, if only half of one: the unlucky remaining three. Lear sat slumped to Deja's left, arms folded across his chest and head lulled back, pretending not to be listening to everything happening around him (which he absolutely was). For all his grumbling anytime somebody tried to keep him updated or—Reapers forbid—get him *involved*, he balked. Scoffed. Murmured nonsense words under his breath peppered with the odd colorful phrase. But he was known to seek the sub-frequencies of chatter out, too.

Like Wren, Lear's face was hidden behind a white mask, but both faces may as well have been bare to Deja's eyes, both determined to make what must work *work*. Wren's face pivoted *ever so slightly* to the next object to be inventoried: the rookie agent beside her. The movement was just a ripple in the gaslight.

Deja'd bet his augur this was the kid's first mission. Unlike the others, her mask was neatly folded upon her lap, protectively cradled in white-gloved hands. She was so focused on *looking* like an agent that she looked more like a child playing dress-up. Her posture was rigid, the lapels of her black uniform jacket laid perfectly flat, large hood folded neatly over her shoulders. Contrast that with Deja's own jacket, which was scuffed to the point of graying. Deja frowned and brushed some dust from his shoulder. No wonder. He hadn't worn the damned thing for half a year.

The train veered to the right and the lamps swayed with a *creak* to the left in time with the gently leaning agents who moved as unconsciously as experienced horse riders.

Another *creak* overhead. Another really-there whisper from across the train.

Deja triple-checked to make sure.

"Demented-level six. In a brand new, single-family suburban home."

Yup, still real.

And still catty.

"Tell me that's not insane." That whisper belonged to one of the agents from the other team just joined to what remained of Deja's through an unwilling marriage. He couldn't remember her name; he only knew her team had been just as decimated as his own this past year.

"Pretty standard these days," another whisper pointed out. That agent's name was Tyre or Joy or something like that. No. Troy. *That* was his name. Deja vaguely remembered him. *Why* he remembered him, he had no clue; dude was half as interesting as a saltine and probably twice as useless in a crisis. Then again, that sheer basicness was, in and of itself, something of an accomplishment and thus pretty memorable. Deja twisted his mouth and tried to recall the woman's name but couldn't—after his time, maybe? He wanted to say it started with a *B*.

She sure sounded like a real *B*.

"And they wonder why we keep losing agents," provisional-ly-B-something said grimly. "This is what happens when we aren't there."

Probably-Troy sighed, tired. They were all tired. Agents were stretched thin. Even the saltines among them. "We are here."

"I mean Omega *South's* not there, you absolute tool," B said. "And it looks like we're finally getting their overflow up North, aren't we?" She didn't bother to hide her occasional, lingering looks Deja's way—the Odd's way—each one charged with resentment and scorn.

She was one of *those* agents, then.

Well, at least she was in good company. Deja didn't look over at Agent Good, the man keeping to himself in the opposite corner. He didn't need to look to know what Good was doing: keeping his eyes closed, mentally preparing himself for the mission ahead. He'd be running and re-running over every bit of minutia in the case file he'd have studied closer than anybody on that train. Certainly closer than Deja, who'd only been allowed a quick glimpse before getting dragged out of his Osiris recovery room and onto this mission last minute. But if agents were spread thin, Odds were spread even thinner. So, here he was.

Funny. Deja didn't think Good had been on Omen's team with the other two agents who'd stopped their whispering. Or Crane's, the masked head agent seated like a stone sentry at the head of the compartment, silent and staring on the rookie's other side. Good had been leading his own team, last Deja heard. Guess that made this an unwilling marriage of *four* families. Deja chanced a glance at him. Good was already masked up. As if activated by Deja's eyes, Good's gloved hand went to the silver mortifier holstered at his hip, checking it was still there before retreating. Then, his face turned to meet Deja's gaze.

Thing was, Deja wasn't the only Odd on that train. Good had an Oddity all his own—a truly remarkable gift. And yet with that gift, Good carried the heaviest burden among any of Omega's resident freaks.

That man alone possessed the arcane ability to project *resting bitch face* while wearing a mask.

And he was doing it now.

For old times' sake, Deja gave Good the victory and looked away first. He let his head fall back against the window and stared dead ahead. All he could see was the suggestion of scenery rippling beyond the windows. A hush fell over the agents, sudden and thick. The creaking, rumbling thrum of the train held the agents' tense silence the way a spouse holds onto old slights—just waiting for a reason to let it break out. *Wanting* a reason.

"You good?"

The rookie agent started at Crane's deep voice. She had that deer-about-to-be-roadkill look in her eyes. The only motion on her face was the occasional twitch and shake from the train carrying them. Her deep gray skin glimmered green in the gaslight—the sole glimpse of color that face had ever or would ever see.

"Yes, Head Agent Crane," the rookie said.

Crane told her, "Just remember your training and you'll be all right." As the rookie nodded, the train passed through a stretch of buildings like they were fog, casting them in total darkness. Both the mask on Crane's face and the one folded on the rookie's lap glimmered, taking just a second too long to disappear from sight. That glimmer returned before anything else, heralding the reemergence of the train into something like light.

Crane's arms were folded across her chest now. The rookie's were held stiffly at her sides, gloved hands gripping the edge of the seat. What had been a wooden bench was now frayed moquette in a pattern of confused circles. She recoiled and moved her hands to her lap—found chewed gum, probably... if she was lucky. Fluorescent lights flickered. The words FUCK REGAN stood above her head like a thought bubble, etched into the cloudy window with ballpoint pen.

The moment the scenery shifted, Deja'd reflexively leaned forward to support his arms on his knees instead. Just like Wren,

Lear, and Good had done. There was a tear in the cushion beside him. Somebody had carved into it with pencil again and again until it went threadbare. He traced over the words with a finger: I WANT TO CHANGE IT ALL. Then he spotted the loose thread on his white glove and picked at it until he felt eyes on him. He looked up.

The rookie hurriedly looked away to stare at an unfortunately mobile-looking puddle of something on the grimy rubber floor. Deja raised an eyebrow. "You gonna give me a name, kid? Or am I gonna have to keep calling you 'rookie' in my inner monologue?"

"Oh," the rookie said, rubbing a hand over her neatly braided black hair. "Izik. Agent-trainee Izik." She offered a handshake across the narrow train car. When Deja just stared at it, she promptly withdrew it with a mumbled apology.

"Don't apologize to him," Crane said, eyes fixed on Deja. "His head doesn't need inflating."

Lear deigned to be social just long enough to say, "Vale gives everybody shit, don't take it personal." He'd know, to be fair.

"My head's fine," Deja said. "Got it checked special and everything, just for you. All shipshape. Cleared for duty."

More or less.

They passed through a block of buildings, and the subway car faded away only to reemerge in the gaslight, wood, and polished metal of an earlier age—minutes and decades removed from their own. Green light rippled over Crane's mask like sun on a pool floor. Her tone was as stony as her posture. "Go back to Osiris and get it checked again," she said.

"Stop gaslighting me, Crane," Deja said. This pun didn't garner so much as a groan—the nonliving lifeblood of all puns. He threw up a white-gloved hand. "Oh, c'mon! Don't you—"

"No," Lear grumbled. "Nobody sees what you did there, Vale. Nobody *ever* sees what you did there." He sniffed and leaned back against the seat, confident there probably wasn't chewed gum or piss soaking into the nineteenth-century cushion. "Why are you here again?"

From his lonely corner of the train, Good said, "I was just wondering that."

Deja rubbed at the dully throbbing scar on his palm through the white glove. "Honestly? Same, buddy."

Good fired a masked glare across the carriage that managed to take his usual resting bitch face and raise it two-and-a-half *fuck-around-and-find-outs.*

Troy—or was it Joy? Toy? Tyre? *Tyre.* No, Roy. No, *Troy.* Whatever. Agent Saltine asked, "Aren't you on probation or something?"

While Probably-Troy had sounded a bit concerned, Wren just sounded amused when she cut in, "For the *second* time?"

"I wasn't on probation, Wren," Deja said. "I was on *leave.* There's a difference."

"Both times?" Wren asked with polite interest. Deja didn't need to see the mischievous twitch of a smile beneath the mask to know it was there. "As I recall, you really earned that first one."

"Allegedly," Deja countered. "I still deny everything."

Lear snorted. "So you *didn't* set Agent Good on fire?"

Deja opened and closed his mouth a few times, then admitted, "Okay, well, yeah. A *little.*" At the horrified look on Izik's face, he added, "*Allegedly,*" and gave the wide-eyed rookie a reassuring nod. In his defense, that had been ages ago—long before they'd even made full agent. There'd been a debate over just how spirit-charged the fire they'd encountered was, so Deja'd experimented with his teammate's arm. You know, the way you'd use a drop of batter to make sure the pan's not so hot it's going to burn the pancakes.

The pan, it turned out, had been too hot for pancakes.

Allegedly.

From the other end of the car, Agent Good (who clung to old grudges the way catastrophic breakfast failure clung to a non-non-stick pan) said, "Fuck you, Vale," before lapsing back into his characteristically moody black crepe of silence.

The carriage around them brightened to match the lightened mood (give or take one pissy little pancake in the corner). Wood paneling gave way to sleek plastic and polished steel. A map of tangled routes and mathematically impossible schedules lit up a pristine wall. The little green light denoting their location in the chaos moved from one stop to the next, and a mechanical bird chirped cheerily overhead.

"All right," Crane said. "Almost there. Let's gear up."

On cue, the agents began their pre-mission rituals. Crane pulled the shining, silver augur from its designated chest pocket. She gave it a quick polish with the heel of her white-gloved hand and replaced it; the chain swayed a moment before stilling. Deja'd bet she'd keep up that habit even if it really were just the innocuous pocket watch it'd been fashioned to look like. A few seats down, Wren took stock of her tether nails for the umpteenth time. Good just stood, straightening his long jacket and managing to look pissed while he did it. All of them checked the silver augurs tucked safely in their chest pockets. All of them checked the mortifiers holstered at their hips, pulling them out to examine its glass chamber and the green fuel swirling within. Wren gave hers a sharp tap with the heel of her hand like that might inspire the faint fumes to form the denser, liquid-like gas it used to be—*should* be.

Deja, whose mortifier had yet to be returned to him, checked his bootlaces. Still tied. Izik, who was too green to have any pre-mission habits yet, just watched and waited, hands tucked neatly beneath her thighs. Her routine needed work. She'd have to find a habit other than checking her bootlaces, though. That was Deja's thing now.

Lear approached Crane. He lowered his voice but not quite enough to avoid Deja's keen ear; unlikely it was *Deja* he was worried about listening in. Tact wasn't his strong suit. "Look. Vale was on my old team and he's a solid agent," he murmured. "And I'm happy to have the pre-mission repartee back, but why was he tacked on last minute? I didn't think this mission called for an Odd." He cast a sidelong look at the rookie.

Crane straightened the sleeves of her stiff, black leather jacket. Like the rest of them, her uniform jacket was knee-length and pretty simple, except for the large, black hood that was functional as much as it was a throwback. But as the head agent, her left lapel was marked with a small silver crescent—less a moon than a scythe without a handle. "Don't worry about it, Agent," she said with an edge of warning. "Just hope you don't have to be grateful he *was*."

But in saying so, Crane only voiced the thought which had them all antsy: If the mission called for resident freak Deja Vale getting plucked from his leave early with next-to-no notice, no rookie had any business being there with them. If Deja had to guess (and since he didn't have time to read much of the case file, he sort of *had* to), he'd say this ghost didn't have any apparent connection to this family, this house, or even this neighborhood. And when a trauma or an attachment couldn't explain that senseless, unending echo, it spelled bad news.

One of only several Odds left at Omega North getting prematurely yanked out of leave spelled *worst* news.

Lear didn't bother saying what they all knew. Like the others, he adjusted his mask to make certain it was secure. Once the black hood went up, his face disappeared to untrained eyes. It was a shape in the nothing that might denote *something*, but only if you looked out of the corner of your eye. Unless, of course, you were one of them.

All agents were masked now. All except Deja. As his gaze skipped over the others, masked faces shifted away from his bare one. Then, each checked their gloves and masks again. Any time an agent noticed someone else doing it, they did it too: falling dominoes of smokers reaching for a cigarette after watching Cary Grant light up on screen. Deja checked his thick, blacker-than-black glasses—far too dark to reflect his own face. Shiny, pristine lenses, unscuffed side guards, and unwarped temples were no comfort. It was a new pair. Untested. Always made him nervous, but not quite nervous like the others were. Some agents had issues with Odds, but most had an issue with *him*. Because his fears looked nothing like theirs.

He dearly wished they did.

A second chirp overhead and the train slowed to a stop. The eight of them stood before the closed doors, rocking slightly until momentum released them. As Crane raised her own large black hood, her featureless face eyed them each in turn for a standard equipment check. Deja brushed his black hair from his face only for it to flop back down again. He was all too aware of Crane's lingering look as he slipped on his glasses and *only* the glasses. Still, Crane said nothing as she checked the rookie's uniform. Twice. Another check of the others. Then, a third check of the rookie.

It wasn't overkill. That uniform was the only shield between the living and them: The nonliving whose every sense screamed, *YOU SHOULDN'T BE HERE.*

But neither should the ghost terrorizing 6 Hemlock Avenue. So, here they were.

Once Crane was satisfied, she nodded, turned back to the door, and raised her fist. After a deep breath, she gave it—

Three.

Sharp.

Knocks.

The train door opened to the Desert of the Living, and they braced themselves against the screaming light and heat of the quiet, suburban night.

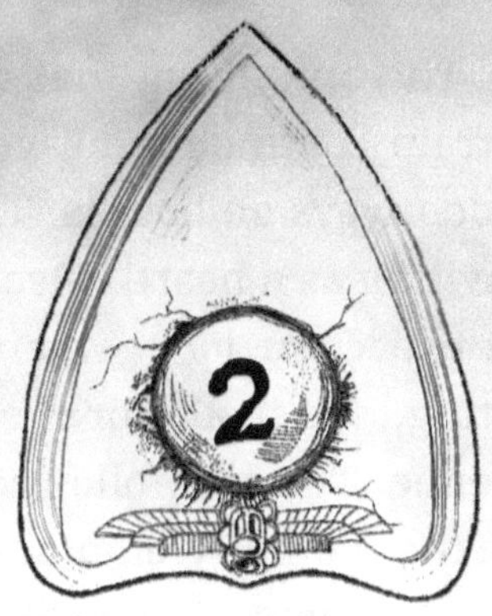

S even black-hooded figures stood on the hazy street, staring up at Deja on the train. Thing was, this was his first time back in the Desert in six months, and he had *no clue* how this was going to go. Head Agent Crane had brought spare gloves and masks, right? She was responsible. That was the sort of thing she'd do. It was the sort of thing *he* was supposed to do, too. He patted his jacket pockets to check for a—

"Hurry up, Vale," Good said.

"Yeah, yeah, I'm coming, pancake," Deja mumbled, still searching his pockets. Ignoring Good's tart, *"The fuck did you just call me?"* and Troy's confused, "What's a pancake?" Deja confirmed that his glasses were secured tight, held his breath.

He took one step... his augur thrummed gently within his chest pocket as it worked to keep him connected to the train and safe from the caustic living world.

Two steps... the moon's heat prickled on his cheeks.

Three steps... the smell of rotting leaves teased like the ghost of perfume from a sofa's second-to-last occupant.

Four steps... boots touched asphalt—more or less.

Deja let out his breath. He'd been half-expecting the road to swallow him up like lava. There was no color to the world—not yet. His glasses were working. The quiet suburban cul-de-sac was far more visible to him than to his fellows, but it was still cloaked by a persistent gray haze. The only thing that could pierce it was the faint green steam the train continually heaved onto the street, and the distant outlines of doorways on houses. They glowed around the edges: faint, gold, as inviting as a hearth. Beckoning to them.

Crane gave Deja an expectant look; when he nodded instead of spontaneously combusting, she made for the distant glowing rectangle of 6 Hemlock Avenue. The rest followed. Deja's steps faltered when he walked out of the motherly embrace of Styx train fog, but he kept going to the porch. There, Crane stopped. Listening. As she did so, Izik discreetly reached out a hand and touched the wall to the right of the glowing door—solid. When she noticed Deja watching her, she rapidly retracted it.

"Okay," Crane said. She nodded to the agent a full hood shorter than the rest—at least. "Wren? Get that tether field up. And keep it tight."

Wren put a hand to the wide belt of tether nails at her waist and pulled one out with a high, metallic note like a song. "Always do."

"Take Lear with you," Crane said. "And remember, this is a demented-level *six*. I don't want any agents alone for *any reason*. Understood?" They all nodded. Crane watched Wren lead Lear back toward the street before asking those who remained, "Ready?" Another collective nod. Crane stepped through the door like it was less than fog. Good and the newcomers followed, but the rookie hesitated.

Those rookie-nerves eclipsed Deja's own, so he gave her a gentle push between the shoulder blades and whispered, "Just stay away from me and you'll be fine." Izik went stiff; Deja gave her a wry smile and explained, "I'm a notorious shit-magnet."

Izik let out a feeble laugh, but she stepped inside all the same. Deja followed to find her standing, stunned, in the hallway. He gave her a firm poke in the arm and led the way to the kitchen where the others had already assembled. They'd all read the file. Well, Deja assumed everyone else had read the file. He'd read as much of the file as he could while being shepherded onto the train by Agent Inquisitor Vex before he could so much as finish his coffee after having been unceremoniously snatched from his Osiris recovery room. His request for his mortifier had just gotten him an unimpressed look and a pair of nightsticks he hadn't even used since training. Off the top of his head, he recalled something about "Clown," "Family of..." *a number*, and "Newmarket, Ontario." "Clown" had seemed like it just might be the operative word in that fleeting glimpse of case file, but Deja couldn't say for certain. AI Vex, the beautiful old bastard, had taken Deja's coffee, thus rendering his judgment questionable at best.

Deja mournfully eyed the ghost of an expensive-looking espresso contraption on the polished marble countertop and the gratuitous, second coffee machine beside it. The rookie was completely oblivious to the fact that she was standing partially inside of both. What was a somewhat blurry shape to Deja may as well not exist to the others. It was always curious to him just what agents could navigate in the Desert without issue: doors, hallways, fireplaces. They glowed to their eyes, subtle but inviting. Walls did not. In some ways, walls were even more of a barrier to them than they were the living. Because unlike them, a living person could always just grab a sledgehammer and force the issue. Walls. Doors. Hearths. There was something primal about those things, maybe. Something so deeply embedded in the primordial consciousness that rodents, insects, wind, and sound—even *ghosts* could figure them out.

But not kitchen counters and not coffee makers.

"So catch me up here," Deja said to Crane. "You and Good are the only ones with chime-capable augurs, yes?"

"Yes."

"And it's a family of five?"

"Four," Crane corrected.

"Slightly better," Deja murmured. "They home or...."

"No. Got scared off to a hotel."

Good scoffed. "Did you even read the file, Vale?"

Deja stared at Good. He'd have sure *liked* to have read the file, but that wasn't exactly an option. No explanation would satisfy Agent Grumpy McSourpuss, so—

A deep *hum* beneath their feet, cradling them. That sudden sense of sinking, of there-ness, swallowed Deja's question. A glance through the glowing glass door to the backyard confirmed that the train was gone, leaving nothing but a last farewell wave of green steam washing over the yard. Its grounding presence was no longer needed.

Lear stepped through the glass, and Wren followed with six fewer nails on her belt, saying, "Tether field's up. Just inside the property line. About a quarter acre." That size didn't give them much space to maneuver, but it made the tether field strong—standard practice for anything above demented-level three, and this was a *six*. They wouldn't be able to move beyond the territory staked out by those six nails until the train came back, but neither would the ghost.

In theory, anyway.

"How much time?" Good asked. Man was clearly having trouble adjusting to no longer being a head agent himself; Crane's sharp glance Good's way told Deja she was thinking much the same thing (and probably far less charitably).

"All goes as planned, three hours," Wren said.

Good nodded. Deja could just about hear his internally grumbled: *Because things always go as planned.* Troy nodded his own simple-saltine understanding; he and his fellow import surveilled the area, hand on their mortifiers. *Sine*—that was her name. Deja had no clue how he knew that, but when did he ever? Lear scoped the hall while Good kept his focus firmly in the kitchen. Curious eyes were still on Deja but darted away the moment Deja glanced Izik's way.

"We've got one OWL planted for us," Crane said. "Refrigerator."

"Right there behind you," Deja said as he took inventory of the vague shapes he knew from experience to be picture frames. "Well," he corrected when Crane turned and ended up standing halfway inside said refrigerator, "*in* you." The curious and persistent fly of a stare buzzed against his cheek. He sighed. "Yes, Agent-trainee I-already-forgot-your-name?" he asked, kindly.

"Oh! Izik. And it's just, um..." Izik hedged.

Deja withheld his sigh. "Please just spit it out."

"Sorry, just—you're just—I mean you—why aren't you—*how* aren't you wearing"—Izik gestured to her own masked and hooded face—"*anything?*"

Agent Good pushed past Deja, tossing out a "Because Vale can't pass up an opportunity to remind us all how much more *special* than us he is," over his shoulder before peeking out the door to the backyard.

"Thanks for that absolutely necessary commentary, Good," Deja said. "You're really on fire with these burns today." To Izik, he added, "Allegedly."

"Stop messing around, Vale," Crane said, "and do that thing you do."

"Well," Deja said, "even with the glasses *on*, I can tell you these people have way more kitchen appliances than one family of four *not* running a panini-and-cappuccino side hustle could possibly need."

Deja ignored Troy's hot-pressed confusion over sandwiches. He couldn't see Izik's eyes go wide, but he could hear that they had. "You can *see?*" she whispered. "I knew about Odds who could do stuff like that but never—that's—*really?* You can *really see?*"

"You're connecting the dots," Deja said. "It's gonna happen for you any minute now, I can just tell." After a moment, he added, "Proud of you," and gave Izik a quick pat on the shoulder.

"*Vale,*" Crane warned.

"Sorry, sorry," Deja said. And he was sorry—well, relative to his own scope of *sorry* which admittedly wasn't much. He cleared his throat and looked around, doing his best to ignore the masked eyes still boring into his neck. He really, *really* wished the first time he used his Oddity in six months *wasn't* under this level of scrutiny, but here they were. Odds must and all that. He took a deep breath, closed his eyes, slid his glasses down his nose and—

Light, brighter than bright, *roared* before him. Sounds, smells, tastes—all crackling in a noxious fume. The mild October moonlight filtering through the patio door beat down on his cheeks like high desert sun. He took comfort in the white gloves on his hands and the fact that he couldn't touch the countertop beneath them. No hardness. No cold marble. No sharp lines. The longer he stayed there, reminding himself of his own incorporeality, the better the shapes of his fellow agents came back into focus. Seven swaths of nothingness outlined by the faintest glimmer of *something*. An interruption in the caustic choke of cleaning products. A fruit fly's shift in trajectory. A lack of dust in the moonlight. And in those uncanny pockets of void lurked the prickling-neck feeling of being watched: seven of them. It wasn't much, but it was far more than the living could see. Most of them, anyway.

Crane's commanding voice was now an echo of a whisper that raised the hair on Deja's arms. "What do you see, Vale?"

Deja didn't answer. He couldn't. He hadn't been in the field since the injuries that took him out of it. Even compared to his fellow Odds, how his Oddity worked was something of a particular mystery. Now, he'd say it depended on building up a tolerance to the heat of the Desert, a tolerance he'd lost—

"Omen!"

"Vale."

Snap.

A white-gloved hand *snapped* in front of his face—Good's. He was staring at him, silent and expectant. For whatever reason, he looked far clearer to Deja's eyes than the others. Maybe because Good was closest. Maybe because he'd known Good the longest. Or maybe Good's expressive masked-resting-bitch-face Oddity was truly just that powerful.

"Yeah," Deja said. "I'm good. Well, *you're* Good; *I'm* fine." At Good's glare—the glare Deja could always see through the mask—Deja mumbled, "It's fine, I'm looking, I'm doing the thing, everybody relax, I'm *fine*."

Good stepped back with a muttered, "Idiot," while Deja looked around. The other agents were clearer now, too. Around them was a tidy but lived-in kitchen furnished with the newest appliances. Sleek black surfaces were marred with tiny fingerprints and the streaks of a hurried attempt at cleaning. Deja stood near a large kitchen table flanked by two benches, one with booster seat. Atop the table was an unopened pumpkin carving kit and one large pumpkin so perfectly round and smooth it might've been wax. The walls had been painted the same gray as the adjoining living room where the fireplace glowed. Its inviting light was gone to his now unshielded eyes, but it would still let him through. Where some might have put a wallpaper border, these people had opted for their children's artwork: A mish-mash of paper shapes and sizes made uniform by a dozen identical, black frames. They'd even framed the macaroni art. Somehow. For some reason.

One half-finished drawing awaited the return of its artist on the table. A child's vision of Halloween. Time would tell if it was good enough for the wall or fridge. The bar seemed pretty low. Purple-crayon bats looked more like winged French bulldogs and the pumpkins were perfectly circular. The only thing that gave it away as a pumpkin patch and not a tangerine patch were the little ghosts: cartoonish, white, and smiling. Deja huffed a grim laugh.

But kids old enough to handle a crayon weren't exactly worrying. At least, not in the way the stacked boxes in the corner were. High chair, car seat, an industrial-scale order of diapers sized for a newborn, all shiny and new. That meant Potential life: A new life waiting to be born and ensouled. It was exactly what ghosts craved—what drove these trapped echoes to such demented violence. If a Potential was in the household, that would certainly explain why the ghost was there, *and* why they'd been sent to neutralize it. Deja liked to think that sort of thing would be in the case file, but he was also a raging cynic. Still. No sense in causing a panic just yet. There were a dozen reasons that new baby stuff could be there. The family could be hosting a shower, or preparing donations, or making utterly unnecessary online purchases to fill the void. But the fact that he—an *Odd*—had been pulled last minute from a leave of absence that was meant to last much longer made him uneasy. Either way, wherever this ghost was, they needed to find it and contain it.

Fast.

"Mrrrrr."

A low whine on the verge of a growl. Deja spun around to find a fluffy white and orange cat with great amber eyes seated on the counter, slit pupils expanding and contracting, bobbed tail twitching. *Shit.* Why had he turned? Why did he have to look the thing in the eyes? He was a senior agent! Why was he the one making the rookie mistakes and not the fucking what's-her-name rookie? *Aisa? Leeza?* Those thoughts cycled on repeat while he struggled to break through the paralysis enough to speak. "Nice kitty..." he pleaded.

Good said, "File didn't mention a cat."

Deja breathed out a weak laugh, eyes fixed on the little menace of the in-between. "Who said anything about a cat?" Good's pissy stare carved a distinct shape into the void and Deja added, "I mean, yes, it is a cat. I'm just, you know"—he swallowed hard—"kind of *immobilized* right now and trying to ease the tension with inappropriate humor. Like I do."

No barrier between worlds was thick enough to mute Good's derisive snort. "Not your best work."

"Thanks, dear."

The cat stared at Deja, unblinking. The ghost of its amputated tail flicked lazily against the dishwasher. Each brush of spectral orange fur against aluminum was sandpaper against Deja's eardrums.

"Where is it?" one agent asked with thinly veiled panic. "What's it doing?" Deja couldn't guess who at this point. Not with that jet engine purr going off six feet in front of him.

Good's voice was distinguishable amidst the roar of threatening cat noises, central heating, and 60-watt lights. "What does the Augury say? Anything?"

"I haven't been taking secret chimes since we've been here, Good." That'd be Crane, probably. Context clues.

"Should I chime them?" Good again.

"You and I are the only ones with chime-capable augurs—don't waste it." Learning that in addition to Crane and Good being the only ones capable of sending communications to the Augury, they *also* had a limited number of chimes allotted to them might have been more surprising to Deja, were he not currently held in ocular deadlock by the reigning feline-staring-contest champion. Which he was.

"Keep the cat distracted, Vale."

"You bet!" Deja obliged as if looking away was absolutely an option he definitely had and he wasn't helplessly paralyzed by feline eyes. Unfortunately, unique gifts came with unique weaknesses: Cats' tendency to pick him out of a lineup of a hundred agents and keep him there was just one of them. And unlike his fellow agents, *he* wasn't protected by a mask. That it was a vulnerability he shared with ghosts was not a bit of irony lost on him.

He really hated irony.

If he got out of this intact, he was going to be having very strong words with whatever idiots compiled that case file he didn't read. Unless he only thought he'd read "clown" and it'd really said "cat." In which case, he was still right. Absolutely the most important word in that case file.

Something flickered. Feline eyes shifted, and so did Deja's, free from their hold at last. Just as the rainbow of magnetic letters pinning report cards and crayon doodles to the huge black fridge began wiggling. With a meow that ripped the very fabric of reality, the cat hopped daintily from the counter and walked off, bobbed tail in the air. It padded down the hall and out the cat door, bell collar clanging like Notre Dame (if Notre Dame were run by sadistic Slipknot enthusiasts).

Deja waited. He counted six of his hesitant breaths, then slid his glasses back up. "It's gone."

The collective relief was as palpable as Deja's sensory calm. He blew out a breath. With the glasses on properly, the cacophony of the Desert was still there but manageably contained. Like the paper jungle landscape pasted to the back of a reptile's habitat: translated by camera and viewed through two panes of glass. The others couldn't even see that much. Hence Lear standing in the middle of the kitchen table with a pumpkin sticking halfway out his ass while he watched the Otherworldly Letters emerge to his sight on the refrigerator, charged by the endless reach of the Augury. That charge made them glow faintly green—a glow Deja could see far better now his glasses were back on.

The magnets made OWL wriggled fitfully. New butterflies emerged from their pupae, figuring out how to pump their wings. Then, a red *M* dragged across the black door... followed by an orange *I*... a pink *N*... and a green *D*.

"Whoa," *Liza? Iza—Izik!* whispered. It would be *Izik's* first time seeing Otherworldly Letters in action.

"Yeah, they're handy," Deja agreed absently. "Doesn't always work out so well, though."

Izik leaned closer and asked "No?" in a hushed voice.

"No. They teach you about Alphabet Crunch? Or Word-i-O's?"

"No," Izik said while the letters continued to sluggishly collect themselves on the fridge.

Deja could've sworn those things used to be faster. Based on Wren's impatient sigh, he wasn't alone. "Well," Deja explained, "rumor has it all that alphabet-themed food had a bit of Augury influence behind it. You know... Eye work."

Izik leaned even closer. "Really?"

"Sure thing," Deja said. "Supersecret marketing outreach and branding division: interworldly, highly classified. Mind you, the Alphabet Crunch isn't *bad*—pre-milk, anyway—but the pasta shapes in all that tomato sauce hardly ever pan out and they stain these"—he held up a white-gloved hand—"like a motherfucker once they're charged."

"Huh! I didn't know there was a—"

"Slower than usual," Lear observed. "They even gonna make it?"

"Shh," Sine hissed. "Just be grateful they still send us *these*."

Wren scoffed. "Oh sure, it's a real comfort. I always feel so informed and prepared these days." She gave her augur a rueful glance. Hers couldn't even send two-way communications anymore. Yet another security precaution.

Lear said, "Hells, I'm just grateful it's right *here*." He turned to Wren. "Remember that Colorado mission two years back? The hotel with the twins? We had to check room after room after room...."

Troy muttered under his breath, "Well, if *Omen* were still here, we wouldn't *need* to rely on just augurs for communications... or one measly OWL."

"Well, Omen is *not* here, is he?" Wren said. "So keep your thoughts to yourself and focus on your job so we don't lose any more Odds, maybe."

"Everyone, shut up," Good snapped as the letters continued their miniature migration. He pointed at Deja. "Especially *you*."

Deja opened his mouth to protest—

"'Mind the cat,'" Crane read.

Deja closed his mouth. Sure enough, that was indeed the colorful message on the fridge:

MIND THE CAT

Lear deadpanned, "Timely."

Then, the pink *A* in Cat shifted downward, followed by *N, D, T, H, E, C, L, O*—

The letters stopped. Some lost their green glow. A pink *C* fell and landed with a pathetic *clack* that only Deja could hear. They all stared: Deja at the fallen letter on the floor, the others at the place it had fallen from.

"'And the *clo*?'" Wren read, frowning. "Or '*Lo,*' now, I guess?"

Troy tilted his head. "Clod?"

Sine snorted. "Only clod we need to be warned about is *you*."

Ignoring this, Lear offered, "'Cloud,' maybe?"

"He–e–e–ey, kiddies!"

All eight agents spun toward the living room archway. There stood a ghost dressed in full clown regalia and hitting every creepy-clowny note from the frayed, orange plastic hair and peeling red nose to the stiff, balloon-fabric pants and polka dot tie. And because this thing had an eye for detail, the red makeup surrounding its mouth and eyes had been smeared to look less like an exaggerated smile and more like a hospital floor where something terrible had happened. When it tilted its head, Deja could make out the sickly green flash of decaying skin. It could barely conceal the jawbone glistening beneath.

A sound like distant metallic hooves—cutlery rattling in the drawers.

BAM!

The drawer shot open and hit the tile floor with a deafening clatter, but not before eight spirit-charged knives—one for each of them—*flew* through the air and embedded themselves in the wall opposite. A warning shot. Unlike the uncharged furniture the agents had been walking through, it was a shot that could *land*.

Crane pulled her silver augur from its pocket and turned it to display the raised *Omega* symbol. "Spectral Presence 780-224-gam-ma-zed, you are unlawfully occupying this residence. By order of the Omega North Inquisitorial Authority, you will surrender your haunt or risk mortification!"

The clown placed its hands jauntily on its hips and tapped its oversized shoe with a stupid little *squeak*. "Naughty, naughty! Bruno's not gonna get *caughty*."

Deja's face contorted as he echoed silently, "'*Not gonna get caughty?*'"

The air shifted once the clown began to rise from the floor—yet another glaring omission in the case file. In sync, all agents took a step back. Even though they hadn't been working as a unit long, four years of identical training guided all eight agents into a defensive formation on instinct. Eight hands hovered at eight holsters on their hips. Of course, Deja's hand found no mortifier. The nightsticks he found there instead weren't much comfort.

Troy warned, "All right, we got a flyer!"

"What gave it away?" Deja asked, interestedly.

Out of the corner of his mouth, Good demanded, "Can you *please* turn it off for twenty fucking minutes, Vale?" When Vale didn't respond with characteristic sarcasm disguised as chagrin, Good's voice lowered. "Vale?" He'd known Deja long enough to take that lack of snark as a very bad omen.

The others couldn't feel it. Not yet. But Deja could.

Someone living was home.

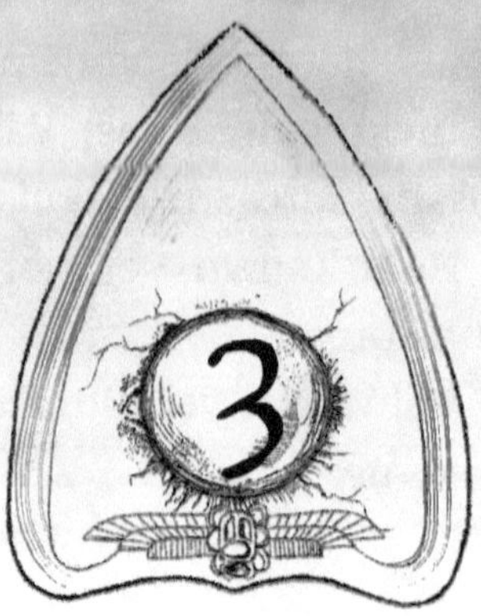

"Cover me," Deja told Good. Once he slid his glasses down his nose, Bruno faded to a vague, angry mist. He could just hear the first words of Good's mortified complaint and another questionable clown rhyme before the sounds of sheer life overwhelmed his focus. The roaring thrum of the fridge, the nattering rustle of leaves in the wind outside. He wanted nothing more than to pull up his hood, turn tail and *run*. But he didn't. He only moved backward through the archway leading to the foyer. As he got closer, his steps took on the rhythm of a beating heart—a *particular* beating heart—and he couldn't have done otherwise if he'd tried. He'd learned long ago not to bother.

A metallic scratch.

A feminine scoff.

The burn of hand sanitizer.

Good backed into the hall to shield Deja from what had just become The Action. He whistled, then Izik was with them too. He may have been a bit of a prick, but the man was known to make the occasional sound judgment call.

The front door opened and a woman in her mid-to-late thirties pushed her way inside. Living energy swelled around her like a storm. Deja held his breath and forced himself to focus. His augur, an agent's last line of defense against lifeburn, heated up with the exertion of shielding its wearer. It had been half a year since Deja'd set foot in the Desert of the Living, and he doubted his tenuous recovery was helping matters. He did have a mask tucked away in his jacket—*pretty* sure he did, anyway—but if he slipped it on now, he may as well not be there. So he forced himself to do what only he could.

He looked.

Deja could just see the woman's head over the mass of shopping bags in her arms. Red hair was done up in a messy bun that was too perfectly imperfect to have taken less than twenty minutes. He could respect that. Life crackled against his eyes like fumes off boiling vinegar, and he turned away to watch her through his peripheral vision. In the archway, Good raised his mortifier, prepared to defend the area. A quick tilt of Deja's head and a glance through his glasses told him Izik's own stance was solid and unmoving, grip on her own mortifier just as steady as Good's.

"I know you don't, but I'm not—no, listen," the living woman said into a device Deja couldn't see, tone as clear as a newscaster's despite the surgical mask covering her mouth. "I—*you* listen. *You* may be satisfied with hotel coffee, but I'm not. Alissa doesn't exactly make *bank* saving puppies from bored nepo-babies' designer purses or whatever the fu—*fudge* she's doing in Buffalo, so least we can do is use that Nespresso she got us, all right? And hey! We were real loud when we called Father Martin!" A pause. Then, a judgy pause. "*So-o-o-o* maybe the poltergeist or Babadook or whatever heard that and got scared off? Like when you just *threaten* to call the cops, you know?"

Over his shoulder, Deja told the others, "They already called a priest."

The woman wrinkled her nose. "No, Matt, we are not *calling your great aunt Rhonda for help*." A forced breath. "Well, I don't give a shi—a *sugar* if she's a professor of corgi puppies and magic fat-burning bagels! You *know* she creeps me out!"

Good hissed a curse; Deja was with him. Priests tended not to be helpful in these situations. Unless by *help* you meant an additional mountain of paperwork once shit inevitably went several blocks of sideways. Judging by the perplexed vibe Izik was giving off, this was a bit of practical knowledge not covered in training these days.

"What *kind* of priest?" Good demanded like Deja'd been the one to call them.

Deja tilted his head, listening while he watched the woman out of the corner of his eye. Anything more would be begging for a sensory overload headache. He scanned the area for information. There were dozens of framed family photos. Deja's brows went up at the sight of the one closest to him: A cheap, white frame with a Polaroid of a crotchety, stone-faced woman with long gray hair standing next to a child. Both seemed to be there under duress and only for long enough to take a photo. Tucked behind it was a postcard addressed to "Matt et al," sent by Aunt Rhonda all the way from Peru. To its right was something Deja hadn't expected to find in a house with such bland decor: A hand-carved mask covered in flaking gold and red paint. It was hard to make out, but he could tell the thing was old. *Very* old. The whole lot—frame, postcard, and mask—had been hung behind a large potted Ficus. Or maybe the plant had been added after the fact in the hopes of never having to actually *look* at the things that filial obligation had left hanging there.

Deja stepped through the plant and left the odd mask behind. A few frames over hung a far larger picture of the Virgin Mary (*not* hidden by a plant), and beside that was a wedding photo—a *cathedral* wedding. The religious knickknacks (Deja spotted four in the foyer alone) looked relatively new. Hauntings would do that to people.

Any confrontation with mortality would, really.

Deja didn't need the confirmation in this white-bread house, but the woman gave it anyway as she dropped the bags unceremoniously to the floor. "I know you do, babe, but he didn't just baptize me, he baptized my *whole family*, for Christ's sake." She swore under her breath, looked up apologetically, and made the sign of the cross over her chest. At least, that's what Deja'd guess she was doing from his limited vantage. A spontaneous fit of Macarena seemed unlikely.

"Catholic," Deja said through a half-laugh, half-sigh of relief. "*Possibly* Episcopalian? Or Anglican, I guess. Either way, we got plenty of time."

Someone Deja could only deduce to be Izik through the distortion of the Desert asked, "Why's that?"

Deja winced at the shrieking sounds of maniacal clown laughter which the living woman behind them was completely oblivious to. *For now.* "Never exactly in a rush, are they? That, and a lot of times these 'exorcists' still insist on using Latin for some reason, whatever Santa or whoever the fuck says otherwise."

The longer Deja looked at Izik, the clearer she became to his eyes—even over the glasses. "So?"

"So," Deja said, "do *you* understand Latin? *At all?*"

Izik hesitated. "I don't think so?"

"Me either, so don't worry about it," Deja said over the living woman's annoyed phone farewell. He groaned once he spotted her unladen (yet very-much-*not*-unladen) figure. One hand tugged off her mask. The other was pressed against her back like it was the only thing keeping her upright. "On second thought," he said mildly, "scratch that bit about plenty of time."

Deja'd been wrong about "clown" being the most important word in that case file. "Expectant" would've been the red-letter word—had it *been* there. *Stupid.* He should've known. Living presences were always difficult to negotiate, but this was so, so much worse. He'd figured it was just the added strain of his injuries or the lack of exposure these past six months, but the almost unreal swell of the woman's stomach fit to burst through her (formerly) oversized U OF T sweatshirt said otherwise.

"She's pregnant," Deja whispered urgently.

"What?" Good said in a tone that made it clear that *no, that had not been in the file.* "*How* pregnant?"

"*Pretty fucking pregnant.*" Deja slid his glasses up his nose. He debated pulling up the hood too. He could already feel the tug of Potential life like an area of low pressure sucking in cold wind from all around it.

And *he* was cold wind.

Izik's composure cracked. She was mumbling under her breath now, pointing her mortifier toward the kitchen archway with a grip so hard it made her arms shake. Good grabbed her wrist. "Have you completely forgotten your training? We've got a confirmed Potential. *Deflecting shots only.* Got that?" When Izik didn't respond, Good said, "You're an Omega agent. That means you were chosen—just like the rest of us. *Act like it.*" Izik nodded and Good finished, "Go tell the others. *Quietly.* And remember, deflecting shots only. We can't risk any drift."

Once Izik ran off, Good pulled his augur from its pocket so fast the silver chain might've snapped. He popped it open and the raised Omega symbol burned white. Good's masked cheeks shone with the green-tinted light of the Hereafter as he held the augur to his mouth. "We've got an unexpected Potential situation. Please advise!"

Deja couldn't hear the other side of the communication. No one but Good could. But the situation was this: Ghosts couldn't be allowed anywhere near an emerging Potential life. Neither, for that matter, could agents. If the process had gotten this messed up, and that baby was born without a designated soul delivery, it would start pulling in spirit-particles from all around with zero regard for whether or not those ensoulments had been signed off on or not. That meant any agent making a shot powerful enough to mortify Bruno would be risking drift. Stray spirit-particles from the disinte-grated ghost would get sucked into that Potential life because that's what Potential life *did*: attract spirit—however broken or demented it was. Agents themselves couldn't ensoul new life because, unlike ghosts, *they'd never died*. They'd never lived. They were *chosen*. But they could still be pulled by Potential life. Even *broken* by it. All too many agents had been lost to oblivion that way, disoriented and sucked out of tether like a hapless swimmer pulled beneath the waves by an undertow and drowned. Those agents didn't end up in the new life. They ended up *nowhere*.

Oblivion.

So, saying the lack of warning re: the Potential life was an over-sight was *quite the understatement.* The fact that Deja had zero interest in getting close to life that raw was just shit-syrup on an already shitty pancake, but he couldn't leave. This baby-onboard was likely what drew a demented ghost to this house in the first place. That Potential was Bruno's one hope for something better than clowning around suburban Toronto and spiraling deeper into rhyming insanity for all of eternity.

The Augur snapped shut in Good's palm and Deja met his gaze. "Well?" Deja asked.

Good didn't respond immediately. His shoulders were tense. Deja repeated the question, and Good answered, "They aren't patching us through. Said to stop wasting chimes when we're on heightened security watch." His tone became more frustrated with every word he added. "But they did remind me that *if* the Potential wasn't in the case file, it's because it's not *due* yet."

Deja rolled his eyes. "Yeah, because babies only ever arrive right on schedule."

"You don't need to tell me, Vale, all right?" Good said and slid his augur back into his pocket.

Deja shook his head, perplexed. What was the good of allowing two agents on scene to maintain chime-connection if they couldn't even get past the bureaucratic gatekeepers in the Warren? The three remaining Omega headquarters, including North, were still shook by the attack on South. Communications had been tightened up even before Deja'd been forced to take leave. Apparently, they'd gotten even tighter since he'd been gone.

Security be damned. If agents couldn't get the information they needed, there was no reason for them *or* Omega itself to exist at all.

Good was a solid agent, but he wasn't going to force the issue. He had too much respect for the chain of command. Deja eyed Good's chest pocket and the chain dangling there. The tether field was tight. It would be enough to keep Good grounded. At least, it would be once Deja got that Potential life out of this house, and he could do that far more ably with the extra protection of dual augurs.

"Cat's back," Deja said.

"What?" Good demanded. "Where?"

As Good spun around, Deja slipped a hand into Good's pocket, unchained the augur and let it drop, stopping its fall with his boot. He kicked it behind him and stepped on it with his other foot just as Good wheeled on him with an accusatory, "I don't see it."

Deja shrugged. "Well, that would mean it doesn't see you either, so... small mercies."

"You—"

Both froze. Trapped not by cat, but by the same horrible recognition. They could all feel it. The pull of life like warm, wet air sucking upward into a gathering of cold, dead cloud. A tornado waiting to happen.

Good said what didn't need to be said. "Potential incoming."

The panicked gasp of the woman as her phone cut out and her water broke only added to the whole redundancy of the comment. The shriek of the clown in the next room was just the worst exclamation point they could've asked for. Deja closed his eyes against the sudden burst of vertigo. It was so severe, he strongly suspected the second augur under his boot was the only thing keeping him upright. "We need to hurry," he gritted. "Grab the kid and watch the door."

"And just what the hells are *you* going to be doing?"

"The sort of shit Vex keeps getting pissy at me for," Deja said, already slipping off his glasses and tucking them into his pocket. The second he did, the strain on his own augur burned against his chest like an overtaxed engine. Good's was a hot coal beneath his heel.

"*No.* Absolutely not."

"You two need to stay on that archway and cover us," Deja said. "We need to get the Potential out of this house and past the tether field. I'm the best option, and whatever issues you have with me, I *know* you know that."

Just as Good opened his mouth to argue, a sharp gust of air blew into the hallway, and the woman shrieked in mixed pain and terror. He nodded once. "Hurry," Good said. "And keep your distance."

"Will do."

Bruno honked and cackled from the living room, and the woman went stiff. Terrified. She'd heard it, too. But she didn't hear the sharp whistle and hissed, "*Izik!*" from Good in the archway.

"Oh, you have got to be fucking kidding me!" the woman cried, leaning hard against the stair railing. "I *hate* clowns! They are so fucking *tacky!*" Okay, so it was less terror and more a sense that her conception of a just, sensible world was being grossly violated in the most inconvenient way possible. Again, Deja could respect that. Reflexively, he reached out when she slipped to the ground with a *crunch,* then recoiled at the scalding life-force his gloves were ill-equipped to handle. So he just watched her growl in frustration as she dug out the cracked smartphone from beneath her ass. She stared at it a moment then wailed, "Oh my God... I'm so *fat!*"

Before Deja could so much as question this woman's priorities, the warning prickle that prey animals felt ghosted over his shoulders. In the reflection of the wedding picture, Good was drawing his mortifier and leveling it; the paltry fuel within the glass could still splash his white gloves with green. For a moment, a stupid little moment, Deja thought that weapon was being pointed *at him*. But then the ominous air swelling in the kitchen archway dissipated in a flurry of crumpled receipts, shopping lists, and crayon doodles of friendly ghosts in patches of perfect pumpkins.

Without glasses filtering out the chaos of life swirling around them, Deja couldn't see the clown much better than this woman could. But if she'd gone so far as to call a priest in this century of Our Science, he'd wager even she'd seen *something* before tonight.

Over her shoulder...

In the shine of the espresso machine...

A laugh heard between sleeping and waking....

Another bad sign. This ghost was willful. *Strong.* The vague feeling of unease paired with white-knuckled readiness told Deja that Izik was back in the hall with them. But now, Deja was too wrapped up in focusing on *not* focusing on the swelling storm of unadulterated *aliveness* before him to confirm it. Their augurs could only absorb and deflect so much. The clown in the next room made a sound far too elated for Deja's tastes and he made his decision—Fatima gambit it was. Vex would give him shit for it, but fuck if it wasn't effective. Well, effective on the sorts of people who considered calling some guy in a curtain to perform an exorcism a reasonable move, anyway.

Deja pushed down what little self-preservation instinct he had, plucked up Good's augur, and knelt two feet beside the woman. He already felt stuck to her like a fly in hot honey. He stared down at his gloved hands—still intact. Had he been Izik, the lifeburn probably would have been breaking apart his fingertips already. He forced his protesting eyes back to the living woman. Moisture plastered once immaculately arranged strands of red hair to her face. If Deja were alive, he was certain he'd be sweating with strain just like she was. He could make out the freckles speckling her terror now. She held onto the railing above her for dear life with one white-knuckled hand while the other clutched the pendant around her neck. Her eyes were shut, face screwed up like a child determined to ignore this nightmare until her mother came to wake her up.

"It's too early," she whispered in a panicked litany, "it's too early, too early, too early—"

The moment Deja spoke, her eyes snapped open. They were blue.

You still got it.

"I am the angel you prayed for," Deja whispered, praying to whatever the fuck it was people prayed to that this lady was the praying sort. And he did this all in an English accent because, for whatever fucking reason, Canadians responded better to that. At least in this province, anyway. It was just another thing on a long list of stuff that Deja found himself knowing that no other Omega agent did. The woman went very, very quiet and held her breath. It was when she closed her eyes again that Deja knew they had a shot because she closed them softly this time, surrendering herself to a higher power. Of course, she was actually surrendering herself to an *adjacent* power.

Her hand unclenched from the locket to rest atop her swollen belly instead. So she was the praying sort after all.

Desperate people always were.

"Listen to me"—Deja glanced at the cross-and-name-engraved locket resting in her sweat-puddled clavicle—"Stephanie. You must be stronger than you have ever been. You must leave this place of evil, *now*." While Stephanie struggled to form words beyond choking coughs of panic, Deja tried to remember just how an English dude would say the word "been." *Bean*? *Ben*?

Stephanie spluttered a half-sobbed, "I can't! I can't even *move*, are you fucking *kidding* me right now?" Blue eyes went wide. "Oh my God, Mr. Angel Man, I am so sorry that was so fucking ru-u-u-ude!" Words disintegrated into a pained shriek and Deja winced against the force of it.

"God asks nothing of you beyond your reach," Deja said over the wooziness blurring his vision and making his left side feel far hotter and far heavier than his right. He checked his hands again to count his fingers. Five and five. But there was a thin spot in the fabric where the lifeburn was already eating through. A hint of gray skin peeked through fraying fabric.

"How can I?" Stephanie demanded between panting breaths. "I'm in fucking *labor*, I can't just—just—*ahhh*!"

Deja threw up a hand in frustration. "Because she's fucking *God*, all right?" he snapped, un-Englishly.

Stephanie went still. "Wait," she said with such levelness Deja began to suspect she'd been faking labor this whole time just to get out of gym class. "God is a *woman*?" Her eyes narrowed. "Weren't you *Australian* a second ago?"

Deja ignored that last question. "She's *God*. She can be whatever the fuck she wants. Now make like an Adidas commercial and just fucking *do it*, all right?"

"That's Nike—"

"I swear to God, Stephanie—"

"Okay, okay!" Stephanie flashed him an apologetic look that, frankly, could've been a little more apologetic given the supposedly angelic recipient. Her lips pursed in determination and she gave a single nod. "I can do this. I can. I can do this!" She looked around hopefully and added, "With a little heavenly help, maybe?"

"I'm not going anywhere," Deja said, wincing. Bruno cackled and a house-shaking *BOOM* sounded from the kitchen. He cleared his throat delicately. "And neither is Bruno the Hell Clown, so let's amp up the sense of urgency here, all right, Steph—?"

Another *BOOM*. Deja and Stephanie both looked to the archway. *She* saw nothing. *Deja* saw Good yelling at somebody to stay focused.

"What was that?" Stephanie demanded.

"Nothing, they're fine," Deja said quickly. "Let's go."

"Huh? *Who's* fine?"

Deja ignored the lecture Izik was now getting from Good and told Stephanie, "Nobody." But as soon as the word left his mouth, Bruno's shrieking rhymes became distressingly clear: "Coffee's a dream with sugar and *screams!*" Deja glanced back at the archway just in time to see the coffee maker in the kitchen become a coffee maker in the living room. When he turned back, he found blue eyes as wide as his own swelling sense of doom.

Apparently, Stephanie's eyes had been wide with indignation. "Was that my *Nespresso?*" she demanded through a shriek.

Deja glared at her. "Priorities!"

Stephanie nodded and tried to push herself up only to wail in pain yet again. Just then, an ear-piercing metallic *eeeeEEEE* rang from the kitchen. They both watched the oven drag across the floor before launching itself at the agents in the living room beyond. Bruno cackled, "Circus and snacks are on the attack!"

Instead of pointing out how that last rhyme was a bit of a reach, Deja said, "Right. We need to go. *Yesterday.*"

But the moment Stephanie attempted to push herself up, pain kept her down. "I can't, I can't, I *can't!*"

"You *can!*" Deja said over the clown's threatening rhymes. He muttered curses under his breath and looked around. Standing out amidst all the other white-framed photos—weddings, proms, Halloweens, graduations, more weddings—was a gilded frame of an elderly woman with kind eyes. A single dried lily withered to little more than a fragile ochre wisp and crunchy green leaves had been tied there with black ribbon. Unlike the Ficus-sequestered photo of creepy Great Aunt Rhonda, this one stood front and center. It didn't hang there out of obligation, but love. Grief. Stuck in the frame was a crinkled bouquet card that read:

FUCK COVID.
Love, Alissa

Deja weighed the relative traumas against one another (ghost grandma versus ghost murder clown) and went for it. "Your grandmother is here! The one who sent me. You can't hear her, but she's here. And she loves you so, *so* very much, Stephanie. Her strength is your strength, so use it and *get up.*"

Stephanie stared up toward the general direction his voice was coming from, tears welling in her eyes. She sniffled. "Which grandma?"

"*Jesus fucking Christ*, Stephanie—the *dead one!*"

"Oh right," Stephanie said. "That makes sense." She sniffled again and addressed the ceiling like her wrinkly hamster of a grandmother was taller than the six-foot Omega agent or something. "Grammy? Is that you?"

"Yes, yes, it's her, now *get up!*"

The biggest *BOOM* yet rattled the hall from floor to chandelier. Two more agents backed into the archway separating their little foyer from the kitchen of chaos. "New message was coming through when it threw the fridge," someone said, voice as distant as a departing crow's caw. A second voice passing in the other direction added, "Faster you get the Potential out of here, the faster we can actually *mortify* this thing!"

"Yeah!" Deja said, gesturing to the panting woman. "I'm clearly working on it!" He cursed under his breath and watched Stephanie struggle to push herself up. The frustration of not being able to touch her, to give her just *one little push* was killing him—figuratively speaking. "Come on, come on, *come on*," he muttered as her sweat-slick palms squeaked their way up the wainscoting. Once she was up, she clutched to the banister like a young squirrel waiting out a storm on a branch. *Reach...* step. *Reach...* step. *Reach...* step. After a lot of panting and twice as much swearing, her hand finally clasped the front doorknob. "Come on, Steph. You got this."

"I got this," Stephanie echoed. "I got this, Gram."

Finally, the door was open. Stephanie supported her weight on the polished brass knob a few moments before stumbling onto the front porch. Just as she made to sit, Deja told her, "No, keep going! Get to the street."

Stephanie gritted, "You want me to give birth in the fucking *street?*"

"Oh, I'm sorry," Deja said, placing an ironic hand to his heart. "Did you want to turn around and give birth on a nice comfy couch while a *psychotic clown ghost* helps you out with your *breathing?*"

Stephanie considered this a moment, lips pursing to a pout. "No," she murmured, and waddling operations resumed. She made it to a patch of leaf-covered grass halfway to the empty, suburban street before collapsing to her knees. "I *can't*—"

"It's all right, it's all right," Deja said. "We can make this work, just stay calm. You know... relative to your whole"—he waved a hand vaguely at her—"*situation.*" He looked around, twisting back and forth. "Shit, where's your phone?"

"Inside."

Deja threw his head back and shouted, "*Goddamnit!*"

"You swear an awful lot for an angel."

Deja leveled her with an unimpressed look she could not see, but it didn't matter. His tone got it across. "Got a wide sample size, do you? Huh, Stephanie? Meet many angels at *Pilates*, do we?"

Stephanie's lips pressed to a tight line. "Hot yoga. It's better for my back." When the angel didn't dignify that with a response, she mumbled a petulant, "*No.*"

"What about your neighbors?" Deja asked, eyeing one of the six iron nails containing the gently shimmering tether field just within the yard's borders. He couldn't risk touching it. Too dangerous. It took a certain sort of agent—a very skilled, very *brave* agent—to do tether work. Wren was one such agent. Deja Vale was not. He looked to the two nearest houses in the cul-de-sac of cookie-cutter Neo-Colonials, both safe beyond the tether field's reach—beyond *Bruno's* reach. One had half-assed Halloween decorations, but the other was so elaborately decorated that Deja started to wonder if they hadn't gotten ballsy with a Ouija board and summoned this clown fucker themselves. That did happen sometimes.

String lights decorated both porches. None of them were on. "Where are they?" Deja asked.

"Camping," Stephanie gritted between pants. "The Kemps, anyway."

"Seriously? It's *October*."

Stephanie rolled her eyes. "I know. They're the worst. Bully us into buying Girl Guide cookies every year... like they're not gonna outsell every other kid in the troop already because Kelsey works as a receptionist at a bariatric surgery center and always sells out the back of her *Te-hehs-hehsl—*" Her eyes clenched shut as she struggled to finish and failed, cheeks puffing up to power a growl more menacing than any cat's.

"Fuck," Deja muttered, scanning the area for a dog walker or something. Across the street from the household of overly competitive neighbors was another white house with string lights lining the porch. Garbage bag ghosts fluttered where they'd been strung from the trees. At least, he assumed it was ghosts. The bags, being pale purple, spoiled the effect. He could smell the caustic artificial lavender scent from there. A huge Canadian flag on a comically tall pole flapped fitfully.

But there was also light upstairs, rippling and blue. A TV in the dark.

"Who's that?" Deja asked urgently. "Next to Jenny Craig?"

"Mrs. Chapman," Stephanie groaned between rapid breaths. "She's, like, a hundred and not exactly all there upstairs."

"Yeah, well, in my experience, people 'not exactly all there upstairs' tend to be the most help in these sorts of situations," Deja said mildly. He looked back and forth between Stephanie and the twenty-odd yards separating her from Mrs. Chapman's grocery-store-cleaning-aisle of a property.

"Maybe?" Three panting breaths. "She did use to be an army nurse or whatever, but the smell of those bags makes me wanna puke."

Deja brightened a bit. "Army nurse? Really?"

"Or maybe navy, I don't fucking *know*! It's how she met the admiral, all right? Who is dead and cannot help, by the way, *Mr. Nosy-wings*."

"Okay, okay, I got it. Shut up and keep your knees squeezed together or something." Deja pulled Good's augur from his pocket and popped it open with a click. Not much happened. "Oh, shit, right," he mumbled and slid his glasses back on to reveal the ghostly green vapor spilling from his palm and the agitated voice halfway through demanding, "*—already have your orders, Agent Good! What is it now?*"

Deja scoffed, turned to Stephanie, and lowered his glasses just long enough to say, "If you could hear the sass this woman was serving me, Stephanie? You would be demanding to speak to a manager *as we push*, I guarantee it."

Stephanie sniffled. "What woman?"

Deja blinked at her. She'd probably had enough metaphysical-crisis fodder to last three lifetimes, so he only said, "Don't worry about it," and pushed his glasses back up. "*Please* just listen! I've got an emergency here with a—"

"*Wait a bone-picking minute. This isn't Agent Good!*"

"No," Deja admitted, "I'm afraid this is the *opposite* of Agent Good—*fuck!*" The omega on the augur lit up white-hot, and he dropped it with a hiss to the grass. He swore again when he realized what was about to happen. With an elaborate string of curses at everyone from the Augury to tailless cats and Jenny Craig, Deja plucked it up and flung it in the general direction of the porch. It smoked and chirped menacingly before exploding into a pile of ash, scattering with the last dregs of Deja's faith in Hereafter bureaucracy.

A misplaced augur was a hell of a sin for an agent, but that particular purgatory of paperwork would be Good's problem, not Deja's. Good was a top agent. He really ought to have been keeping a better eye on his equipment. That happy thought was pushed from Deja's mind by the life burning against his side and the shouts from inside the house followed by the CRASH of breaking glass—

A coffee maker sailed through the air... then landed on the lawn and came tumbling toward them before wobbling to a pathetic stop six feet from Stephanie. Under her exhausted, crestfallen gaze, a large part that looked like it just might be important fell off. She made a dejected little sound. "My Nespresso," she said lamely, her hopes and dreams shattering behind her eyes like a coffee maker through a window. Deja looked up at the Nespresso-shaped hole in the less metaphorical window. Lights flickered within. No, they weren't coming from inside. They were reflected on the *outside*. Mrs. Chapman's porch lights had turned on. Red and purple splashed fitfully across the white siding of her house.

But even if the Augury *had* deigned to grace them with more Otherworldly letters, that couldn't be an OWL—not so far outside the tether field. It was just a confused old lady with electricity on the fritz. She'd probably tried to plug them in but couldn't do it firmly enough to get the thingy to stick in the outlet. Deja glanced over at two of the iron nails Wren had meticulously driven into the front corners of the yard—just where they were meant to be. OWLs couldn't reach outside that boundary any more than he or Bruno could.

And yet, there it was—speaking to him in rap code. One or two letters might be a coincidence, but not *five*. Not six. Not *all of them*. Maybe Vex had been alerted to the communication breach and intervened—gotten on the Augury's ass to protect his agents. That would explain why the message was coming in the rap code only taught to agents, *and* why it was coming at all.

It still didn't give him a *how.*

Which only left one possibility, really. It was just a possibility Deja didn't want to face and it left him scrambling at implausible theories instead. But he had to face it. Those lights weren't really flickering. It had been months since he'd been dogged by voices, sights, and smells that weren't really there. That progress may have held up within the walls of the Hereafter, but under the duress of the Desert of the Living, his recovery had proven faulty. His still-fractured mind was creating messages where there was only silence, same way it had after he'd first woken up in Osiris only to be told half his team was gone—and he wasn't. He'd known it was too soon to be going back into the field. But when Vex had shown up and handed him his augur, Deja'd let himself hope he'd been wrong.

He hadn't been.

Deja forced back his sigh and glanced down at Stephanie. Her sweaty brow pinched as she looked around in confusion at her angel's sudden silence. Any moment now, that confusion would give way to the realization that she'd been abandoned, then to sadness, then to terror. But why shouldn't he abandon her? He couldn't help her. He couldn't help his team. He couldn't remember that last mission, but he was certain he'd have tried to help them—knew from the three wounds that agents Vyne, Ivy, and Thorne had torn from his world that he'd failed. Miserably.

Just read it. What could it hurt?

Deja's mouth tightened. With one last look at Stephanie, he determined to save his maudlin internal spiral for the train ride home and looked back at the impossible message flickering in the lights.

Stephanie's voice was small. "Are you still there—?"

Deja held up a hand she couldn't see. "Shh, hold on a sec." Amazed though he was at just how pissy Stephanie could make relief sound, he ignored her to count raps under his breath. "It's a message." He squinted and translated, "*M... I... N—*"

"What? What message? Where? Is it Grammy? What's she saying? Is Gramp-gramp there, too? And Shadow? And Baxter—?"

Deja shot Stephanie an invisible-yet-effective look and she mumbled an apology (again, not looking terribly apologetic—probably pretty new at this whole devout Catholic thing). He counted blinks, his mind scrambling for the rap code they'd all had drilled into their heads during training. Of course, if his broken subconscious were able to *speak* code, it didn't seem fair that his conscious mind would be struggling so hard to *read* it. "'Mind... the... cat,'" Deja translated. "'Mind the cat.' 'Mind the cat?' Seriously? That's *it*—gah!"

Hardly ten feet away was the cat. It stared at him a moment, sat, lifted a hind leg like it was stretching for a marathon, and began to lick itself. If that impossible message across the street had been merely the product of Deja's addled mind, his addled mind was far better informed than the rest of him. But that revelation could be tabled for later. Right now, he needed to keep that cat from *looking at him.*

"Call the cat, call the cat!" Deja hissed, fighting the urge to step away from the beast of chaos—and Stephanie in the process.

"It's not our cat," Stephanie said. "I'm allergic to cats. We don't have a cat."

Deja demanded, "The fuck did you install a tiny door for? *Feng shui?*" A blank stare. "Whose cat is it, then?"

"Mrs. Chap—*ahhh!*" Stephanie wailed into the darkness.

A door opened and closed across the street. A tiny old lady stood on the porch, squinting into the night. "Sandy, dear?" a feeble voice called. "Is that you?"

"Stephanie," Deja and Stephanie both corrected automatically— Deja unheard, Stephanie through a growl of mixed pain and the dissipation of her last shred of patience for anybody not offering drugs or a new iPhone.

Mrs. Chapman's wispy, white curls glinted red and purple with a second incoming message, and Deja groaned. Again, he did his best to count the flashes over the added strain of Potential life—now *without* the added protection of Good's augur and *with* the rising chaos in the house behind him. He thought he heard Good's yelled, "Where the fuck is my augur?" between the bangs and shouts, but that may have been a guilty imagination. Of course, the subsequent, "Izik! Clock!" followed by a series of unfortunate sounds that just screamed *exploded grandfather clock* made him think he wasn't just hearing things.

Not more than usual, anyway.

"'And... the... crown,'" Deja read in the flickering lights. He narrowed his eyes; maybe he'd been wrong. Maybe he really had been just hallucinating. *Unhelpfully.* "The *crown*?" he repeated under his breath. "Why in the name of Reapers' billowing black ball—"

"He-e-e-ey, KIDDIES!"

Deja took his earlier thought back. Sometimes, your first instinct really was best.

Clown absolutely had been the most important word in that case file.

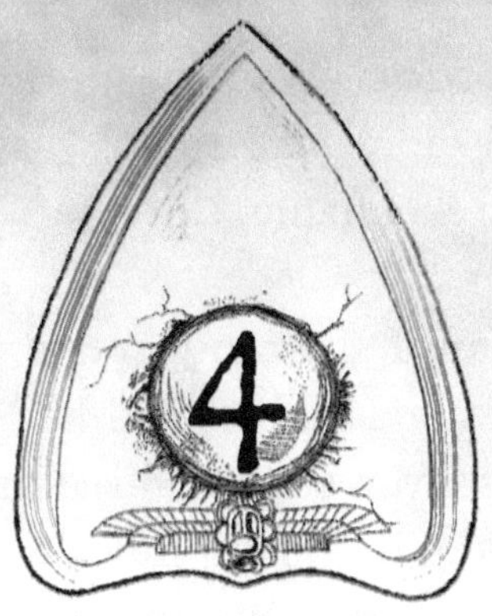

"**B**runo's not *sa-a-a-ad*," the clown called out from a second-story window. "Bruno's *ma-a-a-ad*."

"*Well rhymed.*" Deja sighed and slid his glasses back up his nose. Distantly, he could hear the crunch of the red leaves Stephanie was gripping in her fists. Sense the fear beneath muted groans of pain. She didn't sound hopeless, though. He couldn't see her clearly anymore but he knew she was being brave.

Now, he *could* see Izik. The rookie was on the porch, leaning hard against a column, leg possibly broken (possibly via exploding grandfather clock). Even though she could barely manage to stand, she was waving frantically with one hand and holding a death grip on her mortifier with the other. Given her full-body sigh of relief once Deja waved back, the poor kid must've been waving for some time.

Izik called out, "I can't get closer!"

Deja nodded, not surprised. Even without an injury, a rookie agent had no business getting that close to Potential life. Especially not one so close to the edge of the tether field. The whole situation was a recipe for oblivion. Of course, Deja wasn't much better off. *He* just had next-to-no sense of self-preservation.

Izik yelled, "Crane's pissed you went off on your own and took the Potential outside without clearing it with her!"

Again, Deja nodded. Still not surprised.

"And Good's pissed you stole his augur—"

"Yeah!" Deja called back. "We can run through the list of grievances on the train ride home, all right? Just do your best to keep Bruno, here, away from Stephanie. Got it?"

"Who?"

Deja glared at Izik until she ran through some basic deductions. Then, Izik gave a single nod and leveled her mortifier at Stephanie, eyes focused and steady. Even she could see the living woman now, if only as a swirling nexus of imminent life.

Deja rolled his shoulders and cracked his neck, hoping Mrs. Chapman hadn't gone back inside to finish the Wheel, and had the good sense to call for an ambulance. Or sushi. Hell, he'd take a creepy white van offering candy and kitties at this point. He looked over at the cat. Still licking itself. The ins and outs of just how cats could muddy the waters weren't known. At least, not to agents—fuck only knows what the Augury knew that they weren't sharing with the rest of the class. But what Deja *did* know for certain was this: Potential ensoulment was a delicate business.

And cats had a rare talent for mucking up a delicate business.

As if it could hear Deja's less-than-flattering thought train (and maybe it could for all he knew), the cat glanced up at him, paralyzing him for just a moment before deciding he wasn't worth its time. It daintily switched legs and resumed licking its phantom balls. That suited Deja just fine. Bruno was just as liable to be frozen by that stare as he was. So long as the cat stuck around Stephanie, it became just a little less likely the clown would claim that Potential life. *A little less likely* might just be enough to prevent tragedy.

As Bruno squirmed its way out the window with an incongruously cheerful *honk* and *squeak*, the vague presence of another life approached from behind—fainter than most, but very much there. Deja's augur burned so hot against his chest that when he moved, the skin behind the pocket *stuck*. The absence of his mortifier panged like a lost limb, tingling in grief-struck confusion on his hip. So, he pulled out the weapon he *was* allowed to carry: a super useful pair of nightsticks.

Under his breath, Deja mockingly echoed Agent Inquisitor Vex's parting words, "'You don't need a mortifier, Agent Vale. This is why we work in teams!" He flicked his wrists and the shining black rods extended from one foot to three with a metallic *snick.* The length seemed paltry now that he was met with the prospect of said length being the only thing separating Bruno's demented clown face from his own face. He gave one an experimental toss to reacquaint himself with the weight and continued his AI impression. "An agent as experienced as you should have *no trouble* stopping a demented-level-six ghost from ensouling an utterly helpless Potential life with a pair of *useless fucking sticks!*"

So it hadn't been a word-for-word recitation, but he'd caught the gist.

Deja forced his legs to move away from the Potential behind him and back toward the house. Every step away from that swirling life felt like trudging through wet cement. He managed it, but not without cost. The pain in his eyes, hand, and abdomen screamed at him with more force than they had in months. But he did it.

"All right, Bruno," Deja panted, gesturing with a nightstick; the shallow engraved symbols briefly shimmered to life when the light shifted. "I've got a lot of repressed emotions and it's been a real messed up couple months"—also why he didn't think he could be blamed for engaging a ghost like this, but that wasn't super relevant just now and would probably be up for debate later anyway—"We doing this or what, clown?"

Bruno wasn't dissuaded. It sailed downward and landed with a cyclone of spirit-charged leaves on the other side of the yard. It eyed the nightsticks with a leering, smudged grin. Jawbone glinted in the moonlight through the makeup when it chided, "Naughty boys shouldn't have toys."

"Funny you should say that, 'cause that's almost word-for-word what my boss told me this morning."

Red-ringed eyes shifted to the cat. While Deja couldn't sense Stephanie as much more than a weak pulse, the new, un-souled life roared at him like a fast-approaching train. The cat was next to her. If its furious purring was any indication, it was getting some serious skritches.

That smeared clown-smile flickered. "Out of my way," Bruno growled.

Deja's brows went up. "Seriously? You telling me you couldn't find a rhyme for 'way,' my dude? Seems like 'No time to play' would've been low-hanging—*shit!*"

Deja jumped to the side, narrowly avoiding the bright red and white bullet train of pissed off clown ghost spiraling toward him. Once Bruno reached the edge of the tether field, it turned to face him once more, bobbing in the air like a demented pool toy.

Sure would've been nice if agents could fly, too, but that was just an occupational hazard of not being undead, untethered, and absolutely bat-shit insane. Deja moved to stand between Bruno and Stephanie, prepared to hold his ground.

Bruno laughed madly and dove toward him, then careened off at the last moment. A sizzling green burst of mortifying energy sailed past, nearly taking a chunk of Deja's ear with it.

"Watch it, kid!" Deja yelled toward the porch. Something smelled off. He patted the side of his head where the hair was just a little shorter than it had been moments ago. Rumor was mortifiers didn't pack quite the same punch they used to, thanks to dwindling fuel reserves. Such rumors were little comfort when faced with a terrified rookie who was faced with a demented-level-six clown.

Izik called back, "Sorry!"

"Yeesh...." Deja twirled the nightsticks in his hands, gearing up for another pass from the cackling ball of fast-food-burger-wrapper-colored fury. "Any word from the Augury, kid?"

"No! Another message *was* coming through on the fridge before the ghost threw it!"

"Yeah. *I heard.*"

Izik added, "Troy took it full-on! He's knocked out, but Sine says he's fine!" A beat. "Probably!"

"*Great.*" Deja batted at the clown's legs whenever Bruno sailed past. They squeaked.

"Someone should call the police!" said the old woman who'd inserted herself like a terry-robed garden gnome. She was watching the clown sail around the yard with the indignation only old people met with rising milk prices seemed able to perfect.

"No shit, lady, what the hell do you think we—" Deja stopped short and placed a hand to his glasses. They were still on. Stephanie was still absent minus the sense of Potential swelling inside her (and rapidly on its way to being very much *outside* her). And yet, here Mrs. Chapman was, plain as day. "Fuck," he said, "when did *you* die?"

"Die, dear?" Mrs. Chapman asked, blinking in confusion. "Oh, I'm not dead. Now my husband, *he's* dead. Married sixty-four years, if you can believe that. Just coming up on sixty-five when the Corona— oh, here comes that nasty clown man again!"

"Thanks," Deja said through a breath of exertion. Mrs. Chapman was making cooing noises at the cat. "That's your cat?" he asked, shifting his focus to the clown careening around the yard like he was riding on the rollercoaster from hell.

"Yes, this is Mr. Peepers!"

"Of course it is," Deja said. "Think you can do me a favor and keep Mr. Peepers by Stephanie?"

"You mean 'Sandy,' officer," Mrs. Chapman corrected, kindly.

"Yeah, sure. My mistake, ma'am. Just keep Mr. Pebbles—"

"Peepers—"

"Whatever—by *Sandy.*" Deja gave her a pointed look and she gave him a gnarled thumbs-up in return. "And stay away from that baby or I'll"—he scrambled a moment before settling on—"arrest you and your... *cat.*"

"Oh, you don't have to worry about me, officer!" Mrs. Chapman assured him. "I was a nurse with the army! Served—"

But Deja never learned where or for how long she served, because the clown had taken to the skies and looped back toward him, manic laughter and honks trailing behind it like vapor from a jet. Even if

Deja hit Bruno with his nightsticks perfectly, even if Izik managed a singularly perfect shot from the porch (while missing her fellow agent) and mortified Bruno into a million little pieces, there was no guarantee that none of those clown's maniacal spirit-particles wouldn't drift and weasel their way into that Potential—certainly not with Izik's angle. Their best hope was if the clown didn't realize it held all the cards: jokers and all.

"Mrrrrr."

Deja chanced a glance from the bright ball of menace sailing toward him to see Mr. Peepers staring up at Bruno, too, spectral tail twitching dangerously. With a quick check his gloves were on securely and a muttered, "I hate it here," Deja wincingly reached down, grabbed the cat by the scruff, did his best to hold it away from his own body and *hurled* it clownward.

Mr. Peepers sailed through the air with a great *yowl* that sent Bruno skittering toward the neighbor's house with a yowl of its own. Mr. Peepers landed daintily in a pile of leaves where it kicked out its feet and shot an indignant glare Deja's way that paralyzed him for only a moment before stomping off.

Deja wasn't aware he *could* toss a cat until he'd done it, but luckily he could.

"Angel!"

That word came from the living, but the sheer desperation of it pierced the veil between worlds. Deja slid his glasses down his nose to find Stephanie gripping her own spread knees for dear life, face as red as her hair and both dripping with sweat. Mrs. Chapman was kneeling beside her, nearly a whole foot away from her own spectral presence. She was close, too.

"Help me, please!" Stephanie begged, reaching out a shaking hand to nothing. "Hold my hand!"

Deja shook his head. "I can't—I'm so sorry, but—" A roar of exertion choked off his explanation, and that Potential's pull got stronger. An ominous awareness, the sort of primal warning that reminded prey animals just how far down they rested on the food chain, swept up Deja's spine. He forced himself to take three steps back. Each one was a struggle that only made that warning feeling *worse.* But he kept taking those mile-long steps and watched in wide-eyed silence as Stephanie's face screwed up, inflating like a balloon before letting loose a *roar,* and then—

Four things happened in rapid succession.

Mrs. Chapman let out a little "Oh!" of surprise then keeled over. Dead.

A baby slid out between Stephanie's legs to lie in the grass. Silent. Unmoving.

A *crack!* ripped through the air as one of Deja's lenses shattered.

And Agent Good shouted, "Vale! Catch!"

Deja turned, clocked the mortifier spinning toward him and scrambled to catch it. He flipped it around by the trigger and fuel swirled to life within the glass, flooding his gloves with green light. He leveled the weapon, aimed, and fired—just in time to blow apart the screaming clown careening toward them.

The baby cried.

Deja watched, paralyzed, as the mortified essence of what had been Bruno the Clown glimmered in the night before landing in the grass. He searched out the old lady, but she was gone. He lowered his glasses and darted toward Stephanie. She was sobbing with sheer relief, cradling the now *wailing* baby with exhausted arms. Beside her lay a corpse. Deja didn't need to replace his glasses to know where Mrs. Chapman had gone. The essence of what had been the doddering old admiral's widow was now a shrieking, red-haired baby, still tethered to its mother and shining with... birth juices or whatever the hell it was babies propelled themselves out with these days.

Deja swallowed down his dread. "I'm here; you did perfect, Stephanie." He glanced over his shoulder at the porch and raised his broken glasses. Agent Good stood beside the rookie. Both looked as horrified as Deja felt.

He hadn't gotten Stephanie out of the tether field in time.

"He's so beautiful," Stephanie said through a sniffling laugh. "And strong!"

"Yeah," Deja agreed distantly. "Just like his mom." But he wasn't looking at her. He was looking at the surge of green mist spilling into the street. Eyes were in the area. Exhaustion pressed down on Deja's shoulders. It was all he could do to keep his eyes open, to ignore the quiet but insistent whispers in the back of his mind.

Far realer whispering and hissing noises came from the porch. Good was gesturing pointedly at him. Deja frowned in confusion. Once he caught on, he hurled the borrowed mortifier back. Good reached for it but missed, then watched the weapon sail through the open door and skitter down the hall before turning back with a *Really?* tilt of his head.

Twin ethereal voices spoke. "*Agent Vale.*"

If logic weren't enough, the fact that those two voices spoke in perfect sync would have been proof plenty. It was Eyes, all right. Though, Deja'd never actually heard Eyes *speak* to him in the field before. He didn't even realize they ever spoke to any agent—Separation of Reaper Powers and all that. But he was too exhausted to be curious. He braced himself and looked to the source of dual voices. There was nothing there but an odd circle on the lawn: A space six feet across within which the autumn leaves on the ground weren't red and brown but shades of gray. Deja cleared his throat and asked, "Yeah?"

"Nicely done."

Deja blinked. "What? Seriously? I—" He cut himself off as the disintegrated particles that had been Bruno the Clown converged into a spiral then disappeared into the circle. Before Deja could so much as ask for an explanation, the circle of gray moved away, returning to the source of that surging green. Then, the mist was all gone... and the unseen pair of Eyes had gone with it.

"Well," Deja said. "That was, um, certainly something." He slid down his glasses to find Stephanie pulling faces and making burbling noises at the half asleep, half grimacing infant. "Steph, babe… get yourself a therapist. And I don't mean Father What's-his-name. Kid, too. Trauma like that's intergenerational—and you really gotta watch out for that intergenerational trauma. It'll sneak up on you."

"'Kay," Stephanie said, far more focused on the miracle of a baby's fist clenching around her finger. "What's your name? How about"—a pleased gasp—"*Bruno?*" she offered, mischievous smile in full force. "God sure works in mysterious ways, doesn't she?"

Deja stared down at Stephanie. Something like pride blossomed in his chest. She was on her own now. "On second thought," he said, words happily ignored, "you'll be fine."

THE MOOD ON the train ride back was a confused mix of relief, exhaustion, and irritation. Apparently, Agent Sine had taken a charged panini press to the face. But as she hadn't taken a *fridge,* it fell to her to sit beside Agent Troy and press linen soaked with Q-salve to the side of his pale-haired head. He looked only half-aware as he sipped feebly at a precious vial of aether; its green glint splashed against his white-gloved hand.

The vials used to be bigger.

Izik was on their other side, sitting with broken leg outstretched beside her, looking vaguely stunned. But that was a guess, really; she still hadn't taken off her mask. Somebody had deigned to give her a bottle of aether too—probably in the hopes a bit of nourishment might help with the shock, if not the broken leg. But it just rested, untouched in her lap. Next to her, Lear kept wrinkling his nose like a bunny in a vain attempt to fix his mask-mussed dark mustache without having to go through the monumental effort of uncrossing his arms. Wren and Deja sat across from them, exchanging subtle looks while they pretended to not pay attention to the barely hushed argument at the other end of the train. Deja was too grateful to have something to listen to other than the persistent ringing in his ears to be grateful it wasn't him getting dragged by the head agent. *For once.*

Crane and Good were still masked. They hadn't even had time to push back their hoods before the whispering fight started. It had begun with Crane's clipped: "Good? A word," and Good's resigned, "Fine." It had since devolved into a back-and-forth over Good's "delusion" that he was still head agent despite the lack of rank insignia on his jacket lapel—something Crane, funnily enough being head agent and everything, did have—and that his issuing orders to Izik and Vale had been tantamount to insubordination and he was lucky nobody had gotten lost to oblivion. It was then that Deja got a scattered glimpse of the events that had taken place inside while he himself had been in the yard with the living: former and otherwise.

Good had taken it upon himself to order Vale out on his own, directly countermanding Crane's order that no agents were to be on their own. This was true only in the sense that Good hadn't physically restrained the Odd when Deja'd declared his intent to do just that, but Good didn't point that out to Crane. Then, after Deja'd already gone outside, Good had ordered Izik to cover Vale when he himself couldn't. And, according to Crane's simmering summary, he'd explicitly told Izik that *Crane was wrong* when she'd questioned Good's order to stay away from the fight and keep an eye on Deja instead. *Alone.*

Then, Good had pointed out that it was only when Crane had ordered Izik to abandon her Good-mandated post and join the fight that she'd nearly been taken out by a flying grandfather clock and broken her leg. Crane didn't take this well. Hence her return salvo: Every protocol he'd violated, all delivered with the tone one used to level threats.

Good had born this with what passed for grace in his world. He'd remained silent, but with fists clenched. It was when Crane had made the point that Deja Vale, one of only five Odds left at Omega North, could have been lost due to Good's *ego* that Good's period of silent grace ended with a snapped, "Orders from a head agent don't supersede those of the Inquisitorial Authority!"

And then it became a lot more challenging to pretend they weren't all listening—a fact that didn't go unnoticed by Crane and Good. The next thing Good said was so quiet, Deja'd be amazed if *Crane* had heard him. Whatever it was, it made her shake her head in silent fury before saying, "You can risk agents under *your* watch. Not *mine.*" And with that, she turned on her heel and took a seat on a bench across from Deja and Wren. A few moments after that, Good came over and cast Deja a challenging look before taking the seat on his other side.

Good folded his arms across his chest and let his head fall back against the window with a *thunk.* Deja himself had done much the same thing when he'd first sat down. Now that the battle was over and there was nothing to protect, his exhaustion weighed upon him like chains. He flexed his right hand; whether the pain was from newly acquired lifeburn or an old wound, he couldn't say. He was too tired to care at that point.

Deja caught Wren's sidelong look and let gravity tilt his head a little more in her direction. "So," he began cautiously, "is it just me, or have ghosts gotten more demented since I've been gone?"

Wren scoffed. "That, or we're getting *weaker.*"

Deja didn't even think Lear was conscious until he spoke up from the other side of the compartment, "Don't say that. Come on."

Wren shrugged, silent.

It was Troy who chimed in, "She's not wrong. You saw those OWLs. It was like they could barely even *function.* What good are they if it takes them longer to warn us than a threat does to… *threaten?*"

Wren gestured to her holstered mortifier with its barely-there wisp of green in the canister. "Don't know why we bothered with deflecting shots at all when our mortifiers can barely *mortify* anymore."

"Except they did," Crane pointed out levelly. "The ghost got mortified in the end."

Sine narrowed her eyes and asked, "True, but at what range?"

Deja opened his mouth to answer just as Good did—both were interrupted by the rookie of all people. "About ten yards," Izik said. "From the porch to the edge of the tether field was about ten yards, right? And that's where Agent Good shot it from."

Deja's mouth fell open. A sharp jab in his side from Good made him close it. The tension clouding the compartment began to retreat at last as Sine, amazingly enough, seemed mollified by this. So did Lear, Troy, Wren—even *Crane*. It was a lie, of course. *Why* Izik had lied was of much more interest to Deja at the moment. When Izik removed her mask at last, it occurred to Deja that she'd waited to do so until *after* she'd made that lie.

"So, ghosts are just getting more demented," Deja said. "Noted." Wren gave a small, derisive snort. Deja leaned a little closer to grumble, "Granted, that can't be helped, I guess. But they really didn't think to warn us about the ensoulment, huh?" He plucked absently at the stray lifeburn-singed threads on his glove. The train passed through a stretch of mountain; it reemerged with wood-paneled walls and electric lamps.

On his other side, Good tugged off his mask to reveal a pale face that might've been handsome—pretty, even—if he weren't so *pissed off* all the time. His neatly coiffed hair looked nearly black in the faint light of the train. Whenever Good's mask came off, even after all these years, Deja was always caught off guard: He looked so much younger than he sounded. Delicate and severe.

Good rubbed at a sore spot on his smooth jaw and muttered, "You knew what you needed to," casting Crane a sidelong look. The head agent was listening, clearly, but remained silent.

"I'm just saying," Deja persisted in a low voice, "*knowing* that Mrs. Chapman—"

"Who—?"

"Forget it—was scheduled for ensoulment in Stephanie's baby would've made things way easier," Deja finished.

Good shrugged and Wren sighed. She brushed a stray strand of hair that had escaped from its neat, light plait from her face. Even grimacing, her mouth always seemed ready to twitch in wry amusement, whatever the situation.

On Wren's other side, Crane's own sigh rang with strained patience as she tugged off her own mask. Once the warm electric light morphed into gaslight, her dark, bald head and high cheekbones took on the same green glow as the augur chain crossing her chest. "It's not our department," she said, tone infuriatingly reasonable. "Strange as it may seem—"

"Dangerous, more like," Deja cut in.

Crane shot him a warning look and pressed onward, "To us and our limited point of view, perhaps. The Augury and Inquisitorial Authority know what they're doing. I don't suppose it's occurred to you that they know things you don't about what happened to Omega South? That there's good *reasons* for not sharing every detail? Especially not over interworldly channels?"

"Has it ever occurred to you that there *aren't*?" Deja grumbled back.

At once, the tense atmosphere that had only just begun to relax crackled once more.

Crane hissed, "*Agent Vale*"—Deja so seldom heard anybody else's name getting *hissed*—"watch yourself. You *know* how crucial the Separation of Reaper Powers is to our mandate."

"Yeah, yeah, I know... it's just that woman and that baby very nearly could've—" Deja sighed and muttered, "Never mind."

"I *know* you were worried for that Potential," Crane assured Deja (even as the comment seemed directed at Good). "That's why *I* wasn't. Understand?"

"Oh, Crane," Deja said. "You do say the sweetest things."

While Crane rolled her eyes, Good took the opportunity to whisper with terrifying simplicity, "If you ever snatch my equipment again, I will personally shove it down your throat and rip it out your *Odd ass*."

"But frankly, Crane," Deja continued, bumping his shoulder against Good's far stiffer one, "you could manage to learn a thing or two about sweet talk from my little pancake over here."

"Fuck you, Vale," Good growled, half-heartedly.

"Fuck you too, dear."

"Oh right," Crane said, staring longingly at the past when she'd forgotten about that inconvenient detail. "*That.* You're both going to have to"—she plowed through the twin sounds of protest—"check in, report the lost augur, and"—the sounds of protest swelled like an orchestra but she was thoroughly unbothered—"you know what? Go ahead and submit the mission report while you're at it." She sniffed, rested her head against the cushion behind her, and closed her eyes. "Since you're so keen on being a head agent again, Good."

Deja and Good released twin mournful sighs. Good's was followed up with a sidelong glare at Deja. Good turned away to face the window—guy looked in danger of cracking a tooth. "Already in trouble with the AIs and it only took one mission with *you.*"

Deja defensively scrunched his shoulders. "What? I was just doing my *job*—"

"Yeah?" Good demanded. "That what you were doing? Your job?"

"Yeah! I was!" Deja shot back. "And good thing a *freak* was there to do it, too!" He huffed a dry laugh. "I doubt Mrs. Chapman could've even made it up Stephanie's driveway before she croaked, so *you're fucking welcome*, you ungrateful asshat."

Good turned away to face the train windows opposite once more, severe mask firmly in place. Fluorescent lights flickered on, giving his pale skin an almost sallow tinge. It had been years since Good had been promoted to head agent and transferred from their first team to lead his own. But with the enmity Good seemed to have for his former teammate these days, Good may well have requested a transfer even if he hadn't been promoted.

It hadn't always been that way and Deja hated that it stung now. But if they were going to be teamed up on a more permanent basis, they'd have to mend whatever bridge had burned down without Deja even realizing it had been a fire hazard in the first place. So, he said, "Thanks, by the way. For trusting me with your—"

"You have got to be fucking joking—"

"What! I can't even *thank* you?"

"No!" Good gritted. "Because I didn't *do* anything, understand? And if I had? It wouldn't've been for *your benefit.* You got that?"

"Noted. And I'm touched by your lack of trust. *Truly.*"

They sat in tense silence for several more minutes, keenly aware that their volume had crept above a controlled whisper and now *they* were the center of attention. Deja caught Izik's eye; she didn't look away this time, but gave him a small, cautious smile. Deja gave her a tired, half-hearted one in return.

Crane asked, "All right, Vale? You look a bit... *worn.*"

Deja shrugged off the fact that he was barely able to remain upright in his seat. "I'm dandy."

"Good," Crane said, even as she skeptically eyed his face. Whatever she'd discerned there resulted in Deja getting some aether, too. She didn't do it lightly; they'd been rationing that stuff more carefully long before Deja'd been taken out of action.

Deja stared down at the vial in his hands, willing them to move. The after-effects of life-exposure had settled on him like a wet wool blanket, but his mind wouldn't quiet. Never knew how. He opened his mouth and—

"Shut up and rest, Lifeburn," Good cut him off.

"You're right, Good. I'm sorry." Deja bit back a smirk. "I'll stop *clowning* around." When Good's glare intensified, Deja added, "I know you're *juggling* a lot right now."

Izik choked on her aether and Crane gave her a sharp clap on the back. Whether it was meant to be helpful or a reprimand was anybody's guess.

More silence.

Then, Deja cleared his throat. "Crane? I get that the Separation of Reaper Powers is, like, a big deal and everything, but remember when they used to let us wear those sick black robes and carry *scythes*—?"

Sine made a sound *so* scandalized, Deja almost checked to make sure Stephanie hadn't managed to sneak onboard somehow—and then gotten her busted panini press sat on by Troy's equally busted ass.

Crane just gave Deja a level look. "No, and neither do you."

"Well, not *personally*, no," Deja admitted. "I'm just saying a scythe would've been a hell of a lot more effective than a nightstick. Or a mortifier, for that matter."

"Thirteen hells, do you even know *how* to shut up?" Good demanded, while Sine clutched her nonliving pearls in one hand and pressed a linen pad to her panini-pressed cheek with the other.

More tired silence followed. In the end, it was Izik who broke it: "Harder to throw though," she pointed out. "A scythe, I mean." Her eyes flicked to Good. "Allegedly."

Deja grinned at Good's impotent glare and uncorked his vial of aether. As the flavorless green liquid edged out the pain behind his eyes, he watched the shadows of the living shift through narrow panes of time-stained glass.

THE SARATOGA SPIRITUALIST SOCIETY

AN ANTHOLOGY OF PRIMARY SOURCES

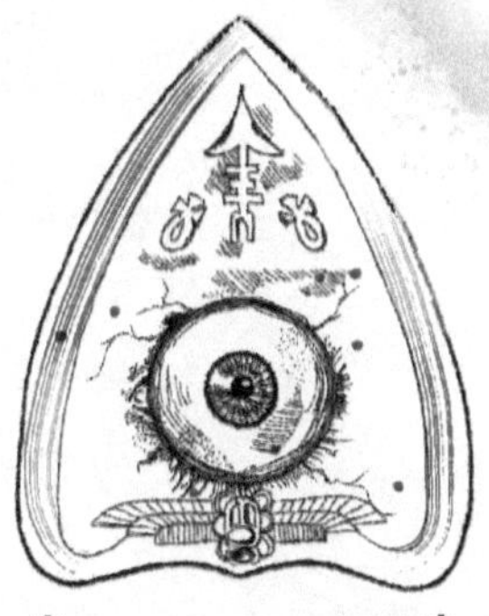

MORS AEQUAT

The first two pages of a letter of unknown length from the wife of Professor Abraham Jude Davis Holmes, Ursula Sarah Davis Holmes, written to her longtime friend, Cat. There is debate as to whom "Cat" refers, but most scholars agree it is addressed to her second cousin, Catherine Eleanor Putnam, while some suggest it is Catherine Fox of the famed (and infamous) Fox Sisters (see Hill 1960, Snodgrass 1971, Cheong 1985, et al).[1]

The letter is dated October 17th, 1877: six weeks following the ostensible birth of her first child, X. Davis Holmes (1869–1870). It is one of only six letters by Ursula remaining from the Saratoga Period of the Davis Holmes family, collected here for the first time.

----

1. This is, however, a mere flight of fancy as there is no record of any association between the two women. The author also notes that Catherine Fox (1837-1892) was known by her family and friends as "Kate" rather than "Cat."

October 11ᵗʰ 1877

My dearest Cat,

As I write, I'm sitting at my desk by the window, watching the last leaves fight the inevitable. There's a chill in the air and has been for weeks now. But still the leaves cling there, shaking and trembling on the bough like so many orphans in a Dickens novel. The bedroom fire is warm and generous, the blanket on my lap thick and warm, but I've insisted my desk be moved here by the window where I can feel the chill.

Your letters are the only respite I have, my dear one.

Abraham has still not held his son. He's such a beautiful, happy baby. He never cries. He has his father's eyes, but I fear my precious boy will never know it if his father never looks at him.

Abraham was meant to be his name, as you well know. Abraham Jude Davis Holmes the third. But my husband, in all his wisdom, has decided to remain a junior rather than claim the title of second.

Already, Abraham speaks of trying for another. <u>Why??</u> is what I wish to ask but of course I dare not. Why would you wish for another son when you can't even bear the sound of the first's cries?

Praise God for my Delia. She has been such a comfort to me, even upon the loss of her own father. I even insisted our family doctor examine her eye. He balked, of course, but you well know how tiresome I can be when I choose! He told me she will never see out of that eye again, poor thing.

I'm loath to admit that half the love my baby boy will see reflected back at him will be from that one, dark eye. The other half from my own.

Such a loving gaze would have been better <u>green</u>.

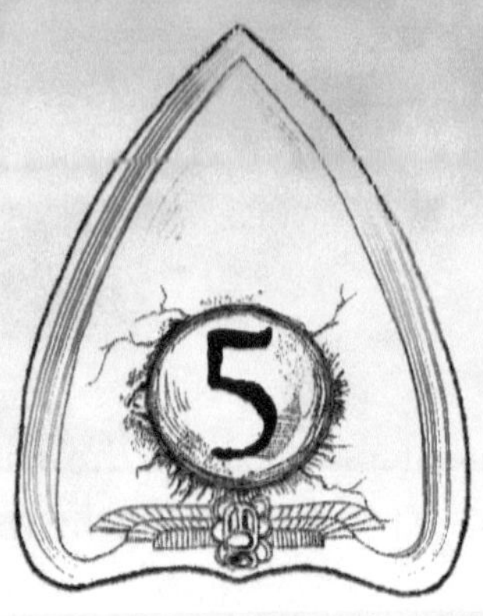

It was the nature of Deja's Oddity that he could bear to see what his fellow agents could not. Before his first train ride to the Desert of the Living, he'd been warned to prepare himself for the sensory shock. Truth was, once he got past the initial disorientation, it wasn't the colors of the living world he found shocking. At least, not when he was at full strength and the colors were harmless—muted by glasses if not his own peculiar talents. No, it was returning to the train that shocked him. Even worse was stepping foot in the Hereafter itself. Seeing just how black and white their world really was? *That* was the real shock.

But it never lasted.

Deja took in the hundred shades of gray, broken up only by the green-tinted mist clouding the boarding platform. With every passing moment, a new shade of gray emerged to his perception. The train let out a heave of steam so thick that Deja's first step off the train was guided more by hope and habit than anything else. His boot hit firm floor, and he kept walking until the train's green plumes gave way to the familiar sights and sounds of Styx Station. Beyond the simple tiled boarding platform were dozens of crisscrossing tracks, each one disappearing into any of the hundred dark tunnels which peppered the cavernous place. That great, stone beehive was Styx Station: The nexus of all things interworldly, nestled in the base of Omega Headquarters.

After even that brief exposure to the Desert of the Living, the cool grays of the station interior were a welcome respite on Deja's bare face. Lingering lifeburn flushed his cheeks and stung his hands like a slap frozen in time. Another train pulled in, bringing with it more cooling green mist. Deja closed his eyes at the fleeting kiss of relief.

"Wow." Good paused at the top of the train steps. "You looked like shit on the train," he said, "but you *really* look like shit now."

Deja didn't bother arguing the point. It was probably true. He just shrugged and offered a weak, "Noted." He frowned when Crane's voice called Good's name from inside the compartment.

Good glanced over his shoulder before turning back to Deja with a warning point. "Stay right there."

Deja scrunched his nose. "What are you, my babysitter?"

Good ignored this and disappeared inside. Deja folded his arms across his chest and leaned against the train. Waiting. A low, whine-tinged groan rumbled against his back. Metallic footsteps echoed then Agents Sine and Troy emerged. Troy gave him a curt yet respectful nod. Sine, on the other hand, paused just long enough to say, "I'll be submitting my own mission report"—she lowered her voice—"and it will be very, very detailed. *Freak.*"

"You do that," Deja said. Once she blended into the crowd of milling agents, constables, and conductors, he muttered, "Personality of the year, right there."

"Right?" Wren said as she debarked. "I've been working with her and Troy a few months now. They're not bad people. They're just scared, like everybody else around here."

"Shitty people usually are."

Wren gave him a chiding look. "You know what I mean."

"Yeah... I know what you mean. At least Crane doesn't think I'm a complete disgrace."

"And that's the head agent you've got fooled there. No mean accomplishment." Wren narrowed her eyes. "What's wrong?"

"They're not wrong. It's too soon. I had no business being back out there."

Wren looked down a moment, preparing herself to ask the question that so many memories clung to like ghosts. "You really don't remember? Any of it?"

Deja's response was mechanical, the way a response given a thousand times always was, polished flat with each repetition. "No. I remember leaving Styx station with five other agents and waking up months later only to find out that three of us didn't make it back."

Wren nodded, taking this in. It wasn't news. "Lucky you," she said grimly. "If I could've chosen to forget, I would've."

Deja hadn't asked Wren about what happened. Even if he hadn't been told that Wren wasn't close to the events that led to the loss of Ivy, Vyne, and Thorne, he still wouldn't have. The mention of it made her close in upon herself. A trapped animal prodded in a cage, recoiling to avoid the stabs it couldn't escape. "I'm sorry," Deja told her. He meant it.

Wren shook her head and turned to face him fully. "Don't be sorry. Whatever anyone else says, whatever you can't remember, know this: You're the reason as many of our team made it back as we did. Including *me*. Understand?"

Deja stared at her. It was the first time he'd heard her say anything about that mission—the first time he'd heard her speak so openly, so passionately about *anything*. When Wren gave him an expectant look, he nodded, dumbly. Wren squeezed his arm and said, "Crane and Lear are taking Izik to Osiris now. You should go, too. You look like you're about to pass out. *Again*."

"Thanks."

"And good luck with that report," Wren said, backing away. "I don't envy you."

"You sure you don't wanna stick around and help me with—okay, then." Watching Wren disappear into the crowd, Deja murmured, "So that was a *no*."

Another train, sleek and black, departed the station. Green clouds crawled across the shining black and gray tile floor then settled on his boots. He debated disappearing into the sea of agents and con-ductors like Wren had. Avoid Good's unique brand of acerbic melo-drama and any other scenes. He could practically hear Agent Inquis-itor Vex's grating sigh, see the disappointed-but-unsurprised twist to his mouth, made all the more obvious by the fitful twitch of a silver mustache.

Of course, being the supreme agent and tactical mind he was, AI Vex had anticipated that very urge. Deja didn't have to imagine those sighs and twitches. He could just see them for himself. Beyond the plumes of green steam and traveling agents, Vex stood sentry at the bottom of the grand staircase that led to the even grander atrium of Omega headquarters. Even as his white-piped, black overcoat bil-lowed in the breeze of departing trains, his silver hair and beard stayed perfectly still, like they'd been carved from the same granite as the rest of his stony face.

Deja just caught Good's muttered, "I hate you," as he came down the steps.

"Agent Good? Agent Vale?" Vex called out, deep voice as steady as a lighthouse in a storm. "With me."

Deja glanced over his shoulder, debating if he couldn't slip onto another train just before it left. Make a new un-life for himself in the caboose.

"Best possible speed, Vale!"

"Coming, sir!" Deja said, jogging to catch up with Good.

Vex began talking just as Deja got in earshot, eyes focused dead ahead as they climbed. "Anything unusual to report?"

Good cast a sidelong look at Deja and let him answer.

"Um…" Deja began, earning him a snort of disbelief from his teammate. "Unofficially or officially?" Good elbowed him and he added, "Sir," before shooting Good a miffed look.

Vex stopped halfway up the stairs to look down at Deja. He eyed him for several eternities. Then, his mustache gave an agi-tated twitch and he turned back, resuming his upward climb. The two agents were powerless to do anything but follow him through the great marble archway that led to Omega headquarters. Above, a motto had been laid to rest within black shadows carved into stone:

MORS AEQUAT

Equal in death.

THE INQUISITORIAL WING wasn't on the top floor of Omega Head-quarters, but it was certainly up there. As the elevator climbed, polished abalone buttons gleamed brighter, and the floor shifted from gray tile to silver-flecked marble. Deja was pushed forward when flat steel against his back became plush velvet. A *chime* declared their arrival; the hall that greeted them looked much the same as the elevator. Here, the walls were less liable to change than most others. The polished woods and gleaming metals you'd only catch the occasional glimpse of on Styx trains and elevators had taken a liking to the upper floors and settled in for the long haul.

A black and white marble floor expanded like an endless chessboard. An infinity of black doors stood like rooks with their framing pillars of gray, carved stone. Vex led the way to the fifth door on the left. He pulled out his augur and pressed it to the gleaming plaque: AGENT INQUISITOR VEX. *Click.* The door swung open with a deep groan and Vex gestured inside. "Gentlemen."

Deja, who'd been sent to this very office on a near-weekly basis during training (and a biweekly basis after that), felt right at home and took a seat on one of the simple black chairs waiting before the matching desk (though the color was barely visible beneath the piles of papers). Good, on the other hand, stepped gingerly inside, eyeing the shifting green and silver ripples of sky beyond the pair of lancet windows. The moon was a great black crescent offset against gleaming green light just barely visible from Deja's seat. But he could see the moon's mouth opening to the left and knew it was waning. Usually was.

Good's eyes shifted to Deja and narrowed. Deja suppressed a roll of his own eyes and looked to the agent inquisitor now seated at the desk before them, neutral face staring back at him. Once the heavy door finally closed, a single gray eyebrow lifted. Good cleared his throat and began, "Well, sir, there were some unforeseen complications, but I believe the Augury was ultimately satisfied with how events turned out."

Vex considered this a moment, then folded his hands across the desk. "And the ghost?"

"Batshit," Deja said, just as Good answered, "Mortified."

Vex blinked once. Very, very slowly. "Mortified," he echoed, bearded chin shifting downward a degree. "A story needs a beginning as well as an ending, Agents."

Good cleared his throat. "Well, sir, there was an unexpected birth taking place, and that ghost"—he glanced at Deja—"who really was particularly demented, sir—was determined to claim the Potential. It overpowered two of our agents and almost did exactly that, so moving the Potential outside became the pri—"

"You moved the Potential outside," Vex said. "How?" Good's eyes shifted sideways and Vex sighed. "Let me hazard a guess, Agent Vale. You pretended to be *God* again."

"No," Deja defended in a small voice. He shifted in his seat a bit. "An *angel.*" Under his breath, he added, "And her dead grandmother."

Vex just stared while Good muttered, "Good Reaper," under his breath.

Deja scrunched his shoulders. "What? It's not against *my* programming to impersonate a deity." When the blank staring and world-weary headshaking only continued, Deja shrunk a bit. "*Return of the Jedi...?* Star Wars?"—he shrunk a bit more—"laser-night-sticks? Space-mortifiers go *pew pew*—ow!"

Good forced an opening by stomping on Deja's foot. "Sir, we weren't prepared for a Poten—"

"How close was this particularly demented ghost to the Potential at the time of said mortification?" Vex asked.

Good's lips disappeared into a thin line. When Vex's other silver eyebrow went up to join its fellow, Good admitted, "Too close, sir."

"How close is 'too close?'"

"Imminently ensouling, sir," Good said.

Vex had the look of a man struggling to not sigh. "And who mortified this particularly demented ghost?"

Good went silent. Lying to Crane was one thing. Lying to Vex, the AI who'd taught them everything they knew about being an agent, was something else.

"I see," Vex said, turning to Deja. "Was there something unclear in the terms of your return from leave?" he asked, not unkindly... but not kindly, either. That was his trick. He didn't make you feel intimidated by his supervision. He made you feel guilty enough that you started *supervising yourself*. Contrary as Deja was, it often worked.

"No, sir," Deja hedged, "but the circumstances were—"

"What circumstances could have possibly justified your commandeering a mortifier against my orders"—Vex's gray eyes narrowed—"and *using it*?"

"If I may, sir," Good interjected. "It was a call that I made. For the good of the Potential."

Vex's mustache twitched at that. "I'm listening."

"I could've made the shot," Good said, "but, the trajectory would've made spirit-particle drift far more likely. Vale, being between the attacking ghost and the Potential, could make a direct, high impact shot forcing any errant particles back long enough for the designated ensoulment to take place, whole and unsullied."

Vex took a few moments to digest this. "I see.... And this was your thought process at the time?"

"It was, sir," Good lied. Deja knew he'd lied, though he didn't know it was a lie until he'd heard Good make it. What was the thought process there? Deja'd guess that Good had attempted the shot himself only to find the blast too weak to land (that may or may not have been exacerbated by the lack of grounding force his auger *should* have provided—allegedly). Or maybe a thought process wasn't there at all. Maybe the urgency of the situation demanded instinctive action, not careful consideration.

Not that instinctive action was really Good's style.

Judging from the tightening corners of Vex's mouth, he suspected the lie, too. "And your augur?"

"Broke off its chain in the fight, sir," Good said. "Just as I was about to contact the Augury."

That was technically true, though committing a rather crucial *by whom*. A misplaced augur was no simple error. There was a reason they'd been built to self-detonate at the first hint of anything amiss, and an agent losing theirs in the field was far from just embarrassing. It was damn-near incriminating. Years ago, Deja might've thought Good was protecting him with the lie of omission. Really, the lie was protecting Good himself. Deja just didn't know from *what.* All the story needed was to tie one last thread: Something doubtlessly on the books long before that clown had even gotten its crazy comeuppance. It was the detail that likely inspired Vex to meet them at the station himself.

"I was closest and retrieved it," Deja explained. "I wasn't really thinking, I guess, and finished the contact Good started. Naturally, it didn't go through. That was my mistake. I was trying to save us precious seconds and ended up costing us instead. Reflex. Guess my muscle memory hasn't had time to catch up with the new..." he trailed off a moment, searching for a politic turn of phrase before landing on, "interworldly communication policies. I didn't realize an agent using a teammate's augur would trigger detonation."

Vex stared at him. Vaguely, Deja wondered if two people who were so often at odds had ever lied harder on the disliked party's behalf. It was for the greater good. It was selfish. It was incidentally something approximating loyalty. Or maybe in their case, nostalgia.

Good's glare simmered far beneath the surface. Based on how tense his neck looked, Deja'd guess it was roiling somewhere in his cervical spine.

Just mutual self-interest, then.

"Anything else I should know?" Vex asked. In the ensuing silence, his gray eyes moved like the pendulum of a grandfather clock (pre-explosion) from Good... to Deja... and back to Good. "Agent Good? I trust you understand the seriousness of a compromised augur?"

Good's already straight posture straightened more. Must've hurt. "Yes, sir."

Vex continued, "And that by allowing your augur out of your control, you put not only yourself but all of Omega North at risk?"

Deja opened his mouth to protest the over-exaggeration, but Good headed him off. "I do, sir."

"Given the *complexity* of the situation," Vex said, "I will only be placing you on probation."

Just as Good asked, "For how long, sir?" Deja spluttered, "That is overkill!" Good shot Deja a sideways look, and Deja snapped his mouth shut.

"Until I deem it long enough." Vex opened a drawer, pulled out a black form, and slid it across the desk. He gave it two quick taps with his fingers and leaned back. "You'll need to requisition a new augur," he said. "Today, Agent. We can't spare agents at the moment—probation or no—and we certainly can't spare an Odd."

Deja's furrowed brow went unnoticed.

"Yes, sir," Good said through a breath of relief. He took the form and neatly folded it.

"Give us a moment," Vex said. "But don't go far. I need somebody to ensure Agent Vale, here, actually *makes it* to Osiris."

"Yes, sir," Good said. "I'll be waiting just outside." And with that, Good stood, gave a quick bow of his head, and left them to it. Vex watched the door open and close, waiting for the hollow thud and metallic click.

Thud.

Click.

Vex forced a short breath. "What in thirteen hells happened to you, Vale? I send you on one mission—*one mission*—and you come back looking like you found a maternity ward and *rolled around in it*."

Deja snorted and gestured to his own face. In doing so, he spotted the pearlescent sheen of lifeburn on the pad of his thumb through frayed fabric. "That bad, huh?" At the grim set to Vex's mouth, Deja said, "I did what I had to."

"Your lack of self-preservation instinct is concerning to say the least," Vex said tightly. "Have you learned nothing? You are *meant* to be keeping your distance."

Deja scrunched his nose and pointed out, "Well, then you *probably* should've given me a ranged weapon instead of a melee one."

Vex pinned him with an unimpressed look. "I meant from the *living.* And I wasn't expecting you to *use* them. Those nightsticks were given as an absolute last resort."

"And it was," Deja said. "Just like Good tossing me his mortifier was last resort." He hesitated a moment. "Sir? I get why I was sent in, and I get Sine, Troy, and Crane being tacked on to"—he stopped short of saying, 'replace Ivy, Thorne, and Vyne'—"fill out our numbers... but why was Good added?"

It was clear from the twitching mustache that Vex was perfectly aware of what Deja was perfectly aware of. Deja made a sound that was less a sigh, more a balloon animal deflating. "*Seriously?*" he asked, not bothering to cloak his own petulance. "A babysitter?"

"You were recovering for *months*, Agent Vale, and have only returned to the field on a probationary basis. Against *my protests*, I might add. Agent Good's addition to your team is what you might call a compromise."

"So that's why Good was there, then," Deja said. "To look after me." Vex's only response was to release a world-weary breath. So, Deja continued, mouth helpless under the sway of a brain with precious little to do for six months other than undergo examination after examination, pace, and sleep. "But Good was promoted to head agent. Why was Crane—" He stopped at Vex's double-time mustache twitching. "Wait. Was Good *demoted* in order to babysit me? No wonder he's pissed! I ruined his career by proxy. Thanks for that, by the way. Love this new dynamic. *Love it.*"

Vex waited patiently for Deja to shut up. "Agent Good understands the importance of his duties. You need not concern yourself."

"Right." That was that sorted, then. At least, as sorted as it was going to get here and now. Which left only a dozen other issues—one glaring issue in particular. Deja debated if he wanted to say what he was about to say. It went quick. "Sir, we went in without enough information. I get *me* not knowing everything, being brought in last minute and all, but not even the *head agent* knew there was a Potential involved. Let alone that it was due to be ensouled by a neighbor." He blew out a flustered sound and scrambled for words, filtering and sorting each one by relative appropriateness only to find *none* of them qualified for the appropriate column. He threw up a hand and finished, "The Augury fucked us."

"The Augury fucked you," Vex echoed flatly.

"Right in the ass. Repeatedly and with no flirtation. I mean, an agent in the field picks up another agent's augur to call for *emergency guidance* and the response is *immediate detonation*? On what grounds?"

"Security policy grounds."

"Fuck-agents-in-the-asinine policy, maybe."

Vex placed a finger to his upper lip like it was the only thing keeping his mustache from breaking ranks from his beard and twitching off his face so it could strangle the man across from him. "Agents only need be informed of details when they *need* to know," Vex explained, tone infuriatingly reasonable. "The Augury had no reason to believe the ensoulment was in peril. And they *weren't wrong*."

"You don't think knowing that, *one*"—Deja ticked numbers on his fingers, taking the opportunity to make sure he still had them— "that baby was about to pop, and *two*, it was scheduled for ensoulment by its imminently dying neighbor wasn't pertinent information that we *needed to know*?"

"The Separation of Reaper Powers is crucial to the—"

"Yeah, I know," Deja said, rubbing his eyes.

"*Do* you?"

Deja fought the urge to roll his eyes and recited, "The Separation of Reaper Powers provides the checks and balances required to ensure equality in death…. *Morse kumquat* and all that." Black spots dotted his vision and he rubbed his eyes again. Didn't help.

"*Mors Aequat*," Vex corrected. "If the Augury didn't contact you to provide additional information, it was only because they knew there was no need to. Moreover, you know that any contact between worlds is always a risk, but never more so than now. And with a living resident in such close proximity? Doing so would have been even riskier. That is why we sent our *best agents.* Why we sent *you*—"

The black dots behind Deja's eyes merged then reddened around the edges, forming a dozen eclipses.

"*Where are you? Are you*—"

"—listening? Agent Vale?"

"Hm?" Deja looked up. "Sorry, I just—sorry. Tired. Too much life-exposure." He clenched his eyes shut a moment then opened them. He blinked. He blinked twice more. "So, the reason we didn't receive *any* contact from the Augury was because they knew about the woman coming home and trusted us to be able to handle it? That's what you're telling me?"

"That's what I'm telling you." Vex lowered his voice and leaned forward a fraction. "You are a superlative agent, Vale, who has been placed on a team of likewise superlative agents. From your perspective, all you can see are limitations: What you can and can't do, what you can and can't know. But there are reasons for those limitations, and you are not the only agent facing them. The attack on Omega South was… a *devastating* blow to all we exist to protect and preserve. It may take centuries to recover, if indeed we ever can. We cannot allow it to happen again. *We cannot afford to lose Omega North.*"

Deja lapsed into silence. The fall of Omega South had left the Hereafter three quarters of a whole. The great machine that worked tirelessly to protect the living from spectral threats was operating at 75% capacity—at best. Each quarter was separated by impassable forests, oceans, deserts, and tundras. Deja didn't even know how they were sure of the existence of Omega East and West at all. Communication between Omega headquarters was next to nonexistent—at least, for agents. But even *they* had heard what happened—just enough to show them that what they'd all believed to be eternal and unchanging could fall. But while agents could only speculate on the shape of events, the consequences were far clearer. Deja tried to read that originating shape from the shadow it cast:

The tightened restrictions on interworldly communications.

The redaction of case file information granted to agents.

The rationing of aether.

The weakness of a mortifier shot.

The unexpected strength of a ghost.

The sluggishness of rainbow magnets on a refrigerator door.

The fear.

But what about the lights? The warning flicker in a code that, so far as he knew, only agents learned? Maybe it had been just another hallucination.

But what if it hadn't been?

"Agent?"

Deja formed one letter with his lips, then shifted course. "Sir, are you saying that what happened to South could happen here?"

Vex eyed him carefully. "We all must do our part to ensure that does not happen, Agent."

Deja nodded, silently tracing shapes in the shadows. If Omega had reason to believe the fall of South had something to do with interworldly communications being breached or compromised, then interworldly communications would be made more secure. Made perfect sense. And if the stakes *were* that high, Agent Inquisitor Vex would *never* have risked compromising the security—the very *existence* of Omega North—by doing something so unorthodox as initiating an unsanctioned OWL communication. Which meant it wasn't Vex who'd found some new way of warning his agent in the flickering red and purple lights as Deja'd dared hope.

Now, he didn't have the first *clue* of who it could be if not his own addled mind.

But he did know where he'd have to start looking to find out. It just so happened to be the place whose security had become everyone's priority: The Augury. That plan was dead in the water already.

"Right," Deja said, clapping his hands to his thighs and moving to stand. "Okay. Makes sense." He sat back down. "Wait, you *didn't* want me going?"

"No."

Deja's jaw tightened. "I told you," he said quietly. "I'm fine." Vex remained silent. "The dreams haven't come back."

Vex gave him a careful look. "It is only a dream if you're *asleep*, Deja." Deja's face shuttered and Vex sighed. "How many times do I have to tell you that neither putting you on leave nor choosing not to reissue your mortifier was a punishment before you believe me?"

"No, yeah," Deja said, looking down at his worn gloves. "I know."

"I want you to allow Agent Good to escort you to Osiris where you will undergo whatever treatment or restrictions they advise," Vex said. Before Deja could protest, he continued, "That is a direct order, Agent."

Something whispered against Deja's ear; he shooed the nonexistent fly away. "Understood, sir."

"Good." Vex opened a drawer, pulled out a form, plucked up a silver pen, and scribbled his elaborate constellation of a signature before sliding the paper forward. "Requisition yourself some new gloves. *After* your assiduous attention to your own healing." Gray eyes swept up and down Deja and he asked, "Anything else compromised?"

"Glasses," Deja said with a small shrug. "Cracked during the birth."

Vex's brows went up at that. "Really." His mouth twisted into a wry grimace and he added in a mutter, "I'll skip the I-told-you-sos and just trust you to attend to that." Then he turned his attention to the hundred black files on his desk and flicked one open. "Get it done. *Sharpish.* I won't waste my time telling you to take better care of yourself—*again*—but for my sanity, if not your own sake, please put some M-balm on your face next time. Or Q. *Something*. You look worn as *life*."

Deja nodded. "Got it, sir." He hesitated a moment, then ventured, "I really don't need Agent Good to—"

With gaze still fixed on the swath of papers before him, Vex snapped his fingers and the door swung open—Good stumbled through, arms rapidly uncrossing. He cleared his throat and straightened his hair with a valiant attempt at dignity. "Sir?" Good asked.

"Agent Good, escort Agent Vale to Osiris immediately. Dismissed," Vex said, mind already lost in the forest of forms before him and unreachable by mundane means.

Deja stood from his seat and eyed the neatly folded form clasped in Good's left hand. Though he couldn't see the contents on Good's augur requisition form, he could guess where the agent was meant to take it. Deja folded his own form with a mumbled, "Goody." He cast a last glance at Vex. The pleading look Deja tunneled into the man's head went utterly unregistered. Funny—the scorn-filled death glare burrowing into his own spine was coming through loud and clear. He glanced over his shoulder to take Good's ire straight in the face. Deja didn't know what the middle-ground between passive aggression and aggressive aggression was, but here it was: Staring at him like he was an invasive species of beetle destroying Good's prize-winning cucumber patch.

"Let's go," Good said.

Deja stepped forward and swayed a little. He waved a hand dismissively at Good and said, "I'm fine, I'm fine, I'm coming," and pushed past him into the unending chess game of a hallway.

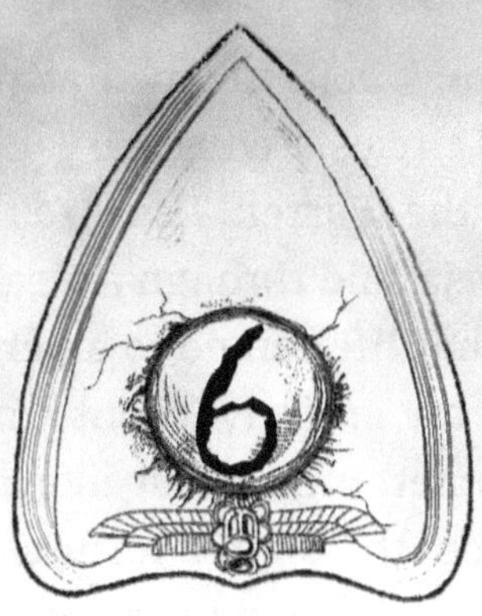

Once amidst the gleaming abalone, wood, and plush velvet of the elevator again, Deja opened his mouth to speak. His lips had barely managed to part before Good headed him off: "Don't you dare act like the put-upon one here, all right?"

Deja bit his lip, obligingly. He only thought the things he'd have said otherwise: That it wasn't Deja's fault Good had been tasked with babysitter duty. That Deja would have dearly loved for anyone else—no really, anyone—to have been tasked with said duty. That if Good really resented it all that much, the best course of action (in Deja's mind) would be to let Deja go on his merry way *not* to Osiris, how he wanted. But he didn't. He just watched Good pound his fist against a button, snatch the form from Deja's hands, and quickly scan it.

"You're going to need an overseer to sign off on this," Good said and unceremoniously shoved the paper at Deja.

"Since when does a little field damage need a signature besides an *AI's*?" Deja asked, doing his best to straighten the paper of Good-induced wrinkles.

"Since you went on vacation." Good narrowed his eyes and asked, "How often do you even work?" almost like he was genuinely interested or something. But past experience of this particular Goodly mood told Deja otherwise. This was confirmed when Deja opened his mouth (again) only to get headed off (again): "Just go take it to Requisitions and wait for somebody to tell you what to do."

"Helpful. Thank you." Deja frowned at the one button glowing amidst hundreds of dull circles. "What are you doing? Warren's on—"

"*We're* not going to the Warren. *I* am. *You* are going to Osiris."

"Right, silly me," Deja said through a weak laugh. He gestured to his own face. "Crazy what life can do to a person, huh?"

The response was an entirely silent and entirely predictable scowl. A glimmer of something almost like *color* caught Deja's eye. He glanced at the source: the signed form clasped in Good's gloved hand. That form, unlike Deja's own, was addressed to the section of the Warren that handled all things Augury: The division that (among other things) tracked Otherworldly Letters. Just like the interworldly communications it managed, the Augury was kept under far tighter lock and key than it had been just a year ago. Its bureaucratic under-belly in the Warren wouldn't be any different.

Deja wasn't famous for his strict adherence to protocol, but even *he* had reservations about poking around the Augury to satisfy his own... he wasn't even sure. *Reservations re: his own fitness for the field* felt less accurate than *compulsion*. Still. There was a difference between an agent *infiltrating* a highly secure department in the Warren, and an agent just *helping out.* For instance, by relieving a colleague of the hassle of requisitioning a new augur. After all, it *was Deja's fault* Good's augur had detonated. Least he could do.

Allegedly.

Deja swayed on his feet, convincingly. And the reason it was con-vincing was because it was genuine. When Good reflexively shot out a steadying hand, his form made a crisp-paper *crackle* against Deja's arm. "Watch it..." Good warned.

"I'm fine," Deja insisted, waving his own requisition form at Good. "I don't need Osiris, all right? I just need to slap some Q on my face, and get myself a nice, stiff—" He stumbled forward and landed, hard, into Good's chest, forcing his back against the wall.

"You have got to be fucking kidding me right now," Good growled as he tried to get Deja off without injuring him further. Deja was a pain in the ass, *but* as one of only five remaining Odds, he was also a precious ass-pain—and part of Good's present job description. But then Good's need to have Deja off of him won out, and Deja ended up on his knees on the elevator floor. The form fell from his limp hand like the last leaf off a dead tree.

Good knelt beside him. "Don't need Osiris, huh?" he said, snatching up Deja's form and hoisting him to his feet with a grunt. "You are an absolute *child,* you know that?"

By the time the elevator had reached the Osiris lobby and opened its doors with an incongruously cheerful *ding!* gleaming wood had given way to stainless steel, simple and clean. Deja gave Good a fleeting, grateful look which reflected back at him in the mirror finish of the opening doors. He winced at the pearlescent glimmer on his face. "Thanks," he said, snatching the Augury requisition form from Good's hand. "I can handle walking from here."

Good was already herding Deja out the elevator before he said, "Oh, no you don't."

Deja paused over the threshold and reached out a hand to steady himself, swiping a hundred buttons in the process. He slumped against the door struggling to close through him and held up a hand to stave off Good's incoming tirade. "Okay," Deja said breathlessly, "you may have a point." He winced. "I think—" he cut himself off with a grimace.

"What."

In a whisper that Deja himself could barely hear, he admitted, "I think I might need a wheelchair."

"*What?*"

Deja closed his eyes and took a deep breath before repeating the admission.

Good scoffed. "First reasonable thing you've said all day." He took Deja by the shoulders to prop him against the hallway wall. When Deja began to lean precariously to one side, Good readjusted him, then waited. Satisfied Deja would be stable for at least a few minutes, he strode off, down the gleaming white hall to the equally white reception desk.

Deja's half-hearted wave went ignored. He blew out a hair-fluttering breath and looked around. His nose scrunched. The smell was unmistakable and unavoidable. Caustic. Sickly sweet. *Medicinal.* As a building, Osiris was a monument unto itself. It would have been about a ten-minute trek to get here, had they walked, but the elevators (like the trains) weren't bound by the same limitations as them.

This was the first of twenty-five floors that made up Osiris, but they all looked the same: sterile, bright, white. Every six feet there hung a bright glass lamp that left nothing beyond the collective reach of their garish light. Polished marble floors gleamed with such a force that those lights might have been built into the ground, too. The monotony of matching white walls was only broken up by the small gray plaques attempting to distinguish one place from the next, and the people passing in matching, efficient paces.

A technician approached from the other end of the hall, one of dozens skilled in the art of keeping the guardians of the Hereafter intact and in shape. However many times Deja had to deal with them (and it was *a lot of times*), he never felt comfortable around them. It wasn't the crisp, hooded white jackets of their uniforms, or the patronizing air of superiority, and not even the muffled echo with which they com-municated said patronizing air of superiority. It was the *masks*. Hard, long-beaked, and white, their masks kept everyone else at a distance. Never permitting a closer glimpse into their two small eye holes that might have revealed anything other than two unfeeling black *nothings* boring into you like surgical steel pinning a frog to its dissection tray.

Deja held his breath when the technician approached. They passed him by without sparing a look, white jacket flapping behind them. Deja let that breath out and watched their departure. The tech-nician stopped at the high front desk to make a quick comment to the attendant, interrupting her conversation with Good. Good looked to be on the verge of getting *animated* when he was mollified by the arrival of another attendant in standard prim white uniform with short cape, pert cap, and porcelain mask. Unlike the technicians', her mask's owl-like beak and round black eyes made her look more curious than grave. And once Good explained what was needed, she became *actually* curious. Her white mask pivoted toward Deja before giving Good a solemn nod.

The only other elevator opened with a *ding.* Two technicians stepped out. The first was quietly muttering something about needing more elevators which earned a weary sigh of agreement from their fellow. Behind them, the wood paneling inside the elevator shifted to stainless steel, covered with grime and graffiti. Painted over the static of gray symbols, tags, and insults stood two huge words.

Red ones.

That red was so bright it had no place anywhere but the Desert of the Living. It felt obscene to read it. But Deja couldn't catch more than the first overly large letters of each word before the doors closed: *M* and *M.*

"Hey," Deja said to one of the passing technicians, "did you see anything in the elevator—" He stopped suddenly at the subtle, surprised jumps they made (doubtlessly at his appearance). The source of said appearance would go a long way toward explaining just why he was seeing impossible things in elevators. "Never mind," he said. "Carry on, Magisters."

Carry on they did. Hurriedly.

Stay out of Osiris—

Deja turned toward the source of the sound. No one there. He rubbed absently at the lifeburn on his knuckles and stared at the twin elevators. *It means nothing,* he assured himself. *You know lifeburn does strange things. Your glasses broke. Of course your eyes took damage. There is nothing there but the afterimage of the Desert burned onto your retinas. It'll heal. It'll pass.*

It's not like before.

A light flashed above the elevator they'd taken. Deja watched it painstakingly stop on every. Single. Floor. It had only managed eighteen of one hundred and sixty-nine since he'd hit the buttons. Beside it, its partner moved four floors up, stalled, then descended. Three floors above... two floors above.... The moment Good turned to follow the attendant to fetch a wheelchair, Deja leaned over and tapped the button to summon the elevator. He waited for Good to take hold of the wheelchair, then made his move.

Deja nodded to the agent emerging from the elevator and slipped inside, quickly slapping the lone, dull gray button labeled with a peeling rabbit. Good wouldn't be able to take the stairs to follow him because Deja would no longer be in the same building. He wouldn't even be on the same square of the Hex anymore. Deja just caught sight of Good's face as it rapidly cycled through three stages of grief before the scratched and smudged doors closed, reconnecting the bifurcated phone number of somebody's mother who could offer a "good time." Deja folded his arms across his chest and leaned back against the metal wall and hoped no unimaginative marker graffiti was printing itself on his jacket.

As the elevator began to move down, Deja just caught the shouted, "Are you fucking kidding me, Vale?" before his descent to bureaucratic hell began.

Ding... ding... ding... the elevator counted the floors away. Deja shared a raised brow with the sharp-eyed man reflected in the stainless-yet-stained steel door. He leaned closer, running a hand over his stubbled cheek, and winced. The more protruding parts of his face—his cheekbones, chin, and the tip of his nose—looked delicate and shining. Like a Christmas ornament passed down by clutching fingers through the generations until its lead paint faded to reveal the sheen of glass beneath. He pressed two fingers to his right cheekbone and hissed.

No wonder the technicians had jumped. And no wonder Good had actually believed his lie about needing a wheelchair.

Agent Deja Vale really did look like shit.

ONCE THE ELEVATOR slipped from Osiris to the Warren, overhead lights flickered... dimmed... then went out. A half-hearted thrum of fluorescence revealed stark metal, unadorned and unmarked, nothing reflected in its dull doors and walls.

Bzzzzzzzz—zz—zz—zz. The fluorescent hum became a fitful buzz and Deja looked up. It sounded like a fly had gotten trapped within the light fixture, struggling to get out. There might even have been something black skittering behind the foggy plastic, dancing back and forth before going dead still with a final, buzzing flicker of darkness.

The elevator stopped. The doors opened slowly. Painfully so. They dug into the floor with a metallic screech so quiet, Deja might've only imagined the sound. He was known to do that. With a bracing breath, he stepped out. The Warren didn't have distinct floors because it wasn't a building like Omega Headquarters or Osiris. It was a network of tunnels, splayed out beneath the buildings of the Hereafter, connecting it all in a sprawling, bureaucratic web. If it did have its own structure emerging above to mark its official place in the world, Deja'd never seen it. It would probably look a lot like this entryway: Dull, gray, and simple with an odd mix of plain concrete and the occasional swath of raw rock on the wall and floor. Faint green mist drifted throughout the place. That combined with the water dripping from the ceiling to collect in puddles on the concrete below gave the uncanny sense of being underground—that the entire endless complex had been dug out. *Clawed* out.

This gray glimpse of Warren was the entry point for the dozens of other tunnels that managed the cogs and gears of the Hereafter. A drop of water landed on Deja's cheek and he winced, looking up. A simple, gray sign above the one gray-brick-lined archway ahead of him read: *PROCESSING*. It was gated with the same dull metal as the elevator. The gate part, at least, was new. Or it wasn't, and he'd just never seen it *closed* before. He leaned to the side for a better look past the iron bars to the tunnel stretching beyond. There was no one else in this little bureaucratic purgatory. The Warren was sure to be packed with rabbits, but he couldn't see any. They must have had their own way of getting in an out that had nothing to do with the elevators.

It wasn't clear which name came first—if the Warren were so called because it employed rabbits, or if the rabbits were so called because they worked in the Warren. Most people unacquainted with rabbits would probably guess the former. But once seeing for themselves just how twitchy and helpless rabbits looked all the time, they'd join Deja in uncertainty.

Deja strode up to the gate. It didn't open. His mouth twisted as he searched out a means of communicating with whomever managed the thing. He spotted a round indent by the lock with a carved Omega symbol—just the size of his augur. Sure enough, he pressed it there, and the gate opened.

It only took a dozen yards for the tunnel to open up. When Deja stepped out, he nearly jumped; flanking either side of the entrance was a constable. Apart from the lack of hood, mask, and augur, they wore a uniform not unlike his own. But everything from the boots to the jacket to the gloves to the crisp caps was gray. Both masked faces were fixed dead ahead. Neither gave so much as a tilt in Deja's direction. He scoffed. So much for added security. He waited a few moments for one to stop him. When nobody did, he walked out into the huge, cavernous hall.

The place was filled with rows upon rows of desks, and at each one sat a rabbit. Rabbits were paper-pushers. They *were* people—or people-shaped, at least—but to Deja, they always seemed more like *hamsters* spinning the wheels that moved the cogs of this whole operation, typing up and shifting the endless forms and stamps that (one would suppose from the scandalized looks and invisible-pearl-clutching their absence engendered), held the very fabric of existence together. If true, the only thing standing between them and the barren vacuum of non-existence was the Warren and its countless counting desks. Each desk was equipped with a spirit-writer, utilized by the meek rabbit tethered to it. Figuratively speaking... maybe. Didn't matter. What mattered now was that somebody down there knew what trees to start shaking to find out just where those Halloween-light messages in Toronto might've come from.

If they'd really been there at all.

For the most part, the agent uniform granted Deja enough sheer intimidation power to sail past most gatekeepers. He didn't even have to flash an augur, usually. An impatient wave and pointed look were plenty for most guards and overseers; at least, it had been last time he'd visited the Warren. He didn't know what to make of this brave new world of heightened security and gates.

Hopefully an augur wouldn't be required for entry again, because *Good* didn't have an augur. And, while a nice thought, that meant that, for the moment, Deja didn't have one, either. Not if he wanted Good's form to give him legitimate reason to visit the tunnel handling OWLs. He warily eyed the next row of gates, one barring each of the six tunnels that led beyond.

Deja pushed back his shoulders and walked with purpose to the first gatekeeper, Janis. He didn't make a habit of coming down here. No agents did. But when he did come down (usually because he was being disciplined via errand), he always dealt with at least Janis, Overseer of Processing. Janis could be a problem. Unlike every other rabbit in this place, she knew *everybody*. She knew who Deja was and who he wasn't.

Namely, *Good*.

As an overseer, Janis was a supervising rabbit of a sort. She could talk and make eye contact and everything. Her large circular desk stood above the smaller ones under her watch. Connecting it to the walls and ceiling was a network of pneumatic tubes, ready to deliver and dispatch communiques as needed. They made Janis look like a large insect seated amidst a great, tropical plant. If that tropical plant were mostly drab gray wood and copper that had burnished to such extremes that it had long surpassed the colorful green phase and jumped into something like a dark, murky gray-brown that might have had a hint of red or green to it—if you squinted.

Deja squinted at it now.

A short distance beyond Janis's massive desk stood a tall gate in the same burnished-to-gray copper as everything else. Through that, Deja could just make out yet more rabbits dutifully gnawing away at their workloads and utterly oblivious to anything that wasn't a particular form with the requisite stamps. He wrinkled his nose at the rows of gray desks extending endlessly into any of a dozen different tunnels, their walls and floors just as gray as anything else.

The only color came from the spirit-writers' occasional, pathetic puff of green smoke. Peering out from beneath identical neat gray caps were a hundred singularly focused faces, each one singularly focused *down*. All wore the same neat gray vest over the same neat gray shirt, and those neat gray shirts had been fixed with identical neat gray ribbons—ribbons knotted *so* tightly, they looked less like ties than a hundred identical, neat gray nooses.

Janis was a large woman with eyes that recognized everyone and hands that could find any desk or department amidst the tangle of tubes. A gray cap teetered upon short, sleek gray hair. The rabbit badge pinned to her lapel gleamed green in the light of incoming messages. It was so brightly polished, Deja could hardly see the small, raised eye in the design.

Janis reached for an incoming message, not looking at Deja as she immediately transferred it to another tube. She twisted the planch-ette beneath to orient it toward its designated destination, pushed a lever, and sent it on its way. "How's the world, Vale?" she asked, eyes still focused on her work.

"Not much different," Deja said, leaning casually against her desk. "Black appliances are back in. Seems like half the houses I go to these days have black doors or black cabinets, too. And *air fryers*."

"What's an air—" Janis looked up and her eyes went wide. "What happened to your face?" It looked like she was debating recoiling in disgust or leaning closer in morbid curiosity. Indecision kept her hovering and she just stared.

"That bad, huh?" Deja asked. Janis gave him what passed for a concerned look in these parts, and Deja batted her almost-worry away. "I'll take care of it, I just need to cross a few T's first. And no, it's got nothing to do with my face." He waved Good's form. "Not last I checked, anyway."

Janis craned her neck just far enough to peek over the desk at the form. Deja used it to gesture to the tunnel behind him and asked, "I go this way for augur requisition orders, yeah?" already walking backward toward the next gate.

Janis nodded. "Needs a stamp first."

Deja made a silent, "*Ah,*" and smacked himself on the head with his stampless form. "Right, sorry." He did his best to keep the name on top concealed with his fingertips, but there was no need. Janis's eyes were honed in on his lifeburned face. She missed the ink pad twice before managing it. "You sure you're okay?" Morbid curiosity won out and she leaned a little closer.

"Just left Osiris," Deja said as he retrieved the form at a speed optimized to reduce suspicion, quick-yet-restrained. "It looks worse than it is."

"Right," Janis said, already back to work. "You know where you're going?"

"Sure do!" Deja made for the next gate and immediately bumped into a passing rabbit. He ignored the startled squeak—but not the sharp *thud.* The sound cut through the background buzz of typing hands and shuffling papers like a thunderclap.

Deja looked down. For a moment, he thought he'd spotted a flash of color, but there was none: Only a gray, clothbound book on an equally gray, concrete floor. The rabbit who'd dropped it mumbled apologies or explanations or both under her breath. Deja couldn't make the words out. Just the tone. She ducked down, grabbed the book, carefully slipped it into her gray vest, and scampered off. Deja followed her with his eyes until she took her seat at a distant desk.

Odd. He didn't know rabbits could read. It occurred to him he was standing in a department of rabbits typing away at spirit-writers. *Of course, they could read.* He just didn't realize it would ever occur to them to *do* it. It was only when Janis cleared her throat that Deja noticed the gate had already opened. "Sorry," he said, giving Janis a wave she couldn't be bothered to look at. "Take it easy."

Deja cast one last look over the endless rows of desks, and the startled rabbit who'd just taken her seat.

Beyond her, one of the constables turned their head.

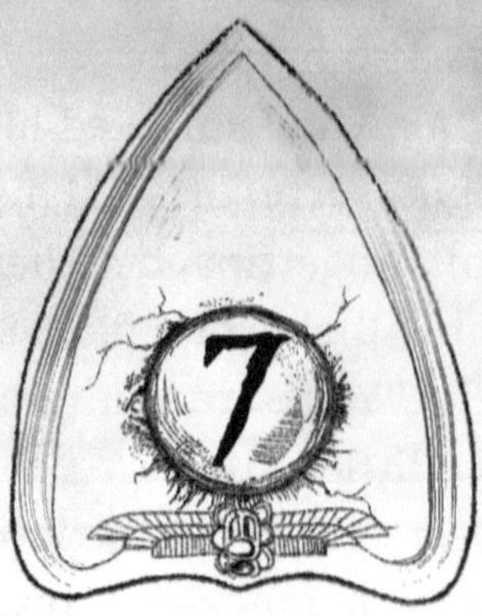

It was often said that Deja thought he was more charming than he actually was. So far, that theory was holding water.

The wide tunnel he passed through now was populated by rabbits busy determining which other tunnel of rabbits upon whom they could pawn off whatever had just landed on their desk. Every ten yards or so, a brick-lined archway (gated) branched off to another tunnel. These days, each was manned by one or two constables. Again, no guard took notice of him—not so far as he could tell. Likewise, not one rabbit spared him so much as a glance when he passed their desks. Every blank eye remained fixed solely on their spirit-writers. There was the occasional flicker of movement when a communique would descend the tube, or a response was sent elsewhere, but that was it.

Deja paused, looking down at a very small woman hunched over her desk. Gnarled fingers moved over the burnished copper keys of her spirit-writer surprisingly fast, considering only two of those fingers actually typed. Deja cleared his throat to no effect. "Acquisitions? Augurs?"

"This isn't Acquisitions," she said, not looking up. *Press. Press. Press.*

"And where would that be?"

Press. Press. Press. "In Acquisitions."

"And *where*, pray tell, is Acquisitions?" Deja asked with a warmth in no way merited by the situation.

"This is not Acquisitions."

"So true," Deja said through a pained smile. He mouthed a silent, "*Yikes*," to himself and backed away. Out of the corner of his eye, he spotted an overseer: A tall woman with a stack of papers in her arms, marching at the determined pace of people who knew where they were going. A glance at the carved eye above the round (and gated) tunnel opening from which she'd just emerged told him she'd come from an Augury-related wing.

Deja made straight for her. She moved to the left to avoid him; he did the same. She moved to the right; he did the same. "After you," he said, gesturing to the right. She moved to the right; he did the same, plowing straight into her path and sending an autumn flurry of papers flying around them. He released his hold on the form he'd borrowed from Good and gasped in mortification.

"Jeepers, I am just so *sorry!*" Deja knelt down to help gather the papers. He gestured to his own face and offered a wan smile. "Lifeburn. Does things to a guy. Darn it all, my AI really does need this form filed"—he picked up papers, eyeing them one at a time—"this it? No. This one? Nuh-uh." He shuffled through the dozens of near-identical black pages scribed with silver ink and said, "It's a black piece of paper—silver ink," utterly unhelpfully.

He spotted the symbol of the Augury, a silver planchette containing a lidless eye, and held it up, squinting at it. First glance told him it was a log of chime requests at various locations, including a recent field op in Toronto—quite possibly his own. Just three were listed: one chime patched through, two chimes denied (one *emphatically*). He recognized Agent Good's Omega identification code beside the chime that had been patched through to the Augury. His eyes darted around for an issuing department or name with signing power. Hands feverishly attempted to snatch back the paper and Deja ignored them, pulling the paper just out of reach as he asked, "Does this look like a requisition form to you—" The overseer finally managed to snatch back the paper with a glare. "So that's a 'no,' I take it? Ah!" He plucked up the requisition form and gave the rabbit a winning smile. "This is me. I'll get out of your fur, shall I?"

"Funny," she grumbled, "real original," and stomped away, reshuffling the papers into some semblance of order. Deja just caught the fluffy tail-end of a devastating commentary on agents, their entitled attitudes, and something about their pathological narcissism. Or pathological Darwinism. Hard to say at that distance.

He'd also caught a glimpse of a few other fluffy tail-ends on that document. The first was the name of the mediating department: Otherworldly Letters - Dispatch. It was a department he'd never had reason to visit before, but chances were it was the one he needed now. Made sense. More useful was the second—the issuing desk number for that one accepted chime from Good: 0101. If that had been the desk of the rabbit who'd handled the successful Augury communication that Good had evidently managed, then maybe they would be the one to know who might have—or *could* have—used those string lights to contact him. Maybe *that* had been the one communication request that hadn't been denied? But no. Good's augur had already detonated at that point. There was no reason to expect confusion over which agent had (allegedly) stolen whoever else's augur. But if Deja's terse exchange with an Augury representative explaining why he wasn't being patched through to a higher-up hadn't qualified as an accepted chime, why wouldn't Good's *own* terse exchange with an Augury representative about how *he* wasn't being patched through to a higher-up be the same?

Unless Good had managed another chime on that mission that Deja hadn't seen because Deja wasn't with him at the time. Which left all of one minute (if that) when Good entered the house before Deja himself had. Curious as it was, that wasn't the priority. Figuring out just where that impossible OWL in the string lights had come from—if not Deja's own broken mind—was the priority. He cast a rueful eye at the gate barring access to all things Augury.

Then he remembered what he was actually here for and looked down at Good's now-crumpled form. How hard should he sell the Agent-Good shtick? The only person in the Warren he could recognize by name was Janis. Hopefully, it was mutual. While trying his best to smooth out the wrinkles, Deja approached the next wrought iron gate. From the center stared a lidless eye, naillike lashes latched into the ironwork like a menacing spider. Granted, it had been some time since Deja'd had reason to be in the Warren, and the Augury-mediating departments weren't exactly an old haunt of his, but he could've sworn that gate was new. He eyed the dark but pristine metal. Certainly didn't look *old*—

"YES?"

"Fuck!" Deja jumped back, recoiling from the great, snaking periscope that had descended before him, nearly poking him in the face with its big green eye. It looked disturbingly real—and *wet*—but it was just as unblinking as the one in the gate. Somehow, it managed to scowl without the aid of eyebrows. Impressive, really.

And incredibly off-putting.

A tinny voice barked at him, "State your business, Agent!" Each hard sound rattled like rocks down the metal pipe.

"My AI sent me down to acquisition a new augur?"

The eye pressed closer to Deja's face, forcing him to either recoil or find out if that eye was *squishy* or not. "Name?"

"Agent Good."

"Do you have acquisition form Beta-Z-19?"

Deja held up the form up in front of his face like a shield. "Oh, sorry," he murmured, rotating it to face right-side-up.

Silence. Then, a sticky *tap* against the paper. "Proceed to Tunnel Six, Agent Good." The snake closed back in on itself with a metallic shuffle like Satan's Slinky.

Deja blinked and turned the paper over. A smudged, white eye had been printed on the top right corner. He really hoped it was a stamp that existed *separately* from the cranky eyeball snake. "Will do," he said distantly, edging through the barely opened gate like a fat raccoon through a closed dumpster lid. "Thanks."

AUGURY - ACQUISITIONS was the second tunnel on the right, and Deja blew right past it. Once neatly laid bricks gave way to rougher hewn stone, he started squinting at each increasingly faded sign he passed: Interdepartmental Disputes, Intradepartmental Disputes, Engineering – Augurs, Depositions, Destinations, Cross-plane Communications—

Deja hung a sharp right and stepped through a portal to a whole other nexus of tunnels. A fat drop of water (hopefully) hit his cheek, and he winced, looking up. Faded gray brick dissolved into shadows— shadows, he suspected, that no being had ever entered and no being ever would. He wiped his cheek and made for the paltry light of what was (yet more hopefully) a relevant department. His shoulders relaxed at the next faded sign, *Otherworldly Letters – Dispatch*, and he stepped in.

Given that OWLs were used by every agent on every mission, it was shocking to see just how few occupied desks there were—far fewer than any other department he'd passed. There were about a hundred desks, but only a third were occupied. Just as gray as the others, just as neatly lined. But, given the scattered white cups and saucers placed deliberately on the floors and desks, he'd guess mysterious drippage was more of an issue here than elsewhere.

Rabbits moved in sync like waves on a mournful sea.

Type type type.

Push the lever.

Pull out the paper.

Slip into the tray.

Plume of green smoke.

Pull the lever.

Type type type.

Deja approached the frontmost desk, labeled DESK 0000. Beyond the shoulder-height, peeling gray partition that framed every desk, sat a pale-skinned man with eyes so wrinkled and hooded, Deja could hardly find them. He was scanning through the massive document spilling onto the floor beside him. Deja could just make out a list of something or other, each and every item neatly crossed out until you reached the man's hands. The man crossed out an item. The massive paper snake shed its skin, and all items rustled downward. He crossed out another item.

"Hello," Deja said brightly. The man nearly jumped out of his seat; Deja mouthed an apology. "Say, if I had a concern about a recent Augury communique, who'd be the one to poke?" When met with a glassy-eyed look, Deja gave him a reassuring smile. "I don't mean that literally. Can you *imagine*?" His smile flickered at the visible discomfort before him. "Please stop imagining it. I can tell you're still doing it and I need you to stop." The stare didn't abate, but Deja's forced politeness sure did. "Look," he said flatly, "I'm sorry to disrupt your eternal tedium, but if you could help me with my inquiries instead of just staring at me like I'm a giant demented Canadian hell-clown, I'd appreciate it."

Upon the word *clown*, there followed a marked offbeat in the uniform rhythm of typing hands and shifting papers. Just the briefest flicker of eyes looking *at* Deja and not *through* him. A shark's fin disrupting that sad sea.

"You know what? Thanks anyway," Deja said, pushing himself away from the desk to make for the only rabbit alone in their row. As he walked past four rows of downcast eyes, he noted the desk numbers along the way and only stopped once he reached the least pathetic thing there.

A pair of very dark, very sharp eyes.

Said eyes belonged to a youngish-looking man with waves of dark hair that had been combed into something approximating submission. His features looked more sculpted than carved from mid-toned skin. It was a face that seemed to pick up the pathetic light of his little lamp far better than the metal keys at his fingertips. Even softened as they were by thick lashes, those eyes still managed to look like the sharpest things in the whole Warren. Now, those eyes were singularly focused on his task: compiling lists of individual letters. Just letters. In a list. That went on forever. At the top of that list was an address in Schenectady, New York.

The spirit-writer made a feeble chirping noise, and the rabbit plucked the black paper from the device. He folded it and placed it in a smoking tray neatly labeled: *Outgoing.* The paper disintegrated in flameless fire then disappeared, leaving nothing but a fresh layer of ash to the soot already caking the tray. That inanimate tray was the only outgoing thing there so far as Deja could tell. Unless he counted the white saucer precariously situated on the floor two feet away, delegated with catching the occasional drop of water from the ceiling. Its jaunty angle managed a bit of personality.

Deja's eyes moved to the faded desk plaque: 0044. Then he eyed the rabbit pin fixed to the rabbit's gray lapel, dull with patina except for the raised eye. Deja could barely make out what he could only guess was a name etched on the bar beneath—not that he'd realized anybody but overseers *had* names—but if he had to guess from the somewhat clear J and A, he'd say it was—

"Jamie? Can I call you Jamie?"

"Not for any reason I can see," Not-Jamie said, still not looking at him.

"Fair enough." Deja picked up an empty teacup and examined it. A faint green ring from bygone aether lined the bottom; it didn't seem like it'd been used for anything but catching ceiling drips for some time. He didn't realize rabbits drank aether, either. Judging from how coagulated it looked, they hadn't been recently. He didn't realize aether *could* coagulate.

He was just realizing all sorts of shit today.

A grating sigh. "Looking for prints, are we?" the rabbit asked.

Deja replaced the cup with a careful *clink*. "Why in thirteen hells would I do that?"

The response was a look that said as clearly as any words could: *because that's what agents do.*

Deja had been curious about the impossible OWL, Good's one accepted chime, and this particular rabbit—in that order. But now he was rabbit-*curiouser. So* rabbit-curious, that the lingering vertigo of lifeburn could hardly get a word in edgewise. Just as he opened his mouth to ask for the rabbit's real name, he was cut off by a statement that almost made him forget his reason for being there entirely.

"I know why you were sent to me," Not-Jamie said. "Contrary to what you people think, I'm not actually stupid."

Deja opened and closed his mouth a few times. "I didn't think you were." His brow furrowed. "And if you know why I was sent to you, that makes precisely one of us."

"*Right.*" Not-Jamie continued typing a few moments, then paused to point out, "Last I checked, I'm not a *ghost,* so I don't really see how I fall into your jurisdiction. Are we done here, *Agent...*?"

"Good," Deja answered. "And I'm not investigating you."

"I'm sure whoever's in charge of your performance review will be relieved to hear it, because you are doing a real bang-up job."

"Wow, you're really coming for me today, huh?"

"About as much as any rabbit ever could, sure." *Type, type, type.*

Deja stared at him in tight-lipped silence for what might've been sixteen rabbit heartbeats. "Okay, I'm going to need you to stop being so sarcastic because *I'm* usually the sarcastic"—he plowed through the rabbit's whispered, "*Wow,*" and continued—"one in these sorts of exchanges."

"Well, well, we're quite easily threatened, aren't we?" the rabbit observed without breaking his typing speed for a moment. "*Shock-ing.*"

"Well, yeah... you did see the gloves, right?" Deja asked, holding up a hand and giving his fingers a pointed wiggle. "I've been led to believe my ilk are all pathological Darwinists."

The rabbit's brow arched like he'd been considering looking at the gloves, decided he didn't, in fact, *care* and continued typing. Just as Deja was about to push himself away from the partition, the rabbit said, "That form you're holding is an Acquisitions form. This is not Acquisitions." He gave a small shrug that spoke to efforts not being made on this agent's behalf. "I'm sure you didn't need a lowly rabbit telling you that, what with your well-honed skills of observation and all." He worked in silence a little while longer before adding, "Skip dealing with Locke today, if you can. She got chewed out by the Augury and she's looking to spread the frustration. Curio's much easier to deal with. Desk on the right."

"Oh."

The rabbit did look up at him then, eyes bright and focused. That look hit Deja with the uncanny sense that this must be how mathematical problems feel when undertaken by someone who knows how integers work. He swallowed. Not-Jamie just kept staring. Then, in a rare stroke of mercy, the rabbit observed, "You don't sound pleased."

"I, uh… no! That is good to know. Thanks." Deja gave the partition a little pat and took a few steps back, whistling an awkward tune. The rabbit's eyes were back to his spirit-writer before Deja could so much as wave. He took another few steps until the rabbit disappeared from his view. Then—

"You're back," the rabbit observed blankly, not looking up. "*Lucky me.*"

"Thought just your feet were lucky."

Eyes shifted to him, narrowed, then returned to their task.

"I've got a question," Deja said, "concerning *Otherworldly Letters.* You know Alphabet Crunch?"

"In theory."

"Uh-huh. Word-i-O's?"

"In theory."

"Alphabet rainbow refrigerator magnets?"

"Depends," the rabbit droned. "Are they rainbow alphabet magnets that go on a refrigerator? Or alphabet magnets specifically made for rainbow refrigerators exclusively?"

"Yes."

"In theory."

"Uh-huh. How about rap codes?" The rabbit's typing pace slowed a fraction; Deja kept going. "And how would any of those things make their way into the Desert, unauthorized and outside a tether field without a Warren record in these our securest of times?"

"In theory?" Not-Jamie's eyes shifted to Deja's just long enough for the Agent to nod once before returning to his spirit-writer.

"Purely hypothetically, yeah."

Long hands stilled above burnished keys. The rabbit leaned back and folded his arms across his chest. He chewed his bottom lip thoughtfully a moment, eyes drifting to the sooty tray beside him. Then he just said, "That is way above my pay grade," and got back to work.

Deja's brow pinched. "You people get paid?"

A small snort.

"Gotcha." Deja looked at the number on the desk again: still 0044. The desk that had approved Good's completed augur communique was 0101. He squinted up the aisle, counting silently to himself as he determined which row said desk would be in. Given that only the first third of desks were occupied, it was most likely empty. "Hey, Peter—"

"—not my name—"

"—where's Desk 0101?"

"Not here," was all the rabbit said. When Deja stared at him—and didn't *stop* staring—he spoke with the flat tone of somebody reciting from rote, "There are one-hundred and one desks, including the Overseer's at the front: Desk 0000."

"But a chime was patched through by somebody at Desk 0101," Deja said, narrowing his eyes. No response. He began striding up the aisle, head swiveling as he noted the numbers: 0041, 0042.... Once he reached the last row, he turned right to begin at Desk 091, then walked back along the empty desks all the way to—

Desk 0100.

Deja stared at it. Then he stared at the place Desk 0101 *would* be, assuming there was any consistency in numbering logic. Just a blank stone wall. Water dripped from the ceiling and landed in the divot its fellow drips had been carving into the stone for some years now. Nobody'd bothered to put down a saucer to collect those because nobody was *there*.

Deja forced a breath, muttered, "Right," and strode back to the desk of Not-Jamie. He channeled Good. Surly as he could manage without spraining something, he folded his arms across his chest and cleared his throat. Nothing but the continued *click clack* of typing fingers responded. "Okay, answer me this, Bugs—"

"Not my name—"

"Where *would* I be able to find Desk 0101 if not here?" When Not-Jamie looked up, Deja offered him his best impression of an expectant and agitated Agent Good. Not-Jamie raised him a brief but eloquent *Go fuck yourself* glare and returned to his work.

"Fine." Deja tossed a flat, "Thanks," behind him and began to walk away—

"Mind the saucer."

Deja froze, mid-step. *Type, type, type.* Deja shifted his booted foot from its trajectory of testing the structural integrity of Warren crockery to land on faded, damp brick instead.

A flash of red in the cup. Deja blinked and stared down at it. Nothing. Then it was there again like a splash of scarlet tea—a stain in the shape of a letter. *M.* Just like the elevator. He waited for more letters but none came, only the occasional ripple against white when a water drop fell from the ceiling.

Deja rubbed at his lifeburned eyes and kept walking. The still-terrified rabbit seated at Desk 0000 was trying very, very hard not to look at him. As Deja left, he struggled to parse out what it would mean if that impossible message in the flickering string lights *hadn't* been a hallucination. That thought carved the same shape in his mind as the message itself:

Mind the cat.

NOT-JAMIE WASN'T just a mystery. He was also a liar and a sadist. *Locke* would have been the Overseer to visit. *Curio* was the one with a vendetta against the universe.

Curio was the spectacled rabbit before Deja now, sassing him through the gate separating them. "And how was it the augur came to be terminated?" he asked—for the fourth coney time.

"Well," Deja said as reasonably as he could manage under extreme interrogatory distress that no amount of training could have prepared him for, "I assume one of *you* good people triggered its termination, thereby risking the safety of me and my fellow agents—not to mention the living and near-living present."

"Don't take that tone with me, Agent"—Curio looked at Deja for the first time—"why does your face look like that?"

"Field damage. What's your excuse?"

Curio gasped. Glasses slid down his long nose to pinch the nostrils shut, forcing his simmering rage out in a whistle like a clogged teakettle. His mouth twisted into an impressive knot as he reached for Deja's form. He gave it a spite-laden stamp before passing it back. "Your new augur will be ready in two to three weeks."

Deja spluttered, "Two to three *weeks*?"

"Since you look like somebody who can't multiply with his shoes on, that'll be twelve to eighteen days."

"You expect me to do my job—preserving the balance of souls, protecting the realms of the living, dead, and in-between—without an *augur*?" Deja demanded. "For *two to three weeks*?"

"Or twelve to eighteen days, yes," Curio said with a brittle smile. "Do you think we just keep un-honed augurs *lying about*? Do you have any idea how long it takes to craft a new augur? To hone a new augur to its agent's spiritual signature? How much work it takes to ensure the security of chimes? No? Well maybe *next* time, you'll be a little more careful with valuable Augury-issued equipment!" He eyed Deja up and down, withering gaze lingering on lifeburn-speckled gloves. "But I won't hold my breath. Good day, Agent Good."

"Yeah, sure. *Good day*," Deja grumbled, leaving the bureaucratic hound of Hades behind.

But it was not a good day.

Agent Good—the *real* Agent Good—stood before Deja, arms folded across his chest. Deja'd really have to step up his Agent-Good-impersonation game in future. *He'd* just looked pissy. But *Good's* face was fixed into a look of quiet disdain so powerful, they could've molded dramatic masks from it. His resting bitch face had clawed its way out of hibernation and was now *active* bitch face.

Good active-bitchily grabbed Deja by the arm and dragged him bodily from the Augury Acquisitions department and into the dripping hall outside. He spun on Deja and tightened his grip. Deja winced; the man was gripping him on an old wound. Or so he'd guess; he couldn't actually remember getting it.

"Would you care to explain to me," Good gritted, "just why *Agent Good* was in the Augury department pursuing some sort of investigation in *Otherworldly Letters?*" Another squeeze of Deja's arm. "While on *fucking probation?* Because of *Agent Vale?*"

Deja blinked at him. "Wow, that was fast—"

Good gave his arm another yank and Deja grimaced in pain. "Answer the fucking question, Vale!"

"Love to, sweetie, but I think I'm about to—"

Deja didn't need to say, 'Pass out.'

He saved them all some time and just *did it.*

"**V**ale...."

Deja wrinkled his nose: One nostril at the prospect of ending his sweet unconsciousness, the other at the familiar stink of an Osiris recovery room. One of two faces would be waiting for him when he opened his eyes, and he was looking forward to precisely *none of them*.

"Hello, Vale."

That wasn't Good *or* Vex. Deja blinked. Ever's round-cheeked, strong-jawed (and seldom-amused) face looked down at him. "Remember me?"

"Unfortunately."

Ever gave him an annoyed look. Thick arms folded across a broad chest, making her look even more physically formidable. No small feat, considering. She was both far larger and taller than him—than Good, too. Always gave Deja a small, petty sort of satisfaction knowing that this *freak* could easily kick Good's ass in the training square. And Deja's ass too, but that was less satisfying knowledge.

Pale brows went up and Ever asked, "You do know why I have to ask, yes?"

"I see what you did there, Ever. Clever you."

Ever forced a smile, brief and brittle. The feeling was mutual.

Ever always looked like she knew something Deja didn't. Now, she probably did.

It was a low bar these days.

Deja grimaced at the medicinal *blegh* caking his mouth; it made his breath smell sickly sweet. Experience warned him that special brand of *eau de fuck you* would cling to his nostrils for days yet. Still, he'd take the burning smells of the Desert over the persistent stink of M-balm any day. He touched his face and felt two linens there, one on each cheek. That checked out. A glance down his bare torso told him another had been plastered over his heart—couldn't say *why*, though. A fourth was on his abdomen, obscuring part of the black sigil framing his navel. The intertwining words that formed the sigil were eclipsed from noon to four o'clock. Didn't matter. Those words represented sounds far too ancient and hallowed or whatever to be remembered. So he'd been told.

More or less.

"You know," Ever mused, "yours is more elaborate than mine?"

Deja narrowed his eyes at the sigil on his own abdomen. It was more elaborate than *his*, too. He glanced over at Ever's stomach as if he could see her sigil through the uniform. When foiled by physics, his gaze shifted to her hip instead; there was no holster there. Unlike Deja, it probably wasn't because *her* mortifier had been taken away; *she* may never have needed one. Deja'd never worked with Ever in the field. There were a hundred times having an agent at his side who could deal a devastating punch to any ghosts getting fresh would have been handy, but *no*. Odds like them were distributed amongst the teams, though plenty would prefer that not be the case. For some, because they'd like to have two or even three such agents watching their backs. Others—far more, probably—because they'd rather have no "special" agents at all.

Wren was of the former category. The man lighting up the doorway with the force of his scowl might just be acting treasurer of the latter. Good's scowl faded (relatively speaking) when he addressed the Odd who'd never set him on fire (allegedly). "Any escape attempts?"

Ever shook her head.

"Petty crimes?"

"Only in his Odd little dreams." Ever gave Good an ironic smile. "Which I'm sure were *all about you.*"

Except they weren't, because Deja hadn't had any.

Good stared at her. "*Funny.*" To Deja, he said, "Vex is back. On his way here." His eyes shifted downward and his expression faltered. Deja followed his gaze; it led to his own bare abdomen. And it tickled. When Deja cleared his throat, Good tossed a pair of new, pristine gloves at his bandaged face.

Deja plucked them up with a murmured, "Thanks," then frowned at Ever. Both of them were Odds, but they were hardly close. It was hard getting close to their own kind with the whole one-Freak-per-team policy. But here she was, sitting at his bedside… maybe had been all afternoon. "How long have you been here?" he asked.

Ever straightened in her chair. "Well, I haven't been here for *days,* if that's—"

"*Days*—?!" Deja demanded, rising from the bed only to be shoved back down by a person far larger, far stronger than him.

"Right," Ever said primly as she effortlessly pinned a struggling Deja to the bed. "I'm out. And if you need him carried *out* of here, Good? Do it yourself this time."

Deja stopped struggling to stare at her, then he stared at Good. His eyeballs didn't particularly like what they found there so they retreated back to Ever. "You carried me out of the Warren all the way here?"

Ever's only answer was a look straddling the border between patient and withering—the sort adults gave children during games of hide-and-seek when asked, *But how did you know I was hiding behind the hat stand, Aunty Odd?*

Good warned, "Almost here."

Ever released Deja, stood, and straightened the cuffs of her jacket. "That's my cue." A quick nod to Deja. "Vale."

"Ever," Deja said. He was still incredibly confused but knew enough to be equally grateful. "Thanks."

Ever didn't respond. In the doorway, she leaned toward Good to whisper something Deja couldn't hear. But he could see the jaw-clenching nod Good gave in response. Then, Ever was gone.

Not a minute later, Vex had arrived. "Gentlemen. Happy to see you actually exercising some self-preservation and staying in bed... *for once.*"

Over Vex's shoulder, Deja just caught Good's valiant (and failed) attempt at suppressing an eyeroll.

"So," Vex said, turning to Good, "any complications in requisitioning your augur, Agent?"

"Not as such, no." Good's lie, shocking though it was, rolled over Deja like overheard small talk about the weather they weren't having. But that may have just been the mental sluggishness. He grimaced at the mortar and pestle on the table beside him. The remnants of whatever concoction he'd been anointed with lingered in black dust in the porcelain bowl. Certainly explained said sluggishness and the feeling his hands had been replaced with balloon animals fashioned by Bruno the Clownfetti Pile.

Good cleared his throat. "It'll take another one to two weeks"— he gave Vex a wry look—"if you can believe that." It was the second time Good had lied for Deja that week. But, given that Good had been tasked with watching after Deja and kept *failing miserably*, he was hardly in the running for any Martyr of the Year awards.

Deja resisted the urge to get out of bed to suss out the contents of whatever in thirteen hells he'd been dosed with. If the choice was between getting berated by Vex and gross black stuff, he wanted some more of the latter.

You really don't, a small voice whispered. And it whispered from a place that smelled like chalk.

No, Deja agreed silently. He didn't want more of it. Fuck knows he'd already had plenty these past six months.

"Unfortunately, I *can* believe it." Vex rubbed a hand across his beard, considering. "Now that I'm back, I'll see if I can't get that expedited."

"I'd appreciate that, sir."

"It's entirely selfish, I assure you," Vex told Good, silver brows rising. "I've just gotten one of my best out of Osiris only for him to end up back in his recovery bed."

Deja looked around. It *could* be the same room he'd had before—same white walls, same linen sheets, same medicinal smells, same pristine white instruments—but then, each room looked identical. Only the position of the door and window might change. He frowned and tried to remember if the window had always been to his right. Seemed like an easy enough thing to remember, but that was M-balm for you.

"I can hardly afford to have another of my best without his augur." Vex turned his focus to Deja and said sternly, "Heed the advice of your technicians, Agent. If I have to waste Agent Good's considerable abilities on babysitting you *indefinitely,* you will find me most *unhappy.*"

Deja nodded. "Understood, sir."

"Wonderful," Vex said flatly. "And see about getting those glasses fixed, Agent. With any luck, I'll have Good's augur ready for him by week's end. I expect you to be field-ready when he is."

Good balked. "Sir, shouldn't—*all due respect*—shouldn't Vale—"

"If the events of this past year have proven anything, Good," Vex said, "it is that Osiris has its limits in what it can and cannot accomplish, whether through the healing arts, negotiation, pleading, bribery, or otherwise." His pointed look in Deja's direction was as good as a declaration: *behold the limit.*

Good looked as close to shocked as he'd ever allowed himself to look before an agent inquisitor.

So, it *wasn't* just Deja confused at the sudden change in tune, then. Small comfort. And, happy as Deja was to be declared competent enough to return to the field, he did wonder just why it was Vex—who'd told him only days ago that he'd been *against* sending Deja back to the Desert—wanted him out of Osiris *now.*

No answers could be found on Vex's face, just his usual, stony composure. And beard. "I want you both back out there and I want you out there *as a team.* Like it or not, you do perform rather well together."

Good looked to be desperately searching for some counterpoint—any reason for why he should be moved back to whichever team he'd come from, or why Deja should be locked up in some backroom in Osiris and never let out to see the black light of the moon again. In the end, he only said, "Understood, sir," and watched their AI leave. Deja counted ten of Vex's departing footsteps before Good turned back to him. He raised a finger in a warning point, opened his mouth, sighed one of his more grating sighs, then turned to leave with a muttered, "Not even fucking worth it."

Deja was inclined to agree. He rolled his head to the side and stared at that mortar and pestle again. An acrid, medicinal scent lingered there. Unless it was just the aftertaste haunting the back of his throat. It tasted like things he couldn't remember. Long after the physical injuries of that Last Mission healed beyond stiffness and ghosting pain, the fear remained—and always, *always* that smell and taste. Deja ran his tongue along the back of his teeth as if he could scrub it away.

You didn't see anything. You only thought you saw color because of the lifeburn on your eyes. It could happen to anyone. You aren't losing your grip. You're fine.

But the fear stayed, stubborn as the cloying stink of medicinal herbs. Given just how carefully Vex had Good watching him now, Deja wasn't alone in that fear.

"Agent?" A white-caped, white-masked attendant entered. She presented a neat, white bag and carefully placed it on the end of his bed. "M-balm, bandages, and technician instructions are inside," she said, her voice like a morning chirp. "Don't remove your bandages until tomorrow morning. Contact us if you have any questions."

Deja pushed himself onto his elbows. "I can leave?"

"Yes, agent," she said with faint surprise.

"That's it? Nothing else? No dietary restrictions? No orders to stay away from booze? Nothing?"

The attendant stared down at him. Even behind the mask, her abject confusion was plain. After a long, awkward while, she finally managed a tremulous, "Sorry?"

Deja took mercy on her. "*Never mind.*"

HABITS HAVE A way of shaping the world. Deja had spent far too many months aimlessly pacing the twenty-first floor of Osiris for his feet to take him anywhere else but right back there. Certainly not while his mind was so distracted, anyway. Floor 21 was for long-term stays, as he himself had been just last week. Marion, so far as he knew, still was. She was an Odd like him. Like Ever. Like Omen had been before he was lost like so many others who'd been lost, too. But Marion wasn't quite here, either. Like Deja, her mission had gone sideways. Unlike Deja, she'd never woken up.

When Deja stepped out of the stairwell and into the hall, he hadn't expected to see anybody—least of all the rookie. But there Izik was, walking up the hall and toward the stairwell where he stood, her eyes downcast. She noticed him once she got about ten feet away and went still as a bunny who'd clocked a dog. Deja himself looked around to make sure he really was in the correct wing. The sign marking this as the wing for long-term stays glinted obligingly above him. He asked Izik, "Have you been here this whole time?"

"What?" Izik asked. Deja nodded at the sign, and Izik shook her head. "No. Just came back for a checkup."

"Gotcha..." Deja said, still a bit baffled by her presence. "And did it, uh... check up?"

"Uh-huh. Leg's still attached." Just to prove it, Izik gave her foot a wiggle.

"Good, good," Deja said absently. "So, you can walk okay?"

"Mhmm."

"Any pain?"

Deja looked past Izik's increasingly confused face. Marion's door was just a dozen steps away. He didn't particularly want to have to explain to this kid just who Marion was and what brought him there—or anything, really. The odd emptiness in his chest tunneled there by the M–balm joined the subtle ache behind his eyes in a symphony of *no thank you.* So, he just nodded once, said, "Right, well, see you around," and walked around Izik to get to the elevators.

Footsteps followed him. Deja closed his eyes and took a breath. *This kid lied for you. You don't need to be bestest buds, but the least you could do is not be a complete Good about it.* When Izik called after him, "What about you? Are *you* okay?" he stopped, turned, and waited for her to catch up.

"Yeah," Deja said as he summoned the elevator. "More or less."

"Good. I'm glad." Izik folded her hands in front of her and stared at the floor numbers glinting above the elevator, counting down its arrival.

"So... you, uh... like being an agent?"

The elevator door opened, and Deja gestured inside; Izik entered and he followed after. "Um, yeah," Izik said, very unconvincingly. "It's certainly interesting."

"Interesting is only a word people use when they're trying not to say something else."

Izik's eyes fell. "Maybe."

"Come on, kid," Deja said through a sigh. "Spit it out."

Izik shrugged. "I'm grateful I was chosen. I am. I just wasn't exactly hoping to get injured my first time in the field is all."

"That's it?" Deja scoffed. "Injuries just show you're invested. Don't sweat it."

"Really?" Izik asked, looking up once more.

The doors opened to the lobby. Deja stepped out as he assured her, "Absolutely. Now, if you *never* got injured, that would be cause for concern. But you got it out of the way right from the off so you don't even need to worry about it now. Good job."

"Oh. Well, how often do you think I should get injured, then? To show I'm dedicated."

Deja hummed, considering. He'd just been about to ask her if she knew the difference between *biennial* and *biannual* when Osiris's front doors burst open.

Two attendants carried a stretcher inside. Whoever—or whatever—laid there was concealed by a thin linen sheet. "Hold the elevator!" one shouted.

Deja immediately shifted to the side and held the door open.

A technician strode from the other end of the hall and demanded, "What happened here?" voice clipped.

"Lifeburn," one attendant said as she backed into the elevator.

"How much aether's been given?" the technician asked.

The other attendant answered, "None, Magister."

One attendant offered explanation—"There wasn't any"—while the other gave justification: "Something went wrong in the field and her mask failed."

The technician sounded almost fearful then. "Failed? What could have possibly caused that?"

"We don't know." The sheet shrouding whoever it was caught beneath an attendant's foot and slipped off. The attendants and technicians were far too focused on helping her to fix it.

It was Agent Sine.

At least, Deja thought it was. All but a narrow stretch of skin along the left side of her face was shining black and peeling. Pieces of her fell away and disintegrated to nothing before they could even hit the floor. Her left eye stared blankly at the ceiling. Her right eye was gone. So was her right ear and right hand. Her left hand twitched on the stretcher beside her. There was a repetition and rhythm to the fitful movements of Sine's fingers. She was rapping out a word in code, over and over and over.

FREAK.

Those fingers disintegrated before Deja's widening eyes.

Until the elevator doors closed, Deja didn't realize he'd pulled away. He rubbed at the old wound on his palm in a futile attempt to soothe the sudden pain away. It did fade, but not because of anything he'd done.

Izik stared dead ahead. She'd have had lifeburn explained to her in training, but she wouldn't have seen it before. Not like that. Deja considered asking if she was okay but there was no point. Who *would* be okay? Well, Deja would. And that was the problem. Nothing terrified agents more than the prospect of being caught in the violent light and heat of the living world without protection—unless you were him. And they hated him for it. Izik had been friendly to him before—bizarrely *loyal*, even—but that was over now. Because now, Izik could better understand the fear that kept so many agents at his arm's length.

The Odd who didn't burn like they did.

The freak who reminded them of their worst fears by just existing.

Izik was still staring at the doors.

Deja cleared his throat. "Kid?" Still staring. "You sure you want to be an Omega agent?"

Izik didn't look much like she did. Glassy eyes stayed fixed on the doors as she answered, "I was chosen. Wasn't I?"

"Yeah," Deja said. "Guess we all were." *Sine included.* He gave Izik's arm a poke. She didn't move. He really ought to just leave her alone with her fears, but he couldn't. He poked her again. Izik flashed him an unsure, apologetic look then resumed walking beside him.

Once outside Osiris, Deja asked, "Did you see the message that Sine was rapping? With her right hand?"

"Was she?" Izik asked. Just when Deja began to wonder if *that* hadn't been a mental fabrication on his part, Izik explained, "They didn't teach us any code."

"Really?" Deja frowned then conceded, "I guess we don't use it much apart from giving each other shit on missions, but still."

"What was she saying?"

Deja shrugged. "Not sure."

"I see...." Izik walked beside him in silence a while before asking, "Are you heading back to barracks?"

"No," Deja said. "I don't stay there."

Izik's surprise pierced her earlier shock. "I didn't know that."

Deja shrugged again. A few more steps. "You okay?" When Izik nodded, he said, "Then I'll see you around," and walked on.

"Agent Vale?"

Deja braced himself. He turned.

"You're really incredible," Izik said.

Deja stared at her. It was his turn to stand there in shocked silence, and Izik's turn to walk away. He watched her go down the wide white stairs, all the way across the square, and disappear through a stone archway before he managed to compose himself. He couldn't remember the last time anyone had called him *incredible*, let alone in reference to his Oddity. Probably never.

Deja resumed walking. It only took a few steps for that minor shock to fade. Now, Sine's charred and disintegrating face came into nauseating focus. She had only just come back from their Toronto mission, but she'd already had time to debrief, brief, go out into the field yet again *and* come back? Deja really had been in that Osiris bed for far longer than he'd realized. That, or when they'd said agents were spread thin—aether, too—they'd meant it.

He'd just beheld the consequences.

Sine wasn't going to make it. Deja could see that. He couldn't shake the feeling that she wouldn't be the last casualty, either. As he made his way across the neat stone of Osiris Square, he forced himself not to look up at the massive, white technician statue looming over him. Just how he forced himself not to look at the faces of the agents passing him by—any of whom might be next.

It probably wouldn't be Deja, was the thing. Many agents resented that.

But not nearly as much as he did.

DEJA HARDLY REMEMBERED making the trek from Osiris Square to the winding, cobbled stone and thick, green fog of the Floating

District, but it was little surprise he'd ended up in this bar. Quiet music whispered and warbled in fits and starts from the geriatric gramophone gasping jazz in the corner. That warbling quality could just as easily have been a product of Lonnie Johnson and friends as the antique playing it. Deja turned the empty glass over in his hands, examining his reflection. Flecks of pearlescent sheen still marred his gray skin like freckles painted a few shades off on an otherwise handsome portrait. Well... *he* thought he was handsome, anyway.

"Your glasses are dirty," Deja said, critically eyeing a splotch of silvery gray on his reflected cheek.

"That's your face, sweetie-pops."

Deja shot the woman behind the bar a look. Darling Dear just kept polishing glasses, her entire being indifferent as ever. He turned his attention back to his reflection in the glass and demanded, "What?" more to himself than any nearby bartenders. When he spotted some lingering lifeburn *beneath* stubble, his face fell. "Yeah...."

Darling polished on. Ukiyo was her establishment. It had been something of an underground institution in the Hereafter's Floating District long before Deja'd arrived (so he'd been told) and it would still be there long after he'd gone (so he was reminded when he got obnoxious). Like the trains and elevators, much of the Floating District never seemed content to stay the same. Also like them, there were some things that never changed. The drifting, green-tinged fog that always blanketed the narrow streets and dark alleyways... the smell of smoke... the barest glow of green light that seemed to emit from the gutters themselves.

But Ukiyo was different. That bar knew itself. So rich and real was the feel of the place, there was even a sense of *color* like nowhere else. You couldn't see it, obviously, but you still knew when you passed through the black *noren* curtain at the door and took your seat at that bar and shared a nod with Darling Dear that her dark lips were painted *red*. A red as sharp as her dress. You knew the dust on the bottles concealed deep greens and ambers. You knew the polished brass was real *brass*. It was precisely that uncanny feature that brought Deja back again and again. And maybe that was what kept everyone else away.

A second feature that also brought Deja back again and again.

Every now and then, Ukiyo's walls and furniture would give way to the occasional flicker of another time. A fully grown cat pretending to be overpowered for the sake of a kitten's fun. But for the most part, it maintained its American Prohibition-era flair—quite possibly out of Darling Dear's fondness for irony more than anything else. But even when it consented to shift for a time, it was always a little too dark. A little too grimy. Nobody else seemed to frequent the place, but *somebody* must have been leaving all those sticky spots on the bar. It wasn't just *Deja.*

He grimaced and shifted his arm away from one such sticky splotch. It took some doing.

"You got hit pretty bad, huh," Darling said. "I suppose it's understandable you wouldn't know better, seeing as how you're you... but they do make stuff for that, you know."

"Yeah," Deja said absently, "they gave it to me a couple hours ago."

Darling gave the lack of bandages on Deja's face a pointed look. "Pretty sure it's meant to stay on at least overnight."

Deja's mouth twisted. "Oh right... I knew I was forgetting something. You know what I need? A personal rabbit."

Darling let out a single, sharp laugh and stepped out from behind the bar. At Deja's bemused look, she just shrugged. "Trust me, it was funny. The fact that you don't understand why it was funny just adds to my mirth." Deja craned in his stool to ask the woman now wiping down tables why she looked so amused and Darling scolded, "Don't ruin this for me, Vale. Just drink your juice."

"Love to," Deja said, eyeing his empty glass. "But can't."

"Guess I shouldn't be shocked a man who can't even be bothered with basic containment procedure would be *impatient.*" But Darling grudgingly returned to the bar to pull out a dusty carafe of from beneath it all the same. And when she poured it out, she glared the whole three fingers' worth of deep, black liquid.

"I think your apple juice has been afflicted."

"Not apple," Darling said, finishing her pour with an artful twist of the bottle. "Pomegranate. Thought you could use a change."

She'd thought wrong. "Pomegranate, huh? Little rich for my non-existent blood."

"Just drink it, Vale. You know," Darling continued, taking up the self-satisfied tone of people laden with gossip and/or the secret to perfectly chewy chocolate chip cookies, "that fellow in the corner? He's a rabbit. Maybe he's looking for some *personal* work."

"Funny." Deja took three deep sips of juice, and the wooziness of M-balm faded a little more. Pomegranate might've been even more effective than apple (not that he'd be admitting it). Other agents always seemed perfectly content to stick to sipping vials of aether, but the green stuff was never able to wash away the taste of medicine like a glass of juice could—and *that* wasn't even being rationed.

"Do I look like I'm joking?"

"No," Deja said, "but then you did drop that one on me about the agent, the Reaper, and the rabbit walking into a bar that one time, and your face looked, well... how it always looks. Which is this." He gestured to Darling's heavily painted face with his glass. "That's it. That's the range."

Darling stared at him for a while with that same, impenetrable face. "What are you even doing here, Vale?"

"You're the only one in these parts serving juice at reasonable, nonexistent prices?" Deja offered. Darling wasn't buying it. He reached into his chest pocket and pulled out the broken glasses. He gave them a flourish before placing them on the bar. "All right, you caught me. I do like the juice, though," he added, charitably.

Penciled brows went up as Darling plucked up the glasses. She examined them with a low whistle. "Wow, Vale. Guess that explains one or two things, huh? You *do know* you don't *have* to get so close to the living, right?"

Deja sighed. "Yeah, so they keep telling me. Except I sorta had to in this case. See, protecting the unborn is kind of my raisin detour."

"*Raison d'être*," Darling corrected absently, focus now absorbed by the glasses. Her hand reached blindly beneath the bar before reemerging with an eye loupe. She popped it on and let out another low whistle. "That's impressive. Even for you." Her bare eye shifted to Deja. "This was a Potential that did this, you said?"

"After a fashion. Birth."

The loupe fell from Darling's eye—Deja reached forward and caught it. "You were at a *birth*?" she hissed.

"Not on *purpose*," Deja defended. He held out the loupe on a bare palm. "Little muffin was done cooking, what d'you want me to say?"

Darling's painted mouth twisted. She plucked the loupe from Deja's hand and fixed it back in place. Her mouth twisted in the other direction as she examined the glasses. "And you won't wear a hood, huh?" she asked in the manner of people who already know the answer and don't care for it.

"No, I can't *hear* with the hood up."

"Hm…" Darling hummed and turned the glasses over. "What about a hat?"

"Wouldn't stay on." After a moment, Deja admitted, "And it'd mess up my hair."

"Poor you." Darling said, removing the loupe. "You're in luck. After last time, I started stocking *spares*."

"You're the best, Darling. I don't care what everyone else over at Omega says about you."

Darling blankly stared at him. "Yule?" she called, eyes still fixed on Deja. "Take care of this sad sack of lifeburn, would you?" And with that, she slipped into a doorway that may or may not have existed until she'd needed it.

Deja leaned back with thinly veiled amusement when a young man who looked like he'd been summoned from the pages of an erotic novel pranced over with all the eagerness one would expect from a supernaturally enslaved cover model.

"What can I get you?" Yule chirped.

Deja leaned over the bar to check for a wagging tail and found none. "Apple juice."

Yule frowned. Pretty eyes glazed over with the effort of calculation. The effort failed. "You mean..." he began cautiously, "like... *brandy?*"

"What?" Deja said, face scrunching. "No. Fucking *apple juice*, dude."

"Sorry," Darling's voice called out (unapologetic) from beyond the door. "He's new."

Deja scoffed. "Hate to tell you, Darling, but I think his issues run deeper than *novelty*." He raised his empty glass to Yule and added, "But kudos on almost knowing where brandy comes from!" Yule brightened at that, and Deja shook his head at the purity of optimism before him.

"Well, you take the help you can get," Darling said, returning with a new pair of glasses. She slid them across the bar. "Beggars can't be choosers." She gave Yule a sideways look; he was looking back at her with pleading eyes. She sighed and reached beneath the bar to pull out a carafe of juice. Before it passed from her long-nailed hands to his, Deja almost caught a glimpse of amber sheen within. All that color was gone once Yule poured it out.

Deja accepted the glass from Yule with a half-ironic, "Cheers." To Darling, he said, "I guess he is sorta cute in a 'Labrador who's always dropping drool-soaked tennis balls into your lap' kinda way." He continued eyeing Yule as the man began polishing a rag with a second rag. "Think he knows any tricks?"

Darling deadpanned, "Get off our dicks and drink your juice, Vale."

"Yes, ma'am." Deja took a sip of juice and craned on his stool to look around. The only movement came from the half-hearted fluttering of the half-curtain hanging in the doorway and the rippling of its white-printed moon reflected on a black, cotton lake. The place was empty—as usual. A pang shot from his navel up his spine and he turned back with a wince. He knew Darling was full of headless-horseshit when she'd said a rabbit was there but it didn't hurt to check. Not these days. Stranger things and all that.

Yule cheerfully placed a bowl of nuts before Deja. When he caught the agent's eye, he smiled. Brightly. Then, he leaned over to the side to call out, "Can I get you anything else?"

Deja frowned and looked up at the rows of bottles lining the shelves before him. Sure enough, reflected upon the glass face of the port was a sliver of somebody seated in the corner, just between the dust and fingerprints. He forced himself to power through the pain in his abdomen and craned to look. In a shadowy corner sat a person with legs neatly crossed, reading a book. An empty glass stood beside his resting hand.

That was a rabbit, all right. In the *wild.*

And it wasn't just any rabbit.

Under his breath, Deja said, "Well, wind my augur and fuck me sideways."

"Sorry?"

Deja told Yule, "That was just for me. You don't—you don't need to listen to that sorta stuff."

"Got it!"

"Say," Deja asked Yule, "what's that rabbit over there been drinking?"

Yule didn't answer him. He just continued diligently polishing the bowl of nuts that didn't need polishing, head bowed.

"I *am* talking to you now," Deja clarified. Didn't help. "Yule?"

"Oh, sorry," Yule said, smiling shyly but no less brilliantly. "Sidecars. He's been drinking sidecars."

"Sidecars," Deja echoed. "What in thirteen hells is a sidecar?" When Yule opened his mouth to explain—or try to—Deja batted a hand. "Never mind. Just make me one, yeah?"

Yule flashed Deja a proud-Labrador-retriever smile and obliged with what was probably a glass of brandy.

UKIYO WAS KNOWN to make the occasional, subtle change. But as Deja approached the rabbit in the corner, for the first time ever, the change took place beneath his feet.

He was walking on *stone.*

Another step, and the table ahead lost its clean lines and Deco details to be replaced by a simple, blocky structure of rough-hewn wood. Deja pulled out a similarly blocky chair and took a seat that went, unsurprisingly, unremarked. He slid the sidecar across the table before leaning back and folding his arms across his chest. He reconsidered, then reached out to orient the twist of lemon to the rabbit's 3 o'clock before leaning back again.

True to form, Not-Jamie didn't look up for any of this. Sharp eyes remained focused on the book perched on his knee. He turned a page.

"So," Deja asked. "Did it hurt?"

One of the rabbit's black brows twitched, but there was no other sign of recognition—not beyond a general annoyed vibe, anyway.

"I asked if it hurt?" Deja pressed. When the rabbit finally lowered himself to looking up a fraction, Deja finished, "When you clawed your way out of hell?"

The rabbit's eyes rose just far enough to give Deja an unimpressed look before returning to his book, but not before the lingering whiskey-smell of Ukiyo whispered to Deja that those eyes were brown. Not-Jamie turned another page. *Implausibly fast reader.* But then, maybe not. Letters were sort of his entire existence.

So Deja'd thought.

"That was some trick," Deja said. "Convincing me to go out of my way to visit the overseer on a bureaucratic rampage. He was a real piece of work, you'll be pleased to know."

"Did I do that?" Not-Jamie said, uninterested. "My mistake."

Deja craned his neck to try and get a better look at the book. The cover was concealed, but he could spot the author's name at the top of the page: Dickens. "Who around here reads *Dickens?*" he asked. "Or *anything?*"

"Nobody committing any crimes or doing anything irregular." Another page-turn.

Deja reached forward and slid the sidecar a little closer. "Got you a drink. *Mind the garnish.*"

Another subtle twitch of eyebrow. The rabbit looked up. "Is there something I can help you with, Agent Good? I have no Osiris training, I'm afraid."

Deja gestured to his own face. "This has already been taken care of, don't worry about it."

The rabbit's brows went up in an expression that clearly said, *I wasn't worried.* All his lips said was, "If you say so."

"And you *can* help me," Deja said, "by answering a few questions."

"More questions," Not-Jamie said flatly, eyes falling back to his book. "Goody."

Deja folded his arms on the table and leaned forward to whisper, "I still wanna know how an unauthorized OWL gets past the Augury and into the Desert."

"I'm sure you would, Agent, but that is still above my pay grade."

"I would *also* like to know," Deja pressed, "how a rabbit comes to know the rap code not even taught to most agents these days, let alone get that code transferred to some string lights *outside a tether field.*"

Not-Jamie clicked his tongue and turned a page. "Well, that's *definitely* above my pay grade." He looked up a moment to 'helpfully' add, "And I'm not on the clock—we do get off it, you know," before returning to Dickens once more.

"Oh, for—will you at least tell me your *name*?"

"Certainly. Just as soon as you tell me *yours.*"

Deja watched the rabbit turn a page in stunned silence. Not-Jamie almost managed to finish those next two pages before Deja finally asked, "Who *are you*?" He narrowed his eyes and amended, "*What* are you?"

The rabbit looked up. His eyes held Deja's own as he closed the book with a quiet, dusty *thump.* "Me?" A small shrug. "I'm nobody."

"Tell me your name," Deja whispered.

The rabbit gave him a chiding look. "What makes you think *nobody* needs a name?"

"*Please.*"

Sharp eyes moved to the untouched sidecar glinting beside the empty glass. "Thanks for the drink, Agent Good, but I'll pass—"

"Vale," Deja cut in. "My name is Deja Vale." The subtle smile he got as payment might've been genuine.

"I'm sure it is," the rabbit said. "Good night."

Deja stood when the rabbit did and nearly overturned his chair in the process. He hurriedly righted it. "Where are you going?"

The rabbit sighed and held the book to his chest. "Typical agent," he said, looking genuinely disappointed. "Doesn't even occur to you to wonder where all those rabbits come from each day, does it?"

Deja'd have sooner asked how the *moon* had shown up before wondering where rabbits came from each morning and went to each night—before, anyway. Now, he asked, "Where do they come from?"

"Where indeed," the rabbit said wistfully. "Go home, Agent Deja Vale. Or better yet, back to Osiris. Lifeburn is not a thing to be taken lightly. Not for you." Once he reached the door he added, "And I wasn't lying. Belligerent as he is, Curio really was the better option."

Deja was too stunned to respond or try to stop the rabbit from pushing past the short, black curtains hanging in the door and stepping out into the foggy night. Fabric kept on fluttering for what felt like ages. And long after they finally settled, Deja was still too stunned to do anything but stare at their paltry imitation of a moon in a lake.

"Get down!"

Deja threw himself to the polished concrete floor just in time to miss the spirit-charged coping saw. Just who the kerf was distributing saws amongst the student populace was a mystery to be tabled for a later, ghostless time. The concrete against his cheek smushed his question: "No OWLs yet?"

"Nope," was the response. "Not a one."

Deja groaned and pushed himself up. "Great," he grumbled. "Just swell." He'd begun brushing dust that could never have been there from his jacket when a green glow across the large shop room warned him of the imminently flying wrenches. He waited for them to signal their trajectory before dropping back down. "I really, really hate schools," he told the floor.

"Why does that not surprise me?"

Deja shot a look at Agent Thorne, whose face was pressed to the concrete just like his. "You know what you can do with those wrenches?"

Thorne snorted and pushed herself off the floor. "Come on, Vale," she said with unmerited cheer. "Time to get up! The ghosts are calling!"

Deja opened his eyes. The Hereafter that greeted him was one without Agent Thorne. Or Ivy. Or Vyne. The temptation to close his eyes and go back to that world with them, with the memory of them, buzzed in his hands like a habit deferred. It was those habits (long neglected but no less powerful for it) that propelled him from his stiff mattress and toward the rest of his day. He washed. He shaved. The ticking clock of his routine only stuttered on the Osiris-issued jar of M-balm waiting for him, shining and black on the sink. Thing was tiny. Not quite dollhouse proportions, but close. It said a lot about just how distasteful the stuff was that, even knowing as he did about the recent scarcity, it took Deja all of two seconds' consideration before he tossed it into the trash with a disdainful flick of his fingers. Even the sight of the foul stuff made him smell that sickly sweet stench.

Deja's scrunched-nose grimace stared back at him as he washed away what he could of the memory of M-balm from his face and hands. "Gross," he muttered and gave his hands an extra wash— then froze. A gray hair. Above his temple. When he went to pluck it, he noticed his fingers looked far more delicate than they usually did. A bit paler. But when he held his hand up to examine it, it was his usual, long-fingered, mid-toned gray hand that met him. He turned it to count the freckles on the back. Two, as usual. And no signs of lifeburn or other trauma to speak of. He rotated his hand; the sheen of scar tissue on his right palm remained. Make that *almost* no signs. But, considering that scar hadn't managed to heal in six months of Osiris treatments, he could only assume it was there to stay.

The turning cogs of morning powered through the disruptions and brought Deja to his small kitchen with its pale appliances and stained counter. It made his hands move for the canister of coffee grounds. Made them reach for a particular, smiley face mug. Made his fingers beat out the same rhythm while he waited for the coffee to brew, made his tongue click the same accompanying tune-like sounds. But once he sat at the island and reached for his smiling mug of coffee, it was only to find a shorter, chipped, faceless mug of *tea*. He stared down at it. The liquid was far paler than it had any right to be. He looked over his shoulder at the fridge. It was still white, but now the oven was the wrong color. Too dark. Smaller. His entire kitchen was smaller, in fact.

Six months was a long time to be gone, but the place had looked normal just last night. Granted, it was dark, and he'd stumbled straight to bed. His brow pinched. *No.* He'd have noticed something like that. He was too paranoid not to. Plenty changed in the Hereafter. Their world was one of impermanence. Its face shifted like eyes blinking and frowns becoming smiles. Change was a fact of existence—one as expected as gravity.

Some things just changed.

Deja's *apartment* didn't.

Deja didn't.

At least, not that he could recall. But there were gaps in memory that felt like gaps in his being. And in those gaps, only fear existed. The fear of not knowing as well as the knowledge that there should have been more. It wasn't just fear of the unknown. There was something deeper, darker, *knowledgeable* in that fear. That fear knew things he did not. Trauma could do that to a mind, the technicians had told him, but he still wanted the knowledge of whatever that trauma might have been *back*. Maybe, just maybe, there were *happy* memories hiding there in the dark, too.

Agent Thorne... he'd broken off with her during missions so many times before they lost her. Had he seen her go? Had she been alone? Was his presence a comfort in the end? Or a liability? Did she make a joke or tell him a story that made him laugh in her last hours—a memory that only he could have carried? Last words as lost to oblivion as she? So much of her and what she'd ventured to share with him and him alone was lost now.

She deserved so much more. A legacy unbroken. A friend so much stronger, so much completer than him.

Deja stared down into his coffee-turned-tea like he might see a hole on his head, reflected in milky white. Memory was all they were, really. Their world. Without his, he felt as tethered here as he did the Desert of the Living. He took a sip from a stranger's morning habit. Before he could stoically accept the fact that he'd now received ample evidence that he was indeed losing his mind, *whatever* insane theories about rabbits and OWLs he'd formulated, light flashed to his left. His augur. The engraved Omega symbol glowed white. Once open, it emitted green light and a distant, rhythmic sound like lapping waves.

Vex's tinny voice penetrated that static like a foghorn. "*Agent Vale?*"

Deja rubbed his temple. "Yeah?"

"*Get to my office, ASAP.*"

Deja frowned and stared down at his half-drunk mug of tea. "You mean 'finish your drink' ASAP, or 'don't bother putting on pants' ASAP."

"*Find a middle ground and get over here, Agent.*"

"You got it, sir." Deja closed his augur with a quiet *snap*, took a sip of tea and promptly regretted it. Down the sink it went to swirl along with the hope that Omega Headquarters might have installed coffee machines at some point during his long recovery and absence. A crestfallen sigh. "I miss Stephanie."

DEJA'S APARTMENT BUILDING stood so perfectly on the transition between the cobbled, winding Floating District and the neatly paved lanes and squares of the Hex that it could have *been* the border. Those meandering alleys were very good at funneling wind and fog. The whole place was like a water wheel too big for anybody to feel it moving. It churned a gust of wind toward Deja now. He raised his hood against it and began the walk through high stone walls and carefully constructed archways. It wasn't until he reached Omega Square that he even saw anyone else.

In matching, toy-soldier pace, four gray-clad constables cut across the square. Deja watched them until they disappeared through another archway. Constables had some purpose, surely. Decoration, maybe? Like having a fleet of cranky lawn gnomes or something. He slowed down as he reached the center of the Omega Square where a massive black stone plinth supported an equally massive, black marble statue—a larger than life and even larger than death *Reaper*.

Any shadow it might have cast was eclipsed by a far greater one. The shadow of the Tower in the Central Hex.

Deja stopped to look up at it. He often did. It was a habit he'd picked up after occasionally catching Vex doing the same. Deja would do it too, trying to suss out just what the agent inquisitor had seen there that made him look so... *sure.* He didn't think he'd managed it. Even so, there was something oddly comforting about the black statue. Unlike the massive statue of the technician guarding Osiris Square, this Reaper didn't feel haughty or intimidating. There wasn't much to the thing, really. Basically just black robes and gloves holding a massive, stone scythe. The void beneath the hood was just that—a void. He doubted very much if a sculptor had bothered to carve a face under there. They wouldn't have dared to presume. What would that face even look like if they had? There were no Reapers left to consult—hadn't been for over a century. Not since the Separation of Reaper Powers was enacted. So really, a sculptor could have carved anything and just *said* it was what a Reaper looked like. Maybe Reapers hadn't even worn robes or carried scythes and that was just a story people told in hushed, reverent tones, fond nostalgia, or eye-rolling contempt for an obsolete past (depending on the teller).

Deja's eyes drifted to the scythe. Even though it was made of the same stone as the rest of the thing, the blade seemed to glint. Omega agents were meant to be that scythe now, metaphorically speaking. The agent inquisitors had become the Reaper's hands. The Augury, the Reaper's eyes. Those who governed the Hereafter from the Tower known as The Twelve Who Are Thirteen, the mind. Deja's mouth twisted, eyes falling down the robes like rain. He didn't know what the rabbits were meant to be. The Reaper's accountants? Feet, maybe? The plinth beneath them? Couldn't be the plaque on it. *MORS AEQUAT* applied to all of them.

Deja gave the statue's foot (or, where the foot would be if it had them) a quick pat and continued to the massive black tower that was Omega Headquarters. The same black stone that made up the wide steps outside lined the atrium, but this stone was polished to a mirror finish that reflected nothing but the green light of the moon outside and the gaslight lanterns within. It only took six minutes of dodging odd looks and hushed whispers from his fellow agents to reach AI Vex's all-too-familiar office and the all-too-familiar Deja-weary sighs of its chief occupant.

Agent Ashe was there, as she often was. A tall, steel-faced woman, she usually accompanied AI Vex. Like Crane had once done, Ashe chiefly trained other agents. Unlike Crane, she hadn't been sent back to the field once agents got stretched thinner and thinner. Instead she was here, holding a case file and staring at Deja with an utterly blank expression. Deja took his seat and stared back. When she lifted a dark brow ever-so-slightly, he cleared his throat and shimmied a little further back into his chair.

"Ashe?" Vex said, and a black file fell before Deja with a little *smack.*

Deja stared down at it. That was a case file, all right. Only, this wasn't a briefing room. This was Vex's office. Apart from Vex and Ashe (who hardly ever went anywhere else and didn't count), Deja was the only one there. But then, the last time he'd been called in for a mission, he'd been wearing a linen robe and drinking coffee in an Osiris recovery room, so he didn't know why he expected normality to reign at this point.

"I was under the impression I was still on leave, sort of," Deja said. "Recovering or whatever."

"Yes," Vex said, "but this case is complicated in an unfortunate way and we are spread very, very thin."

Deja's mouth tightened at the memory of Agent Sine's disintegrating face and her last, tapped word: *FREAK.* "How thin? We talking American or French panca—"

"You will be a team of five—"

"*What?*" Deja demanded, not sure if he should laugh or not. The look Vex was giving him wasn't exactly a tick in the *laugh* column. "*Five?*" Had somebody else been injured on that mission, too? The shock was edged out by dread and he asked, "Who else?"

"Head Agent Crane, along with Agents Good, Wren, and Lear."

No Izik. That was a small relief. And temporary. If a demented-level six mission qualified as a milk run fit for rookies, he shuddered to think what qualified as *too dangerous for fresh meat* these days. "Okay," he said slowly, "Can I ask why?"

"I told you. We are spread thin."

Deja thought back to the Bruno mission aftermath and Sine's thinly veiled threat that she'd be filing her own mission report, doubtlessly in the hopes she'd get him nixed from field duty. Maybe she hadn't had the chance before getting sent off on yet another mission—one that ended with her *like that*. Maybe she had. Maybe it hadn't gone exactly as she'd hoped.

Or maybe it was just as Vex had said. They were spread thin.

Disconcerting as it was to be so undermanned, Deja had to admit it was a solid team. He'd be hard pressed to handpick a better team himself... ornery former comrades aside. Good was hardly a warm and fuzzy, but there was no denying he was, well, *good.* Competence was his most annoying quality. He looked back down at the file that was puffed up with more information than he'd seen in some time. The exact opposite of what he'd come to expect these days. "And, um," he began, squinting at the silver-foil case number stamped on the top right corner, "I'm supposed to *open this*?"

Vex nodded. "And read it, yes."

"Really? I mean, you get why I have to *ask*, right?"

"Yes. It's the attitude I don't get. You know what you need to know and nothing more." Vex gestured to the file. "In this case, you need to know *more*." After a beat, he added a half-hearted, "Congrats."

Deja blew out a hair-fluttering breath and flipped the file open with a quarter-hearted, "Yippee." His eyes darted over the details. Demented-level five. Not great, but not too bad. He skipped the areas peppered with all the usual suspects: "Clear and present danger." *I'll say.* "Belligerent." *I'm about to be.* "Long-term infestation." *Brought to you by Augury procrastination.* "Potential household." *Typical.*

Then, Deja spotted a word he didn't usually see in a case file. Possibly never had before now.

INTERSTATE.

Once Deja looked up, Vex's look of wry apprehension came into unhappy context. He looked back down at the file. He closed it. He opened it just far enough to confirm that he had indeed read the word "*Winnebago*" within the case parameters, and Omega hadn't started selling ad-space in their briefings to fine purveyors of recreational motorhomes. But no. The word was still there, still beside those other more expected words like "nocturnal shrieking," and "mild possession." But, like Vex's face, those words now bore a whole new and terrible context. Said context was a tiny list of *vehicle specifications* scribbled into one corner like an afterthought. *By hand.*

How reassuring. Deja slid the file back toward Vex, gave it a little pat with his hand, and straightened in his chair before offering a delicate, "Oh." He cleared his throat. "I'm afraid to look. Any OWLs?"

Vex gestured over his shoulder and Ashe answered in her usual flat affect, "The mother-to-be has been having inexplicable cravings for Alphabet Crunch cereal."

Wonderful. Not only *was* there a higher power serving as Dungeon Master of Deja's universe, but it had a twisted sense of humor bordering on the sadistic. He could practically see its Cheetos-stained fingerprints all over that black vellum case file.

As if Deja'd said those things instead of just thinking them, Vex said, "You'll manage. Train is scheduled to depart in"—he glanced at the thirteen numerals of the clock over the door—"four minutes." He waved a vague hand and added, "Dismissed," before reaching over his shoulder to receive the next file awaiting his attention.

Ashe didn't shift her eyes from Deja's grimacing face as she passed it over.

"Right," Deja said, clapping his hands to his thighs and standing. He hesitated and watched Vex fill out forms before turning to Ashe to ask, "Can I take this file on the train or—"

"No," Ashe said.

"Just this then?" Deja asked, pointing to the augur in his chest pocket.

"Yes," Ashe said.

Deja mouthed a silent, "*Okie-dokie,*" and turned to leave. Then—"Do I at least get a *morti*—"

Vex and Ashe both said, "Absolutely not."

"*Right.*"

Just as Deja's hand touched the doorknob, he heard Vex's last words, quiet but heavy with warning: "Be careful." A grave pause. "There's a lot riding on this, Vale."

"Yeah," Deja said, tapping the augur in his pocket with a dull *tink.* "Like 19-foot awnings and a solar-powered entertainment—*yes, yes,* I'm leaving, sir."

JESSICA B IS A HO

"You all right?"

Deja stopped tracing over pencil-etched insults on the murky train window and looked to the agent on his right. Wren's hands were poised near the thick belt on her waist like they'd just been interrupted from their task of checking the iron nails strapped there—presumably by Deja's silence. Funny. He'd been under the impression other agents treasured his silences. No, that wasn't fair. Not to Wren, the only other agent apart from Thorne, who'd seemed to enjoy (or, at least especially tolerate) Deja's particular brand of noise.

"Yeah, fine. You?"

"Me? I'm always fine." Wren seemed satisfied by the faint smile that twitched at Deja's mouth and returned her focus to the tethering nails. Once certain all were present and sound, she leaned back in her seat. "So..." she whispered, "is it true Good got landed with probation?"

"I'm not one for gossip, Wren," Deja chided. "You know that."

"Uh-huh. *Sure* you're not." When Deja lapsed back into silence, Wren let out a groan. "Come on… I'd tell *you*."

"Not something to brag about."

"Please. Who's bragging?"

Deja looked around the car. Lear was resting with chin to his chest two seats down. Every now and again he'd sniff, and his mustache would twitch like a cantankerous grandpa. Even if he were only faking indifference, he hardly mattered. Not like Crane or Good did. Those two were seated at the other end, locked in a hushed conversation. Deja couldn't hear their whispers and figured they couldn't hear his. "Not Good, that's for sure."

From his right came Wren's subdued but excited gasp.

From his *left* came Lear's murmured, "*I knew it.*"

Deja snorted a laugh and turned to Lear who just shrugged half-heartedly.

"What?" Lear said. "I'm bored."

"Do you have some super-secret Oddity that lets you tune in to goings-on *just when there's hot goss*? Huh? You messy mustached bitch?"

Lear sniffed and shifted in his seat a bit. As he leaned away from Deja, he muttered, "No clue what you're talking about," and went back to ignoring the existence of a world beyond his seat (but only after discreetly straightening his mustache).

"Uh-huh." Deja's eye-rolling look shifted to Wren. "Just officially," he told her, more quietly. "I sort of got the sense it was a box being checked more than anything. I doubt it'll actually stick. I mean, it's not like they took *his* mortifier."

The amusement that had been dancing in Wren's eyes flickered away. "Well, I don't know. That might just be because we're down two agents this mission."

"Yeah," Deja agreed grimly. "Any word on Sine?"

"No. I was going to check, but I got called in."

Deja nodded. He didn't think Sine would make it. He'd be more worried for her if she *did*. "Do you know what happened?"

"Not really. We were only off the train a few minutes when..." Wren trailed off with a dark look.

Deja's brows went up. "You were there?" Wren nodded, and Deja blew out a breath. They were spread thin as it was and Wren, being a tether wrangler, was more valuable than most. That meant even more missions. "I'm sorry it happened. But I'm glad it wasn't you."

"Thanks," Wren said, a bit surprised. "I'm glad it wasn't you, too." She lowered her voice and Deja had to strain to hear her admission: "If it was going to be anyone, though...."

"You said it," Deja muttered, "not me." He glanced around the train. "Everyone else okay? Who else was there?"

"Me, Sine, Troy, and Thrall." Wren shot Deja a careful, sideways glance. "I'm not clear on what happened; I was working on shifting the tethers. But Thrall wasn't on the train back."

Thrall was gone?

Deja sank back against his seat just as worn plastic gave way to leather beneath him. Why hadn't Vex told him another Odd had been lost to oblivion? There were only four of them now. Truth be told, Deja hadn't known Thrall well. There was only one Odd per team per mission; it made few opportunities for bonding the way he had with Wren or Thorne before she, too, had been lost. Even so, it felt important to know.

"Do you have any idea how it happened?" Deja asked.

Wren's gaze shifted to the gaslight sputtering fitfully in its lamp. She stared at it, silent, until it settled. "I wasn't briefed. I only know what I've heard, and well...." She shrugged and Deja understood: Her information was mostly hearsay, and hearsay where *freaks* were concerned tended to skew less toward fact and more toward resentment. Even hysteria.

Still, he wanted to know. Even if it wasn't true, maybe he could discern the shape of real events from the edges of rumor.

"They're saying something went wrong," Wren said, "with his... with his *Oddity.*"

Deja frowned. Thrall's Oddity was odd, even by Odd standards. He captured gazes—not unlike a cat that way. Ghosts were easier to shoot when they couldn't look at the agents aiming the mortifiers because they were stuck staring at that one Odd. But Thrall could control it. If he couldn't, he wouldn't be in the field—

You're in the field, aren't you?

Can you *control it?*

Deja stared at his hands. He willed the words YOU ARE IN CONTROL again and again until he could almost see them typing across his white gloves. The urge to write those words out on his thigh itched in his fingers. Instead, he traced out two dot-eyes and an arching frown.

A smaller hand briefly touched his. Less a comforting gesture than a reprimand. "That's only what I've heard, Vale."

Maybe it was just a rumor. But Vex deciding it best *not* to tell Deja, combined with Sine's twitching last word—*Freak*—painted a horrifying picture. Another touch on Deja's hand. A question. He could only nod in answer.

"So, there it is," Wren said. "Spread thin is now spread *thinner.* Otherwise, I really don't think Good would even *be* here, let alone with his weapon."

Deja's brows went up. "What? Really? For a first offense—if it can even be *called* an offense?" The corners of Wren's mouth tightened and Deja blinked at her. "Isn't it? His first offense?" Wren didn't answer, and Deja glanced Good's way; Crane was done with him now. He was sitting with eyes closed but wide awake, assiduously running over every detail from the case file and stacking a matryoshka doll of contingencies upon contingencies.

Wren shifted the tether nail poking into her leg. "All things considered," she said, "you picked a pretty good time to be down and out. Things have been... *tense.*"

"Right." Deja turned his focus back to the window opposite. It was glass now, clean and clear. It glimmered in the lamplight, only where the distant, vague shapes that might have been mountains weren't. "Say," he whispered, "that last mission... the, um, the one where—"

"What about it?"

Deja lowered his voice even more. "I know you don't like to—well—just, quick question. Was it at a school?"

Wren's tone shifted from wary to confused. "Yes… why?" She leaned closer and whispered urgently, "Are you remembering anything?"

Deja shrugged. "Not much. Just the occasional weird dream." He scoffed and muttered, "Forget most of it the second I wake up, but I remember a school. Couldn't even tell if it was just something I'd cooked up in my sleep or what. Seemed like both." He gave her a one-sided smile and lied with a technical truth. "Somehow, I don't think I ever actually forgot my pants on a real mission."

Wren's face was a difficult-to-read maelstrom of emotions that might have been abject confusion, concern, anxiety, or all of the above. She did relax a fraction at Deja's last words, though. "Got it." Then, the tension crept back, but subtly so; Deja could only see it in the flexing of the gloved hands against her thighs. "See anybody?" she asked. "That you remember?"

Deja hesitated. "Yeah. Thorne."

Wren nodded slowly, giving herself time to take the name in. Wren, Deja knew, hadn't been there when whatever had gone wrong had gone wrong. That was the only reason she was still here. Lear, too. It also meant she hadn't been with Thorne in her last moments. Nor with Ivy or Vyne. Like Deja, she had no way of knowing if they'd been alone in the end. Or scared. And, like Deja, that not knowing weighed on her. He could see it in the rigid set of her shoulders. Hear it in the subtle desperation tightening her words when she asked, "Was she—"

"Fine," Deja said. "She was fine. Giving me shit, as usual."

"Good," Wren said with a small, sad smile. "That should be how you remember her." They sat in companionable (if sullen) silence as the maybe-mountains beyond the windows grew, their peaks jutting out in sharp teeth above the seats. A quiet breath of laughter drew Deja's focus back to Wren. "I didn't think it would be, but it's nice to hear her name—"

"All right!" Crane said.

Deja straightened in his seat and looked at the other end of the train where Crane was walking toward the center of the compartment. Behind her, Good pulled on his mask. Wren did the same beside Deja.

"We're approaching the campground," Crane said. She reached into her chest pocket and pulled out her augur to give it a quick polish before replacing it. "This is a Potential mission, so everyone stay on highest alert."

Lear grumbled, "Good of them to *warn* us this time."

Crane's only response was a sharp look. "It'll be evening," she continued like she hadn't been interrupted. "I'm told this campground is fairly popular, but this particular area only has two other groups parked there—four people in addition to the haunted couple."

The sigh of relief that followed was collective—for all but Deja. He fiddled absently with the new pair of glasses in his lap, turning them over slowly and willing his mind to relax to the same speed. It didn't. Something about forests made him uneasy and the ones in the Pacific Northwest were old.

Very old.

"Yes, Vale?"

Deja leaned back in surprise. He'd have leaned back further if he didn't expect Crane would just follow him.

Crane only stared down at him expectantly. "What's on your mind?"

"We just need to hurry, is all," Deja said. as fluorescence replaced the gaslight. "Even if there's not many people in the area, the fact that it's an RV is going to be a problem—knowing our luck, anyway."

"How so?"

"Well, it can *move,* can't it?" Deja looked around the compartment at the nonplussed masks meeting him. Sometimes he forgot just how little of the Desert his comrades could see. How that ignorance altered the ways they not just moved in but *thought* about that other world. Ghosts haunted places people lived—homes, usually. *Mobile* home wasn't exactly a concept that meshed in their minds, let alone what made them mobile: *fuel*. "*And* the thing is basically a 20,000-pound explosion waiting to happen, so the sooner we can get the—"

"Wait," Good cut in. "*What?*"

Deja frowned. "It's got a propane genny, so—"

This time it was Crane who cut him off. "How do you know that?"

Deja's frown deepened; surely he wasn't the only one given the file. "You didn't see the attached vehicle specs? It was pretty detailed. I'm starting to think rabbits have Otherworldly internet access." When this only exacerbated the collective confusion, he explained, "See, the 'internet' is a modern marvel which the discerning Winnebago owner might access with an optional—"

"Thank you, Vale." Crane went stiff a moment and pulled out her augur. Green light splashed her face, highlighting the deep-set furrow to her brow triggered by the message only she could hear. She snapped it shut and slid it back into her pocket. "Well, team, Vale was right. The Potential is en route to a maternity hospital in an ambulance. The haunt is being driven in pursuit."

"The ghost is en route to a *maternity hospital?*" Wren echoed, pitch rising. "I can't tether a Car-V—"

"RV," Deja corrected.

"Whatever—from the off!" Wren continued. "It's too small to stabilize!"

"We've worked with small fields before," Lear pointed out.

"Yes, Lear, you have," Wren said. "Because *I* established a larger field, stabilized it, and then very, *very carefully* tightened it. *Over hours.*" She scoffed like the mission parameters were an insult not just to her, but to the dignity of tether-wrangling itself. "We haven't even *started* and we're already at worst-case scenario!"

Whoever was in charge of transportation must have agreed. The train took a sharp *left* that sent them all swaying to the side. Lear only just steadied himself in time to keep from flying to the stained, gray rubber floor. A deep, creaking ship of a moan shuddered around them.

Once they steadied, Wren shot Deja a wry look. "Guess that explains you, huh?"

"Yeah," Deja agreed. "Just once I'd like to get tapped for my good phone manner, or because they thought I'd enjoy the locale or something." He nodded to her tether nails. "Explains you, too." At Wren's disbelieving snort, Deja said, "No, really. You're the best tether wrangler I've ever worked with."

"So?"

From across the aisle, Crane asked (less with petulance and more with hopeful interest), "So?"

"*So,*" Deja began, "I've got two questions." The train jerked again as he counted off on his gloved fingers. "One: can this train keep up with an RV *and* maintain a more-or-less constant distance"—he held up a second finger and the train gave another lurch—"and two: Wren, have you ever heard of anybody using *shifting tethers* instead of a field?"

Wren gawked at him like he'd spoken in tongues. "Not *success-fully.*"

Deja stared back at her. "Define '*successfully.*'"

The train door swung open to the five agents with a deep belly groan. Wind from speeding traffic whipped Deja's hair around his face and only *his* hair. The others' coats rustled gently in the subtle, interworldly motion of the train itself as it shifted between the paths only it could carve, but not in the wind. Only Deja could feel the wind. He pushed his glasses back up for a bit of respite from the bright moonlight beating down on the freeway, and the caustic smells of exhaust and rubber. Some vehicles bore the inviting glow of doorways, but they were difficult to track at that speed, and it wasn't all of them. Maybe only the most lived-in ones? Still, it might be just enough of an indication for an agent to identify a car and land on it.

More or less.

Good looked out the doorway. "This is insane." For Deja's sake, he got more specific. "*You* are insane."

"Yeah, well," Deja began, flipping a large iron nail in his fingers, "apparently that's a desirable trait in the wide world of Winnebago"—he searched for a ghost-related word beginning with 'W' and settled on—"wauntings."

Good turned to face him fully. "*Wauntings? Weally?*"

Deja couldn't help but smile at him. Standing in the face of open-highway peril, he'd just about forgotten what a *dick* Good had turned into since his promotion, and the *double-dickery* that came with his demotion. There was only what Good *had* been. Namely, half a dick. Five-eighths on a bad day. But before Deja could cling to that nostalgia any tighter, Crane elbowed her way between them, eyeing the open highway that, to her eyes, would only be a blur of flickering shadows.

"All right," Crane said, sharp voice piercing the rushing traffic like a siren. "So long as the train keeps up, we've got some leeway with the tether fields, but stay close to your nails! Clear?" Three nods and one *what-has-my-world-come-to?* stare. "Wren is taking point and planting a tether on the ambulance. Vale, you'll be close behind, tethering the RV. Good and Lear? You follow right behind Vale. Then I'll take the left. Lear, Good, you're on the right. And stay alert! I'm guessing it'll be *soon*."

A pull, subtle but irresistible, tugged them forward. The roar of an ambulance. A red storm surged toward them, sending off spears of light in every direction. Deja cupped his hands over his eyes and watched it between his fingers.

"Vale?"

Deja confirmed what they already knew: "Ambulance." Even if they couldn't see or hear it with the overwhelming clarity that he could, they could all sense the swell of Potential life. The train *lurched* forward and so did they. It heaved a great plume of green steam, struggling to keep pace. It was then that Deja learned Styx trains didn't move on straight paths. And why would they? There were no tracks outside the Hereafter. Its path was less the purposeful stride of a horse and more the winding way of an aquatic beast. No agent knew who or what drove the trains, but it wasn't the conductors always scrambling around Styx Station. Now, Deja couldn't help but think the trains were driving themselves.

A sharp poke in Deja's side. Good was staring at him. Even hidden, his glare spoke volumes: *Pay attention. Idiot.*

"Wren," Crane said. "Ready?"

Wren checked the iron nails lining her belt one last time, then nodded. "Ready."

Crane jerked her head at Deja. "Go on Vale's mark."

"Traffic's gonna slow down in a second, here," Deja said, squinting at the cars ahead. The left lane had been cleared for the ambulance, but an 18-wheeler was struggling to merge over. The ambulance *whooped* agitatedly at it, and each one was deafening. He gritted, "Wait…. Okay, see that door there? Go!"

Wren crouched low, waiting for just the right shift in the cosmos, then leapt from the train, guided by the glow of the doors and the pull of Potential life. For five terrifying seconds, she floated like a cartoon coyote trapped in the Grand Canyon—then she drove a nail into the ambulance roof and held onto it. Her black jacket billowed behind her but settled quickly. The wind couldn't touch her any more than those cars could. New fears replaced the old when it looked like she'd gotten sucked in by the Potential. But then she spotted the glowing doors of a Jeep behind her; she leapt to it and drove a second nail into the hood.

Deja released a sigh of relief that she was still Wren-shaped and not moo-shoo-agent-shaped. "She's tethered and off the ambulance. We're good." So long as the train stayed close, Wren would stay good.

Crane nodded once; she was careful not to show it, but Deja could feel her relief. That relief was short-lived, unfortunately, as the train began to creak beneath their feet, already straining with the effort of following the agent dependent upon its tethering presence. "Right," Crane said. "You're up next, Vale. Got eyes on the RV?"

The RV in question was in hot pursuit of the ambulance, honking at anyone who dared *hint* at coming between them. The customized horn they'd opted for played a clumsy bar of "Rocky Mountain High." Each time it blared at a sneaky sedan or cheeky coup, Deja could only think that John Denver had never sounded so pissed, nor looked so beige.

Deja warily eyed the Minnesota license plate on front— MNTNFVR—and turned to Good. "Do you think that's meant to read, 'mountain fever?' Or 'mountain *forever?*'"

"What are you talking about?"

"The vanity plate is—"

"Just tell me when it's close," Good gritted.

Deja mouthed a silent, "*Fine,*" and turned his attention back to the highway. A sudden gust of wind nearly sent him falling off the train before multiple hands grabbed both of his arms. "It's getting close."

"Are you insane?" Good hissed. "Put your hood and glasses on before you jump!"

"If I do that, I can't *see* properly."

Good demanded, "And what's the point in being able to *see* where you're jumping if you're too constrained by Otherworldly physics to *make it?*"

"Okay, fair point," Deja grumbled. "I'll—" He clicked his tongue, staring at the rapidly approaching caravan of Rocky Mountain fury. "I'll put them on after I jump," he said, sliding his glasses down his nose. "In mid-air."

"In *mid-air?*" Good echoed. His rage collapsed into a series of spluttering noises before he regained enough steam to all but shriek, "*Are you completely in—*"

"Now!" Deja yelled and he leapt from the train, Good close behind. The moment he felt the triple tug of wind, momentum, and gravity, he pushed up his glasses. Next came the regretful litany of, "*Fuck me, fuck me, fuck me,*" as he struggled to get his hood up. Just when he realized he *couldn't* get his hood to stay up, a strong hand yanked him toward the RV, and he landed on the rear of the roof with a hollow metal *thunk*. He reached for his tether, but the RV suddenly changed lanes, sending him sliding off the back. The only thing that kept him off the road was the iron nail he drove into the roof. He laughed his relief. Both Good and Lear stood above him, looking over the edge of the roof with the composure of people who were concerned for the mission, yes, but also not aware they were careening down the highway at 90 plus MPH. Deja opened his mouth to ask for a hand when an 18-wheeler screamed past and he ended up clutched to his tether like an unlucky ladybug clinging to a side-view mirror that had only very recently become distressingly mobile.

"Need a hand?" Lear asked, thoughtfully.

Deja winced, determinedly closing his eyes against the knowledge of the asphalt running beneath them in a river of scraped skin and broken limbs. "Nah," he managed. "There's a ladder here, just—just give me a minute."

"We don't *have* a minute," Good snapped. "*We* can't move on until *your* Odd ass gets up here."

"Fine, *yeesh.*" Deja forced his eyes open, regretted it immediately, and shut them again. In theory, the proximity of the train was keeping them grounded enough that they didn't strictly need the tethers to do anything but contain the ghost. And, in theory, if any of them fell off, their bodies would just follow the path of least resistance and flow back onto the train accompanying them. The augurs ensured it.

In theory.

Deja opened one eye. Speed had filled the painted white dashes beneath him into a solid line. With a last, "Fuck me," he straightened his glasses. It wasn't necessary. Those glasses were far less susceptible to Otherworldly forces than the rest of him. But it made him feel like steps were being taken on the long, fast-moving highway that was *getting his shit together.* "Fuck"—one hand shifted from the tether nail to the shining ladder—"me"—the other hand next—"in"—the RV changed lanes yet again, and Deja swung back with no choice but to grab the nail once more—"the"—he threw caution into the wind and let go, grabbing onto the ladder with both hands—"*ass.*"

Deja climbed up top where Good and Lear were as composed as ever, postures evoking impatient foot-tapping without actually having to do it. "Thanks for the support, guys," Deja said, pulling himself to the roof. He swayed. Good immediately shot out a hand to steady him, gripping his arm with force that would've been punishing in any other circumstance.

"Hurry up and get inside," Good said. "Then me and Lear are off."

"Right." Deja looked down at the subtly glowing port-hole-like hatch at their feet. "Soon as I go down there, our ghost is going to kick up a fuss."

"Yeah," Good said shortly. "We know."

"So, you all need to get into position *first*," Deja said, matching Good tone for tone. "Otherwise we—"

"No," Good cut him off, "we can't risk you flying off this RV."

Lear fiddled with the nail in his pocket. "No, Vale's right. Worse comes to worst, he'll just get sucked back into the train and have to jump again, right? *Maybe* get stuck to a tether if it's closer?"

"Ow!" Deja winced at the tightening grip on his arm. If the *love squeeze* hadn't been enough of an indication, the look burning into his cheek would've been. Good was thinking what Deja was: The rules of metaphysics dictated that an agent would get sucked back onto that train. But Good knew better than most that Deja didn't always follow rules, metaphysical or otherwise.

The vise-grip on his arm relaxed. *A bit.* Good asked, "Can you hold on?"

"Yeah," Deja said, rubbing his arm. "There's all sorts of rails and stuff to hang onto up here. I'll manage."

The train made a shuddering moan like a great ghost of a ship emerging from the deep, and Crane flew toward them with far more grace than any of them had managed. She landed as gently as a moth alighting upon a lantern and demanded, "What is it? Why are you two still here?"

"Metaphysics," Deja answered, just as Good answered, "We're set now."

"I can see some doors," Crane said, staring off at the passing blurs of motion. "But they sure are fast."

Lear agreed with an unenthusiastic grunt.

Over his lenses, Deja looked out at the highway and took a deep breath. There wasn't much there but trees and distant mountains. Each exit road sign advertised campgrounds, ski resorts, and the odd gas station or diner. They approached a buzzing neon sign for a motel, and he winced. It screamed its vacancies at him in red light but soon passed.

Deja clapped his hands together like he was casting a spell to summon optimism. It didn't work. "Okay," he said with 100% contrived confidence. "Best bet is the cars merging. They'll be here longest." He looked around again. "There's really not much on this stretch of highway. Anybody going this way is probably headed home—should be here a while. Crane? How far to the hospital?"

"Last chime placed it at thirty minutes,"Crane said. "And before you ask, no, they did not tell me how much of that was highway."

Good huffed a breath that was as good as a grumbled *typical.*

"Guys?" Wren was waving at them from the jeep ahead. To Deja's eyes, she was drowning in red light and the sounds of sirens. To the others (presumably), she may as well have been waiting for them at a train station.

"Right," Crane said. "Lear? Good? *Go.*"

Good glanced at Deja. "Cars merging on, you said?"

Lear scoffed. "And we're meant to know that *how*?"

"You can see the doors, can't you?" Good pointed to the far right. "They're the ones that show up when a fourth row of cars appears and they're coming toward us."

"Helpful," Lear said. "We coming up on any now, or...."

"Soon," Deja said. "Give it thirty seconds."

"I'm going now," Crane said. "Shouldn't take a minute." She walked up to the front of the RV, eyeing the cars to the left as casually as an apex predator at a petting zoo. Without warning, she leapt... and landed easily on a passing pickup. A moment later, her tether was down, wedged between massive tackle boxes.

"It's time." Good crouched slightly. He glanced at Deja and asked, "Right?"

"Right. Lots of cars coming from"—Deja squinted his eyes and lowered his glasses as far as he dared—"Sleeping Beauty Mountain Ski and Lodge."

"Yes, okay," Lear said, staring off in the same direction, "I see it." He crouched as well and shot Good a last wary glance that made it clear he blamed him for this before he made the jump.

Good watched Lear land before turning to Deja. "You holding on?"

"I'm secure. Go."

Good stared almost longingly at the train before shifting to Deja yet again. "I don't think you should leave the RV—"

"Last car coming in now, Mom."

Good swore under his breath and leapt. He landed neatly on the back of a second (and far rattier) RV, jacket rippling gently behind him before going still. The instant the fourth and fifth tethers were in place, Deja felt it. They all did. It was weaker than a standard field, but the sense of containment, of sinking *there-ness* was unmistakable. It was a presentness Deja himself almost always felt in the Desert of the Living, but a quick look between Good and Lear confirmed it; they stood atop the vehicles just a little more firmly, like they'd gone from weightless to a hundred pounds in an instant.

But when the RV suddenly *jerked* to the left, only very narrowly missing a van, Deja felt about *three*-hundred pounds. He tumbled forward and grabbed onto a railing. In the distance, someone— maybe multiple someones—shouted his name. Deja, however, was too focused on shimmying forward enough to lean over the wind- shield to see just what the fuck the driver was thinking.

When the pale man in the red plaid shirt and Patagonia cap stared straight back at him with sunken white eyes, a few key facts became abundantly clear:

The driver wasn't thinking.

A ghost was doing the thinking for him.

DEJA CLUTCHED TO the RV roof as he struggled to recall Omega mirandizing procedure. "Spectral Presence 799"—there was zero chance of him remembering this ghost's identification code—"num- ber, number, letter, letter! You are hereby ordered to—"

"GET OUT OF HERE!"

Steaming, yellow-green ectoplasm *shot* from the possessed man's gaping mouth and coated the inside of the windshield.

Deja blinked. "Don't you wanna hear your rights?" Spirit-charged wiper fluid spurted at him, and he pulled back with a grumbled, "So that's a *no*, then." He cleared his throat and called out, "Guys? I think we've got a—" He jerked back to avoid the windshield wipers, then nearly tumbled off the roof completely when the RV made a second sharp swerve to the right.

The afflicted's priority at the moment was not to pursue the ambulance, and it certainly wasn't avoiding a crash.

It was getting Deja off that RV.

Deja gritted his teeth and gripped the railing before finishing, "*Possession situation!*" Unfortunately, the horn-ripping rendition of "Rocky Mountain High" drowned out the message. Hopefully, the others had heard him even if he couldn't hear himself, but no. Crane pivoted immediately upon the sound. Ahead of him on the Jeep, Wren was even covering her ears. The horn had been spir-it-charged.

Made sense.

"*Right.* Down we go." Deja released his grip on the railing and let the swerving motion drag him back. Once he reached the glowing access hatch, he slipped down inside the RV like it was nothing but dry cloud. When he pulled off his glasses, he noted a few things.

One, the John Denver/Rocky Mountain obsession was less a discreet aesthetic choice than a lifestyle.

Two, RVs came with *plasma screens* now.

Three, it was indeed a possession situation. (He hadn't been in the field a whole lot lately, so having his initial impressions confirmed was a confidence-boost he very much appreciated.)

Four—a number Deja only added once the driver's head swiveled 180 degrees to unhinge its jaw in an ungodly *shriek*—number three probably should've been number *one*.

That, or the fact that it was the agent *without* a mortifier who was trapped in the RV with the possession-grade ghost driving the twenty-three-ton death wagon down the highway at roughly ninety-five miles per hour.

Prioritization had never been his strong suit.

A foul smell crept toward him, subtle and slow as a morning fog. Unfortunately, that fog was only a herald of terrible things that he did not get paid enough to deal with. He held up his hands in a futile gesture of appeasement and took two slow steps back. "Okay now," he said as calmly as he could manage. "There's no need to do anything that'll damage this lovely sandstone leather interior—*shit!*"

'Shit' was half-vocalized and half-implied by Deja's rapid side-step into one of many expansive vertical-storage options. Unlike the sulphureous bile spewing from the driver's mouth like the worst sort of Hieronymus Bosch painting, the golf bags Deja huddled beside were *not* spirit charged and as immaterial to his legs as that door. Same with the ventilation panels, which was quite handy. He wriggled his way through sleeping rolls and badminton paddles, and shoved his head through an exterior vent. The ambulance was still blaring its way ahead of them, and Crane was still perched on a truck a little way behind.

"Hey, Crane!"

Crane's hooded head turned as rapidly as an owl's—well, not *their* OWLs—"Vale?"

"Yeah, um, quick question!" Deja caught a whiff of otherworldly exhaust that would've made his head turn if the alternative weren't so, *so* much worse. "Afflicteds *don't* have an infinite supply of ectoplasm spew, right?"

Thankfully, Crane didn't ask *why* he was asking that. "Right!"

"Your car's signaling right!" Deja told her. "Shift to the one behind you!" Of course, he had no clue *that* car wasn't hoping to merge, too, but he didn't know for sure that it *was* which would have to do for now. "I think it's safe to say some backup would—*fuck me—!*"

Something told Deja that the thing gripping his arm wasn't Good's loving vise. He really hated being right. He let out a squawk as he was grabbed and *hurled* out-of-bodily into the main cabin to slide through the still-steaming, yellow-green ectoplasm coating the floor, walls, and John Denver albums. It dripped from the ceiling in fat, simmering globs. The plasma screen was now an ectoplasma screen.

Deja automatically shot a hand for his mortifier but, of course, it wasn't there. Even though he already knew the answer, he shouted to the wood-paneled interior, "Why the fuck is the one without the mortifier in the R-fucking-V?" then rolled to the side, just missing a *whack* from a glowing golf club.

It was glowing the same, unearthly green as the *steering wheel*.

Deja rolled into the cubby beneath the Murphy bed. The sharp *clang* of five iron against wood veneer followed him. That was the advantage of possession cases: It may have an earthly body to manipulate the world and hold hostage, but it couldn't move like a ghost could. Not anymore.

Not like Deja could.

Deja pushed himself to his feet and wriggled along through the cabinets and the half an LL-Bean-catalog's worth of outdoor recreation stuffed inside them. The question of just why the walls separating those cabinets were permeable while the exterior walls of the RV were *not* was a fascinating metaphysical discussion—one Future-him would love to have over a bowl of hemp granola, but not now. Now, Present-him needed to get to that steering wheel. He spotted a green cereal box with the subtle glow of any spirit-charged item. "*Yes!*" He shoved his hand inside the box of Alphabet Crunch.

Nothing but sugary dust.

"'Craving for Alphabet Crunch,' huh?" Deja tossed the box aside in disgust. Once he reached another vent, he stuck his head outside. The train was still chugging alongside them, sending up clouds of green steam like a great beast panting in the cold night as it struggled to keep up. Though, it might be struggling to *slow down*. Whenever it surpassed them, it would release a labored moan while it let them catch up. It took Deja a little longer to spot Crane this time. All cars were giving the RV as wide a berth as possible—most, anyway. A black Escalade with Texas plates had places to go, and neither traffic laws re: ambulances—nor possessed Winnebagos—were going to stop it.

"Crane!" Deja called out. "Get to this car! The"—he stopped short of identifying the make and color she couldn't see—"big entitled one I'm sort of pointing at with my face!"

Crane gave him a quick nod and did just that. Once her tether was firmly wedged into the Escalade's hood, she yelled, "What's your status?"

"Steering wheel is spirit-charged and the afflicted is"—Deja winced at the sound of short fingernails clawing at acrylic—"attempting to force its way into my cabinet. I need backup! I can drive this thing if somebody else gets in here and restrains Bougie Jack Torrance." When that reference fell flat, he added, "Please and thank you!"

Some confirmation that back-up was on its way before the cabinet popped open to reveal a head-spinningly pissed off ghost-made-plaid-flesh would've been nice, but you can't have everything you want. That was Deja's thought as he was, yet again, yanked from a cabinet and hurled across the slimy RV. *This* time, he crashed into the plasma screen which, all told, wasn't nearly as bad off as the floor. Once he hit said TV, it flickered to life. An angry British man shouted obscenities in a restaurant; Deja marveled at the fact that an afflicted had bothered spirit-charging a television at all when it was hot on the tail of a Potential-laden ambulance. But then, possessing types really were as dreadfully predictable as all the training manuals said.

They loved a TV.

Deja groaned and peeled himself off the cracked screen that still managed to shriek about raw chicken while the rapidly approaching afflicted shouted, "Get out of here, you hoser!"

Deja's face contorted. "*Hoser*? What are you, nine or *ninet*—ope!" A hand clenched his throat, and he braced himself. The afflicted lifted him upward with frightening ease; Deja could only grip its forearms. He made a valiant effort to support his own weight while his feebly kicking feet doggy-paddled their way clear out of Dignity Bay.

Deja choked out, "State speed limits aren't just for the living, you know." The man raised him higher, and he winced. "Holy *crap*, is that you or *him*?" He glanced at the biceps bulging beneath the plaid and managed a raspy, "How much protein is *in* that granola—"

"Shut up!" the afflicted shouted in a ghastly chorus. Spectral wind whipped around them, sending spirit-charged granola bar wrappers and wrinkled maps flying before the RV door *burst* open—just in time to hurl Deja through it—

—an earth-quaking moan—

—a rush of cool air—

—and as suddenly as Deja was thrown, he was back inside the train. He couldn't say for certain if it had been the pull of the train itself that brought him back onboard, or the fact that the afflicted just so happened to have great aim. Seeing how he had a clear view of the RV through the train's open door, he couldn't rule out the latter. He had no desire to test it again.

Swoll or not, that afflicted was far too strong to be just *one* ghost. Double-affliction was rare enough that it had only been mentioned as *theoretically possible* rather than *something to prepare for* back in training, but it could happen. Naturally, that wasn't in the file.

There just had to be a catch in there somewhere.

Deja rolled his shoulders, grumbling, "It's never in the fucking file," before running back toward the RV. Headlights and honking horns blurred his vision as he sailed through the air. That blurriness only abated a little once he had the side access ladder in his grip.

"Status?"

Wincing, Deja glanced upward to find Crane looking down at him, unruffled as ever. "It's—*shit*—" He stopped short and wove his arms between the rungs. He dearly, *dearly* hoped a vehicle wouldn't show up on the left suitable for *ramming*. Knowing his luck it'd be that giant fucking *Escalade*. "It's a double-afflicted, and they are *not happy!*" The rapid swerving of the possessed RV made it sound like he was singing the warning. Poorly.

"What?" Crane asked sharply. "You're sure—?"

A hand *punched* through a window and grabbed Deja's arm. The power of at least two angry ghosts and one very outdoorsy dude tugged at him with all their combined might, doing their unholy best to get him off that ladder and underneath those massive wheels.

"This—*stop it, bro*—this is probably a bad time to ask, but what's the protocol on afflicted these days?" If the protocols had changed, Deja hadn't been told.

And he hadn't been told twice now, because he'd been yanked off the ladder like a bath-phobic cat from a shower curtain and dragged inside.

"*You,*" the afflicted growled into Deja's face, sickly white eyes bulging, "are a *pest.* Brandon is *ours!*"

"Hey, Puke-happy!"

They both turned.

Good was standing at the rear of the RV, mortifier raised. "*Drop him.*"

The afflicted turned its haunted gaze to Deja once more, considering. It shrugged, said, "Okie-dokie," before obliging Good like the polite Midwesterner he was and flinging Deja toward the door—

Good ran forward. He just managed to grab Deja's ankle and tug him back inside before he could undergo another metaphysical experiment. He shoved Deja to the floor behind him (ignoring the indignant *yelp*) and leveled his weapon once more, crouching low. "That the best you got?" Good shouted. "You puss-faced sack of"—he faltered until Deja offered a whispered insult-assist over his shoulder—"Patagonia!"

Deja snorted a laugh, earning him an over-the-shoulder glare. He mumbled hurriedly, "Sorry, sorry, just—thank you." As the afflicted began stomping toward them with murderous hospitality, Deja said, "Didn't realize you were so protective of me, dear."

"Yeah," Good said shortly. "That was my intention. Protecting *you.*"

Between Possibly-Brandon 3.0's legs, Deja caught a glimpse of the front of the RV where Wren was scrunched down in the driver's seat, doing her best to take control of the wheel without getting noticed. The world made sense again. Unfortunately, Wren couldn't actually *see* where the RV was going—or whom it was going *through*.

Things could be going better.

Deja cast a half-longing, half-unimpressed look at Good's mortifier. Living bodies were a pain in the ass to leave and even *more* of a pain in the ass to possess in the first place. But while you were in there and at peak power, even a full-strength mortifier would do you about as much damage as a can of hairspray. Much like hairspray, taking it straight in the face wasn't existentially threatening.

But it *was* incredibly unpleasant.

Bam!

"Jeez Louise!" Almost-Brandon clapped its hands over its face and stumbled back at the first shot.

Good cursed under his breath. That shot had been weak.

Between casting aspersions on an under-seasoned risotto, the British chef shouted threats and obscenities from the cracked television screen. "Listen here, mate! You'll pay for that in Brandon's blood! He will die screaming and you will—"

"Isn't *that* Brandon?" Deja asked, nodding toward the shrieking tower of plaid.

"That or the Potential, I'm guessing." Good was far less concerned with the TV chef than Deja. He tried to fire his mortifier again only for it to spark fitfully. He hit the back of the glass fuel canister like a diner patron desperate for the last dregs of coagulated ketchup, but it was no use. The pathetic wisp of green within remained pathetic, unmoved by Good's growled, "Damn it!"

"What's wrong with your mortifier?" Deja bit back a grin with only minimal success. "Did you chuck it down a hallway or something?"

Good's responding look was concealed yet scathing, nonetheless. He finally spared the shouting plasma screen a look. "TV's charged, huh? Good to know. Anything else? Apart from the obvious?"

Deja clicked his tongue and looked around, struggling to concentrate over the enraged Midwestern chorus of, "All will pay," and, "Boy, that smarts!" and, "The rivers of Minnesota will run red with Brandon's blood, ya hear?" He gasped his excitement. "Golf club." Good shot out a hand for it, but Deja beat him to it. "Oh, come on, dude. You've already got the mortifier!"

"Yeah!" Good snapped back before pausing to aim another weak chirp of a shot at Brandon's face. "And fat lot of good it's doing"—*Bam!*—"thanks to *you!*"

"Just—just, I don't know! Use the TV!"

"The *TV?*" Good echoed while he fired another shot at the afflicted's face without looking—impressive, really. "You want me to use—"

ScreeEECH! The radio cycled through a dozen tracks before settling on Britney Spears.

Just when Deja found himself silently mouthing along, "*Give me a si-i-i-ign,*" The-Artist-Formerly-Known-as-Brandon geared up for another burst of ectoplasm, and Deja hissed, "Grab the TV! Grab the TV!" but Good was way ahead of him.

Good *yanked* it from the cord and angled it above them while a supernaturally sassy chef shouted about what sissies they were for not being able to handle a little bit of projectile hell-bile any better than the would-be chef now crying blood could handle seasoning a risotto properly. The stuff hit the TV with a sound that Deja could never have predicted, and yet the moment he heard it, made him think, *yes—that is exactly what two quarts of ectoplasm spraying the back of a plasma screen TV would sound like.* Green spoo spilled over the edge and landed on the floor beside them with a plopping *hiss.*

Deja grimaced at the acrid stink of sulphur and mumbled, "I hate it here."

As Britney sang lyrics about getting hit one more time that struck Deja as a bit on-the-nose, the ambulance shrieked and Potential life tugged at Deja's core, forcing him to lean in its direction.

At the same moment, Brandon-cubed let out a throat-ripping

scream of rage. The steering wheel *jerked* to the right in pursuit, straight out of Wren's grasp.

Deja gripped Good's shoulder, hard. "Fuck, it's going for Wren," he said hurriedly. "Shoot it again, *shoot it again!*"

"Shut up!" Good growled and did exactly that. He leaned around the TV and managed to fire a few rapid shots into the afflicted's back, each blast flying with a piercing sound like a hawk's cry. Those shots did look stronger, but Possessed-Brandon didn't seem too bothered until one hit it square in the back of the head. It *bellowed.* The RV swayed, back under Wren's control. And when the afflicted yelled that they were all going to pay for that, Deja heard two voices: Disparate now, like the precision-perfect chorus that the afflicted *had* been was now an untrained community choir.

Deja squinted at it. "Wait a sec, is that a—"

"Help Wren!" Good shouted over the dissonant roar of twin ghosts. "I'll cover you."

"Help Wren? With *what*?"

"With the golf club and your, I don't know, *sarcasm,*" Good snapped. When Deja just stared at him, Good repeated, "I'll cover you, all right? *Go!*"

Then, four sharp bangs sounded from above.

Good looked up.

Deja looked up.

The afflicted looked up.

Wren looked up.

Even the pissed off celebrity chef looked up.

"RV must be fully tethered now," Good said.

"Hurray?"

"Which means the ambulance will've broke far enough ahead of the field that Crane and Lear must be up there with all the tethers. Afflicted's contained in here. Potential's somewhere out there. We can take it out."

"Yeah, well, if this RV catches up again and splits that ambulance in half, it's not really gonna matter *where* it's tethered, is it?"

Good shot him a look, then muttered, "Fair point."

"And anyway," Deja hissed, "I'm not exactly keen on taking out a dozen motorists to subdue *one afflicted*!"

"You think *I am?*" Good snapped back. "*Fuck you*, Vale—"

"Can I get some help up here please?" Wren called as she struggled to regain control of the massive boat of a vehicle. The wheel jerked from left to right in her hands, spirit-charged leather *whirring* against her gloves like a rock climber who'd lost their grasp on a rope. Deja half expected smoke to rise.

"Okay, Brandon—Bran*dons*," Deja corrected. He stood and gave the golf club a quick twirl. "Time to leave the poor Winnebago alone, she's been through enough."

Brandon-question-mark growled, "*You first!*" and craned its head back, jaw opening preternaturally wide.

Deja prepared to dart into the cabinet to avoid the onslaught, but only a yellow-green bubble of spectral sputum appeared. It wobbled pathetically on a waxen lip, then—*pop!* Down a ghostly white chin it dribbled. Spooge steamed faintly on the plaid collar.

Deja glanced down at Good, who was crouched behind the TV. On said TV, the celebrity chef paused his task of force-feeding a contestant under-seasoned risotto just long enough to projectile vomit across the studio kitchen. "Well," Deja muttered over the crescendo of Britney whining overhead, "that was anticlimactic."

Good shrugged. "I'm not complaining."

"*Give me a si-i-i-ign—*"

"Stop singing, Vale, and *go hit it*, already!"

"I'm *sorry*," Deja defended. He hadn't even realized he'd *been* singing. "It's just so damn *catchy*!"

"*Now*, Vale!" Good snapped.

"Right!" Deja tightened his grip on the golf club and darted forward, aiming a solid swing at Brandon's white-eyed face.

Brandon just managed a "You wouldn't *dare* harm us—" before taking a blow to the head *so hard* that what little reserves of ectoplasm it had shot clear out its mouth and splattered the Murphy bed in green. When it spoke again, it was in that strange dissonant chorus once more. "He's *ours*."

"He's really not." Powerless to disobey the orders handed down from the queen of turn-of-the-century teen pop via Dolby surround-sound speakers (with bass module), Deja swung back the golf club to hit that baby *one more time*. But before he could try for an eagle, the RV took a rapid shift to the left that sent Deja flying to the right. He landed with an "*Oof!*" against Good, who landed with a second "*Oof!*" against the possessed TV chef, who was far less Midwestern about things.

"Get *off me!*" Good struggled to free his left arm and level a shot at the afflicted who'd finally reached the *head-spinning phase.* He fired three quick shots.

Not a one even registered to the possessed man stomping toward Wren. Just as it made to grab her, she pointed her own mortifier over her shoulder and fired at its blur of a face. Shouts of enraged pain *shook* the RV. They picked up speed with a growl of rubber before bouncing *off* the road entirely.

Between mortifier shots, Good demanded, "What's happening?"

Deja crawled his way up the wall just far enough to see out the window. "We're driving on the median. It's taking us straight into oncoming traffic!" He winced at the enraged honks and screeching rubber. The ride smoothed out for a few seconds, then they were back in the grass of the roadside, and then the loam of the forest. Reflexively, Deja leaned back to avoid the branches the RV cut through with a thousand whip-cracks of snapping wood. "Guess this is some sort of afflicted shortcut—wait, are we going uphill? Where in the non-living fuck is the—hold on." He narrowed his eyes, then scrambled to the other side to check those windows. "Good?" he called weakly. "Do you know what happened to the—"

BAM!

Just before the RV rammed a massive oak tree and accordioned to half its length, Deja's last thought was:

Train.

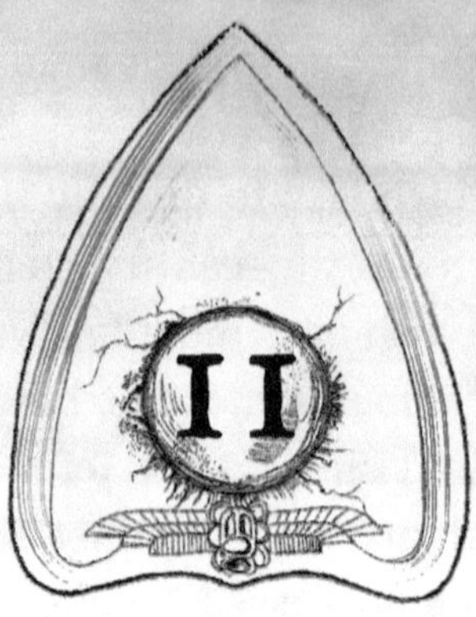

"**I**t's *not even* seasoned, *you absolute numpty! What the f—*"beep! "*—is wrong with you?*"

Deja grimaced against the cracked TV. He kept his eyes closed against the pain throbbing in his head. The celebrity chef's voice was tinny and distant and entirely *too loud.*

Nearby, Britney's distorted voice skipped in answer to the chef's rhetorical question: "*—my mind—my mind—my mind—my—*"

"*Well?*" the chef demanded. "*Are you even listening to me?*"

Deja ignored this and took stock of his injuries. His head was killing him like Britney's loneliness was killing her, and his right side ached so bad you'd think he'd just woken up *under* the RV instead of *in it*... but he seemed to be intact. As much as usual, anyway. He could feel the press of his augur against his chest. It was cold. It shouldn't be. Not outside the walls of the Hereafter. Not with the train close by—

But it wasn't close by.

"*I asked you a question, Vale! Are you listening to me?*"

Deja's eyes shot open. The tiny chef was staring *straight at him.* He pointedly rapped his digital knuckles on the screen with a *donk-donk-donk.* Deja's considerable pain was edged out by the dread-filled recognition that he was hearing and seeing things that couldn't be there.

"*Well?*"

Deja hesitated... then nodded.

"About f—" beep! *"—ing time!"* the chef said, throwing back his head. *"I wasn't even going to do this, you know, but you're so f—"* beep! *"—ing pathetic, here I am, sticking my neck out for you! Again!"*

Deja mumbled to himself, "I've fucking lost it. I've *beyond* fucking lost it."

The chef pointed a stern finger at Deja. *"If you don't shape up, you're going to lose a hell of a lot more than your mind, Vale. Now, you listen and you listen good, you little sh—"* beep! *"Stay out of that forest, yeah? There's"*—a hiss of static—*"for you and"*—a crackle of distortion—*"risk it."*

Deja blinked in confusion. "What?"

The chef gave him a look of strained patience and opened his mouth to speak once more, but most of what came out of the speakers was the distorted death throes of an appliance already past its expiration date. *"—are not ready yet!"* And with that last string of words, the chef disappeared. Just blank, cracked gray remained.

Even Britney had fizzled out.

Deja forced himself up and leaned against the wall only to roll clear out of the RV. Now a crumpled tin can of a wreck, what was left of the walls had become meaningless as barriers. Whoever it was that governed the laws of metaphysics decided that the peeling bits of aluminum no longer counted as proper walls, apparently. He rolled further away from the RV—or tried to. A waylaid tether tugged in his core and he stayed put. The train was nowhere in sight. He needed that tether to ground him now, or he'd risk losing himself to oblivion.

"Shit," Deja hissed, frantically searching the wreckage for one of the iron nails.

Later, it would occur to him that the process would've been far faster with glasses *on*, but with the afflicted coming to a stand with a series of grotesque pops of shifting joints and cracking bones, he couldn't spare the cognitive power.

"Shit, shit, shit!" Deja ran his hands through the busted aluminum and cracked leather and singed fabric and splintered wood to try and find something whole and iron and *helpful*.

"Here."

Good crouched beside him and reached straight through a cushion to grab a tether. "Where's the afflicted?"

"It's right—"

Deja stopped. The afflicted wasn't there anymore. "Shit."

"Not the priority right now," Good said, looking around. "The other tethers must've flown off somewhere because there's none here. You see Wren? Anybody?"

"No. My guess is they are wherever those tethers are. Or on the train, hopefully."

"Where *is* the train?"

"That's just what I was asking when we"—Deja smashed his right fist into his left palm—"took this unfortunate detour."

Good pulled out his augur. When he opened it, no green light splashed his face. He spotted his mortifier beneath a spilled set of golf clubs and picked it up, turning it this way and that. "That's something," he muttered and holstered the weapon. "Take this." He passed Deja the tether. "I'm gonna look for more. And keep an eye out. We know that fucker's around here somewhere."

"Do we?"

"I don't like the tone you used just then."

"Well," Deja explained, "forests—especially old ones like this— they're—well, *you* know. Odd. I don't know how far into the woods we should be expanding this field. If we've even still *got* a field."

"We don't have much choice."

"I know we don't. It's just a feeling, I guess." At Good's short sigh, Deja scrunched his shoulders defensively. "What? The woods are creepy, dark, and deep, all right?"

Over his shoulder, Good said, "You can deal," but he didn't con-tradict the point. Forests were like walls and doors and hearths and tunnels. What they were and what they meant sat so deep in the subconscious that even Good could see them. Parts of them, anyway.

Deja slid his glasses back on and stood. A chill trickled down his neck. It crept along his spine in warning whispers. Or maybe it was the trees doing the whispering. There were hundreds of them. Thousands of them. Sentinels standing guard amidst the faint fog of the forest. A strip of black here, a skeletal hand of branches there. A spirit could get lost for millennia in those whispering woods.

A muffled hoot in the distance.

A glimmer of light flickered, running in a web between shapes in the fog.

Another hoot.

The light flickered back in the opposite direction like a call and response between whatever it was that lived—or unlived—in these woods.

But the longer Deja stared into that endless mist that seemed so far away and yet close enough to touch all at once, he found himself taking his glasses *off.* He felt too exposed with them on—not that the forest was much better without them.

A little way off, Good walked through a stump so decayed, Deja was amazed it could hold the weight of the tennis racket that had landed upon it.

"Found another," Good said, holding up a tether. "Thoughts on where to put it for now?" If Good was asking for Deja's opinion—really asking—that meant he was just as unsettled by this forest as Deja was, even if he didn't want to admit it. But then, Good didn't bother waiting for an answer and just stuck it in his pocket.

A bird sang like metallic chimes. Far away... directly above. No way to know.

Hermit thrush. The name came so suddenly, so inexplicably, the knowledge might've been whispered to him. Didn't matter. That thrush might've been dead... might've been alive. No way to know. It didn't matter. Not to the forest. Bird song broke like glass and faded into rustling pine needles that chimed in the wind in the same, shattering key.

Deja couldn't remember stepping closer. But here he was.

"Hey." Good was speaking to Deja, but his focus was fixed on his own hand pressing lightly against a massive tree—touching it.

That couldn't be good. "Stay focused," he said like he was reminding himself, too. He removed his hand. Unless the tree had *released* it.

"Yeah. Sure. I'm focused." When Good just continued to stare at him, Deja slipped his glasses back on. Jagged lines of light darted under his feet, clouded like veins beneath skin. As he stared at it, he had just the prelude to a thought, sudden and strange but unrelenting:

I want to crawl beneath that soil and bury myself there.

Before that prelude could become an overpowering song commanding him to action, a familiar voice pulled him away.

"We need to find the other tethers, Vale. *Vale!*"

"Yeah," Deja said, forcing his eyes upward. "I'm looking." He did look. He pretended to ignore the growls and screeches that might've just as easily come from flora as fauna and looked. They both did. Deja kept his eyes focused a foot above the ground. High enough to avoid getting sucked into the circulating pulse of the forest, low enough to spot a lost nail.

"*Guys?*"

They stopped.

"*Vale? Good? Anybody?*"

Both spun, looking in opposite directions.

Deja asked, "Was that Wren?"

"Sounded like Wren," Good said cautiously.

Deja looked into the forest. A light flickered then faded, swallowed up by rolling gray fog. It looked uncannily like the endless Gray beyond the walls of the Hereafter. But, unlike that senseless nothing, there was a feeling of something out there. Of some*one.* Deja let out a shuddering breath and took a reflexive step back.

There were places Omega agents couldn't go. Ghosts they couldn't hunt. Every instinct told Deja he was looking at both.

And it was looking right back at him.

If that wasn't Wren, Deja could only hope it was that pair of ghosts. *Ghosts* they understood. *Ghosts* they were equipped to deal with. He cast a glance at Good's holster. Some of them were more equipped than others.

The voice called their names again. And only *their* names.

Deja whispered, "Why would Wren only be calling out for us specifically?"

"Because we're the only ones missing?" Good made a frustrated noise. "But then she wouldn't be calling for 'anybody.' *Damnit*. Ours are the names it *knows*."

"The afflicted might not know the other's names," Deja pointed out, hopefully. "Could be that."

"True... but it's not the afflicted."

As much as Deja hated being right, Good being right was usually worse. "Sure wish I was armed," he muttered.

Good scoffed. "Don't know if it'd do either of us any good." He craned his neck to look around. "Don't suppose the train could even make it in this far?"

"I expect not. If it could, it'd be here. Or we'd be *there*." Deja moved his glasses to rest atop his head. "There's just so much—so much *much* here."

"Sure. Whatever the fuck that even means."

Another breaking-glass melody ghosted through the pine trees overhead. Deja felt cold. "I miss Brandon."

Good snorted. "Of course, you do. Come on. We need to keep looking. Grab that golf club. We can't just wait here. Stay close."

Deja sighed and did as he was told—within reason, anyway. He drifted off to the left where it felt fractionally less ominous.

Good broke off to the right.

Once out of direct eyeshot, Deja said, "Marco."

"Fuck right off, Vale."

But it was an effective way of keeping them somewhat together while expanding their search, so Deja kept doing it. He'd walk off a dozen feet or so and toss out a "Marco," while he searched for a tether or spatter of ectoplasm or some other sign they weren't the only ones out there.

In response, he'd get variations on, "Shut up, Vale," or "Anything yet?" or "This isn't good. Why weren't we pulled back to the train with the others?"

A ripple of light danced up a tree and spread like fleeting fire-works, flashing in the canopy of fog. A smell, deep and rich and sweet and *old,* bloomed in its wake. Something that Deja dearly hoped was a loon called in the distance. Was it the distance? Deja had to stop to take a deep breath before calling out a weak, "Marco."

The hissed response licked Deja's ear, cold and wet.

"Polo."

"SOMEONE WORKED VERY hard on those."

The voice came from within, but he knows the true source is behind him and turns.

It's a large figure in a black, hooded robe. His mind supplies the concept of 'robe' much the way it knew to turn around. Like how it translates images from the retina, flipping them right-side-up. An optical illusion. A trick played on the brain. The vague black before him is an optical illusion, too. Shadow one moment, fabric the next. Less a substance than a trick of the light. He can't see any mouth that might've spoken—can't see *anything* in the void—but he can hear a smile. Sense crinkles at the corners of nonexistent eyes.

He drops the ten-inch spike he'd been holding. It falls to the tile with striking softness, like he'd dropped a square of spider-spun silk instead of iron. "You shouldn't be here," he says, stepping back.

Again, he senses the smile. Another trick on his mind.

"You shouldn't even be *able* to be here, yet here we are," the hooded figure says—again, from inside his head.

He takes another step back.

A faint, fluttering ripple of black. The figure stays still.

"What are you doing?" he asks, cursing the quaver in his voice.

"Nothing," they say. "Waiting, patient." A shrug—a trick of the light. "Perhaps listening... if you've something to say."

"Who are you?"

"I'm nobody. But *you* are—"

"Vale!"

Deja opened his eyes.

Good was staring down at him, mask off. Wavy auburn hair fell into his face, but it couldn't hide the few freckles scattered across his nose or the brown eyes wide with concern.

Deja blinked rapidly and the face was gone, replaced by a hollow hood haloed in gray mist. He opened his mouth to speak but couldn't.

"Don't talk," Good said. At Deja's pointy look, he shot him a glare through the mask. "Yeah, I know. Just *take it easy,* is my point. Don't move."

Deja shifted as well as he could manage to get a sense of where he was beyond *under Good.* The barest wriggle of his shoulders told him he was on the forest loam. Just a little too late to be anything but uncanny, the dried leaves made a rustling sound. Then came the cool press of metal against his chest, followed by a feeling that couldn't be described as anything but his own *there-ness.* Good had pressed his augur to Deja's heart; the silver chain connecting it to his own chest pulled taut between them.

"What happened?" Deja asked, surprised to hear his voice sounded the way it did—mature and sharp (weak as it was in that moment). Did it always sound like that?

An answering voice whispered from nowhere, *No.*

Deja struggled to rise. "We need to get the fuck out of here."

"Agreed." Good tucked his augur back into its pocket and sat back on his heels.

"Any contact?" Deja asked, pushing himself onto his elbows. "Anything?"

Good didn't respond for a few moments. "How long do you think you were out, exactly?"

With a groan, Deja managed to get himself into a seated position. The pops and cracks made his body feel like scrap metal being hammered out. "I dunno. Three years?" He patted the ground around him until he located the golf club.

"More like three minutes. If that."

Deja gave him a small, satisfied smile. "You were worried, huh."

Good looked up like he was praying to some distant star for patience and sighed. "I was worried I'd have to drag you out of here, yes."

"Yeah," Deja said, giving Good a sympathetic pat on the back. "Procedure's a bitch, huh." He looked around. "Any sign of... anything?"

"Thought I heard the train, but..." Good trailed off with a small shrug and stood.

Deja grimaced. They'd *thought* they'd heard a lot of things. That was nothing new for Deja. He just wasn't used to *not* being alone in the mistrust of his senses—a positive indication, to be sure, but it didn't really feel like one.

Good tugged Deja to his feet. He waited all of two seconds to make sure Deja could stand on his own before walking off. "Highway's this way."

"How do you know?" Deja asked, surprised.

Good shrugged. "Feels less, I don't know... fucked up this way."

"Fair enough. Lead on, Gandalf." Deja ignored Good's scoffed, "*Idiot,*" and looked around. Turned out Good was right. That sense he was being watched, that prickling whisper on the back of his neck felt weaker when they walked this way. Odd, considering that strangely sentient forest was now behind them.

So that was the way they walked.

After a long while of *nothing*, Good asked, "Still got your tether?"

"No, I ate it. Was that bad?"

Good didn't dignify that with a response. Unless you counted his quickening stride.

As the path beneath their feet became less accidental and more purposeful, life prickled the tip of Deja's nose like the looming threat of sunburn. "We're close," he said, "to, you know"—a vague wave with the golf club—"where we were."

Good grunted noncommittally and kept moving. "Looks like a path."

"It is. There's trail markers and stuff."

Another grunt.

They kept moving.

Deja didn't bother to ask the rhetorical question dogging him: how the ever nonliving fuck did they get out that far? Surely the RV couldn't have driven that deep into the woods—certainly not over the small but sharp hills they were crossing now. Good didn't know the answer any better than Deja did, but they both knew the shape of it.

Because this was a place they didn't belong.

It belonged to those ghosts they couldn't hunt.

Once they entered a large man-made clearing—some sort of picnic area—a different sort of unease crept in. Not quite as uncanny, not quite as existentially terrifying, but threatening all the same. A familiar sort of threatening that could only be their erstwhile afflicted friend. Joining that feeling was an equally familiar, buzzing burn. Neon. Deja placed a hand to his itching ear and looked up. Beyond this clearing was another larger one, and at its center a cabin fixed with a loud and colorful neon sign. A red and yellow coyote howled at a blue moon. Beneath that fitfully glowing moon were far brighter red letters. They were so bright they even *tasted* red:

THESE WOODS EAT MEN LIKE YOU.

Deja took a step back. He pulled off his glasses and rubbed at his eyes. When he looked again, the howling-coyote sign only said:

COYOTE SYD'S RV PARK

He took a deep breath and glanced at Good to see if he was alone in seeing impossible things. His first indication that something was genuinely wrong was the focus of Good's line of sight—an overturned trashcan. A very unremarkable trashcan. No, not the trashcan. The subtly glowing, not-so-subtly hissing raccoon *inside* the trashcan.

"Oh no," Deja whispered, taking a cautious step back. "It's charged the raccoon."

"I can see that. It's not like it's charged a *bear*, is it?"

Deja scoffed and continued his ginger retreat. "In that case, it is *all you*, buddy. I'm still recovering, probably."

"Please. You're fine. Don't know why you're afraid of a little—*fucking hells!*" Good drew his mortifier and darted to the side, narrowly missing the crazed leap of glowing black-and-gray fury barreling at him. He composed himself with admirable speed and fired three quick shots at the ground, forcing the raccoon charging in for round two to weave from side to side.

Deja really hoped its speed had not been inhibited by the salvo. If that was spirit-charged *slow* raccoon, he did not want to see *fast mode.*

"Vale!" Good shouted. He scrambled up a tree, firing shots over his shoulder. "Help me out here, would you?"

"I thought it was just a raccoon!" Deja called back. Before Good could unleash his retort, he added, "And I'm not exactly armed here, am I?"

"You've got a golf club!"

"What?!" Deja held up the golf club and gave it an indignant shake. "You want me to attack a raccoon with *this?*"

"Yes!"

"No! Just"—Deja waved vaguely at the squat beast scrambling at the side of the tree with its little black hands—"*shoot better!*"

Good did. The raccoon fell to the ground, stunned. The green-glow of eyes that had been casting its black-masked cheeks in light receded.

It came back.

"Shit!" Deja raised the golf club—more as a shield than a weapon—and Good scrambled higher up the tree until he reached a branch to stand upon. He began firing rapid shots down at the thing while it weaved and darted and hissed with supernatural speed.

The raccoon launched itself at the tree, and Deja took a solid swing with the golf club that sent it screeching off into the tree line. It regrouped in a wood pile and came running back on its hind legs like a demented cartoon character. Deja jumped to the side to avoid it, and it was perfectly content to continue the charge at the agent cowering up the tree. Once its paws latched onto the bark, Deja dove forward and drove the tether nail into its tail.

It let out a disturbingly *human* wail, and the green glow melted away. Once the last hair went back to drab gray, the tail passed through the tether like it was nothing but a nightmare. Mrs. Raccoon was wide awake now where nightmares couldn't hurt it.

"Where is it?" Good demanded from the tree. He couldn't see the raccoon now—couldn't watch it adorably scratch at its face and clean its cheeks with its little black hands.

"It's uncharged, it's fine," Deja panted. "Good thing we're the only ones out here, huh? That would've been real embarrassing for you otherwise."

Good landed on the ground with a sound lighter than falling snow. "No clue what you're talking about," he said, straightening his hood with an indignant *snap* of black leather.

"Uh-huh." Deja lowered his glasses a moment and looked around. There didn't seem to be anything remarkable about the area. The raccoon even agreed; it had already scampered off in pursuit of better garbage from less haunted campgrounds.

"We should wait here," Good said.

Deja gave Good a surprised look. But when he saw how heavily Good was now leaning against the tree, he understood. Without more tethers, without that train close by, he was fading dangerously close to oblivion.

Far faster than Deja himself was.

Normally, Wren didn't take up the tether field until the train was there to take them back. Only, the train was nowhere to be seen. Maybe whatever it was that allowed Deja to withstand the burn of life so much better than his teammates was holding him there, too. But he didn't know what would happen to Good if they kept on like this. No one did. That's why they called it being lost to *oblivion*.

Deja sat at the base of the tree and patted the dirt beside him. "Come on. Let's check our augurs."

Good didn't bother putting up a front and collapsed beside him with a ragged sigh. He pulled out his augur and popped it open. The green light of the Hereafter was faint, but it was certainly there. A small improvement. "Agent Good here with Agent Vale. No sign of train or other agents—please advise."

Nothing.

They waited.

Deja unchained his augur and held it against Good's shoulder.

"Thanks," Good mumbled.

"Don't mention it."

They kept waiting.

Beside him, Good rapped code on his knee—too tired to speak. *Anything?*

No, Deja rapped back.

They waited more.

You all right? Deja rapped.

Good's fingers were slow to reply, but somehow managed to come off as pissy anyway. *Shut up.*

Deja rapped, *Marco.*

No.

The campground was silent. The leaves hardly even rustled. It was that silence that made the fervent *tap-tap* of a woodpecker above them so jarring. Deja squinted and watched the bird over his glasses.

Tap-tap—tap-tap-tap—tap—

"Vale, what are you staring—"

"*Shh.*" Deja held up a silencing hand and watched. Listened. Sure, it might've been a coincidence the first time. But once that rap-code word repeated, it was far harder to dismiss. It said:

Wait.

Once Deja mouthed the word, the rhythm shifted: *tap-tap-tap—tap—tap—tap-tap-tappity-tap.*

Stay out of the forest.

The tapping continued, more urgently now.

Train coming.

Again, Deja mouthed the words. Again, the rhythm shifted.

Mind the afflicted—

"Shit," Deja hissed, standing up. "Give me your mortifier—"

"No! Not again!"

"Come *on!* You're in no position to—"

"Neither are you! *You're* the one who *passed out!*"

"Fine," Deja said tartly, refastening his augur to its chain. "Just be ready."

Good scoffed and checked his weapon. "I'm always ready." He shot Deja a look and asked more quietly, "Why?"

Deja didn't say the truth: *Either I'm still hallucinating or I just got an OWL from a woodpecker.* He couldn't say what it was that made him hedge with a casual (if a tad salty), "Common sense?"

But the fact that Good didn't accept this right away—that he continued staring up at Deja with a suspicion that Deja couldn't see but felt as well as any of the living things made manifest to him alone— gave him an unsettling fear rivaled only by that old, old forest.

At last, Good said, "Fine," and gave his mortifier a final check before holding it at the ready position, pointed at the ground between his bent legs. "Don't think two tether nails are going to cut it with this thing."

"No," Deja agreed. "I expect four wouldn't be much better."

"Exactly. What if we kept moving—"

"*No!*" More levelly, Deja said, "No. We're both, well... suboptimal right now. Protocol says to stay put, and we've already moved enough."

"That was different."

"I know, but now we're not in a freaky forest, so we should stay." Deja gave Good a knowing look. "Feeling useless, huh?"

"No," Good said a little too tightly to be believable. "I'm just— *behind you!*" He raised his weapon and fired a shot before scrambling to a stand, leaning against the tree.

The afflicted was back. What remained of its shirt hung in plaid, bloody shreds from broad shoulders. Pale cheeks were streaked with ash and blood that Deja could only assume was Brandon's. Its eyes still bore the distinct, cloudy look of the possessed. When Brandon opened its mouth wide, Deja prepared to leap back. But all that emerged was a coughing burp and an anticlimactic trickle of ecto-plasm that barely even sizzled as it dribbled from the corners of its mouth.

"Seems weaker," Deja said. "I don't know if it's being farther from the RV or the Potential or what, but it is definitely weaker."

"So are we, so don't get too excited."

"True." Deja gave the golf club a twirl and—it fell to the ground with a distinct, this-worldly *thud.* He looked down at it. So did the afflicted.

Good, on the other hand, only said, "Where'd it go?"

"Do you think it did that on purpose?" Deja asked cautiously. "Because that'd be an unfortunate trick." If this afflicted really was composed of multiple ghosts savvy enough to team up to possess one man, he wasn't about to put anything past them.

"No. Ghosts don't have that kind of control. It's running out of juice. Makes sense everything it charged would be, too."

"Well, shit." Deja stared back down at the perfectly ordinary golf club. He glanced at Good and chanced a "Don't suppose you'd—"

"Move over," Good growled, aiming his mortifier. Deja raised his hands and did just that while Good fired shot after shot, straight into the pale, dribbling face.

The afflicted stomped toward them, less like a supercharged human and more like a zombie. It barely bothered wincing at each shot—just kept dragging its limp left foot behind it, grasping its dirty fists like it couldn't tell how far away they were. When a shot hit its left eye, it stopped, head swiveling back and forth. It couldn't even tell where the pain was coming from. And when it moaned in pain, it was with three distinct voices.

Now Deja was sure. It shouldn't have been possible for ghosts to operate with that level of coordination, but no point denying it. Two ghosts were cooperating to possess one man.

And one of those ghosts was a *kid.*

An aura formed along the afflicted's right side like an afterimage. Barely there. Barely *anything.* When it opened its mouth, Deja had to struggle to hear the words that came out. "It *hurts!*" a small voice whined. A child.

Another shot—this time to the right eye.

"I'm not leaving you, sweetie," a stronger, feminine voice said.

Two more shots.

The afflicted went stiff. It didn't even open its mouth, but the child cried out all the same. "No, mom! I'm sorry, mom—mom, I'm scared, mom, please don't—"

Without understanding why, Deja reached for Good and whispered, "Wait, don't—"

One last shot. Straight between the eyes. The white clouding the afflicted's eyes faded, leaving only Brandon's unremarkable blue.

Deja asked, "Did you hear that?"

"Hear what." Good's pseudo-question was a thinly cloaked statement: *Stop talking.*

But if Deja knew how to do that, they'd probably have a stronger working relationship. "Their voices at the end," he said.

Brandon collapsed to his knees, blinking stupidly as he came to living awareness once more. Two ghost's worth of spirit-particles fell to the ground, glimmering weakly. Then, those lights came back. They pulsed like electric veins beneath the dirt, shooting rapidly from east to west. An answering pulse from the other direction swept past in a thread-thin hand and, just like that, the spirit-particles were *gone.* Only Brandon remained.

And also the phone vibrating in the pocket of his dirty khakis.

Deja stared at the ground. "Can you see spirit-particles?"

"No," Good said. "But it's not like there's a Potential around, and Eyes couldn't get here to collect them anyway."

Brandon coughed weakly and pulled out his phone. "Hello?" he croaked. *Screams* on the other end made him wince.

Deja winced too. A sharp nudge at his shoulder.

Good jerked his chin. "Train's almost here."

"Shit, really?" Sure enough, green mist was rising over dead leaves and moss. "Good," he said weakly. "That's good."

Good's hum of agreement was barely there.

Deja gave him a cautious, sideways look. "You know we're not the ones who exorcised that afflicted. Those mortifier shots were too weak for that."

Good eyed him a few moments, saying nothing. Then he turned away to stare determinedly in the direction of the approaching train. "Doesn't matter," he said. "It's done."

Deja opened his mouth to argue, then closed it again. He watched Brandon struggle to get a word in—or *out.* At last, the basic factory-issue man managed a feeble, "Sarah?"

Deja slid his glasses down his nose. Crackling on the other end of the line was a frantic woman's voice. "*Nick? Baby, is that really you?*"

"Yeah," the man who was apparently named *Nick* and *not* Brandon croaked. "It's me. Are you all right?"

"*Couldn't be better,*" she said through a wet laugh. "*Your daughter is right here and she's* perfect."

"Already?" Under his breath, Nick mumbled, "How long was I out?"

"*She's gonna be trouble! Impatient one. Couldn't even wait 'til we got off the highway. You wanted to come out and meet your daddy, didn't you, sweetie? Say hi to daddy! Say hi!*"

The baby did not say hi, thankfully. If it had, they'd be back at square one—square negative one, even.

Nick's eyes clenched shut and his mouth followed soon after. He took a deep breath and managed a semblance of vocal composure. "Listen, Sarah"—Deja's face scrunched in confusion as his tired mind caught up to the fact that 'Brandon' was never on that RV, Potential or otherwise—"I don't... I don't know what—"

"*It's okay. Just get here, all right?*"

"All right. I love you." Nick paused. "Do you have cash for a cab?"

The magic of childbirth all but faded from Sarah's voice. "*What?*"

"Never mind."

"*What happened to the RV—*"

"Love you, see you real soon." Nick hung up and slid his phone into his pocket.

Off in the distance, fainter than distant thunder, the RV let out a feeble snippet of "Rocky Mountain High."

Off-key.

Deja looked for it, but it was eclipsed by the train. Compartment doors opened in a flood of green steam to reveal Agents Crane, Wren, and Lear. Deja was too confused to be relieved. "Wait," he asked Good, "if that's Nick, who the fuck is *Brandon?*"

"Probably the Potential. Like I said." Good shouldered past Deja to board the train.

"No. Baby's a girl."

"So?"

"So they're pretty hippy-crunchy, but they don't strike me as quite that progressive."

Good didn't bother responding further.

Deja placed one foot on the first step and hesitated. Inside, Good passed Wren the tether he'd been clinging to then collapsed into a seat.

Crane hurriedly passed him a vial of green aether and demanded, "What happened? Vale makes sense, I suppose, in that he makes no sense." She ignored Deja's muttered "Thanks," and asked Good, "But why didn't *you* rebound to the train?"

Good threw up a hand. "I don't know, Crane. Next time I won't stand so close to him. Happy?"

"Doesn't matter if I'm not, does it." Crane said. "Vale?"

Deja wasn't really listening anymore. Instead, he found himself unable to look away from the forest. He could've sworn he heard something.

The ghost of a horn.

The warning *tap-tap* of a woodpecker.

The buzzing threat of a neon sign.

"Coming?" It wasn't a request.

Deja nodded absently and turned away from the forest. He froze.

By Wren was a glimmer. An impossible glimmer of *red*, just as bright and colorful as any neon sign. It was right there, painted across the windows above her head:

MEMENTO MORIEBARIS

That prickly-neck feeling of being watched dripped down Deja's spine. It only got worse once he saw Lear speak to Wren. He was looking at her, *right at her*, but he paid the red words no more mind than the gaslight flickering overhead, or the knots in the wood beneath him. Unlike that phantom voice in the woods calling their names that Good had heard, Lear couldn't perceive those red words.

Because they weren't really there.

Deja cast a last glance at that leering forest. He could just make out the blue moon of the neon sign, but no words—real or imagined. When he turned back to the train, the painted red words were gone too.

Deja boarded. A whisper rustled through the leaves:
Marco...?
Another whisper licked up Deja's spine and answered:
Deja.

Deja paused halfway through his descent from the train. AI Vex waiting for them at the bottom of the grand staircase of Styx station was becoming a familiar and unwelcome sight. It wasn't that Deja disliked the man—quite the contrary. But agents who weren't in charge generally didn't receive a personal debrief after every mission. He could only hope this was just a short-lived bout of overcautious-ness following his return to the field. With any luck, this would be the end of the paranoid pattern.

It shouldn't be. You shouldn't even be in—

Deja focused on the feel of boots against metal. All things considered, he didn't feel too bad. His head was sore and so was his neck. But, after a bit of rudimentary first aid on the train, he felt basically normal—which *wasn't* normal. *Good* looked worse off than Deja did but was likewise far better off than he should have been. He was still *there.* When Good hadn't even managed to peel himself off his seat upon arrival, Deja'd offered a hand. Naturally, all he'd gotten for his troubles was an exhausted but potent glare. The fact that the man had yet to achieve locomotion was Crane's problem.

Meanwhile, Vex had folded his arms across his chest, still waiting in the rolling, low clouds of fog. Constables standing guard throughout the platform stood a little straighter in his presence.

Deja stepped onto the platform, and the train let out a great plume of green-tinged steam like a breath of relief. The thing may even have sunk a few inches once he'd gotten off. A gaggle of conductors in gray uniforms ran toward it, casting demands at nobody in particular to know just what in Tartarus had happened to their most precious, most goodest train.

Probably addressing the train.

A conductor shot Deja an accusatory glare. "Wasn't my fault," Deja mumbled, batting green steam from his face.

"It absolutely was," Wren said as she debarked. She looked around the platform. "Pretty dead, huh?"

Deja hummed absently. She wasn't wrong. Six other trains waited in their tunnels like beasts of burden taking a rest to nibble hay before they were needed again. Even before Deja'd landed in Osiris for six months, Omega had adopted a policy of only dispatching one team at a time. So, usually, the next team due out was waiting in the wings. None was. Just conductors and constables. Deja couldn't say for certain that was something he'd never seen before. Maybe he just hadn't noticed. But if agents were spread thin enough that the standard eight-agent teams that had already been reduced to seven were being reduced again to as few as *five,* it'd be naïve to call it random happenstance.

"How's the face?" Wren asked, gesturing to her own cheeks. "Looks much better than last time." She gave him a quick pat on the back and followed Lear toward the exit.

Footsteps echoed behind Deja, followed by Good's ragged sigh. In that sigh was the same thought Deja'd been keeping to himself: This better not become a routine. Of course, in Good's case, that was far less likely. Good was on probation. Vex summoning Good was hardly unusual. Deja and Good shared a quick glance and followed the man to his office—where Good's probation was officially lifted not five minutes later. Deja was relieved by the confirmation of his suspicion: The punishment was just a box being checked. A formal necessity.

That relief was short-lived.

"What do you *mean* I'm still not being issued my mortifier?" Deja demanded, barely managing to resist the urge to stand from his chair.

Two sharp knocks on the door spared Vex having to answer

beyond a withering sigh of forced patience. He waved a hand and Ashe opened the door. "Chief Inquisitor," she said.

Vex cleared his throat and echoed, "Chief Inquisitor."

Deja twisted in his chair, then went stiff. Standing in the doorway was Chief Inquisitor Hiero, a woman with a voice as soothing as a death sentence, and eyes as dull and lifeless as her white hair. Until they weren't. Those eyes sharpened once they moved to Deja. He held his breath the way children did when passing a graveyard.

"Ah," Hiero said. "Agent Vale. You've recovered." Her eyes moved to Good before returning to Vex, and Deja envied the man the shield his desk provided. "Are you finished with Agent Good, Inquisitor?"

"In a moment. I have one question for him, then he is yours." Vex folded his hands upon the table and turned to Good. "Agent Good," he began in a depositional tone, "is it fair to say that without Agent Vale's Oddity, your success in managing the mobile situation would have been made far less likely, if not impossible?"

Deja's mouth fell open and he shut it again. His eyes shifted sideways to Good, expecting to see him looking just as perplexed as he himself was. Only, Good wasn't perplexed. He just considered the question carefully.

Over the silence of that careful consideration came the subtly impatient sigh of the chief inquisitor behind him.

At last, Good said, "Yes, sir. Without his particular Oddity, I think it unlikely we'd have managed to follow the afflicted *and* eliminate the threat to the Potential."

"I see," Vex said. "And the afflicted was en route to a *maternity hospital*, yes?"

"That's correct, sir."

"Thank you, Agent Good." Vex gave his superior a look fanged with politeness. "He is all yours, Chief Inquisitor."

Hiero's tone was equally polite. *Aggressively* so. "Thank you, Agent Inquisitor." She gestured to Good, and he stood immediately—then wobbled before steadying himself on the chair. Hiero ignored this. "I will leave you to your... *Odd meeting*." And with that, she left.

Good hesitated on his chair-crutch and cleared his throat awkwardly.

Vex nodded. "Once you are done, take yourself to Osiris. Dismissed, Agent."

Good inclined his head to Vex and offered a quiet, "Sir," before following Hiero.

Deja watched him leave. Just beyond the swinging door, Crane stood waiting. He kept staring long after the door clicked closed. "Since when does the Chief Inquisitor *personally fetch agents?*"

"I suspect," Vex said diplomatically, "when the Chief Inquisitor has reason to." He passed a form to Ashe. "Take this to AI Oathe. And make sure she signs it immediately. Otherwise, we'll be waiting on *doomsday* for it."

Once the door clicked shut after Ashe, Deja folded his arms across his chest. "So, was me not getting my mortifier back your call? Or Happy-go-lucky over there."

"Don't be absurd," Vex said, pen scribbling away. "Agent Ashe had nothing to do with it." Deja stared at him until he looked up. "Agent," Vex said wearily. "You—"

"Yeah, yeah, I know. *I'm not being punished.*" In the spirit of intra-team cooperation, Deja did not add, 'Unlike Good.'

"We are only being cautious."

Deja understood that bit. It was just who constituted 'we' that was his question. He had another. "And, uh... how long are we going to be 'cautious' for?"

The twitch of Vex's mustache said, 'indefinitely.' What he actually said was, "Until such time as I deem it appropriate. So, from your debrief, the mission went as well as it could—clearly. But how are you? Any lingering symptoms of lifeburn? Other issues?" There was no need for Vex to be more specific. He meant: *Are you still seeing and hearing things you shouldn't?*

The mission had gone well. That was the important thing—the *only* important thing. Good (surprisingly enough) had been right; had Deja not been there, their mission could've gone south very, very quickly.

Deja shook his head. "I had a headache and some bruises courtesy of our afflicted friend, but nothing some Q on the ride back couldn't clear up."

"And your separation from the train and tethers? How did you fare then? No symptoms?"

"Not like before," Deja said carefully, "if that's what you mean." It felt like a lie. What didn't was his added, "Good seemed much worse off than me. But he was basically fine, too. Just tired."

Vex leaned back in his chair. "Yes," he said, "that is interesting…. Was Good the agent closest to you at the time?"

"During the crash?" Deja asked; Vex nodded. "Think so."

Vex steepled his fingers in front of his face and stared at a point halfway between them. "And you do not know for how long you were untethered?"

"No, it was—"

"Disorienting, yes," Vex finished for him, nodding again. "You truly suffered no ill effects after failing to rebound to the train?"

Deja'd heard things that weren't there. But they were the same things Good had heard.

Until they weren't.

"We told you about the voice," Deja said. "Again, I didn't experience anything like I did before. It wasn't a hallucination. Just a feeling."

"A feeling," Vex echoed. "Describe it."

Deja shrugged and blew out a long breath. "I guess… like… we didn't belong there." An aftershock of the cold being-watched feeling brushed his cheek and whispered, *But it wanted us.*

"I see…. Did you have a question for me, Agent?"

"That obvious, huh?"

"Perhaps," Vex mused. "You *always* have questions. Whether you *voice* them is a different matter."

"Fair enough." Deja ran his tongue along the back of his teeth as he debated whether he wanted to voice this one, or whether it would only confirm Vex's fears that Deja was no longer suited for the field.

That he couldn't be trusted to manage the costs of his Oddity and stay in control. That he was a danger to his fellow agents and the living they sought to protect. Like Thrall had been. Like Deja might have always been. Maybe Wren had been wrong. Maybe he wasn't the reason so many of his team had survived. Maybe *he* was the reason Ivy, Vyne, and Thorne had—

"Deja?" Vex asked quietly. "Consider yourself ordered to tell me what's on that peculiar mind of yours."

Deja cleared his throat. "I heard about Thrall, is all."

Vex's face shifted in understanding. "From Agent Wren, I take it?"

Deja nodded. "Said she didn't know much more than what she'd heard."

"That being?"

"That being something went wrong," Deja admitted like he was confessing to his own failing. "With his Oddity." He stopped short of adding, *'And it's true. Which is why you didn't tell me.'*

"Yes and no," Vex said. "As you are well aware, your gifts, they… they come with a cost. Weaknesses. And, tragically, we did not understand the full scope of Thrall's weaknesses. Nor the cost."

Deja stayed quiet. That was the reason, then. What all these personal briefs and debriefs were about: Keeping tabs on his Oddity. Its costs and weaknesses. *His* costs and weaknesses. It was plain from Vex's almost regretful eyes that the man could see the thoughts crossing Deja's mind like they'd been tattooed on his face. Bizarre (and unfamiliar) as it was, Deja was embarrassed by that. No. *Ashamed.* That was it.

Vex endured that silent shame for as long as he could. Then, he ended it with, "You may find this ironic, but I want you to ensure that Agent Good makes it to Osiris."

Deja scrunched his nose. "*Is* that irony?"

Vex stared at him a while. Then, "I never know."

"I really hate irony—"

"So you've said. You are dismissed, Agent."

Deja gave Vex a last nod and left. As he passed through that infinite chessboard of a hallway, that feeling—that prickly-neck, being-watched feeling—was back in full force. He summoned the elevator and looked over his shoulder. Nothing there. It was only when he saw nothing on the elevator walls, too—no warning messages, no splash of impossible red—that he finally stopped looking for the hungry eyes behind the dread.

LEANING AGAINST A WALL of the atrium, Deja waited for Good, as ordered. Dozens of agents milled about, each one in a hurry. He paid them no mind—just stared up at the massive portrait of the first governor crowning the elevators like a sentry. A judgmental one. Which was impressive, given the subject's eyes were concealed by a white blindfold. The plaque beneath named him *The First of The Twelve Who Are Thirteen* and nothing more. Where a given name might have been was instead the ubiquitous phrase that governed all the Hereafter did: *MORS AEQUAT.* Equal in death.

The governors, collectively known as The Twelve Who Are Thirteen (even though it's much more of a pain to say than just *governors*) were said to be the mind driving the engine of the Hereafter. The Augury were the eyes. The Inquisitorial Authority, the hands. Omega agents, the scythe. But it was that man, whatever his name really was, who was credited with that drawing and quartering of Reaper powers into separate parts. Lest he be lauded, his eyes were covered. His name left unwritten. He'd insisted on it, so they said. Such was his devotion to the edict *equal in death.*

That's what AI Oathe had told Deja and the rest of his training cadre upon their first visit to Omega Headquarters, anyway. Deja'd asked just why the guy had such a massive portrait if he was so *un-lauded.* The response had been an entirely predictable series of eye rolls from his fellow agents-in-training, a startled shuffle from Good, and a less expected but utterly delightful squawk from AI Oathe. Poor woman. She'd doubtlessly been thrilled when that particular little freak had been passed off to AI Vex's charge instead of hers.

The feeble smile that had twitched to life on Deja's face at the memory collapsed. *FREAK.* That's what Sine had chosen to rap out in her final excruciating moments. That was her last word. Then, Deja'd assumed it was a final insult. Still might have been. But it was also something else. An explanation. An *accusation.*

A Freak did this to me.

A Freak like you.

"Vale?"

Deja lowered his gaze from the utterly uncelebrated and unre-marked governor looming in abject non-acknowledgment. Good was weaving through milling agents to get to him. "Vex asked me to—"

"Yeah," Good muttered, not stopping. "He just told me. Let's get this over with."

"You went back to—okay, okay! I was just asking, *yeesh.*" Deja jogged ahead to push open one of the massive doors and hold it open. This only earned him a second glare. "Right." He followed Good across the square at what he decided was a safe distance, sharing a commiserating look with the tall Reaper statue as they passed. But when Good veered right, Deja (risking great bodily harm) clasped Good's sleeve and guided him to the left instead. "Wrong side of the Hex, buddy."

Rather than admit Deja was right, Good just resumed his stride in the appropriate direction. Deja increased his buffer distance and followed to Osiris Square.

The building of Osiris itself rose from the ground in a massive monolith of white marble. Wide but shallow stairs in that same pristine white fell from brass-framed doors like a spill frozen in time. Whole place felt frozen in time. The only clocks were those pinned to the uniforms of the technicians and attendants. Even the moon, whose waning might've given a sense of one day passing to the next, never looked like more than a sliver from within. That's how narrow the windows were.

Good consented to be escorted to the lobby, but no further. After he explained his presence to the attendant sitting sentry at the front desk, he shot Deja a pointed look that said as clearly as anything: *You can go now.* When Deja only watched the attendant summon the considerable paperwork required, that pointed look elevated to a glare that added: *why in thirteen hells are you still here—fuck off, you Odd piece of shit.*

So, Deja did fuck off. But he didn't leave Osiris. He summoned the elevator to pay a visit to one of the few people who might be able to help him untangle the mess of his mind. Marion, being unconscious, was a great listener—even when she hadn't been unconscious, actually. Deja rubbed at his sore shoulder. The elevator opened silently onto the twenty-first floor. He kept his own steps quiet on his way down the gleaming white hall. Hushed voices crept around the corner, and he stopped.

"—another governor to see him," one voice said.

"I don't understand what they're doing here," another said.

"I don't either," said the first. "But one has been down there almost every day this week."

"The same one?"

A scoff. "Who can tell? They all look the same under those massive—"

A *shh.* Not playful. Fearful. Upon the pitter-patter of cautious feet, Deja resumed walking and turned the corner to find a pair of startled attendants. One quickly adjusted her short-beaked mask.

"Hi," Deja said. "Is Agent Sine still here?"

A blank pair of masks stared at him. One attendant adjusted her cape and answered carefully, "No, Agent."

Gone, then. Lost to oblivion. There was no way she'd have left Osiris as anything but a memory. Deja took his leave. As he made his way toward Marion's room, the warmth of a stare caressed his neck.

When he turned, the attendants were already gone.

"HEY, MARE." Deja closed the white door behind him. Before taking his usual seat at Marion's bedside, he walked to the narrow lancet windows. It had become something of a ritual of his to write a message there in the fog—just in case Marion woke up confused and frightened. Something to let her know she wasn't alone. It wasn't a friendly message he found himself squeezing into the tight space, but a spontaneous lament:

AND THEN THERE WERE FOUR.

His finger dragged on the last stroke, period squeaking into a comma. The words only lasted a few seconds, like Osiris itself had swallowed them whole.

Deja pulled a chair to Marion's bedside and stared at her mask-like face. Had he looked like that after his own catastrophic mission? Not peaceful. Marion didn't look peaceful. She looked *unpainted*. Like a blank porcelain mask waiting to be finished. A doll waiting for rouge.

The technicians didn't know what to do with the Odd, clearly. The fact they had (apparently) known what to do with Deja (more or less) was actually pretty astounding. How were technicians to know what to do with an injury that was the first and last of its kind? For a patient who was the first and last of her kind?

An Odd laid low by her own Oddity.

Because that's what happened. Nobody had to tell Deja so. He could read between the lines of Vex and Wren's tight-lipped looks and sympathetic eyes. He only felt himself proved right each time Vex nagged Deja over his internal state, or fussed to make sure he wasn't on the road to wherever Marion was now. Or Thrall.

Only four Odds remained and Marion was one of them. Several had been lost while Deja was in Osiris, including Omen, the Odd from Troy and Sine's old team. Had Omen fallen upon his own sword the way Marion and Thrall had? How? He could see how Thrall's Oddity could have gone wrong. He'd been able to capture the gazes of ghosts, but sometimes of the living, too. If there'd been enough living present, and he'd lost control of the situation, it's possible Thrall could have been pinned down. Wren had told him Thrall wasn't on the train ride back.

Maybe whoever was head agent had made the decision to leave him behind.

It was all too believable.

There was Hart, too. The Odd from Good's last team. Deja hadn't heard details on Hart's loss—or *anything*, actually. He'd asked Vex, but all he'd gotten was a useless, "A tragic accident." But, like Thrall, Deja could imagine her Oddity going wrong. She made herself an irresistible target to ghosts. It didn't take Deja's odd imagination to work that one out. But all Omen's Oddity did was allow him to see OWLs in places not specifically prepared by the Augury. It made him very useful on missions where agents had to cover a large area like a hospital or campus. It was also hard to imagine how such an Oddity could have led to his demise.

Deja's mouth twisted sadly. He'd always liked Omen. And Marion. Ever had always seemed a bit untouchable, though. Marion had told him once that she suspected Ever resented her own Oddity and took it out on the others. Hard to imagine Ever being self-conscious about anything. Still, Marion always had a knack for interpreting other people's inner worlds. Part of that might have been her Oddity, but Deja figured it was just *her*.

Deja envied her that. Good was an enigma to him now. Or, maybe that's just what Deja told himself to avoid grim likelihoods. Like, the likelihood that Good had harbored a deep-seated resentment of Odds this whole time and only now let it show. And that was the better of two options. The other possibility sat heavy on his chest like three stone slabs—one for each lost teammate—pinning him down and suffocating him any moment he dared give it credence. Like now.

Deja's eyes moved to Marion's unmoving hands. Once, those fingers had moved with incredible grace. With just some flicks and flourishes, she could bring ghosts under her control, powerless to make any motion that Marion didn't make for them. But something had gone terribly wrong. New agent training. "A tragic accident." The course of events was sketchy at best by virtue of where that training exercise had taken place: The Gray.

Beyond the winding ring of the Floating District, three rings of walls bordered the Hereafter. The Gray was the vast space between the second and third—the last bastion of something like order before the emptiness beyond. So far as Deja could tell, the Gray had no use beyond a proving ground for would-be agents, and a place for constables to patrol. Give them something to do. The Gray wasn't as dangerous as the Desert of the Living; it couldn't tear an agent apart like the Desert had done Sine. That didn't mean it was safe, which is why that's where their kind got sent to learn the importance of keeping their augurs close and staying within the tether field after the train left. The Gray was their first glimpse of what could happen to them if they didn't—of what it felt like to be utterly, irrevocably *lost.* In that fog of senselessness, it was hard enough holding onto the knowledge of who you were and what you were doing there *without* keeping track of anyone else. But that was the challenge: Learn to keep an eye on your fellow agents—and ghosts—under duress.

Someone had failed to keep an eye on Marion.

Or else she'd just lost control. And now she was here.

"Mare...." Shame strangled Deja's confession. Chasing after that shame was the urge to make a gratuitous sarcastic observation. A scavenger after scraps that just made it worse. He'd lost Vyne and Thorne and Ivy. He felt terrible admitting it, but Thorne hurt the worst. They were gone. Staring at Marion, knowing she'd likely never wake up, was an entirely different sort of hurt. Less a lost limb than an open wound unable to heal. Until the foreign body digging into the flesh was removed, it could only pulse and fester. He took a deep breath and pushed past the confused half-grief.

"I'm guessing nobody told you, but we lost Thrall," Deja managed. "So now it's just you, me, Ever, and Sygil who's left." He huffed a hollow laugh. "I don't know what's happening around here anymore. I feel like I don't recognize this world I woke up in... like I didn't really wake up at all."

Deja sighed and rubbed a hand over his eyes before resting his head on it. "Fuck, Mare.... I wish you could just tell me what it is I'm really thinking. Sort my brain out for me. Because the damned thing is, I'm still see—"

A whisper *hushed* him into silence. Red ghosted along his peripheral vision. Against the wall was a shiny cart bearing jars of medicinal balms and tinctures. The jar of Q usually labelled with its contents bore a warning instead:

You are not alone.

Deja blinked once and it was gone, replaced with a neat label—*QUINA*—and the dusty smell of chalk. The door he'd closed just minutes ago, though, was open a crack. Then, like he'd pushed it with his very glance, it closed with a faint *click.*

Someone had deigned to visit with the freak after all.

Unless they were there to do something else.

There'd been no other agents at Styx station when they'd returned from their mission the day before, but that wasn't to say nobody was around. Constables were everywhere. Deja couldn't swing a cat—living or dead—without hitting one. Always in pairs, they traced their plotted courses through the halls of Omega. Only, they didn't seem to have a purpose beyond *being there.* And it wasn't just Styx Station and Headquarters. Deja passed a dozen more on the wide, black steps outside Omega. Some gave him a nod of acknowledgment, some a lingering masked look, but most ignored him entirely. Deja'd seen them stationed outside buildings or patrolling the Hex before, but they'd always seemed more *ceremonial* than anything else.

He'd never seen them *here.*

Deja slowed his pace as he approached the Floating District. Not a pair, but a *trio* of gray-clad constables were walking at a clipped pace from the direction he was headed, arms swinging in sync. Deja waited for them to disappear around a corner before letting the rolling green fog pull him into a winding alley. The deeper into the Floating District he walked, the rougher his steps became. Soon, the cobbled and jagged pavers beneath could only be called *rock.* The green mist that always clung to the lower places seemed to be funneled here. Maybe by the gentle, downward slope of the streets, maybe by the chiller air. Maybe there was just more space for it here where shadows grew darker. *Deeper.*

A lantern hanging outside a small tavern broke up that deep dark, swaying gently in whatever force it was that pushed all this mist down the alleys. The *creak... creak* of its chain was the only sound, the soft glow of green the only color. Until it wasn't. Deja froze when he spotted it—*red*—gone as quickly as it had appeared. He followed it back up the street. He turned down an alley, and another, and another and—there it was. *Red*. Gone again already, but he was sure of it. He stared up at the second story window where he'd seen it.

Lace curtains fluttered. A woman stood in the dimly lit room beyond them. Naked, furiously brushing her hair, and growling unheard things at the mirror before her—a mirror where she wasn't reflected. Decency demanded Deja look away but he couldn't. He was certain he must've seen somebody else in all these doors and windows of the Floating District, but he'd never marked it before. Not outside Ukiyo. The woman had stopped brushing. Her face was staring at him from the mirror—a mirror where her face now was. She clutched at her breasts and belly, shielding them. She began to cry.

Deja called out, "Wait—"

The light went out.

Another flash of red. Lower.

Deja took off at a jog to follow the source of that impossible color. Another flash led him down another alley and then another, its glint skipping along a path of puddles. Those stepping-stone puddles led him to a book held in the hands of a rabbit, just outside Ukiyo. And he wasn't the only person who'd noticed her. A pair of constables blocked her path to or from wherever she was going. Presumably, one of those ends was the Warren. The other, wherever it was rabbits went to at night and came from each morning that he'd never thought to think about before getting scolded by a nameless rabbit with a thing for snark and sidecars.

Deja mentally stuttered. He couldn't even remember the last time he'd spared a thought for the stranger.

The constable's question snapped him out of it. "And where are we headed, little rabbit?"

His partner jerked her head behind her. "Warren's this way."

The rabbit kept her head bowed, holding the book protectively against her stomach. It was a faded, peeling gray now, but Deja knew, he *knew* that book had been red just moments ago.

"What's this?"

It was only when the constable actually reached for the book that the rabbit acknowledged their existence at all. She opened her mouth to protest, then meekly bowed her head as the book was plucked away by a gloved hand—Deja's.

He turned it over to examine the cover: Dickens. *Stories for Christmas.* His brows shot up. "Silly rabbit, books are for kids." He eyed the two constables expectantly. "Nothing? I mean, okay, it's not Alphabet Crunch, but come on; learn your cereal culture." After a pause, he admitted, "All right, you got me. The reference really didn't work. It made no sense. It's just, well... *rabbit-adjacent.*"

Even with the masks, the constables had the distinct look of people who'd never considered the possibility of current events and so had never planned for it. They didn't strike him as the plan-on-the-go type.

"So... can I help you?" Deja asked them. When their only response was a shared glance, he assured them, "This book is not haunted." He flipped through the pages, eyes scanning for any sign of color and finding none. "Not possessed, not a ghost-in-disguise, not anything but some words on some pages thought up by an English dude long dead and reproduced by somebody at some point after that." Deja held it up. "Or are you on some sort of special, secret rabbit-harassment duty I don't know about?"

A constable finally spoke up. "No, sir. Just keeping an eye out." Her eyes shifted to the rabbit. "Making sure everything's secure."

Deja scoffed. "Who's insecure? This place is perfectly secure."

"Well," she countered, "said that about Omega South, too, didn't they?"

"*Did* they?" Deja challenged. "Go be insecure someplace else, all right? You're annoying me."

They only hesitated a few moments before striding off with the sort of upright, surly posture clearly meant to let Deja (and anyone else in the area) know that leaving was *their* idea. It wasn't, of course. Before an agent, those constables were tidily outranked.

Deja shook his head. He eyed the dull metal rabbit pinned to the rabbit's gray vest. Where he'd expected to find a name, there was only a string of letters and numbers. With a frown, he held out the book. "Where are you headed?" No response. Deja jiggled the book pointedly in front of her. When she didn't reach for it, he sighed. "Look, I'm not trying to hassle you. I'm trying to help you get where you're going. Want me to leave you alone?"

Hesitation. Then, the smallest nod.

"All right, fair enough." Deja extended the book a little closer. This time, she took it. "Have a better night," he said.

Another nod. She walked away, trailed by a suitably small voice barely audible over Ukiyo's creaking lantern chain. "You too, Deja Vale."

Ukiyo, mercifully, was absent any constables. Deja didn't know how much trouble he'd get into for chucking one out a bar and into a gutter, but that was knowledge he could do without. He pushed past the curtain fluttering in the doorway. Rows of bottles and brass fixtures gleamed in the dark like candles in a church, reflecting just enough light to guide him to the bar that was always empty. He took his seat and glanced at a large, squat bottle of liquor. This time, there was no rabbit reflected in the glass. Not that he'd been expecting to see Not-Jamie. He'd been there hundreds of times, after all, and had only seen the rabbit there once. Now he thought of it, he didn't even think to *look* for him until he'd taken his seat. His sudden disappointment slipped out in a quiet sigh all the same.

"Rough night?"

Deja looked up to find yet another freshly appointed, bright-eyed and bushy-tailed piece of bartending ass smiling politely at him. He shook his head to himself as he took in the black vest, crisp oxford shirt, and neatly tucked tie. "That is such a bartender thing to say."

The bartender brightened even more. "Thank you!"

Deja huffed a small laugh in spite of himself.

"I'm Yule," the bartender said, ignoring Deja's murmured, "Of course, you are, sweetie," and finishing, "What can I get you?"

"Apple juice. Neat."

Yule's pretty face pinched. "We have brandy."

"And there it is," Deja said under his breath. More clearly, he said, "So close. Try again."

"Vale...." Darling Dear emerged from the back room with a warning look, wiping her hands on a bar rag. "You haunting this place or something?"

"Funny. Don't really have the demented rage for a good haunt, I'm afraid."

Darling gave him an ironic smile and reached beneath the bar for a crystal carafe. She uncorked it and muttered, "Could've fooled me," before pouring him a glass. She slid it to Yule 2.0, who obligingly added a speared cranberry garnish then placed it on a black napkin before the agent.

With a sweet smile, Deja said, "Kindly fuck yourself."

"Charming." Darling gave Yule a pointed look and jerked her head over her shoulder. The man nodded and hopped to, slipping into the backroom whence Darling had emerged.

Deja stared down into his abyss of a drink, searching out a glimmer of deep amber. Nothing but gray. He plucked up the garnish and dropped it inside with a sad little *plop*. "You know," he mused, "I never had a reason to form any sort of opinions on constables. But *now*, I'm starting to think they might just be assholes."

"What gave it away?" Darling asked.

"They're all over the place. Not even *doing* anything. And I know that, because they've got all the free time in the world to *harass rabbits*."

One of Darling's fine eyebrows arched at that. "You don't say. Well, these are uncertain times we're not living in."

"Yeah, I guess… but where did they even come from?" Deja asked, not really aiming the question at anyone in particular. "These the last survivors of Omega South, or something?"

"Definitely not." Darling pressed her palms against the edge of the bar and rapped her long nails on the wood. "Border, I'd wager."

"The border," Deja echoed.

"Mhmm."

"Huh." Deja took a slow sip of his drink, considering. "I've never really been over there—just once or thrice in training. The Gray, anyway."

"Well, why would you? *You* passed *your* agent training." After a moment, Darling added, "Somehow."

Deja bit back a smirk. "Sure did. And unlike some chirpy Christmas-themed bartenders I could mention, I didn't have to rely on my stunning good looks to do it."

Darling smacked him across the cheek with a *new* rag she might have just summoned from nothingness for that express purpose. "Watch it…."

"*Please.* What are you gonna do, *ban your only patron?*"

Darling ignored this and folded her arms across the bar to lean in closer. "All right, honey, I have to ask. If you don't have stunning good looks, how *did* you avoid border duty? I suppose your Oddity comes in handy, but with observation skills *that* woeful, there had to be *something else.* A bribe, perhaps?"

That's when Deja realized the bar had lost its smooth varnish beneath his gloved hands. Ever-present sticky splotches of evaporated liquor were now rough knots of wood. He turned.

His rabbit was back.

And he was reading a *red book.*

"GET YOU A DRINK?" Deja asked, tugging off his gloves. He took a seat in the rough-hewn wooden chair across from the rabbit whose name wasn't Jamie. Beside the delicate hand resting on the table (when it wasn't turning pages) was a martini glass, empty of all but a twist of lemon. It looked as out of place on that table as Deja surely did.

The rabbit didn't spare a glance for the agent. "Lifeburn again?" He turned the page.

Deja's brow lifted at that. Even Vex hadn't noticed, and Deja'd had a whole day more to heal since then. "Not as bad as last time."

And unlike last time, Not-Jamie actually seemed to care either way. His response lacked its previous, marked disdain at any rate. "Good." Still, his eyes were focused on the book—the *gray* book— resting on his folded legs. He turned a page.

Deja leaned forward just far enough to catch the author's name at the top of the page. Dickens again. "It was a weird mission," he said. "Don't know if that's something rabbits hear about or talk about."

Another turn of the page. "Oh?"

"Is it?" Deja asked. "Something you talk about?"

A shrug. "We don't talk about much of anything."

"But you *read*."

"Professionally, yes."

"Is that what this is?" Deja nodded to the book. "Taking your work home with you?"

"Oh, I don't live here, Agent," the rabbit said. "I just like cognac."

Deja's mouth twisted into a smile as wry as the rabbit's favored drink. "Guess so. You gonna tell me your name tonight? Or should I just start calling you 'Sidecar' in my head."

"Now, now," the rabbit provisionally known as Sidecar said, "I'm sure you can come up with a better name than that."

"It's an improvement on what I was going with before, trust me."

"And that was?"

"I'll tell you mine if you tell me yours. As I recall, that was the deal last time. Or was that a lie?"

"No," the rabbit said lightly. He turned another page with a sound like rustling autumn leaves. For a moment, Deja could smell them.

It was funny; for all the thought Deja hadn't devoted to this man, he couldn't shake the uncanny sense of familiarity now he was here.

Like he'd known this rabbit for years. Decades, even. When the pace of turning pages slowed, Deja looked at them. Index finger and thumb framed a one-line paragraph:

For the first time the hand appeared to shake.

The real one didn't, though. It seemed far stiller than so many words on that page. More permanent.

"Please," Deja said. "Will you *please* tell me your name? Anything but *nobody*?"

At long last, the rabbit looked up. He closed his book and laid a hand upon it. "Jamais."

"Jamais," Deja echoed, testing out the feel of it. Tasted... French? "Thank you."

Jamais inclined his head. "You're welcome, Deja."

"All right, Jamais. Don't suppose there's any point in asking if manipulating television personalities is something your department's had in the works?"

"Probably not."

"In that case, can I get you another drink?"

"All right."

"Sidecar?"

"What are *you* drinking?"

"Me?" Deja lifted his glass. "Apple juice."

Jamais laughed. And when he did, his eyes lit up brighter than any gaslight could. It became Deja's personal mission to earn that laugh as much as possible. "That sounds good," he said, eyes still smiling. "I'll have the apple juice."

"You got it."

Darling Dear gave Deja an unreadable look when he ordered her best vintage, but she poured it. When Deja returned and slid Jamais the crystal tumbler across the table, the juice glittered gold in the candlelight. His hand went still, reluctant to let go of that tiny world of color. It wasn't until a slightly smaller, brown hand covered his dusky olive one that Deja released it.

"Thank you," Jamais said.

Deja stared at him. "Your cheeks are red."

"It's a bit warm in here so close to the candles. Yours are red, too." Even as Jamais said it, the color began to fade from his face, retreating to smooth grays. Deja could only assume his had as well. Jamais's eyes narrowed slightly. "Are you all right?"

"Fine."

"You're certain?"

Deja blew out a laugh. "Absolutely fucking not, no." He waved a dismissive hand and added, "But it's probably above your imaginary pay grade, so don't worry about it."

Jamais accepted this and opened his book once more. Again, that flash of red. It disappeared beneath open, ivory pages. Again, the smell of leaves. *That* lingered. They sat in silence a while. Jamais reading, Deja sipping his drink and watching Jamais read. Vaguely, Deja knew Darling Dear's eyes were fixed on him but he ignored it. He was so fascinated by the autumn rustle of turning pages he couldn't even make himself turn to check.

The flashing lights at Stephanie's house could've been explained by a mind overtaxed from lifeburn. *Mind the clown* wasn't exactly an earth-shattering revelation. He could've told himself that. Maybe he *did* tell himself that. Maybe he even could've told himself to stay out of that forest and dreamt up the TV chef's warning words. But he wasn't really lifeburned then. Not beyond the usual Desert exposure. That was *nothing* compared to staying by a pregnant person's side.

The book was red again. Deja could see the color there, just along the edge.

You're not ready yet, the television had said. And then there was the neon sign's buzzing threat: *These woods eat men like you.*

Why would he tell himself that?

Why would *anyone* tell him that?

Deja could chock it up to his dwindling sanity—his Oddity finally starting to take its toll. But even if he blamed his warped mind for the flashes of color he kept seeing, the whispers he kept hearing, and the warnings he kept reading, that didn't explain why he was seeing words in a language he didn't understand. His mind could have made up some Latin-sounding nonsense like *memento moriebaris*, sure. Still wasn't buying it.

Deja watched Jamais turn another page in an impossibly red book. "So," he ventured, "you seem... bookish. Can you read Latin?"

Jamais looked up. "Can I read Latin?"

Deja nodded. But when the rabbit opened his mouth to answer, Deja headed him off with a "Assuming it's not above your pay grade."

Jamais's eyes crinkled in a silent laugh. "No. In fact, it's just within my pay grade."

"Do you really get paid?"

Jamais gave a small shrug. "We all get paid."

"'We' as in the collective of rabbits? Or the royal we?"

Jamais closed his book again and placed it on the table with a soft, gray *thud*. "If you don't get paid, Agent, why work so hard? Why risk so much?"

Deja leaned back in surprise. "It's—it's my *duty*," he said. "My whole *purpose*. I was chosen for this. What I do—what agents do—it matters. It means something."

Jamais inclined his head. "There you are." Even as Deja frowned in confusion, he felt he understood. This was confirmed when Jamais said, "A lot of people would kill to feel like that."

"You mean you don't?" Dozens of empty rabbit eyes stared back at Deja from his memories. Hard to imagine how a rabbit could feel otherwise, really. "It is important," he said hurriedly. "What you all do, I mean. In the Warren."

Jamais hummed in absent agreement. "Maybe."

Recalling those handy (and *by* hand) details squeezed into that last case file, Deja added, "I couldn't do what I do without all of you."

Another hum. "Maybe." But this time, a faint smile twitched at one side of his lips when he did. "Can I ask you a question?"

"Sure, shoot."

Jamais folded his arms across the table and leaned forward, face thoughtful. "What's it like? Doing what you do."

Deja twisted his mouth and considered this. "Uh, well, I guess it's dangerous, so we're always—"

"No, I don't mean *agents*," Jamais said with the patience of a teacher. "I mean *you*. And what only *you* can do."

"Oh." *Well, that was disappointing.* There was always a curiosity about him and the other Odds—*more* now that they were quickly becoming something of an endangered species. "Why do you want to know?" he asked warily.

"Is it wrong of me to want to know?"

Deja gave a one-sided shrug. "I suppose not." He let out a long sigh and looked up. The ceiling was full of beams now, and they looked thick enough to hold up all of Headquarters. "It's... I guess it's just not something I go out of my way to think about."

"Because it makes you different?"

"Maybe," Deja said, not really believing it.

It did make him different. But it also made him a liability in a way he hadn't begun to appreciate until he'd heard about Thrall. Add that to Omen, and then to Marion's condition, and tack on Deja's own experiences of the aftermath of his Oddity—the pain, the disorientation, the exhaustion—it was difficult to think he was anything *but* a potential burden on any mission. At *best*.

That was something Deja could barely admit to himself, let alone to a strange rabbit in a bar. He'd been reluctant to think deeply about his own Oddity long before it occurred to him that he might be a liability to his team. And there was something about the quiet expectation on Jamais's face that made Deja think that was precisely what he wanted Deja to do—think deeply. To consider the burning core that this newfound fear of endangering his team had latched onto and coalesced around like debris about a newly forming planet.

Jamais had to speak again to draw Deja out from his frantically orbiting thoughts. "Then why?"

Deja couldn't say. He really couldn't. But of all the things in his world, he thought of Stephanie. He thought back to the newly purchased crosses and prayer plaques decorating her hallway. To her childlike desperation to believe an angel was there, that her grandmother was there, that there was a *There* for her grandmother to come visit *from.* Hers was a distinctively living impulse that always struck Deja as silly. Probably for no reason other than the fact that it indicated a fear of an unknown that wasn't unknown to him—not totally, anyway. But as he stared at a knot in the wood to avoid Jamais's expectant eyes, that impulse didn't seem quite so silly anymore.

Deja faced the stare. "I don't know."

Jamais nodded slowly, eyes bright and focused. Again, Deja had that sense that he was a problem being worked out. A knot untied. *Effectively.* He was compelled to say more. To defend himself from being untied any further. To appease those eyes.

"When I'm in the Desert," Deja said slowly, quietly, "and I take off the glasses and look—see—it's... it's too much. It's always too much." He exposed the blossom-like scar on his palm to the candlelight. It made him want to put his gloves back on. "Everything is loud and bright and... and *invasive.* It's like I'm being ripped out of myself and forced back in all at once. And I think it's—" He stopped short and looked up.

Jamais was looking back at him with soft, understanding eyes. "It's what?" he asked, voice just as soft as his gaze.

Deja came untied. "I think that might be what it feels like. For them, I mean. The living."

"You feel alive?"

"No," Deja confessed as the thought occurred to him for the first time, in incontrovertible red letters. Like Jamais had unburied it himself. "I feel like I'm *dying.*"

"But isn't that the same thing?"

Footsteps approached from behind and, for a moment, it felt like a heartbeat—like *having* a heartbeat. Deja reached for his glass and took three quick sips while the source of those beating steps spoke.

"Get you anything else?" Darling asked. She was asking Jamais.

Had to be. Deja didn't get that sort of treatment.

"I'm quite all right," Jamais said, smiling kindly at her. "Thank you, Darling."

A long-nailed hand squeezed Deja's shoulder, and he looked up. Darling's deep red lips were pursed in a frown. As she said, "Vale?" the color faded from all but the knowledge it was there. "All right?"

"Yeah." Deja cleared his throat and stood from the chair. It shifted in a way it hadn't before and when he stepped away, a lighter, leather-cushioned chair had taken its place. "I'm gonna call it a night."

Darling's lips twisted. "Why don't you let me give your glasses a quick look first?"

The rustle of dried leaves against Deja's shins. The sweet smell of decay, of damp earth.

Jamais was gone. The book was gone. A pair of crystal glasses and the echo of shame were all that remained of Deja's confession.

"Yeah, actually," Deja said, staring at the empty glass. "That'd be great. Thanks."

The second letter by Ursula composed during the Davis Holmes' Saratoga Period, and the only letter to survive in its entirety (being only one page). It is dated October 22nd 1877, eleven days after the first. There is no suggestion that answering correspondence has been received in the meantime, granting further credence to the theory that "Cat" refers to Ursula's second cousin, whose body was found in the Hudson River on New Year's Day, 1880. Authorities were unable to determine a precise time of death, as that autumn had been one of the coldest on record, and the body frozen. Thus, it is entirely possible that Catherine was deceased as early as October the year previous (cf. Merecki 1983).

October 22nd 1877

My dearest Cat,

The house is freezing and no wonder with all the comings and goings! I have hardly seen hair nor tail of Abraham for over a week now. How could a father ignore his son so callously? One would think his cries were wind in the night.

The nights used to be our time. After Abraham's lectures and meetings and correspondence was done, dinner eaten, and the cook gone home, my husband would sit in his chair with me at his feet, petting my hair with such a kind, loving hand and tell me the most marvelous of things. Miracles. But now my nights are filled with footsteps I don't recognize.

Tonight, I saw a woman among the strangers. She wore all black and a mourning veil, so I couldn't see her face. Even so, I could feel her eyes on me from behind all that confounding lace, and I rushed back up the stairs immediately. I had Delia move the crib to my bedroom, and locked the door.

I didn't sleep. I held him all night.

What a blessing that horrible woman didn't care to see her great-nephew!

When will you come see me?

Yours for eternity and beyond,

When Deja was next summoned via augur to Omega Headquarters—a proper briefing room this time—he dared a bit of relief that normality was returning. But when he stepped off the elevator and saw Agent Inquisitor Oathe heading into that briefing room, the relief faded. It usually did these days. Honestly, he didn't know why he ever bothered experiencing it anymore. Such a waste of emotional energy.

A pair of agents on their way to the elevator gave him a quick glance. Deja nodded an acknowledgment that wasn't returned. Whispers rose while the elevator doors closed.

"—*only three left,*" one agent said.

At least, Deja hoped it was an agent who'd said it.

Three left?

Deja strode toward Vex's closed door. He raised his fist to knock, then stopped at the sound of raised voices. One belonged to Vex: "—against everything we—"

It was the sharp voice of Chief Inquisitor Hiero that cut him off: "We are already receiving reports that Omega West is in danger of imminent attack! Every vulnerability, every weak link, every risk to security must be eliminated *without hesitation!*"

"Chief Inquisitor," Vex said (it was harder to hear him now his tone had become more reasonable). "Omega's—"

"I will not let your sentimentalism put our mission at risk! You haven't changed, Vex. It's always the same with you lot. It's as if you really think a *Reaper* is going to come—"

"Vale?"

Deja narrowly avoided banging his knee on the door.

Wren was giving him a half-knowing, half-chiding look. She pulled out her augur and glanced at it. "I realize punctuality isn't your Oddity, but—"

"Right," Deja said, already walking past her to the meeting room. "Briefing. Getting briefed now. Briefly."

Wren hurried after. At the last stretch, she jogged ahead to slip into the room before him.

"Hey—"

"Agent Vale?" Oathe said, strong jaw gritted. Amazing her enunciation was so impeccable—like, *metaphysically* amazing. "You're late."

Deja opened and closed his mouth a few times. Wren, who was already seated at the long table, had a cat-who'd-caught-the-ghost sort of look. He apologized and sat beside her. Across from them, Good emanated both an eye roll and an impatient tut without actually having to do either. Impressive. The question of why Good was bothering to suppress his disdain at all was answered by the silver scythe pinned to his lapel. Whatever Hiero had pulled Good away to discuss after their last debrief, it had gone very, very well for Good. He was a head agent again.

At the front of the room, Oathe straightened so suddenly, Deja'd expected a spinal *snap.* "Now then! This mission is of the utmost importance and *delicacy.* It falls to you, Omega Agents, you chosen few, the scythe of the"—Deja only half-listened as she waxed poetic about the scythe of the Reaper this, and the hand of the Reaper that, and the... whatever-body-part of the Reaper compelled her to make a little speech whenever presented with the opportunity.

He glanced at the door. Shut. There were only three agents in the room. That one of said agents was himself didn't give him much confidence. He didn't feel terribly *delicate,* something this mission apparently required. He tuned in to Oathe's soliloquy, caught, "The fate of Omega North, nay *the world,*" and promptly tuned out again.

Good's face was so devoid of expression, Deja worried he might start smoking from the ears with the effort of maintaining composure. Really ought to have gotten out that eye roll while he'd had the chance, poor guy.

Smack. A single case file dropped onto the table. It was thin. Good reached for it, pulled it toward himself, and flipped it open. "Three ghosts?" he read aloud. "Western New York?"

"Three ghosts?" Deja echoed in faint disgust. "What, *one per agent?*"

Agent Inquisitor Oathe blinked her hawkish eyes at him; the movement hardly had any impact on her face. "Were you tuned out for the 'We're spread thin' segment of this meeting?" she asked tartly.

Abso-reapin'-lutely. Deja leaned back and stared at his superior. He should've known better than to expect a real answer from anyone but Vex (and even then he only got one half the time). When he'd first arrived, he'd hoped this more standard briefing in a standard room was a positively standard indication that things were edging back toward—well, *standard.* Now, he just found himself smacked in the face with the reason that only Wren and Good had been summoned there. He'd assumed Crane and Lear were just late. It hadn't even occurred to him to *hope* that was the reason, because he never would've imagined anything else being the case.

Silly him.

It wasn't the first time he'd heard all that, of course. Saying how thinly spread they were had become the choicest topic for elevator small talk.

"Hey, Dale!"

"Hey, Vale! How goes it?"

"Oh you know, spread thinner than crepe batter!"

"And how! Well, see you around!"

"Not if they spread me any thinner, you won't!"

Not that anybody ever made small talk with him in elevators, but he had heard it. Thing about small talk was, it didn't need reasons or speculation. Small talk didn't mean you questioned *why* the rain wasn't falling. It only meant pointing out that it didn't.

"Sure is dry, huh?"

"Sure is, Dale. Sure is."

The halls he'd walked to get here had hardly been empty of agents, was the thing. Hell, he'd bumped into two in the lobby.

Both flustered.

Both spread thin.

"I was not tuned out, sir," Deja lied, diplomatically. "But if this mission is of the"—he struggled to recall Oathe's particular turn of phrase—"utmost delicacy and importance, maybe a fourth teammate would be helpful?"

"The *delicacy* is precisely why only *three* of you are being sent in," Oathe said. "As I've already *explained*. There are twin Potentials involved. And while they will not be present when you are sent in"—Deja scoffed his skepticism, but Oathe plowed through—"they *are* expected within two months."

"Within two months," Deja parroted flatly. "Then why the urgency?"—it was his turn to plow past Good's scoff at the flagrant insubordination—"Why the gravity and daintiness or whatever?"

Oathe stared down at him, her lips pressed so tightly together it was like they'd been erased. Her look spoke volumes. It said, *I am so glad this freak was not assigned to me,* and *Why in Reaper's robes have I been cursed with this freak now? In this our time of utmost importance and delicacy?* "That," she managed at last (though it looked like it took all her force of will and patience to do it), "is none of your concern. What I *can* tell you is this: You three have been handpicked for this mission... and it comes from the top." Deja opened his mouth, but Oathe headed him off, "The *very top.*" She punctuated this with a significant, and somewhat threatening, look.

That shut Deja up. Oathe probably wouldn't have bothered to tell them, had she not been so desperate to do just that. And she did look pleased with herself. Deja glanced over at Good for confirmation he'd read that right. Good looked up from the case file for the first time since he'd gotten his newly-reinstated-as-head-agent hands on it. Even

Wren looked chagrined. This mission hadn't come from the Inquisitorial Authority or even the Augury. It had come from The Twelve Who Are Thirteen. The *governors.*

It didn't get any more *top* than the Tower.

Deja sat silent, stunned. Next to him, Wren stared dazedly out the windows at the green and gray clouds beyond like she might catch a glimpse of the Tower. It just so happened they were in one of the few windowed rooms in the Hereafter *without* at least a partial view of it.

Across from her, Good had returned to scanning the file, scant as it was. His brow pinched. "There's three different demented levels listed here."

Oathe pivoted to him like an owl who'd just heard a mouse snap a pine needle beneath its tiny paw. "Was there a question, Head Agent Good?"

Good turned a page. "No, sir."

Carefully, Wren asked, "We're just going to find out which is a level seven when we get there, then?"

"The others are only a one and a two," Oathe reminded them with forced patience. "The difference should be simple to discern for agents as experienced as yourselves."

"Augurs?" Good asked, sensibly.

"Given the priority of this mission," Oathe said, "all of your augurs will be equipped to receive chimes, and yours, Head Agent Good, will have full chime-capability. And there will be one OWL on premises, activated only as necessary. For security reasons." Her attention turned to Deja, whose eyebrows were in danger of disappearing into his bangs. "What about you, Vale? Any more *pressing questions* I can clear up?"

Plenty. Just how much further was Omega willing to cleave down their teams? Why was Oathe their AI now? Was the change permanent? Did Vex approve it? Did Vex even *know* about this mission? And what in thirteen hells was so urgent about these three ghosts that they were sending in what could only be called a *specialized strike team*, handpicked by the governors themselves? Why had the governors even gotten involved in the first place? Why would they *choose them*? How did they even *know* them?

As for questions Oathe *would* clear up, there was only one. "Yes," Deja said. "When do we leave?"

Deja should have guessed the answer: *Now.*

He followed Good and Wren to the elevators, struck dumb by the oddness of the whole situation. Just as the doors opened and Good and Wren stepped inside, Vex emerged from his office. He was alone now, headed for the office next to his: Oathe's.

"Sir?" Deja called out, ignoring Good's order to get his Odd ass back in the elevator. Vex turned and Deja jogged forward to meet him. "Sir," Deja repeated more quietly. "Did something happen to Marion? I overheard an agent mention—"

"No," Vex said, face grim. "But we did lose Agent Sygil."

Deja sank at the confirmation. Yet-another Odd had been lost. The solid floor shifted like fine sand beneath his feet.

"Later, Agent. You have a mission and I have my own duties to attend to."

"With just *three agents*?"

Vex clapped a hand on Deja's arm. "Fear not, Agent." His tone became wistful, even *reverent* when he added, "Back in the Age of Reapers, no one worked on teams *at all.*"

"Yeah, well," Deja grumbled, "back in the day, we didn't have our scythes and hands and eyes and hearts or whatever separated and doled out between several *departments.*"

Vex's eyes glinted briefly. "I have every faith in you, Agent Deja Vale. Now go." He gave Deja's arm a last squeeze and left him for Oathe's (presumably empty) office.

A tart voice called from the elevator, "Vale!"

"Yeah, yeah," Deja called back. "I'm coming; don't get your head–agent knickers in a twist, Scary Poppins." He slipped into the elevator and glanced at Good. "Why you bother glaring at me, I have no idea. It never works."

DEJA STEPPED FROM the departing train and looked around the small parking lot outside the veterinary clinic. He winced at the evening sunlight reflected back at him by car mirrors and held a hand over his exposed eyes. The last person to leave the vet was ushering the last dog into the last car in the parking lot. A pickup truck and a beat-up sedan were parked around the back, nestled behind the dumpsters. Employees, probably. He craned his head around to glance up and down the street. Somebody could be catching a ride, but it was unlikely anybody was walking to work this far out in the boonies. If he had to guess, the closest residence was miles away.

So why the hell was this so *urgent*? Thinly spread as they were, it was only him, Good, and Wren. Wren could handle a tether field on her own, no problem. If it weren't for the fact that it was *three* ghosts in that veterinary clinic, he'd have pushed for just the pair of them. But, as it was, *Head Agent* Good was scoping out the perimeter.

Good liked perimeters. They made him feel safe and happy. Like a hug. But instead of interpersonal contact, it was the loving embrace of a tactical grid.

Deja watched the sun set over the gabled roof of Pierce & Sons Animal Hospital. It was a small practice. Maybe an old bed and breakfast by the look of it. Sunflowers just past their prime grew in abundance around the parking lot. In full bloom, they'd probably have made the peeling, white wood siding look charmingly rustic rather than decrepit.

Unless you were a ghost. Then the peeling paint probably made it look charmingly decrepit rather than rustic.

A blue metal sign post caught Deja's eye. Historical plaques were always handy.

Chastity Holmes Halfway Home for Wayward Girls, est. 1877
"Mortify therefore your members which are upon the earth; fornication, uncleanness, inordinate affection, evil concupiscence, and covetousness, which is idolatry."
Colossians 3:5

Deja wrinkled his nose and mouthed, "*Charming.*"

Wren approached from the other side of the building, walking through the back of a pickup truck to get to him. "Tether field's in place. I kept it tight, so it's strong but we've only got an hour and a half, tops. Anything?"

"Not really," Deja said. "Sun's set, so that's nice."

Wren eyed him curiously.

"Yes?"

"Nothing," Wren said with a shrug. "Just trying to remember the last time I heard somebody bring up a sunset outside a case file."

Deja didn't know what to say to the fact that, to her, sunset was only a word marking a time of Desert day. His augur chirped at his chest; he pulled it out. "Yeah?" When nothing happened but muffled whispers, he rolled his eyes at himself and slipped on his glasses. "So sorry, babes, what was that?"

"*Computer*," a distant voice said with the clipped tone of somebody who'd only just said it two seconds ago.

"Helpful." Deja snapped his augur shut. "OWL is set up on a computer," he told Wren.

"Where?"

Deja just shrugged.

"Right. How many computers could one vet have?" she asked, hopefully.

"These days? A lot. Maybe we'll get lucky and this place runs on paper and rotary phones."

Wren was silent a little while. "Are... rotary phones obsolete?"

"Unless you're just cool like that, yes," Deja said as Good came around the other side of the building at his usual brusque pace.

"Welp," Wren said, clapping her hands together. "Let's hope they're *cool like that*."

"Doubt it."

"Dare to dream, Vale," Wren said.

As Good approached, he looked over the parking lot, probably counting the car doors glowing amidst the gray fog that shrouded the Desert to his eyes. "Two cars?"

"Two cars," Deja confirmed.

"Hm. Not ideal," Good said. "We'll make do. If these people are still working nights, it can't be—"

That bad, he'd been about to say when the back door burst open. A harried woman in pink scrubs rushed out and called over her shoulder, "Yeah, good-fucking-luck, Brenda," before scrambling toward her car. She made the sign of the cross as soon as she took her seat and tore out of there so fast, Deja nearly forgot she couldn't hit him.

But when Good grabbed him by the arm and *yanked* him back, Deja realized she *could have.*

"Charged the car," Good said. "*Shit.*"

"Great," Wren said. "Not even inside yet and they know we're here."

"Maybe," Good said with uncharacteristic optimism, "maybe not. Could just be they're so deranged they're charging everything in sight."

Scratch that on the optimism.

Deja sniffed. Smoke. One glance at the too-close wisps of cloud on that deepening, indigo-gray sky told him there was something on fire in there. He could taste ash. It was hard to tell if it was spirit-fire or mundane. If the former, they could only hope it was just *one* of the ghosts who'd gone pyro-capable.

A second-floor window shattered. Fresh plumes of smoke twirled out, followed by an unearthly shriek. Smoke tinged *green.* And with that, Deja's optimism was gone, too. Not that he'd shown up with any; all his emotional energy got blown on relief that morning.

He sighed. "It's never in the fucking file."

GETTING A GOOD look at the vet waiting room through the sheer *stink* of the place was not easy. An ammonia-burn haze hung over everything like heat off a desert parking lot. If desert parking lots sprayed you in the eyes with scared-dog perfume.

Deja covered his nose with a gloved hand and powered through. The first thing he noticed was the faintly glowing fireplace on the north wall. Even boarded up, it still invited them. *And* ghosts. Above it hung a plasma screen TV running through its screensaver: Photos of employees' pets and favorite patients. Deja eyed it warily, half expecting the pair of Siamese cats who'd just popped up to freeze him in place with their blue eyes. They didn't. Chairs and couches designed with waterproofing in mind were scattered about. Painted word art declared in big, cursive letters things like: SANDY TOES AND SALTY KISSES and THE BEACH IS CALLING. Seashells and starfish drove the theme home. Considering just how landlocked they were in rural, western New York, it was an interesting choice.

An interruption to the beachy vibe came in the form of a felt board sign propped up on an easel near the reception desk. Stuck-on white letters warned of the upcoming Thanksgiving holiday and asked guests to please cooperate with their masking policy and fill out the forms provided in the entryway. Deja eyed a small, resin lighthouse set on the reception window counter. Beside it was a mason jar decorated to look like a tropical cocktail and filled with ballpoint pens, each affixed with its own cocktail umbrella. An unlit candle sat in stark contrast beside it. *"When this candle is lit, please be quiet and respectful,"* the small sign beside it read. *"Someone is saying goodbye to a beloved friend."*

Deja peeked through the plexiglass and into the dark room beyond as best he could. There was a table covered in gift bags and wrapped gifts, each a slight variation on the theme *pink*. A hand-painted pink sign declared, *OH BABY, IT'S TWINS!* and a gigantic card rested, open on the table. He couldn't make out the constellation of hand-written notes and signatures, but the huge blocky letters congratulating Dr. and Mrs. Pierce were visible even from there.

"Computer's in there," Deja said. "One of them, anyway." He spotted a door to the side and walked over, leaning halfway through before slipping inside. There were *two* computers. A rainbow of encouraging post-it notes peppered the closer monitor. He squinted at a pink one. *MAKE GOOD CHOICES!* it said. The "i" in choices was dotted with a tiny heart because *of course, it was.*

The ammonia stink burned more sharply in there. It seemed to be leaking out from beneath another door across the room. Deja pulled the spare mask from his pocket and held it to his face. Once the smell degraded from *olfactory hellfire* to *did the dog pee?* he rolled his eyes at himself for not thinking of it sooner.

Wren and Good stared at him from the doorway.

"What?" Deja demanded. "It stinks of terrified dog and antiseptic in here"—a wince—"I can taste it in my *eyeballs*." When the two just shared a significant glance, he demanded again, "*What?*"

Wren hesitated a moment. "Just...."

Good finished the thought she was too politic to state. "What is the point of you now?"

Deja glowered. "Oh, fuck right off, Good." A metallic skittering noise scratched from the other side of the door where the stink was harshest. "You hear that?"

"No," Wren said. "And that's good, right?"

"Possibly." Good jerked his chin at Deja. "Go investigate."

"Why me?"

"Because I'm going to check for OWLs," Good said. At Deja's pointed look, he added, "And Wren is helping."

Wren shrugged. If Deja had to guess, he'd venture neither of his comrades was any keener on running into spirit-charged fire than he was. Good in particular had a history (*allegedly*). At least the fire wasn't strong enough to spread.

Yet.

"Fine," Deja said. "Send the one who can smell deeper into the smells!" With a last grumble about olfactory torture and toxic workplace conditions, he stepped through the next door and into a long room lined with cages. Examination tables ran up the middle like a stainless steel spine. As he passed the cages (some empty, some not), a large, fluffy white dog with pointed ears and bright eyes barked like mad—*at him*. Deja winced and covered his left ear against the piercing ring of it. Even once the other dogs joined in, the sound was nothing compared to the *smell*. He pressed the mask tighter over his nose and mouth. Only one dog wasn't barking: An old golden retriever lying on the bottom of the cage, watery brown eyes lined with flecks of white fur. Those eyes were focused on the door leading outside and the small window showing just a hint of setting sun beyond. The dog's eyes shifted; Deja followed the gaze to find Good in the doorway.

"Well?" Good asked. "Anything?"

"Sure." Deja jerked his head at the golden retriever. "This dog is staring at you."

"What are you talking about?" Good asked with the tone of someone not seeking answers so much as pointing out an unfortunate turn of events (like Deja speaking, for instance).

Deja pointed to the cage. The dog gave its fluffy tail a single, weak twitch. "There's a dog there, yeah?"

"If you say so," Good said slowly.

"And it's staring at you. Like, *right at you*, dude."

"Dogs are irrelevant. Let me know if a cat shows up."

Wren's hesitant voice trailed from the next room. "Cat?" Silence, then, "If it does, it should be in one of those little carriers, right?"

"Cats go on leashes now," Deja called back. At Wren's skeptical scoff, he added, "Not all of them, but some of them definitely go on leashes."

Good shook his head to himself. It might've been disappointment in the world, disappointment with Deja, or both. Who was Deja kidding? It was both.

"Sure, Vale," Wren said. She stuck her head through the door. "I'm going to check the tethers again. I've got a bad feeling about all this." When Good only stared at her, she pretended to rephrase it as a question. "Good?"

Deja'd never actually seen the wonder that was Good's masked-yet-unmistakably-bitchy stare directed at anyone but *him* before, but here it was, aimed straight at Wren. A few more seconds of increasingly tense silence later, Good muttered, "Fine, go," then peeked through a storage room door.

Skitter skitter click.

Deja spun toward the door at the other end of the hall and called out a mask-muffled, "Hello?"

Silence.

Then, a tiny but cheerful voice called back, "Hello!" through the door.

With a grumbled, "Damnit," Deja strode to the door and stuck his head inside. It was a narrow stairwell. In a rare moment of complaisance he, frankly, thought deserved commendation, he pulled back to inform the head agent of his intentions.

Good was gone.

Deja scoffed. "Great." He made the charitable choice to check one more room before running off on his own (as was his usual custom). Good was in the lobby, staring out the window. "Good?"

Good didn't look away from the window. "What?"

"Whatcha got there, buddy?"

"Nothing," Good said flatly, not tearing his eyes away from "nothing" for a moment.

"Right..." Deja said, already backing away whence he came.

The little voice welcomed him back with a "Hello!" and Deja followed it upstairs to a large office. After a moment's consideration of his current orientation, Deja stuck his own head out the window to catch a glimpse of "nothing" himself.

It was Wren. She was standing on the edge of the tether field, back facing the vet. Deja watched her with a frown. She wasn't adjusting the tethers. She was just standing there.

Deja murmured, "What the..." trailing off before he clocked yet another computer. He pushed up his glasses and eyed the large monitor for a whole minute. Nothing. No messages, no instructions, no suggestions, no solicitations for questions and/or comments... no OWLs. Deja slid down his glasses once more. "Helpful," he muttered before reaching out to type: *THANKS FOR NOTHING.* His fingertips passed through the keys.

"Hello!" the voice said again.

Deja spun around. Nothing. With one hand on his nightsticks, he crept across the room. Amidst the towers of shelves and filing cabinets was something draped beneath a large, heart-covered pink sheet. He reached for one corner and *yanked* it off before stepping back.

It was a huge bird cage.

Inside that bird cage was a suitably large, white cockatoo... or pink cockatoo. Most of its feathers were missing. Even with the little red sweater (which probably used to be a sock), that much was clear. The only feathers remaining were the small, pearly ones around its eyes and cheeks, and the massive, yellow crest atop its head. Tiny emergent pins of white sticking out of its pink wing nubs somehow made it look even more like a plucked chicken than if it had been cleanly bald. Its great, gray beak opened a crack as it surveilled the room with wings held aloft and crest stuck straight up in the bird equivalent of a cat's raised hackles. Only, instead of preparing for attack, it was preparing to experiment with innovations in desperation-fueled featherless flight. It gave a little wiggle of its two-piece McNugget wings like a warning.

Deja ignored that warning and leaned closer to the cage. A hand-written sign read:

HELLO! MY NAME IS ORLANDO PLUME.

"Oh my gerbils. Adorable." His smile faded once he spotted the second sign to the right:

HELLO! MY NAME IS KEIRA BITELEY!

In parentheses was added:

FOR A REASON!

Deja leaned back. "Where the fuck *is* Keira—"

"What in thirteen hells are you doing?"

Deja placed a hand over his heart. "Dude!" he hissed. "Do not sneak up on me like that!"

Good ignored this like any number of things he couldn't perceive through the mask. "What are you staring at?"

"Birds." Deja shook off his indignation and gestured to the cage. "There's a bald cockatoo in here, and the sign says there's a second one. But it's not here."

"I really hate birds."

Deja's face contorted. "Where would you even get a reason to feel any sort of way about *birds*?" he demanded. "And who the fuck hates *birds*, anyway?"

A dark, deep growl of a voice answered: "*God!*"

Both agents spun around. The erstwhile and *clearly possessed* red-tailed, gray parrot rose from its file cabinet perch to flap its wings, sending supernatural wind bellowing around the office. As shit-laden newspaper, blank forms, and encouraging post-it notes flew around them, Deja couldn't help but wonder just why it was he *didn't* hate birds.

And when Keira Biteley screeched toward them—talons first—he decided that now he did.

So much.

D eja darted toward the closet at the other end of the office to get—

Bam.

"*Fuck,*" he hissed, rubbing his nose. Probably should've made sure the door wasn't spirit-charged first. Too late for that. The green-glowing knob did give a promising jiggle in his hand, though, so that was nice.

The parrot's beak opened wide, letting out six buzzing black flies and an unearthly shriek before *launching* toward him. At the last moment, Deja ducked to the side and tugged the door open—

Thud.

He trapped the parrot in the closet and *slammed* the door shut. He'd barely managed to close and lock it in time to avoid the eight spirit-charged claws headed straight for his face. A second *thud* against the door, more befitting a Rottweiler than a bird. Deja braced his back against it.

Good joined him. "What *was* that?"

Thud. Another bid for unholy freedom was underway. Deja pressed back with all his might. Furious talons scratching at the wood may as well have been clawing inside his eardrums. He could practically feel it digging into his back. "Keira Biteley, I presume," he answered between grunts of exertion. "Please stop looking at me like I'm insane. *I* didn't name the fucking thing."

Good's retort was cut off by a second avian *slam* behind them.

Click clack.

Deja searched out the source of the noise. Orlando Plume was cowering in a corner at the bottom of his cage, little raw chicken-tender wings aquiver. "Me too, little buddy," Deja grumbled just as Keira threw herself at the door with all the force of a pissed off moped.

Click click clack.

That wasn't the bird. It was the computer keyboard.

"Stay here," Deja said.

Good spluttered, "Are you *fucking kid—*" But the true potential of his insult was strangled off by the necessity of channeling all that verbal rage into possessed–bird containment.

Deja debated freeing Orlando Plume as he passed. Half the things in the room looked to be spirit-charged so he probably could. Then again, *liberating* a flightless bird from what was, essentially, a defensible fortress would be a dick-move. Considering the damage they were likely about to deal to Keira 'I need a young priest and an old priest' Biteley, he didn't need that on his animal-relations ledger. But when Orlando began *squawking* a noise so loud it made that fluffy white dog's barking sound like a whisper, he reconsidered.

Deja slapped his hands over his ears. He spun on the parrot and shouted, "If you don't shut up, Orlando, I'm gonna get *real old fashioned* with my augury!"

Orlando went silent.

With a neat, "*Thank you,*" Deja took a seat at the computer desk. Once he slid his glasses on, he smelled smoke. "Shit." The window was open a crack, letting the barest green–gray haze creep in. Given how well this mission was already going, he didn't dare hope it was a low–energy fire started by one of the less demented ghosts. Even if it weren't spreading rapidly now, he had to assume it *would* be.

Because of course, it would be.

Computer keys clicked and clacked. Silence a few moments... then, they began shifting again—hopefully from the beginning. "Mind the parrot," Deja read aloud. "*Thanks. No, really*," he typed back. "You've been *such* a help." Deja scowled at the incoming message. "No, *you* go fuck yourself!"

"Vale!" Good snapped from the door he was still struggling to keep closed. "What are you doing?"

"Well, dear, I'm just—" Deja stopped short and frowned down at the keyboard's question. "Am I forgetting somebody? Who the—shit." He twisted in his chair and pushed past Good's burgeoning demand for an explanation with, "Where's Brenda?"

Good stared at him, ignoring the fervent scratching at his back. "Who's Brenda?" A moment's hesitation. "Not another bird, is it?"

Deja closed his eyes just long enough to take a deep breath in and out. "Brenda's the employee who's still here."

Good stared at him again, longer this time. He opened his mouth, closed it, thought hard, then opened it again to say, "In the on-fire building?"

"Well, that was my next question. You ever heard of a living person harmed by spirit fire?"

Good shook his head. "No, but then it doesn't really *come up*."

"Yeah. Brenda should be safe, at least." Deja winced. "Relatively speaking."

Good braced against another *thud* and muttered, "Bully for *Brenda*."

Deja lowered his glasses and sniffed. He sniffed again. The sharp tang of urine and disinfectant wasn't enough to cover the smoke. "Well, it's moot because I smell mundane smoke, too. We need to figure out if Brenda's still here."

"No," Good said. "If Brenda can't figure out that being in an on-fire building is bad for her health, then that's not on *us*. She's a big girl." He paused. "I assume."

"I didn't see her. She could be tiny. She could be huge. She could be—"

Another *thud* shifted the door behind Good, and he pressed harder against it. "I meant an *adult.*"

"Oh. Well, in my defense, you could have been way more specific." Deja rolled his eyes at Good's invisible-yet-potent glare. "Yeah, yeah, all right. I take your point. But if she *is* here, and she *does* spot a fire, she's more likely than not gonna be contacting the fire department, and that's more living wild cards than we wanna be dealing with right now."

Good clicked his tongue, reluctantly conceding the point.

"For all we know, there's a precinct of expectant-mother firefighters out there, and that's why we're here in the first place."

"What?"

"I don't know, dude! Stranger things and all that!"

"Fine," Good said shortly. "We look for Brandon—"

"Brenda—"

"Does not matter. What we really need to be looking for is OWLs. If the Augury's got intel on whether that bird is just charged or actually poss—"

"Wait, what?" Deja cut in with a confused laugh. "What do you mean, 'keep an eye out for OWLs?'"

Good stared at him. After a good four seconds of silent insults, he said, "I do not know how to be any clearer."

Deja gestured to the computer.

"What?"

Deja turned to the computer, stared at it, then turned back to Good. "Computer," he said, jerking his head toward it.

"So? There's two more downstairs, you said. And I couldn't see any of them either, so it's not an OWL, is it?" Suspicious silence. "What now?"

"I, uh... nothing," Deja said over the sounds of muffled hell-parrot rage. "Just observing. You know... doing that thing I do." He looked around the room, nodding his head at various objects. "Yup. All sorts of otherworldly stuff in here. File cabinets, lamps, picture frames... motivational posters...."

"Please just shut up."

Then, a very flustered and faintly singed Agent Wren burst through the door. "What in thirteen hells have you two beendoing up here? Holding hands and reminiscing?"

As Good answered, "No," Deja answered, "Maybe."

Good glared at Deja, then at Wren. He pressed harder against the door. "What have *you* been doing?" he countered.

"Fighting our *demented-level seven* afflicted," Wren said levelly. "*Alone.*"

Good folded his arms across his chest. "Unless Brenda's a bird"—he jerked against another *thud*—"I'd say you drew the winning hand here."

"Huh?" Wren looked between them, nonplussed. "What are you talking about? What bird?"

The keys click-clacked again. This time, all three agents' heads turned to look at the now-glowing green letters on the computer screen:

That bird.

IT WAS HARD to say who squawked louder—the afflicted parrot emerging from the vent or Good. One thing *was* clear: Keira Biteley wasn't spirit-charged. Keira Biteley was *possessed.*

Good held one arm protectively across his face while waving around his mortifier with the other. Any time the parrot was in danger of taking a hit, its wings billowed up a miniature-yet-mighty gale that sent the agents tumbling over spirit-charged furniture and slamming into walls.

Wren slipped behind the only file cabinet sturdy enough to not have moved and eyed it warily. Deja took meager shelter beside a stack of empty dog crates. He replaced his glasses, and his stomach dropped. The office hardly looked different. Almost *everything* had been spirit-charged. "I think it's safe to say we've got a problem," he said before ducking to avoid an incoming cockatoo-shaped lamp.

Had Good wanted to scold Deja for pointing out the obvious, he couldn't. Keira Biteley was circling above him like a slaughter-happy ceiling fan, cackling madly. Good dove to the ground beside a dog crate and held his mortifier against his chest. He jerked his chin at Wren. "You're *sure* that afflicted you saw was a level-7?"

"A level-1 or 2 couldn't possess a functioning adult," Wren pointed out. "Maybe the numbers we got were wrong."

Good nodded grimly. "Could be."

Deja asked Wren, "Thoughts? Plans?" More hopefully, "Escape plans?"

"Well," Wren began before pausing to shield herself from a fresh burst of wind, "I'm guessing it doesn't take much in the way of power to possess a parrot. Leaves more energy for"—she gestured at the myriad glowing green objects around them—"other pursuits. So maybe this *is* the two?" She winced at a wall-shaking squawk and amended, "Or three—?"

CRACK!

With all the force of a cannonball, an urn shot across the room and hit the wall. It shattered, releasing gray ashes like sullen snow.

Wren's shoulders sank. "Never mind."

"I'm guessing this thing's at *least* a five," Deja said. "Apart from the"—he winced when another urn joined the first in an even larger explosion of morbid pet confetti—"obvious, parrots aren't as simple as the hamsters and raccoons and shit we've seen in the past."

"Hey!" Good cut in. "Why in the ever-loving afterlife are we hosting a metaphysical discussion while being actively pursued by a possessed fucking *hell parrot* in an *on-fire building?!*" When Deja looked to be in danger of actually answering the question, Good shook his head in disgust and snapped, "Shut up! We need a plan. The thing's more-or-less contained for now. I say if we can't find a way to take it out fast, we leave it contained and *move on*."

"Right." Wren held her mortifier at the ready. "Agreed."

"All I need is a few good, clear shots," Good said, "and we put this thing to bed."

Then, Good and Wren's faces both turned expectantly toward Deja.

Deja slumped against the kennel. "Come on, *really*?"

Wren scrunched her shoulders. "Good's the best shot of all of us."

Deja shot back, "And *you*?"

"Me? *I* do tethers," Wren said, "this is what *you're* good at."

"Being a *target*?" Deja demanded, voice going high. "I'm good at *being a target*?"

Good said, "Hells, you're tempting me right now."

Wren shot Good a silencing look, then told Deja, "You're the only one without a mortifier. We shoot, you distract! Simple."

"Fine!" Deja shook his head to himself and grumbled, "*Simple*," under his breath. "*Right.*" Engaging ghosts wasn't exactly procedure... by which he meant it was, in fact, the precise *opposite* of procedure (or so it had been explained to him roughly forty-two times). But considering how much louder AIs got when bitching about the extraprocedurality of engaging the *living*, Deja'd say what he was about to do barely hit a *six* on the Inquisitorial Authority scale of *Whoa, whoa, whoa, you did what?* He stepped out from his hiding place and rolled his shoulders.

Keira Biteley loomed from its perch atop a bookcase that had since moved away from the wall to stand crookedly in the middle of the floor. Gray talons clenched so hard, the wood protested with a feeble *creak...creak...crack!* Its head ratcheted with a sickening *crunch* 180 degrees to face Deja, white eyes staring dead at him.

"Okay," Deja said in his second-best distraction voice (first-best would have been too dangerous, unarmed as he was). "You *do know* the neck-twisty thing is infinitely less impressive when you're possessing a *bird*, right? It's—*gah!*" Deja dove to the other side of the office and scrambled behind another bookcase to avoid the dozen pens flying point-first in his direction. "Point taken," he murmured. Just when he got his bearings, the bookcase groaned ominously, then *rushed* toward him. It pushed him across the floor and *slammed* him against the far wall. Deja clenched his jaw and pushed back. The bookcase pushed even harder. Cheap plywood gave way against his hands, and the entire thing collapsed around him in a splintered heap.

A purr-like chirp. Deja lowered his glasses. Orlando Plume's yellow crest was shot straight up, wings held half an inch from his body; wide black eyes shot back and forth like he was watching an interdimensional tennis match. Another chirp. When that failed to soothe, he started shushing himself. "*Shh... shh....*"

"Hey, little buddy," Deja said. "You—"

"KYAAACHHH!" came Orlando Plume's single, eardrum-imploding *shriek.*

"Yeah, great, thanks," Deja muttered, rubbing his ears.

From somewhere behind the gray-feathered tempest making its demented way toward him, Deja just caught Good's shouted, "Keep it there!" before eight claws made for his face. Deja grabbed hold of the bird's gray, scaly feet in his gloved hands and held on.

"That's perfect!" came Wren's encouraging shout.

Deja gasped out, "I hate it here," as he attempted to hold on while also keeping his face and hands away from the beak gnashing at him with single-minded determination. "Nope, nope, nope!" He winced and leaned his head back to avoid a bite. "Keira Biteley, no! Bad parrot!" Another bite. "I sense the good in you!" He jerked his head toward the now constantly squawking cockatoo. "Look at your boyfriend! Look at how pathetic he looks in his stupid little sock sweater!"

The parrot *did* stop. And it *did* turn its head toward the cage. Deja actually felt hopeful a moment before it *kept* turning its head all 360-degrees of the way toward the other agents, its neck *pop-pop-popping* like somebody had just danced across Satan's bubble wrap.

Good and Wren both stood at the other end of the office, arms raised and steady, mortifiers pointed dead at the bird. Before Deja could request that his comrades kindly *not* shoot the spirit-disintegrating energy at *him*, twin blasts echoed in the room and Deja wincingly turned away, hoping for the best. It was nice having hands for as long as he did.

Silence and stillness.

He needn't have worried. At least, not on the mortifier front.

The parrot blinked its white eyes open before letting loose a noise that could only be described as the sound a pterodactyl might make in comparable circumstances. It certainly *felt* like trying to wrangle a pterodactyl. Keira Biteley earned its name and sank its beak into Deja's right hand. He let out a dinosaur noise of his own and *flung* the parrot off of him. It flew madly, totally independent of any logic of gravity or flight mechanics, and circled the office.

Upside down.

Deja clutched his hand to his chest and shouted, "Wren!" over the din of afflicted and mundane parrots. "The window!"

"What about it!" Wren pointedly gestured to her presently incorporeal self.

"If it's gonna open the window," Deja said, "it's going to *get* charged!"

"Oh—"

Before Wren could even finish, Good darted toward the window to stand between Keira Biteley and unholy freedom. But before he could raise his mortifier, the parrot was on him, gnashing at his masked face and hissing obscenities about various vet techs, their mothers, and what it was going to do to them in hell once they all got there.

Wren dove forward to help pull the thing off Good, but a sudden burst of spectral wind threw her off. She landed with a deafening *crack* against the wall opposite, crumpling atop a dog crate.

White birdy eyes rolled madly, its jaw unhinged. "Kiss kiss!"

Good growled back, "Polly wanna *go to hell*?" and shoved the barrel of his mortifier into its open beak. He pulled the trigger. The earthly parrot fell through his hands and landed with a *thud* on the floor.

A thud only Deja could hear.

The green hue of spirit-charged matter faded.

There came a second, barely-there *thud* as Wren fell through the dog crate and landed on the floor. "I'm all right!" she called out, un–all–rightly.

Good rolled his shoulders indignantly and stared down at the parrot—or to his eyes, where the parrot *had* been.

Deja glanced over his glasses to see the thing lying flat on its back, wings spread like an angel, harmless feet pointed skyward. Its eyes weren't rolling and demented white but shuttered behind soft gray lids. When those eyes snapped open, Deja jumped back. They were yellow now. He watched, stunned, while the parrot righted itself, gave its feathers an indignant ruffle, then waddled across the room with a little *tick tick tick* of claws on wood. Keira Biteley went straight to her cage and began her ascent, beak first. From his corner, Orlando Plume shushed himself again. Keira Biteley responded with the soft whisper of a stolen woman's voice, "You're okay… you're okay…."

Deja clutched his injured hand tighter to his chest. The pain was less like a new wound than a reminder the old one was there, but the burn of the Desert was already creeping past the beak–shaped hole in his glove. He pressed his mask to it like both bandage and shield. "Fucker *bit me!*"

From across the office, Keira Biteley just laughed.

"Oh, fuck off, Keira!"

"You're you, you'll be fine," Good said, already ignoring Deja's war wound in favor of the window. "Probably." He stuck his head outside and looked around.

"Funny," Deja said. "You know, when *Crane's* head agent, she usually brings *spare gloves*."

"I did."

Deja scowled, then frowned when Good's face turned back to him, silent. "What is it?" Deja grimaced. "More parrots?"

"Brahma, you said?" Good asked.

"*Brenda.*"

Good jerked his head toward the window. "That her? *It?*"

"Move." Deja stepped forward and pushed past Good to look. A short, stocky woman in magenta scrubs was hauling wood from a pile of pallets in the parking lot to stack them against the wall. She looked up with white eyes. And *hissed.*

Deja stepped back from the window with a murmured, "Bummer."

Good tilted his head as he watched the living (if occupied) entity he could now see. "It's going back inside."

Wren checked her mortifier and re-holstered it. "You guys are just going to love that one. A real peach."

"So," Deja began conversationally, "you think Brenda's really possessed? Or in a cult?"

Good pointed out, "*I* can see it."

Wren shrugged. "Two things can be true."

"Fair point." Deja stuck his head outside once more and looked around. He squinted. Smoke rose in the distance, glinting in the setting sun. A pickup truck had been driven from the parking lot and crashed into the cornfield across the way.

Because nobody had been *driving* it once it crossed the street.

"Tether field's holding up so far," Deja observed, "so, that's something." He turned to Wren. "Good job."

"Thanks," Wren said, cheerfully. "I did something a tad experimental to make the field last longer and went with a—"

"*Again*," Good cut in. "Now? Really?"

Wren went silent. She shot Good a look then mumbled, "Yes, all right... just nice to be appreciated for my craft is all."

"I'll save any appreciation for the train ride home," Good said flatly.

Brenda was back outside now, depositing cardboard crates of paper atop the pyre-in-progress. "Why's it doing that, you think?" Deja mused, earning him twin scoffs of incredulity. "Oh, what," he said, jerking his head at Wren. "*Tether Queen* here wants a gold star mid-mission and *I'm* the weirdo for trying to parse out a motive?"

"The *why* doesn't matter," Good said. "It's a ghost. We stop it. End of."

"Yeah, in a larger sense, I'm with you," Deja said. "But if an afflicted is lighting up a building with more than spirit fire, there's likely a reason."

Wren clicked her tongue and conceded, "And the reason isn't likely to be good."

Good scoffed. "Such as? Ghosts don't have *reasons.* Only chaos and destruction. It's what they *do.*"

"Sometimes," Deja said. "Sometimes it's chaos and destruction with a particular chaotic and destructive *aim*."

"Like forcing their way into a Potential, maybe," Good said. "But there's none here. Ghosts *have* no other aim. They're not *capable* of it."

"So why the urgency?" Deja asked. "Why send us at all if there's not an immediate threat? Why not give it a few weeks? Or months? However long it'd take for more agents to become available."

"I get you've got a bizarre need to question protocol, Vale, but if there was some darker purpose we needed to thwart specifically, we'd have been informed."

"*Would* we?" Deja countered.

"Not if they didn't *know*," Wren said. "Not if that ghost just came up with it." She turned to Deja. "You're the creative one. What would *you* do? If *you* were a ghost—"

"*Wren*," Good hissed.

Wren shot Good a challenging look then turned back to Deja. "Well, Vale? What would *you* do?"

"Uh, well," Deja began, staring out the window to watch the afflicted gather wood. It struggled with a pallet for a bit before managing to free it from the tangle. "My goal would be to stay among the living as long as possible, right? Wait for an opportunity to claim a Potential life."

"And how would you do that?"

"I'd have to avoid getting caught or mortified," Deja said. "Either break through the tether field or eliminate the agents." He nodded in the direction of the still-steaming pickup truck. "Only, I'm not strong enough to push through a tether field—" He stopped short, the words crumbling away with his horrified realization. "The Twelve Who Are Thirteen are involved, right? They're the ones who sent us here. Why?"

"Why does it matter?" Good demanded, patience beyond thin.

"What if they're involved because these ghosts aren't *like* other ghosts," Deja explained. "This building's old. These ghosts could have been here a long time—long before this vet was ever a vet.

Back when it was a halfway house for slutty independent-thinkers or whatever." Good's glare intensified behind the mask, and Deja added, "Meaning, they're old. They might know things."

Good said, "So?" but his previous skepticism and irritation was steadily giving way to something more like dread.

"So," Deja said, "if they've been here that long, and all they wanted was a Potential, they'd have claimed one by now. What if they're not here because they're hoping for a baby expressway to life town? What if they're here because of what's always here even when the people leave? Because it's *defensible.*"

"No way," Wren said. "Nothing like that's been reported in *decades.* Longer, even."

Good nodded grimly. "A century."

"But what if that's how long these ghosts have been here?" Deja countered.

The agents shared a look, then looked back out at the parking lot where the afflicted was digging around its pockets for something.

A lighter.

"Oh, Styx," Wren said.

"Yeah," Good agreed reluctantly. "It's going to try an animal sacrifice."

While the Desert of the Living burned down forests and culled oceans to fuel its Industrial Revolution, the Hereafter made its own strides. Gone were the Reapers of old. Now, they had agents. And with protective uniforms, tethers, and a train always waiting in the wings, there wasn't much a living being could do to even *reach* let alone *harm* an Omega agent. Not that anyone ever really tried anymore. Not in the jurisdiction of Omega North, anyway. These days, the protocol for dealing with interworldly assault was hardly even covered beyond how to avoid startling priests mid-exorcism, and Ouija board etiquette.

That was a mistake. Some things were too old, too primal to guard against. Too powerful to stay forgotten long. Things like blood. Like sacrifice. Like the transition of living to dead and back again. It was rare to come across any living person who knew how to channel those things—who'd ever even think *to* channel those things.

Brenda, with her Hello Kitty lanyard and magenta scrubs, would never know to channel those things. But the ghost possessing her sure as shit *did.* Deja had no idea what it was planning to do with all that energy once it harnessed it. None of them did. How could they?

They'd never been *taught.*

A new sense of urgency tensed the agents, muzzling them into a cautious hush. Deja could barely hear Wren's question: "Should we call the train?"

Good shook his head. "No." His gaze was fixed on the afflicted standing before the flames of its handiwork, as unbothered by Brenda's lack of protection as the ghost.

Deja watched the skin of its knuckles peel and flexed his own hand. The prelude to a burn radiated from the parrot's bite like some sort of ancient, rose-ringed plague. "Good," he said, "maybe we *should* call the—"

"No," Good repeated, sharper this time. "This situation is too dangerous to continue unchecked." He placed a hand over his augur through his jacket. His thumb brushed against it like a child soothing themselves with a beloved doll. "We can't risk interworldly communication until we know what we're dealing with."

Wren stared out the window, looking haunted. "Guess we have to worry about the vents now."

She was absolutely right; Deja'd forgotten about that. With a ghost this old and this well-established, they had to assume it had embedded itself in the building. Could travel through ventilation ducts. Maybe even something as narrow as a pipe. Deja said so.

Good completed the list they only knew theoretically. "Drains, too."

"How old do you suppose that ghost is?" Wren asked.

"Right now," Deja said, "I'm more worried about what else it *knows*... and taught any of the others. That ghost in the parrot was not a demented-level two. It was a five, minimum."

"There's no way this is all just an Augury mix-up," Wren said. "Not something *this big.*"

"What are you saying?" Good demanded, just as Wren mumbled, "Oh no," to herself, once she'd followed the logical trajectory she'd charted with the observation.

Wren held a hand in front of her face like she was about to start biting her fingernails through the gloves. "If these ghosts know enough to cloak how powerful they are, then they can probably cloak their *numbers*, too." She shook her head. "There's more of them. Bound to be."

"Granted," Good said, "I'm with you on the Augury. We have to assume these ghosts can skew their levels. That's safest. But if they could cloak their numbers, why not hide completely? Why not—" Good stopped short, and Deja knew they'd all just realized the same thing.

Wren's sleeve brushed against Deja's arm as she stood just a little closer to him. Might've been him standing closer to her, actually. He needed to know this was real and not some lifeburn-induced nightmare. One so, *so* different from everything they'd been taught about the limitations of ghosts. Ghosts couldn't plan. Planning meant thinking of a future. Echoes knew no future. Their tortured world was an ever-yet-never-present past. Mindless repetition. Shrieks and pain and spite trapped forever, chasing the source of wounds long since scabbed over and moved on—without them. Less rational than an animal. *Demented.* And yet, if there were another explanation, Deja would love to hear it. His desperate confusion echoed back at him from two masked faces, both as frozen in place as he felt. He said, "They *wanted us to come.*"

"That's that, then," Good said. "Nobody summons the train. Nobody uses their augurs for anything. Clear?"

"But *why*?" Wren demanded, but her tone screamed another question: *How.* "Why would they want us here?"

Good stepped away from the window. "Let's not find out. Come on. Time to move. We need to find a way to get all these animals out. Or find *all* these ghosts and get them contained." He strode through the door, not bothering to check if the others were following. They were. As he made his way down the stairs, mortifier at the ready, he whispered, "Vale? Think you can get those dogs out? The way you got that Potential out in Toronto?"

Deja blew out a helpless breath. "I don't know, maybe. You think they're religious? You're right—not the time—sorry. And I think so. But only if the cages are open or spirit-charged already. If these ghosts want dead animals, I don't see them being so obliging."

"Try anyway," Good said. He stopped before the door leading to the kennels. "This is it through here?" Deja nodded. "Afflicted went in and out of *some* door more than once. Might be in there. Might even be charged enough for you to open it. Try to get those animals out, but don't try too long. I don't want you wasting your time when you could be helping me and Wren contain these ghosts."

Wren examined her weapon and asked, "Where do you want me?"

"Let's not split up more than we need to," Good said. "I don't want anybody getting more than one doorway past anybody else. And remember, no augurs."

"Not even to *receive* chimes?" Wren asked. "Surely *that's* not against protocol?"

Good's tone left no room for debate. "It is now."

Wren debated anyway. "An *exception* then."

"No. Can't risk it. We don't know what these ghosts are capable of."

Deja didn't voice the surprise he felt. That had been the second-to-last thing he'd have expected to hear from Agent 'Ghosts are dumb' Good.

Good shot him a look and demanded, "What is it, Vale?"

"Nothing," Deja said. "I agree completely."

Wren murmured, "Spooky."

"All right," Deja said. "I'm going in."

Good gave him one short nod and leveled his mortifier. "We're right behind you."

Deja stuck his head through the door first. No sign of ghosts or afflicted. Even with his glasses on, he could hear dogs barking—desperately. He stepped through and slid his glasses down his nose. Dogs were scratching at the bars. Some were gnawing on them and no wonder. Smoke already filled the room, collecting on the floor at their paws like dandelion seeds. Could those trapped animals sense just how horrific the threat had become? Or did they just know they were *trapped?*

Only the golden retriever wasn't moving. She hadn't even bothered to get up from the floor. Her big round eyes were still open, still staring at the door leading outside. Deja pushed up his glasses and cursed once the bar handle became a blur. "Outside door's not charged."

Foolish hope tugged in Deja's chest when Good pointed out, "I can see the kennel doors."

"That's surprising, no?" Wren asked. "Maybe they were hoping to spread them out?"

"Nah," Good said. "Ghosts don't make plans that careful. Must be frantic. Charging things all over the place."

Ah, yes. That sounded much more like his Good. Deja slid his glasses down his nose and squatted in front of the closest cage on the bottom row. The large white dog stopped gnawing on the bars and went stiff, tilting its head from left to right, pointy ears perked. Deja gave the lock an experimental poke and the dog gave its fluffy white coil of a tail a single, cautious flutter. "I can touch it"—his shoulders sagged in relief—"and open it—"

The dog immediately pushed its way out, darted forward, and began scratching at the door to the outside.

"Help me out, would you?" Deja said over his shoulder, already moving to the next cage to free a small mutt.

The first thing Good did was move to an empty kennel.

"No dog," Deja said. "Nope, next—no, down one. Yes. Only bottom row has dogs. And *this* one up here," he said, straightening to unlock the door of a tiny dog with big ears standing from its pointy head like shaggy, brown butterflies. The moment Deja got close, the poor thing only shook harder. He pulled the door open and gave the dog a sympathetic look. "Can you make it down?" he asked, not even knowing if the dog could hear him. "Come on, you can do it! Come on!"

The dog stepped back a few inches, front paws bouncing with a *snick snick snick* of claws on metal.

"C'mon! C'mon sweetie!" Deja said in the highest, least threatening voice he could manage. "You can do it! Hop down! C'mon! Yes! Good boy! Or girl! It could not matter less!" The dog scrambled down to the floor before darting under an exam table. "So brave," he sighed, and moved on.

Within minutes, all dogs were out but one. The golden's kennel was open, but she wasn't budging. Deja grimaced. The smoke was thicker now, dense enough to make the signs instructing employees to sanitize nail clippers between uses hard to read.

"Might be too sick or injured," Deja said over the sounds of dogs barking and scratching at the door. "Post-op, maybe."

Good hummed an acknowledgment, looking down and just to the left of where the golden really was. "One dog might not be enough to do anything."

"Oh, like you'd *know*?" Deja countered with a harshness that surprised him.

Even Good seemed surprised, but he also had to concede the point. "No, I would not know. Let's focus on getting these ones out for now."

"If nothing else," Wren said, "they might last a little longer *not* in cages."

Good began to speak, then stopped. He held up a silencing hand and looked around. "Vale," he hissed. "Glasses."

Deja nodded and pushed them up. The moment he did, the dogs disappeared and Wren's tense stance emerged. Like Good, she was looking around, grip on her mortifier tightening.

Pipes rattled.

A low *hiss* moved behind the walls before coalescing into whispering, sing-song words. "*Law man, law man, have you any wife? Anyone to cry for you in the afterlife?*"

Deja spun around. That voice was coming from everywhere and nowhere. He looked up. "Up there. Ventilation shaft."

"I can't see it." Good said, backing up and aiming his mortifier at the ceiling. He followed the trajectory of Deja's point.

"*Gun man, gun man, have you any mother? Anyone to weep and wail for how you didn't love her—?*"

Bam!

Good fired a single shot.

A *swish* like silk dragged over metal.

A quiet laugh.

Another.

Then, a taunting chorus emerged—cackling children who've cornered their prey. It was in the walls now. Whispers aged when they moved. Giggling babies on the left gave way to pained, sickly death rattles on the right.

When next the voice spoke, it was behind Good. *"Brother dear, brother dear, does your brother know? How you plan to end it all with one last loving blow?"*

Good gritted, "Shut up!" and backed up against the kennels, mortifier's aim ghosting along the walls. The muzzle followed the voices until it was aimed straight at Deja. The voices laughing and singing behind Deja laughed louder.

"Little boy, little boy, scared and shaking now. How many ghosts are here—"

Hands. *Dozens* of hands sprung from the cages and *yanked* Good against them with a metal *clang*, pinning him there.

A fleshless ghost pressed its skeletal mouth against Good's ear and hissed, *"Too many to count."*

GHASTLY HANDS SCRAMBLED for Good's left arm—the one holding his mortifier. Some had flesh, some only skin hanging in torn gossamer curtains from bone, but all stank of chemical-cloaked rot. Good *yanked* his arm free and aimed it at his own head.

"What are you doing?" Wren demanded. "You're going to *blow your face off!*"

Good twisted away as best he could, but there were always more hands. "At this point," he managed past the childish fingers clawing at his masked mouth, "it'd be worth it to get these things *off me!*"

Over his glasses, Deja saw the dogs huddled by the door. "Dogs aren't thrilled, either.

Good's face turned to him as well as it could and stared, silently.

Message received.

Wren's mortifier wavered in front of her, searching for the slightest opportunity. A second face emerged over Good's shoulder and she took it, blasting the thing back. It retreated with a rasping shriek. Spirit-particles fell on Good's jacket.

There was no time for optimism. Stainless steel water bowls *sailed* out of two-dozen kennels, glinting with green. The water inside splashed through the agents like harmless rain, but a bowl flying at unreal velocity hit Deja in the temple. A curse told him another had hit Wren.

Click. Creak.

Deja spun. The fluffy white dog with the pointy ears was standing with its paws on the bar handle of the door. The *open* door. It shot Deja a look like it was daring him to call it a *bad dog* before it landed on all fours and shouldered its way outside.

"Door's open! Quick," Deja said. "Grab something charged!"

Wren caught a bowl in mid-air and tossed it to Deja.

Deja dove toward the door and wedged it there with a *clank*. Face on the floor, he sighed his relief. "Nice one." The butterfly-eared toy pranced daintily *around* Deja before hopping over the bowl like it did this every morning between walkies and breakfast. Cats weren't the only animals that knew them then.

They were just the only ones who were *dicks about it.*

Deja got up—he dropped back down to avoid several bowls. Three hit the door behind him, one sailed outside and rolled away.

Good yelled, "Shut the door!"

Deja glanced at the golden retriever still lying in her kennel. "Not yet!"

Two mortifier blasts. A metallic clatter.

Good wrangled himself free of the hands and started shooting kennel doors. A blast that hit a ghost square in the face made it wail, but not disintegrate. "Fuck," Good bit out, checking his weapon. "Stupid fucking thing." He called over his shoulder, "Wren!"

"Got it!" Wren stepped forward, mortifier perfectly level as she fired six quick shots. One ghost disappeared in a burst, but the others faded away, intact. She swore under her breath and darted forward to stick her head inside a kennel. "*Great.* There must be a drainage hole or something on the bottom."

"More ventilation grates, too," Deja confirmed. "At least four."

Pipes rattled. Laughter ran beneath their feet like a subterranean stream. Good kept his eyes on his weapon as he adjusted it. Pointless. Their weapons just weren't as effective as they used to be.

Or these ghosts were just that strong.

"Don't give them time to regroup," Good said. After one last check of the trigger, he raised his mortifier. "This way."

A quiet whimper. It was the golden retriever. Even without his glasses lowered, Deja could hear her feeble whines. While Wren followed Good to the reception room, Deja hesitated.

Good ordered, "Whatever it is, leave it, Vale!"

Deja ignored him and knelt beside the dog, lowering his glasses. "Can you hear me, sweetie?" The golden gave a weak twitch of her tail, chin resting heavily on her front paws. "I need you to be a good girl, okay?" The dog moved to stand, but she collapsed once more with a whimper. Wide brown eyes glistened up at him.

Good's voice was a warning growl from the doorway. "Don't you dare do this, Vale. *Move.* That is an *order!*"

Deja shot him a look and turned back to the dog. "Fuck," he whispered. "I am so, so sorry, girl." Something like heat rose behind his eyes. It faded once he replaced his glasses. Without looking back, he followed Good and Wren to the next room.

At least they'd found the source of the smoke.

Flames crawled up the reception desk. Paint peeled from beach-themed tchotchkes. Even the candle beside the canister of melting pens was lit. *When this candle is lit, please be quiet and respectful,* the sign whispered one last time before the fire consumed it. *Someone is saying goodbye to a beloved friend.*

"Fuck that," Deja said, already turning back.

"Vale! What are you doing? Get back here!"

Deja ignored Good's angry shouts and slipped back into the kennel room. He knelt before the golden's open cage. The moment he tugged off his glasses, his throat tightened. "Okay, girl," he said urgently, "I know you've gotta be in pain and exhausted and just so, *so* done right now. But I need you to push through whatever's keeping you in this cage. Somebody out there loves you very, *very much*. And you need to get out of here and keep living for them, all right? You need to live as long as you can. You need to *get up* and *get out* of this place and you hide. You hear me? You stay in that field just outside the parking lot but you *hide*. And you wait for your family."

Rising smoke stung Deja's nose, and he covered it with a gloved hand. When the dog still didn't move but only closed her eyes, Deja pleaded, "Come on, sweetie, don't do this. You are such a good girl. Come on. You can do it! Come on!"

A twitching tail. A low groan.

"Come on! Get up! That's a good girl, come on!"

The knowledge of a name whispered against Deja's neck. And when Deja said, "Come on, Moxie! Come on, girl!" the dog looked up at him. With shaking legs, she stood. "Yes!" Deja cried. "Yes! Good *girl*, Moxie! Yes! Come on! Follow me!" He stepped back and shepherded the dog toward the door. She ambled stiffly along, head bowed. There was a moment of hesitation, but with a last push of effort, she squeezed through.

"Good girl!" Deja called after her. The dog turned back, and he waved her onward. "Keep going! Get to the field!"

Moxie did. The fluffy white menace emerged from the rows of corn, barking and running in excited circles around the far older dog.

Deja winced at the vise-grip on his arm.

Good snarled, "You are fucking *done*, Agent."

Deja allowed himself to be tugged back into the reception area and slid his glasses back on.

He wished he hadn't.

Though the fire slowly spreading from the reception desk to the chairs in the waiting area was orange for the most part, there was no denying the green haze of the smoke, nor the ghostly green flicker to the flames' edge. It was mundane fire that fed off mundane things, but it moved *exactly* where the ghosts wanted it. Icy heat pushed him back a step. "It's both," he said, staring helplessly at the liminal flames.

A *hiss* ripped through the air. Fire ran up the wall to consume the memorial portrait of Dr. John Pierce Senior. His eyes and mouth went first, expanding into warped wounds.

"I've never seen this before," Good said grimly. "How charged do you think it is?"

The last time Good had asked Deja that, he'd (allegedly) set his arm on fire. Now, all Deja could offer was a helpless shake of his head. Beside him, Wren warily eyed the flames. Its green light was clearest in the glow it cast on her gloves and mask. "It's incidental when it's only going to get *more* charged."

An excellent and horrific point. Deja's dread deepened the longer he watched the flames, alternating looking over and through his glasses. "It's like the two fires are feeding each other."

"At least the dogs are out," Wren said.

"Yeah," Deja agreed, though he didn't feel terribly comforted. Something nagged at him. The ghosts were still expending energy to feed this fire. Whatever Good said—whatever they'd been taught about the limitations of ghost logic—they had a reason. "We need to put this out."

"Well, we really can't, can we?" Wren said. She carefully skirted the fire lighting up the reception desk and slipped partway through the door that led into the office beyond. "Phone is spirit-charged. Maybe we can call for help?"

"Sure," Good said flatly. "Call some priests."

"I don't mean *priests*."

Good reminded her, "They can't hear you."

"No," Deja agreed, "but in a small town like this, maybe just *calling* first responders would be enough to get somebody out here."

Wren didn't wait for Good's approval before running into the office. She plucked up the receiver and asked Deja, "Now what do I do?"

Deja had no idea. He knew something with nines was involved, but whether it was 911 or 999 he had *no idea.* Dialing both couldn't hurt, surely. "Try hitting 9-9-9—no! 9-1-1. Sorry. Try 9-1-1."

Wren nodded and carefully pressed the buttons like it took all her strength to do it. A flicker of movement to Deja's left. The black felt sign was going up now. Only, the white letters no longer spelled out the warning about the Thanksgiving holiday or anything else. Instead, they read:

NO MORE LIVING FOR THE DEAD

Deja raised his glasses, lowered them, then raised them again. No change. "Wait!" he said, and Wren paused, finger halfway to pressing what was probably a random button on a printer. "Look there," he told Good. "Look at that sign board. Do you see anything?"

"What are—"

"Good, *please.*"

Good's head searched the blaze. "What sign?"

Deja didn't know if he was relieved or not. If Good couldn't see it, the sign wasn't spirit-charged. That meant two things: It wasn't the ghosts who'd left the message, but it wasn't an official OWL, either. Which meant it might not be *real.* Even so, Deja knew, *somehow*, it was there to help. Something had to be. *No more living for the dead,* it had said. But now, when he lowered his glasses again, it was just a mundane message once more.

"What if that's exactly what they want?" Deja asked. "More living bodies. *Human* ones."

Wren placed the phone back on the receiver with an unearthly, hollow *clack.* "You think they want people to *see* the fire?"

"And come to help, yeah." Deja scoffed at himself. "These things are playing inter-dimensional chess while we're stuck playing checkers."

Omega agents were all taught the same: The ghosts they hunted were no more capable of reason than a wound. And yet, there were places they couldn't go. Ghosts they couldn't hunt. Now, those ghosts were pushing back against the border between them.

Hunting *them.*

Wren began to argue before Deja held up a silencing hand. He slid his glasses down his nose, listening. Approaching siren. "Doesn't matter anyway. Somebody's on their way." He shook his head to himself and muttered, *"Motives don't matter my Odd ass."*

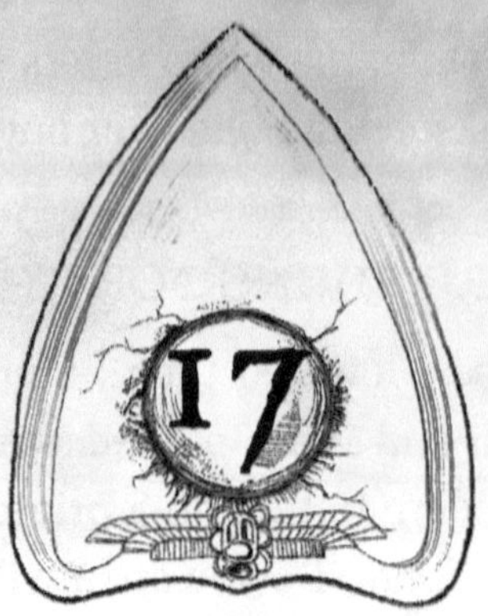

A voice, quiet but sharp, cut through the air like a page torn from a tome. *"Clever tricks won't save you,"* it said. *"Nothing can save you from judgment."*

Green flames rippled in the hearth. Emerging from the defunct fireplace was a ghostly woman, eyes nothing but black, sunken pits. Its tightly coiled bun and simple collared dress hearkened back to the nineteenth-century. The singed flesh peeling from its throat to reveal a frayed spinal cord hearkened back to a nightmare. Good and Wren raised their weapons. Good's, however, was next to useless. After taking up the slack, Wren's probably wouldn't last much longer. Maybe this ghost didn't know that. They needed time. For what exactly, Deja had no idea. He made a play for some anyway.

"Emily Dickinson?" he said cheerfully, "I didn't know you were from New York!"

"Don't engage," Good whispered with an urgency he hadn't had for that possessed parrot upstairs—that he hardly *ever* had. "They're just demented echoes."

"I'm not engaging the demented echo," Deja told him, "I'm *distracting* the demented echo."

Good's lack of retort was chilling. Maybe Deja hadn't been the one Good was trying to convince.

A sound like nails on wood scratched beneath their feet, then faded.

"Stupid boy," the ghost hissed. "You think you're any better than us? Look at you. Hiding beneath your masks like children hiding beneath their blankets from make-believe monsters. You're *pathetic.*"

Good whispered to Wren, "How much time on the tethers?"

"With the influx of ghosts? Maybe another half hour, at the most." Wren frowned and looked down at the return of that scratching-nails sound. It crept toward Good. She tilted her head and listened to it, tracing the sound with her gaze. She jumped back. "It's a circle! Get away from it!"

Deja and Good complied immediately. They didn't know what the plan for that circle was and they didn't need to.

Good demanded, "Where'd it go?"

All three agents looked around, turning frantically. The ghost was gone—probably back up the fireplace like the worst possible version of Santa Claus. Deja slid his glasses down his nose just in time to hear the approaching siren give a last *WHOOP!* then fall silent.

Outside, gravel crunched beneath heavy tires. "Hello?" a lone man's voice called out. "Greenfield Fire Department!" A pause. The voice got closer. "It's Jeff! Jeff Howe!" Another pause. The next question was even closer. "Anybody there? Brenda? I saw the truck! The dogs are all outside in the cornfield, is anybody—"

Jeff Howe appeared in the flesh, wearing a red t-shirt and suspenders. His red-bearded face fell, aghast at the sight. He pulled out a walkie-talkie. "Arnie?" was all he managed before it *shot* out of his hands and skittered across the floor. It came to a stop in the highest of the flames. "What the—*Brenda*?"

They'd missed it. How did they miss it? How the fuck did three agents miss the one afflicted *crawling* along the *on-fire wall?*

What had once been long, brown hair was now singed and curling strands framing a peeling, white-eyed face.

Jeff Howe seemed like a level-headed man, but boy did he *scream.*

Wren fired at the afflicted four times before her mortifier gave out with a pathetic whirring sound like a toy plane falling from the sky. Good ran forward to try and stop Brenda—somehow—but it just scrambled past him, knocking him to the ground. Good hissed and rolled away, just barely avoiding green flames.

Jeff stepped back. Raised hands and terrified screams were no use against such undead fury. The afflicted launched itself at him, grabbed him by the beard and *slammed* his head against the brick wall—

Three.

Hard.

Times.

Jeff dropped to the floor, unmoving. Blood trickled down his forehead and dripped from the tip of his nose to the floor. A matching splatter stained the afflicted's palm. It stared down at it, blinking. Between blinks, Deja could have sworn he spotted a glimmer of brown behind the white. The afflicted tried to form its mouth into a word, but an internal battle ensued over which words to speak; what came out was an awkward, "Geteff."

A gagging cough. "Jeff," she repeated more clearly. That was Brenda. Deja was sure of it.

"Oh God...." Brenda took three steps back and hit the wall. She slid down, breaths coming out in choked gasps. "Oh God, Jeff...." Then, she went stiff, eyes wide and unmoving. Staring. With a thud, she fell to the floor, half-lidded eyes barely visible through the swelling smoke.

Distant laughter rattled in the pipes.

"Are they dead?" Wren asked.

"At least they died outside the circle," Good said. At Deja's look, he added, "I'm being pragmatic."

"*She's* in shock," Deja said, "and I don't think the guy's dead, either. But he might be soon. He is beyond out cold."

The quaver in Wren's usually sure voice sent a chill down Deja's spine. "Guys?"

With one, bleeding, glowing-green hand, Jeff Howe's body was dragging its unconscious self along the floor.

Drag—thud.

Drag—thud.

Drag—thud.

Then, he stopped. His hand fell limp against the wooden floor... just inside the circle.

And it was there that he died.

Deja knew he'd died because the moment he did, ghosts appeared. *Everywhere.*

They came out of places they should never have been able to—not just pipes and vents, but out of the floors. Out of the ceiling. They seeped from the walls with laughs and wails. The clearest, most-fully formed one was the woman who'd scolded them before. It billowed forth from the flames like smoke, toes dragging along the floor as it surged toward them.

Good jumped to the side and pulled out his nightsticks.

Deja did the same, but Wren didn't.

Wren was running toward Deja, hand extended. "Vale! Get back!"

Deja tried. He couldn't move. He couldn't see anything but gray rising all around him. Just as he opened his mouth to try and speak, a strong hand gripped him by the arm and *yanked* him away. He landed hard on his side and skidded across the wooden floor—the floor he could see once more. He pushed himself up and froze all over again. The circle that had only been a memory of scratching sounds now bled onto the wood in a ring like a burn.

Only, it wasn't Deja who was trapped within.

It was Wren.

Deja stared at her with wide eyes. "No," he whispered. "Please, no."

Wren stared back at him. "Vale?" Her voice was as distant as the dogs barking from the field. She tried to pick up her feet. No use. She held her hands in front of her face, but all she could do was stare at them.

Deja knew Wren was staring at her hands because he could just make out her masked face *through* them. "You need to call the train," he told Good.

"No—"

"Fuck you, Good, she's—"

"You don't understand. Even if we did, it *won't come*, Vale." Good shook his head and took a few steps back, staring not at Wren but the circle itself. "We need to find another way."

Deja walked up to the circle and held out a hand. Within, Wren raised her own. Something pushed at him once he got closer. If a Potential was an empty bottle tossed into the sea that sucked in water and all the smaller, weaker creatures within it, this was the opposite. Sealed.

Deja lowered his hand and stepped back.

Wren lowered her own. "You need to go," she said, her voice barely more than an afterthought of sound. Her attention shifted to the ghosts about the room. They weren't trying to stop the agents from inspecting the circle. They must not have had a reason to. They had what they needed and soon they'd have everything they wanted—whatever that was. There was nothing two Omega agents could do. That's what those unbothered ghostly faces said: *There's nothing you scared little boys can do.*

Deja watched ghosts mill about like guests at a party: Not one questioning that they belonged, nor worried they had something else they were meant to do. Beneath their feet, those scratching nails gave way to whispers. Deja couldn't hear the words or understand them. He could only feel them carving themselves into his soles. Green flames rose higher. Heat slapped against his face.

Within the circle, Wren's hood went back. She sank to her knees. Then, she began frantically clawing at her own face to keep the strange, white threads now swarming around her from getting any closer. No. She wasn't trying to keep them away.

She was trying to keep them on.

Good sounded as horrified as Deja felt. "They're unweaving her mask and gloves."

The memory of Sine's crumbling, black face crawled up Deja's throat like bile. "*Fuck!*" He lowered his glasses and looked around in the hopes that what Good couldn't see might help them. If there were a helpful message on the sign, it had been consumed in the flames with the felt and wood. He twirled his nightsticks. If nothing else, they could put a dent in the ghosts' numbers. Do something to stop that fucking chanting beneath their feet.

A hiss of static from behind him.

Even though the power cord had melted, the heat-warped TV was on, rapidly cycling through different channels. Deja narrowed his eyes and watched. No one show or commercial lingered long enough for more than a choked-off syllable or jarring half-note of score. Desperation made him ignore Good's demand to know what he was staring at. Hope kept his eyes glued to the flashing colors.

A woman sang, "*No one, no one, no o-o-o-one c—*"

A weatherman cautioned, "*—should—*"

A cartoon cat yelled, "*—die!*"

A PSA soothed, "*—alone. If you need help, call—*"

Deja turned away from the kind-eyed woman assuring him help was out there even in these dark, unsure times. Good was staring at him like he dared to hope the freak had magicked up a solution, too.

"I need to go in after her," Deja said.

And just like that, Good's hope was crushed. "*Absolutely not.*"

Deja began to speak but the whispered chants swelled to a roar like an approaching tornado, billowing in their jackets. Deja did his best to shift the hair from his eyes and shouted over the wailing, unearthly gale, "I have to. If we all get stuck, there's no helping her!"

"I'm head agent," Good yelled back. "*I'm* going in after her."

"No."

"That wasn't a request, Vale!"

"But I could be more resistant."

"You could be *less!*" Good said. "They went for you first, Vale! You could be *exactly* what they want. I'm going."

They stared at one another, each equally determined not to let the other win—to not let the other lose. It was only when they realized there was a reason for that rising roar that they broke away. The ghosts were no longer casual. No longer unbothered, no longer *sure.*

They were *pissed.*

Two ghosts broke from the churning gears that held Wren in place and rushed toward them.

"Shit," Good hissed, jumping back. He raised his mortifier but he didn't aim it—he *whipped* the ghost across the face with it. *Hard.* The ghost let out a hollow shriek and collapsed at his feet. Good didn't hesitate. With the full force of six-feet's worth of momentum, he brought the mortifier down onto the ghost's head. It disintegrated with a rattling breath. A sound like something taking flight whirred from Good's hand. He stood, rolled his shoulders, raised his mortifier, aimed—

Bam!

The weapon fired three shots before whirring back down, but it was enough. Three ghosts disappeared into smoke. The agents were still outnumbered, but the ghosts were cautious now. An invisible line bisected the circle, and they remained behind it. Reassessing. Regrouping.

It was only when Deja took a step forward that they took a matching step. Deja stepped back. So did the ghosts. Meanwhile, Wren's pale, gray throat was visible past the unraveling silk. Her right glove had unwoven enough to expose her last two fingers. Those fingers weren't disintegrating from Desert exposure, crumbling off in black ash.

They were fading away.

The ghosts were feeding on her—burning her up like a candle. Her neck, though, *was* beginning to glimmer. *Lifeburn.* She wasn't even looking at her fellow agents anymore. In that moment, in every sense that mattered, she knew she was alone.

Deja whispered, "She shouldn't have to be alone."

"What?" Good demanded over the rushing roar of spirit fire and arguing ghosts.

Deja watched pewter skin never meant to touch the Desert burn with each thread of unwoven mask. Wren wasn't like him. She wasn't going to last. The circle seemed to provide some protection, but not enough. At this rate, the Desert would burn Wren away long before she faded. Just like it had Sine. Maybe Good was right. Maybe they did want Deja.

And that was why this might actually *work*.

He took a deep breath.

Good said, "I don't get it. Why are they only trying to stop us now?"

"Because they know it'll work," is what Deja said. But it wasn't what he'd thought.

Because there were some things too old, too primal to guard against. To stay forgotten long. Things like blood.

Things like sacrifice.

Deja ran. If Wren looked up, if she could manage just that much, the last thing she'd see would be *Deja coming for her.*

That she wasn't alone.

RUNNING, RUNNING, RUNNING through the halls. Doors stand out as beckoning rectangles. Walls are a dismissive maze in the fog. A smaller rectangle—glowing, beckoning. A window. Running to the window. Beckoned. Voices. Looking inside.

Recognition. Confusion.

"Omen?"

Steps not taken force him back where he was. Outside now. He spins in the hall. The wall beyond isn't like the others. It's clear and shimmering. Not dismissing. Not beckoning. *Threatening.* A nail has been driven into the heart of it. It begins to glow. To vibrate.

Something has gone horribly, horribly wrong and it's all his fault. He should have known sooner. But he didn't.

And now, it is about to get worse.

His teammates, his *family* call for him around the corner. It's too late to warn them now.

Behind him, from within him, a sigh. Its punctuated by every weary line unseen on their faces.

Together they whisper, "*Memento mori*—"

BAM!

"Wren!"

Deja awoke to the sound of his own, unvoiced scream. He was on his back now. Wren and Good's unmasked faces stared down at him. Only, Wren didn't look quite like herself. A crack extended like a skeletal hand across her throat, its fingers reaching toward her cheeks. It glowed faintly gold how doors and hearths did. Her face looked like someone had tried to fix the broken, lost pieces of her with another, mismatched piece of pottery. It was the eyes that gave it away. They were different colors. They *were* colors. Golden brown on the left, pale blue on the right. Good looked the same: A fusion of darker and lighter skin, wavy auburn and straight black hair, softer and sharper eyes. Both eyes looked familiar.

A jolt of panic. Deja scrambled for his own mask before he realized someone had already taken it. When he looked back up, it was to find two masked faces looking back at him. Of course. Wren was already wearing his mask. The empty waiting room of the veterinary clinic came into focus.

"You all right?" Wren asked.

Deja hesitated. "Probably?"

Good sighed and muttered, "Get up. Train's here."

Deja blinked. He blinked again and pushed himself onto his elbows. The fire, mundane and spirit-charged alike, was gone. The ghosts were gone. Two bodies remained, but they weren't moving and that was certainly a tick in the A-Okay column. In the distance, Orlando Plume screamed. Not because he was in danger, but because that's what he did. Keira Biteley was whistling a mash-up of disparate songs, unruffled. Outside, dogs matched a fleet of approaching sirens with howls and barks, guiding them in.

Deja wasn't sure he wanted to ask what happened, or if he just wanted to be carried onto that train and dropped onto a bench to sleep before the inevitable debrief.

Curiosity won out.

"What happened?" Deja asked, then winced. His throat felt as rough as his voice sounded.

"Hey," Wren warned, her own voice hoarse. "Take it easy." She grasped Deja behind the shoulders and eased him into a sit.

Deja looked at the circle. What had been a bright black ring as thick as blood was nothing but a faded mark on the wood. It was so subtle, it might've been a trick of the light. He put his fingers to it and felt nothing. He didn't know why that was so surprising.

Good's assistance was far less gentle than Wren's. He hoisted Deja to his feet with a grunt. "Save it for the train."

Deja nodded and allowed himself to be steered outside. The train waited for them in the street, breathing out great plumes of green steam into the night. Once they stepped onto the pavement, that fog rolled over their feet. The train opened its door with a breath-like hiss and Deja sighed, half exhausted, half relieved. A gentle hand at his back guided him up the stairs. "Thanks," he said. "I'm all right." The hand didn't leave until he was safely seated on a leather bench.

As soon as the train began to move, Wren tugged off the two masks. The ghost of panic rattled in Deja's chest when he saw just how much her original mask had unwoven—barely half of it left. The fact that Wren hadn't been lost to oblivion was nothing short of miraculous.

Either unaware or unbothered by the horror gripping her teammate, Wren passed Deja his intact mask with a "Thanks. Not that I asked to borrow it or anything."

Good collapsed heavily into a seat across from them. He pulled out his mortifier, closely examining it. "Just be glad Vale managed one point of protocol."

"This time, anyway. I forget it half the time." At the judgment-laden silence, Deja defended, "What? I never *use it.*"

"You used it today," Wren pointed out.

"Yeah, to cover up the dog piss smell," Deja said. "That was less a safety issue than *self-care.*"

"Well," Wren said, "you should always bring it, is my point—"

Good cut in, "He should always *bring it* because it's *protocol.*"

"I will do that, *mom.*" Deja tugged off a glove and placed his fingers to his cheek. It felt oddly cool: lifeburn, but mild. His fingertips ghosted over his own face, taking inventory. It was only when he touched his throat that he grimaced. The skin was cold and a little stiff to the touch.

Wren made a sympathetic sound beside him and stood. "You've got it pretty bad. You stay, rest. I'll grab the stuff."

Good made to stand and told her something, but Deja didn't hear what. Nor did he hear the retort that set Good right back down in his seat. All Deja could hear were the whispers.

Not the M-balm.

"Not the M-balm," Deja said, "just the Q. I'll get too woozy otherwise." At Wren's skeptical look, he added, "Really, Wren. Scarcity's got nothing to do with it; I'm better off with just Q 'til we get back."

Wren's mouth twisted, but she nodded. As she fetched supplies from the cabinet at the end of the compartment (and muttering about how M-balm probably wasn't even an option), Deja caught a glimpse of her neck. The only thing remarkable about it was just how *unre-markable* it looked. A fact confirmed when Wren returned with some bandages and a jar of Q-salve. She struggled to open it and with good reason. The last two fingers of her right glove were empty.

"Wren...."

"It's fine," Wren said. "I'll get it taken care of once we get back."

Past experience kept Deja from asking if she were in pain. Anytime he had in the past, he'd just gotten a look he did not care for: Mostly blank, but a little sharp around the edges, too. It felt wrong.

Deja shared a glance with Good. He was still masked, but his own tension was obvious. "So," Deja began as Wren dabbed soothing salve to his throat. It smelled bitter, but it made the air taste sweet. M-balm was so much worse that he never complained—not even to himself. He asked, "Anybody gonna tell me what happened?"

"No idea," was Good's gruff reply.

"That's it?" Deja asked. "Seriously?"

Good shrugged. "All I saw was you ran into the circle, then I couldn't see anything."

"What do you mean, you couldn't see me?"

"I mean the whole place lit up and I couldn't see a damned thing," Good said like he was defending himself against a murder charge or something. "Couldn't hear anything, either. Couldn't even hear myself *yelling*."

"Yeah?" Deja asked. "What were you yelling?"

Wren snorted. "Mostly what an insubordinate idiot you are, I'm guessing."

"Then," Good continued, determined to ignore the interruptions, "I got a chime giving us the all clear. Ghosts were gone. Everything was like it was before the ghosts and circle and fire showed up."

"Well, sort of," Deja said grimly. "The whole place was still burnt to hell."

A man was still dead.

Good shrugged, indifferent. He couldn't see any of that, of course. To his eyes, the waiting room really was exactly the same as when they'd found it.

And that was as much as anybody who didn't outrank Good was going to get.

Deja turned to Wren. "Are you all right?"

Wren looked unsure, but an all right sort of unsure. "I don't really know what happened. Look up—not with your *eyes*; tilt your head back." Deja obliged with a muttered apology, and Wren dabbed salve beneath his chin. "That whole situation was just insane."

A scoff from Good: *An understatement.*

"And OWLs were no help," Wren continued. "Just *two words* from the Augury until it was all over. Turn your head—other way." She shook her head to herself as she worked. "We got lucky. That's it. *Lucky.*"

"Yeah," Deja agreed absently as Wren took his hand in hers to bandage it. "Lucky."

THE TRAIN RIDE back was long—most of it motionless. By the look of things, they were stuck somewhere close to the Hereafter if not Styx itself. Even if Good hadn't finally de-masked, his agitation would have been glaring. His glances at Wren and Deja were discreet but frequent. He had two injured and compromised teammates—*subordinates*—and they were stuck.

Deja watched Good walk toward the doors and stare out. He blinked. When he opened his eyes, Good was on the other side of the compartment, whispering with Wren. Deja rubbed his eyes and ignored Good's tight-mouthed look. While Good walked back toward the door (presumably in the hopes that if he just looked annoyed enough they'd open), Wren whispered, "Get some rest, Vale. It could be a while."

Deja'd been about to say he didn't need rest, *she* did, when heavy lids snuffed out the gaslight of the compartment. His eyes opened. Electric light glinted on neat plastic and stainless steel.

"—non-standard occurrences before I worry," Head Agent Ivy told the agent seated closest to her. "And this delay is beyond non-standard. It's a high school, Wren, not a papal exorcism college." She was standing at the door where Good had been moments ago, staring out the small window with arms folded across her chest. She glanced over her shoulder at Lear and asked, "Still pretending you're not listening, Lear?"

Lear was leaning back in the corner, eyes closed. He didn't open them when he grumbled, "Maybe."

Beside Lear, Vyne rolled her eyes.

A quiet snort from Deja's left drew his gaze there. It was Agent Thorne. Concern had dulled the ever-present glint to her eyes. "You good, Vale?"

Deja stared at her. *Didn't she know? Didn't they all know?* "Thorne," he said feebly.

Thorne gave him a furrow-browed smile. "Yeah?"

Deja opened and closed his mouth as he struggled to find the words. And once he did, they came out tight and strained. "Don't you remember?"

Thorne frowned but her eyes were smiling, expecting a joke. "Remember what?"

"*Remember that you're—*"

"Dead," Wren said. Her voice was so much louder, so much clearer than the others had been that Deja was shocked he hadn't realized he'd been dreaming before now. His shoulders jerked and his head snapped up. To his right, Wren closed her augur with a huff. "Try yours again."

Good was pacing the length of the compartment. He looked at Deja just long enough to note that he was conscious and pulled out his augur. "Agent Good here, do we have an—" The green light rippling over his face shifted, and Good narrowed his eyes. "Understood." He returned his augur to its pocket and relayed the message. "Trains are backed up. Won't say how long the delay could be."

Wren's brows shot up. "Backed up? *How?*"

Good shrugged and resumed his pacing. "I don't know, Wren," he said tightly. "My guess is there's a problem on the tracks." He reached the doors, pivoted, and walked up the compartment again. "Or they're expecting a train with higher priority than us. Or *both.*"

No one said what they all feared it to be: An attack on Omega North.

Deja rubbed a hand over his eyes. He hadn't wanted to use the M-balm; it made his head feel inflated. No denying its effectiveness though. He touched the bandage covering his throat and winced. A worried look at Wren reflected his own concern back at him.

"You all right?" they both asked at the same time. Wren answered with a wry smile, Deja with a shrug.

Good kept a careful, sidelong eye on both of them as he paced—something he kept up for some time.

"Get all your steps in yet?" Deja asked after another thirty minutes.

Good gave him a barbed look. Deja hadn't been counting for the first few minutes, but since he'd started to, he'd counted one hundred and ninety-six laps: *back and forth, back and forth.* The compartment had been filled with woods and leathers but had since degraded to frayed polyester seats and smudge-speckled stainless steel. The lights flickered, then dimmed. Then—

"*Are you there?*"

"*Memento mori—*"

"—look at him!" Wren hissed. "Forget *rationing*, he needs more aether! Chime somebody again!" She was standing before Good at the end of the compartment, gesturing at Deja.

"I'm fine," Deja said. "Just tired."

Wren looked skeptical.

"Sorry for being cagey," Deja added. "Didn't mean to ruffle your feathers."

Good stared at Deja a while, considering. "He's punning," he told Wren. "He's fine."

"You sure?" Wren countered. "Because I'm pretty sure Omega could be going down in flames and Vale would still say something like... like—I don't even know!"

Good offered, "We need to smoke out the culprit?"

Deja rasped out, "*Nice*," earning him a flat look from Good. "I really am fine," he assured Wren.

Wren rejoined him on the bench. "Sure," she murmured.

Good may have *said* Deja was fine, but he resumed his agitated pacing all the same.

Deja peeled back the bandage to inspect his reflection in the window across the way. He couldn't see much past the pen-carved words and smeared handprints—except for something *red*. When Deja leaned forward and the red shifted, he realized it was the reflection of something beside *him* and twisted in his seat.

It was Wren's hands. The gloves loaned to her by Good were no longer a pristine white. The palms and fingers were coated in red. On the edge of panic, Deja inspected his own hands. Turning them over revealed the same red, so deep and brilliant it was *grotesque*.

"What are you looking at?"

Deja ignored Wren and craned to look at Good, but Good's gloves were concealed by his folded arms. As the man paced past the window, Deja saw red again. It wasn't just on their hands anymore. It was two words, dripping above his and Wren's heads:

MEMENTO MORIEBARIS

"Vale?"

Deja ignored Wren and twisted in his seat. Streaky handprints and clouded glass, nothing more. A hand clasped his shoulder. Wren was staring at him with curiosity edging on concern. Deja looked at her hands: plain white gloves. Perfectly normal... like his.

"I'm fine," Deja said. "Just going a bit stir-crazy."

"How's the throat? Looks a little better."

Deja just stared at the window, watching for another trace of impossible red. *You're tired. You're lifeburned. You only just woke up from a dream. Sleeping people dream. Normal people get tired. Injured. It's not like before.*

Wren nudged him in the shoulder, and Deja answered absently, "Not bad at all." He folded up the linen pad and stuck it in his pocket. "How's the hand?"

"Not bad at all," Wren parroted with a small smile. At Deja's dubious look, she amended, "I *will* be okay. They'll fix me up. Always do. Don't worry."

Good's pace quickened. "Not if we can't get you there fast enough."

Wren watched Good pace with a *seriously?* look. "I didn't thank you," she told Deja. "Before, I mean."

Deja shrugged. "It's just a mask, Wren."

Wren gave Deja a *seriously?* look all his own.

"Ah. That bit."

"Yeah," Wren said. "*That bit.*"

"You don't have to thank me. I was doing what any agent would do for a teammate."

Wren's mouth twisted wryly. "I don't know about that," she whispered.

Deja waited for Good's pacing to bring him back to the door where he always lingered a while to stare out the window before continuing. "Good was *going* to do it—no, really," Deja insisted. "I had to fight him for the right to do something reckless and stupid. You wouldn't think I'd have to. I mean, that's basically *my brand* but..." he trailed off and didn't finish the thought.

Good was walking toward them again... and past them... and toward them....

Wren's skeptical look unfurled into something like surprise before settling into mild confusion. "Oh. Well, that's... huh." As Good stopped at the door and stared out yet again, she eyed him thoughtfully. "Wonder if it was really me he was being reckless for, though."

Deja's face scrunched. "The fuck does that mean?" he demanded, fruitlessly. His loud sigh morphed into a louder groan.

"You got plans, Vale?" Wren asked. "Is your entire purpose for being keeping you from something?"

"Yeah." Deja held up his damaged glove in a bandaged hand. "I've got a hot date with a rabbit named Janis to talk dirty about some field damage."

"Oh, well then," Wren said archly. "Don't let me or Good keep you."

Just when it seemed like Good's internal friction over his own impotence might actually cause him to burst into flame, the train doors opened. He didn't even wait for the doors to open all the way before forcing his way through. "About damn time."

The other two exited at a less existentially threatened pace. Deja surveilled the area for anything to explain the hold-up. Far more constables were milling about the rolling, green fog of Styx than usual, but that was a sign of the shifting times more than anything else. He spotted movement. A train slipping away into one of many tunnels that lined the cavernous, tiled walls like honeycomb. Only, it didn't look like the others. All he could make out was its retreating caboose, but he could still see that much; it looked even darker than the blackness it had disappeared into. As Deja stared after it, an odd sort of dread whispered against his neck. It warned of ancient threats to his ancestors—brightly colored snakes and alluring but toxic flowers.

"Coming?"

Deja did. Wren bumped against his elbow with her shoulder, and Deja smiled at her. "Glad you're here, Wren."

Wren smiled back. "You too." Her smile became more mischievous. "Whatever everybody else says about you."

"Fuck off, Wren." When Wren walked off with a quick bounce in her step, Deja followed and called after her, "You ruined it. We were having a moment and you just puked ectoplasm all over it." He couldn't make his annoyance sound convincing. Not when all he could feel was warning pangs of grief, and the quiet relief that he hadn't been made to feel it in full.

Not for her.

Not yet.

There was a simple enough explanation for the excess of constables at Omega.

The Twelve Who Are Thirteen had arrived.

Deja stood in the grand atrium of Headquarters, stuck to the wall like so many other limpets: agents, constables, agent inquisitors, technicians, and even the odd conductor or Osiris attendant. But no rabbits. He frowned. He didn't see *any* rabbits. Warren-wide meeting, perhaps? Coordinating whatever it was the Warren did to prepare for a visit from the governors? With an odd sort of sick feeling (that might've been the after-effects of lifeburn) he realized he didn't know if that was *unusual* or not.

The massive front doors opened wide to the Hereafter, and the always-waning moonlight stretched across the black marble floor. Two dozen constables stood between the crowd of agents and the other custodians of the Hereafter who'd been caught unawares in the midst of their mundane days. Before them were a dozen Eyes, standing as still as dolls in their white hooded jackets and black porcelain masks. Six pairs of them: One with a white lidless eye painted on their mask's left side, the other with one painted on the right. Deja narrowed his eyes at the closest one Their head swiveled just a hair. and Deja knew that painted eye was staring at him. He looked away.

A deep *gong* heralded the entrance of the governors, felt more by their feet than heard by their ears. Everyone stood a little straighter.

Well, most everyone. Deja slouched a little more on principle and sighed out his frustration at the delay. Most (Vex especially) met The Twelve Who Are Thirteen with a solemn reverence.

Deja couldn't get past the fact that the acronymic form of their title spelled *TWAT*. He snorted to himself. Somebody kicked his foot; Wren was giving him a warning, sideways look. Deja replied with a pointedly cocked eyebrow. They'd already been delayed by all this pomp and circumstance. Deja was in no hurry to get himself to Osiris, but he wasn't going to tolerate any more delay in getting *Wren* there.

He was about to tell Wren so when six of The Twelve Who Are Thirteen governors entered. As they moved, six long, hooded cloaks, gossamer-light and colorless, rippled behind them like an afterimage. Deja didn't realize they knew *how* to walk. Good on them. But then, he couldn't actually see any feet. They could be floating for all he knew. It was only when the procession turned right to make for the single, grand elevator reserved for their use alone that Deja saw the white-masked faces beneath the hoods. They'd barely been carved, with only the subtlest suggestion of eyes, nose, and mouth.

A pair of blank, white eyes pivoted sharply toward Deja. He stood a little straighter. Not out of respect.

Out of instinct.

That mask turned away, but Deja didn't relax. He kept watch on the six pairs of Eyes who followed the governors inside, their movements as graceful as dreamt-of dancers.

The elevator doors closed behind the procession with a second, deep *gong.* Chatter swept across the hall like sudden desert rain. Even the constables relaxed their stances.

Out of the corner of his mouth, Deja said, "Don't suppose there's any point in wondering what they're doing here?" Deja looked around and frowned. "Where's Good?"

"Debrief. Ordered us both to Osiris while you were ignoring him."

Deja ignored the bit about Osiris, too. "A debrief? Really?" he asked, not sure if he should be jealous or grateful. "How the fuck did he manage to slip away so fast?"

"I don't know, Vale," Wren said neatly, "probably because he didn't spend five minutes standing on the train and gawking like a slack-jawed idiot."

Deja gave her a look. "It was two minutes tops, come on." He clicked his tongue, debating. Vex would want to speak with him. But with the commotion of The Twelve Who Are Thirteen's surprise (to him) arrival, he'd been kicked several rungs down the priority ladder. The predictable commotion was presently clogging up the elevators and would be for a while.

"C'mon," Deja said, taking Wren by her uninjured hand. "At this rate, the long way to Osiris will be shorter."

"I can wait, it's fine."

Deja tugged at Wren's hand and muttered, "That makes exactly one of us, Wren."

"All right," Wren said through a long-suffering sigh, but she allowed herself to be pulled through the crowd all the same. "If it's for *you*."

Deja scoffed. "Considering what I'd have done after two more minutes of that? I think it's safe to say this is for *everybody*."

As they walked down the black stone steps spilling forth from Omega Headquarters and across the square, Deja kept a close eye on Wren. And because he was keeping a close eye on Wren, it was clear she was keeping just as close an eye on him. Her attention was only drawn away while they passed the large black Reaper statue standing sentry in the square. Not so she could look up at it.

So she could look away from it.

They slipped through one archway, down a lane, then another archway. When Deja led them to a shortcut through an alley, Wren said, "Slow down, Vale."

Deja turned to her with a pointed look. He already knew the admonition wasn't because *Wren* needed to slow down. It was because Wren thought *Deja* needed to slow down. He didn't. He was fine. Wren was neither bothered nor convinced by Deja's miffed look.

"I *will* knock you unconscious," Wren warned. "With the state of you, it wouldn't even be hard. Test me, Vale. Go on. *Test me*."

Even with Deja walking at a gratuitously slow pace, they still reached Osiris Square in decent time. Deja'd never liked the place. Now that he'd spent so many months trapped inside, he liked it even less. It came as no surprise that his distaste showed.

Wren stopped on the first white step. "I'm really fine on my own. You don't have to come with me." Her mouth twisted wryly. "Since I know better than to hope you'll get your hand and throat looked at."

"All they'll do is slap it with M-balm and wrap it in linen, and I've got plenty of all that crap back at mine." Technically true. It's not like he'd taken out the trash.

Wren rolled her eyes and continued back up the stairs. Osiris Square was so silent, each footstep clapped in the air like melting ice sliding off a roof. "If you do have a stock," she called out without looking back, "it's because you never *use it*."

"Touché." Deja followed Wren. Even those shallow steps had him nearly out of breath. He pretended this wasn't an indication that he really ought to check himself in, and remained a solid six feet behind her as she approached the front desk.

The attendant tilted her head when Wren approached—as if the mask didn't make her look bird-like enough. Deja waited for her to *hoot*, too. She didn't. She only asked Wren for her name, her symptoms, their severity.

Wren tugged off her glove, held up a three-fingered hand, and said, "Severe-adjacent." The attendant stiffened, and Wren added, "I can walk. Just tell me where to go."

"Floor 9," the attendant said, writing something so fast, Deja'd be amazed if it were legible to herself let alone anyone else. "The attendant at the desk will direct you further, Agent. And thank you for your service in maintaining the balance between worlds." The rip of paper tore through the air, echoing through the huge atrium like an entire book was being sundered, one page after the other—*rip, rip, rip, rip, rip....*

Deja grimaced and turned away in a vain attempt to shield himself from the sound.

Wren approached him, sheet of white paper in hand. "Well, Vale, this is my stop."

Obligingly, Deja pushed the button. The elevator opened with a single, perfunctory *ding.* "Your chariot, Agent," he said, gesturing grandiosely inside.

"Such service," Wren deadpanned. "It's almost like I've been maintaining the balance between worlds or something."

"Or something."

Wren stepped into the elevator with a snort. "Go get treated or get out of here," she said as the doors closed.

"Will do." Deja let his head fall back against the wall with a *thud.* To the right was a hallway, long but not so long he couldn't see the door standing at the end. Deja stared at it. Beyond that innocent white door, the stairwell rose the entire monumental height of the building. Unlike the elevators that moved between buildings, those stairs were contained by the walls surrounding them. They could only ever lead up... or down. He swallowed around the sinking feeling in his chest. It spiraled down his stomach.

He didn't hear the elevator *ding* a second time.

"Vale?"

Ever emerged from the other elevator, brow furrowed in something like concern, and a tiny, almost novelty-sized jar of M-balm in her large hand.

"Rough mission?"

Ever shrugged. "Something like that." She gave Deja's bandaged hand a pointed nod and returned the question. "Rough mission?"

"Usually. You know how it is."

"I suppose all missions are rough when you don't bother to mask up."

"Yeah, well," Deja grumbled, "we can't all put a ghost in a headlock and strangle it into submission, you know. We have to rely on other talents."

"You doing okay out there? Really, I mean."

"*Really?*" Deja echoed doubtfully.

Ever gave him a patient look. "It's not like you're my rival, Vale." And in case he'd mistaken the sentiment for sweetness, she added, "Not when you've got as many lectures and probations as I've gotten commendations."

"Right." Deja twisted his mouth and looked around for anybody other than Ever to talk to. His options were limited. "Do you know if Marion is still here?"

Ever's face settled into something neutral. "She is."

Deja eyed her curiously and asked, "Visit, do you?"

"I peek in every now and again." Ever raised the jar of M-balm like she was toasting with it. "When it's on the way out."

"Touching." Deja pushed himself from the wall. The motion was a nail driven through his palm. He cloaked the grimace of pain with a world-weary sigh and said, "Well, it's been... it's *been*. See you around, Ever."

The corners of Ever's mouth tightened. She opened her mouth to form one shape, revised her thoughts, and formed another instead. "See you around, Vale."

"HEY, MARE," Deja said, closing the door to Marion's room behind him. He walked to the wall opposite and peered outside one of six narrow lancet windows. From that angle, the moon was low in the sky, round and nearly full. It looked like an augur dropped by the clouds, frozen in its fall. But from the bed, the moon was little more than a source of light and shadow, casting bars that stretched across the floor and over Marion's blanket before creeping up the wall opposite. Had it not been for that wall, those shadows might've gone on forever. As it was, they were trapped there in this moment with them. As frozen in place as Marion.

Deja placed a finger on the glass to write a message in the fog, but he couldn't come up with much but: *AND THEN THERE WERE THREE.* Once back in his usual chair, he rolled his eyes at himself... then did it again.

The nearby cart was stocked with ointments, salves, and tinctures, all lined up in neat rows of six. The second-to-last row of small, dark glass jars was not fully stocked. There was only one jar of the M-balm which instinct warned him not to take. But what if that instinct hadn't evolved to avoid a threat? What if it was some other animal entirely? Something soft and stupid. Like hope. Like grief. Even loneliness. Osiris treatments never did him any harm. Apart from make him groggy, the only thing M-balm did was drive away his waking dreams and muffle voices that weren't really there anyway.

What if after all that, you never really wanted *to get better?*

What if you only pretended *to want the dreams and hallucinations to stop?*

What if you are so weak, you couldn't even let the imaginary sight of your lost teammates go?

Buried beneath those questions was a deeper one. One that sneered like the others didn't.

Is that why you lied to Vex?

Because he had lied. Again and again, Deja'd lied to the man. *No symptoms,* he'd said. *Nothing like before,* he'd said. *Everything is normal,* he'd said.

It *was* normal for an agent to get injured or overtired. It *wasn't* normal for an agent to be dogged by visions of impossible things—colors, words, messages. Hells, he'd even gone out of his way to seek *out* those messages. It was almost like he believed if he could just convince himself that those messages were real and not his own broken mind projecting its cracks onto the world, then he really was fine. He was just doing his duty. But he wasn't fine, was he? Those messages *weren't* real. At best, they were a distraction. He didn't have the stomach to contemplate what they were at worst. Thrall and Sygil came to mind, though: his fellow Odds whose Oddities had gone wrong. Gotten them lost to oblivion. He thought of Sine's charred face—the *smell* of it—as she told him exactly what was responsible for the pieces of her crumbling apart and fading away on an elevator floor.

Freak. The freak had done that to her.

Had there been signs before that mission? Signs that Thrall ignored? The way Deja was ignoring the signs now? Was every hallucination just another warning *screaming* at him to stay away from the Desert because he couldn't be trusted anymore?

Maybe *no* Odd could.

Deja released a breath that desperately wanted to be a yell. He rested his elbows on Marion's bed, pressed his face into his hands, and stared at the stars his eyes fashioned out of the blackness.

The messages were right, though....

Deja took another breath, long and deep and loud in the hopes it would drown out the whispering thought. It didn't. Of course not— he didn't want that whispering thought to go away any more than he wanted to stop seeing the people he'd lost. He held his breath and let the whisper dare:

What if it's not a hallucination... what if it's a lost memory coming back?

The last mission, the one he'd forgotten, had been at a school. Wren had confirmed it. And when he'd seen Thorne, or Ivy, or Vyne, it had always been on a train to a mission, or *at* the mission—in a school. So, maybe he was hallucinating.

But maybe he was *remembering*, too.

Which meant he really might be getting better. Just like he'd told Vex.

"What d'you think, Mare?" Deja asked. "That a chance worth taking?"

Marion's answer was silent and still. It was only because of that silent stillness that he heard the very faint *click* of a door opening. A sliver of familiar face peeked through the crack. For a stomach-tugging moment, a moment Deja hated himself for, he really thought it was Thorne peering back at him. But then those eyes widened in a very un–Thorne (but still very familiar) way.

"Oh!" Izik said hurriedly. "Sorry, I'll just—"

Deja called out just as she turned away. "Hey! Get back here, kid."

An internal debate rolled across Izik's shoulders in tension like subtitles. In the end, she decided to submit, eyes betraying the grimace she had too much self-control to reveal on her mouth.

Deja asked, "What are you doing here?"

"Same as you, I'm guessing?" Izik offered like it was a second question. It sort of was, Deja supposed. "Visiting."

"Yeah. Same as me." Deja lifted an eyebrow at the unmoving rookie. "Did you need *privacy* for that or...."

"No!" Izik stepped fully inside and closed the door behind her. "Just wasn't expecting company is all. First time there's been any." She cleared her throat and amended, "Well, second. But I've never seen anybody but you here."

"Shocker," Deja muttered. It wasn't. Freaks weren't exactly popular with their fellow agents. When Deja'd been interred at Osiris himself, he'd made his own visits to Marion after-hours. Ever was around, but she wasn't exactly sentimental. Deja couldn't claim to be sentimental himself, but he'd always gotten on with Marion. And Omen. Even if he hadn't, an unconscious Odd was the closest he ever came to company back then.

Still was, apparently.

"Take a seat, kid," Deja said. "Your awkward-teenager-running-into-a-teacher-in-the-mall energy is killing me."

Izik blinked in confusion but took a seat on the end of the bed all the same. What a trooper. She placed a hand on the linen beside Marion's leg and gave it a small pat: a well-worn greeting. "Any change?"

"No."

"Oh, oka—"

"What are you doing here?"

Izik, to her credit, didn't hedge around her reasons. "She was my teammate," she admitted. It really sounded like an admission the way she said it. "Or, was going to be. I hadn't gone on any real missions yet. But we did training exercises with full agents and—"

"I remember training," Deja interrupted.

"Right," Izik said, eyes drifting down like a dead leaf. First to Marion's face… then Deja's bandaged hand… then her own, resting on the bed. All the while, she did her best to look like she wasn't watching Deja. She was.

"You can't have known her long."

"Suppose not. She was always kind to me though." Izik shrugged. "The other agents can be a bit—" She stopped short, but the tight press of her lips finished the thought: *less kind.*

"New agents are always assholes and old agents get scared," Deja said. "They lose one or two teammates, get handed some new ones, and start doing the math. Try to figure out how long the new teammate's gonna last while the new teammate tries to figure out how long *they're* gonna last."

"Why should that make new agents assholes, though?" More quietly, she added, "Not that I'd noticed that or anything." But as her mouth said the politic words, her face grumbled: *I, too, had noticed that new agents are all assholes.*

"Well, newer agents tend to have a lot to prove. Especially to even newer ones. None of us is any better than anybody else, but I guess when you go through training as intense as that and make it out the other side, you expect a bit more recognition, maybe. Like a gold star or a cookie or something."

"Is that why they don't like you, you think?"

"Me personally, or"—Deja jerked his head at Marion—"people like me."

"Both?"

"Both," Deja echoed through a thin laugh. "Yeah, maybe. Some of us might be *odd,* but none of us is special because we're *all* special. All put through the same ringer. All made to feel like inconsequential tools for four years, before getting handed an augur and sent off to try and *not* get eaten up by a world that doesn't want us there, and reminds us so via combustion any chance it gets. We were all chosen. But we all earned our place, too." The pull at the corners of Izik's mouth inclined him to think she disagreed. He narrowed his eyes at her. "What?"

"Nothing."

"You know what happened?" Deja asked.

Izik frowned. "You mean you don't?"

"No, I do." Deja knew Vex's version of it, anyway: *A tragic accident.* He shrugged and told a half-truth. "Just curious what version of the story *you* got that made you come back here enough times to know Marion doesn't usually get non-me-shaped visitors."

"Oh," Izik said. "I just got the sense we're not really supposed to talk about it, is all."

Deja's brow furrowed. "From *who*?"

"Nobody, honestly. Just a sense."

"Ah. You saw it... didn't you."

A nervous laugh. "What?"

"People don't share gossip around the aether cooler in these parts," Deja said mildly. At Izik's increasing confusion, he explained, "If you weren't meant to know something, you wouldn't be told. Nobody'd be telling you and winking at you to keep quiet. So, if you know what happened, it's because you were there. You saw it."

"What makes you say that?"

"Because you're *here*."

"So are you," Izik pointed out. "And *you* weren't there."

"How do *you* know I wasn't there?" Deja countered smoothly, and Izik pursed her lips. "We're freaks of a feather, Mare and me. But you... *you* keep coming back. Same as any comrade with a heart would." *For any comrade who wasn't a freak,* he didn't say. "So tell me what happened."

Izik worried at her bottom lip as her eyes drifted back to Marion's face. Whatever had happened hadn't been classified—not officially. More likely, it had been swept under the proverbial rug. And this kid hadn't been in the field long enough to fear or resent the Odds like so many of their fellows did. But maybe that wasn't why she was the only visitor. Funny thing was, often it was the same force keeping some away from the twenty-first floor of Osiris that compelled others there again and again and again. *Guilt.*

Only, Deja couldn't tell which way the guilt fell in this case:

Pushing Izik here? Or keeping the others away?

"We were in the Gray," Izik said. "Me and another rookie—Yve—and the agents training with us. It went wrong, is all. They said it does sometimes."

Deja grimaced at the memory of his own training in the Gray. He'd take the burn of the Desert over that emptiness any day. Even Good (who'd been a textbook trainee and never said a word to a superior without a snap to attention and a *Sir!*) had shrunk in upon himself. That place pulled you apart just when you were still at your newest. Your most fragile. After Vex had released the ghost in there with them, there'd even been a moment when Deja'd thought Good was going to let it tear him apart—wanted it to—*anything* to get away from that maddening, empty Gray.

Vex had even been about to step in.

Then Deja did.

That was only their *first* exposure. There'd been plenty more after that. If Izik had been training with fully-fledged agents, she'd have been nearing the end of her four years. Cleared for duty in all but name. As Deja watched her stare at Marion's face, he felt an echo of the creeping insanity of the Gray. Again came the question of just what it was that kept Izik coming back: Guilt? Or the lack of it?

Izik's hand crept a little closer to the pale, still one resting atop the linen sheets. *Guilt, then.* Either someone had stepped in... or someone else hadn't.

"Tell me what happened," Deja said.

Izik hesitated, but not for long. "They released a pair of ghosts. It wasn't my first time in there with a ghost—Yve, either. But it *was* the first time we had one higher than a level two. Or two at once. Or a real team with real agents. Or an..." she trailed off before finishing with a hint of apology, "an Odd."

That raised a dozen questions but Deja didn't interrupt. If agents-in-training were being sent into the Gray with demented-level three ghosts two at a time, then training had taken a real turn since his day. Given how thin agents were spread, it made sense training would be accelerated to compensate. He could only hope this *tragic accident* had shown just how foolhardy that venture was. A darker part of him, a part he didn't think he'd even had a few months before now, suspected that losing an *Odd* wouldn't be inspiring anybody to change tack.

They couldn't seem to *stop* losing Odds, and nothing had been done to change that. Not so far as Deja could see. Unless you counted tightening up communications and decreasing team sizes. But no, they'd been losing *normal* agents, too. It was just that the freaks were few enough in number to start with that their casualties felt less like a tragedy and more like an evolutionary shift. An existential threat. Only three of them remained now, and one third had been lying unconscious in a bed for five months with no sign of waking up.

Deja's own recovery was tenuous at best.

Izik continued, "Right away, it didn't feel right. But it never feels right, does it? The Gray *or* the Desert. Neither of them ever feels right."

"No. That's why they send us there. To get used to feeling like we don't fit in the world."

"I think you're right. But... I'm not sure that was all of it." At Deja's expectant look, Izik explained with the side-stepping tone of somebody trying to assure themselves as much as anybody else, "It's probably just because it was my first time in a real team that things felt off. That's what Crane said. Just nerves."

Deja's brows went up. "Crane was there?"

"Yes. She's been my head agent since I started—*before* I started."

As Deja tried to parse out her team's strange family tree, Izik worried at a loose thread on the linen sheets with a finger.

"Not Sine and Troy, though," Deja said. "They were with Omen. Not Marion."

"Right. I never worked with those guys before that clown mission."

"So you were tacked onto a team with Crane and Marion. Along with another rookie?"

Izik's mouth tightened. "Yes. Yve." There was a distaste to how she spoke the name that Deja hadn't noticed before. Like she'd bitten into what she'd thought was a chocolate chip cookie only to find a raisin.

"And is this Yve person in the field now?"

What had been subtle distaste was now the closest thing to open disdain Deja'd ever seen on Izik's face. "She is," Izik said. "There's just so few of us, so...." The thread broke off in her fingers. She did her best to smooth it out to hide the hole it left behind, but it just kept sticking out.

"Right...." Deja let out a sigh. "Look, kid, I don't have all day. And I can almost guarantee you I'm the only person around here you can kvetch to without getting thought less of, so spill your guts while you can."

Izik's face went stiff before relaxing a fraction. "Okay." She glanced over her shoulder at the closed door. "You know Marion's whole thing, right? She sort of... takes over ghosts the way ghosts take over the living sometimes. Except she doesn't need to be inside them, she can just"—she jerked her arms around like a puppet on strings—"do it?"

"Yeah," Deja said flatly. "I'm familiar with her whole schtick."

A sheepish half-smile. "Right, of course you are. Anyway. The ghosts were... well, they were strong. One of them went for me—a level three—and its face was coming at me, snarling at me like this demented, monstrous thing and I just—I just *froze.* I couldn't move. And this ghost is screaming when suddenly *it's* frozen, too. And I can just see Marion behind it, standing perfectly still in the same position. Holding it there. Crane tells me to get out of the way so Marion can release it, but I'm still just—I still just can't *move.* And then—" She clapped her hands together. "Somebody fired. Shot the thing right in the back. Ghost disintegrated, mortified... and Marion went down."

While Izik gathered the wherewithal to continue, Deja took this in. In a way, Marion really *had* been taken down by her own Oddity.

In taking over a ghost's movements, she'd taken over something else, too. Something that made it so a shot at the ghost was just as good as a shot at her.

Izik stared at him with an almost pleading expression. "Crane ran over to her but I still couldn't—I still couldn't—"

"It's all right," Deja said quietly. "I mean, it's not all right. But you know what I mean."

Izik nodded. She knew what he meant. She just didn't believe him.

Deja ventured, "I take it you know who fired the shot?"

"Yve *says* she didn't, and there's no way to prove otherwise," Izik said. "You've been there. You know what it's like. Even when you *can* see through the Gray, it's still so disorienting. But nobody else says it was them, and I saw how Yve looked when she heard we'd be training with Marion. I doubt anybody else noticed it because they didn't know her at the time, but I did. I could tell she felt some kind of way about it. And she was always—she always had to be so *perfect* all the time. If she messed up? There is *nothing* in this world that could make her own up to it." Her afterthought was so quiet, Deja might have only imagined the muttered, "Prick."

Deja sat in uneasy silence. If Crane suspected anyone on her team of causing harm to a teammate—Odd or not—she wouldn't let it stand. She'd do something about it. Maybe the fact that Crane and Izik were now on an entirely different team *was* the aftermath of that something. Could just be more of this haphazard restructuring from Omega trying to patch over the holes with the few resources it had left.

Deja looked back to Marion's utterly still, uninformative face. It was guilt, then, that brought Izik here again and again. But it probably wasn't what kept the rest of the team away. He didn't have enough optimism left to believe that. "The first time I went into the Gray and saw a ghost, you know what I did?"

Izik looked up at him, a tad hopeful. "Did you freeze, too?"

"Nah," Deja said, batting a hand. "I was pretty much fine, actually." Izik deflated a bit before Deja continued, "But *Good*, though. Good was an entirely different story." Izik's brows went up, and Deja hedged, "*But...* if Good knew I'd told you that story, he would hurl me outside a tether field."

"Oh," Izik said, disappointed.

"Yeah...."

Izik cleared her throat, staring down at Marion.

"Yep..." Deja said distantly, "right past the tether nails."

"Right...."

"So anyway," Deja said, leaning forward in his seat; Izik leaned closer, too. "Good and I had been placed in the same cadre from day one. And he was always just so... *into training,* you know? Like, he could recite any lesson, execute any form perfectly, nail any target, dismantle and reassemble a mortifier blindfolded in record time."

Izik's lip twitched. "You too, I bet."

Deja scoffed, "Yeah, *no.* There's a reason he's called 'Good' and I'm not. So anyway. Naturally, when it came time to go to the Gray, everybody was expecting Good to just knock it out of the park, right?"

Izik frowned. "Knock it out of the park?"

Deja waved an impatient hand and hurriedly translated, "Do really, really well. It's a Desert sports thing, don't worry about it. So we go in: It's him, me, and four other agents-in-training. Vex is supervising us—"

"AI Vex?" Izik interrupted, wide-eyed. "You were trained by AI Vex?"

"As much as I was trained at all, yeah. Not the point. So, we're sent out there, and immediately you can see Good is, well, *not good.* He looks like he's about to pull an afflicted and spew green goo all over the place."

Izik leaned forward with bated breath. "What happened?"

"Well, he did. All over." Deja's hands made a concluding flourish. "And they hadn't even brought the ghost *in* yet." With a groan and a few pops of his spine, he stood and gave his body a few seconds to adjust to the change in position. He rolled his right shoulder before giving Izik a quick clap on hers. "So, don't feel bad for freezing up, is my point. You're not the first, you won't be the last, and you're definitely not the *worst*. That dubious honor is held by none other than Head Agent Good."

Izik gave him a suspicious smile. "You made all that up."

"What?" Deja demanded, voice going high in faux indignation. He began walking backward toward the door. "Why do you think he hates me so much? It's because I never let that fucker forget he painted the Gray green." He turned to leave and threw a "Take it easy, rookie," over his shoulder.

A little laugh followed him into the hallway. An even quieter "Thanks, Agent Vale... you too" tagged along after.

The streets of the Hereafter were seldom crowded, but they were never *this* sparse. Nobody else walked past Deja the entire length of the long, straight street connecting the center of the Hex to the Floating district. At the end, Deja took a sharp turn down an alley you'd barely notice if you didn't know it was there. Smooth stone cobbled beneath his boots, lights dimmed. Fog, green, damp, and dense, licked at his shins. That fog usually pulled Deja through the winding Floating District as nonnegotiably as a swift stream does a paper boat. But that night, when he happened to clock a glowing rectangle two stories above, he stopped against the misty current. He looked.

A middle-aged man in a three-piece suit wobbled on the railing of a narrow balcony. Deja stared up at him. The man stared dead ahead, too-long-socked feet curled over the second rung, knees bent like he was about to jump. *Why?* What could that possibly accomplish? Deja followed the man's line of sight and saw nothing there but more windows and balconies. All dark.

The man choked out, "Gone… all gone," and climbed another rung. He sobbed, open-mouthed, into his sleeve, either oblivious or unbothered by the tears and snot now tethering him to his arm. He looked at Deja. "*Gone.*" He swung a leg over the railing.

"No, wait." Deja rushed forward to—

Nobody. There was nobody there.

Deja looked around, less in search of the crying phantom than potential witnesses of his cracking sanity. Nobody saw. He sniffed, bracing himself against the sudden chill and continued down the familiar, nonsensical current to Ukiyo.

As always, the cracked lantern swayed and creaked outside. As always, inside was nearly empty. Here, at least, that was a familiar comfort. Deja surveilled the corner of the bar where he'd spotted the rabbit before. Nobody there. He tried again, this time out of the corner of his eye—no dice—then the curve of the gramophone. Still nobody there.

With a preemptive sigh of relief, Deja took his seat at the bar. Osiris's medicinal stink was so strong it was practically a taste—one that was finally about to be chased away by something in a glass.

Yule beamed at him from his station. This latest rendition was cheerful as a foil bow on a present, with glinting, silver glasses and neat black hair. "Brandy?" he asked when Deja took a seat before him.

"So close," Deja said, more to himself than the bartender aglow with contrived youthful exuberance. "I'll have an apple juice." Clocking the mild panic tensing Yule's uncannily handsome face, he asked, "You good, sweetie?"

"Darling Dear serves the juice," Yule recited as though from rote. "I can serve brandy." A little more confidently, he added, "And *nuts*."

Deja stared at him. "Uh–huh." He craned in his seat to call out, "Darling Dear? Please come out... I don't know how to explain what juice is."

No response.

He rubbed his hands over his eyes and let his arms fall to the sticky bar with a lame *thud*. "All right," he sighed. "Get me some *nuts*."

"Right away!" Yule continued beaming at the cranky agent as he reached below to extract a simple, black bowl half-filled with almonds.

Deja suppressed a grimace. Then he stopped bothering to suppress anything. "Almonds? *Really?*"

"Almonds are nuts," Yule said, sounding as close to defensive as he could manage (which wasn't very). When Deja just stared back at him, his face flickered with concern. "Are... aren't they?"

"Yeah, Yule, they're *nuts*," Deja said. "The *worst*—oh, fuck it, never mind." He pulled the bowl toward him and began popping nuts through a half-hearted, "Thanks." Another nut. "Go polish something."

Yule smiled and began polishing the bottle of brandy Deja never let him pour.

Nuts weren't nearly as effective as juice at forcing back the Osiris stench, but it was better than nothing so Deja kept munching. His brow furrowed when Yule rotated the bottle he was polishing. Its label was simple and white, but the plain black text didn't read *Brandy.*

It was a bunch of *gibberish.*

Yule noticed the scrutiny and beamed at him.

Deja huffed a laugh and shook his head to himself. *Yule was such a simple creature.* Then, he frowned. A ridiculous thought had just occurred to him. "Say, Yule?" he asked between almonds. "Buddy?"

"More nuts?"

"Not just yet."

"Brandy?"

Deja took a moment to snuff his sarcasm. "I'm good. I've got a question for you: What are you doing here?" Before Yule could answer—*I serve brandy*—Deja added, "I mean, why are *you* here, and not somebody *else.*"

Yule frowned at him in pretty confusion. "Why am I here?" he asked. Deja nodded, and Yule's frowned deepened. He really did look to be considering this. Hard. His answer ended up roughly six blocks south of the one Deja'd been expecting. In fact, it almost made him order a glass of gibberish brandy—a double. Neat. "I... I was chosen," Yule said. "That's why I'm here."

"You were chosen," Deja echoed blankly.

Yule nodded and resumed polishing.

Deja scoffed under his breath. There wasn't much point in asking if that was something Yule'd come up with on his own, or something Darling or somebody else had told him. Yule didn't come up with things on his own, let alone the same answer every Omega agent was given. *You were chosen.* That's what they heard the moment they reported for training, and again when they first stepped foot in HQ. They'd hear it time and again after that, especially during the roughest missions. The ones that carved the question *Why me?* into blankly staring eyes on the train ride home.

They weren't like ghosts. They'd never lived and so they never *died*. But they weren't like the constables or the rabbits, either. Omega agents were special. *They were chosen.* The thought that Yule was also getting that headless-horse shit shoveled down his throat made Deja laugh the sort of laugh you scrambled for when you didn't want to risk *crying in public.* Crying for what? *No idea.* Didn't matter, really.

"So you were chosen," Deja began with an expectant look at Yule.

Yule nodded.

"So answer me this. You've got a job, right? That's what you were chosen for."

Another nod.

"What happens if you can't do that job anymore?"

No nod.

Deja plucked up another almond and waved it vaguely as he posed, "What happens if you, say... oh, I don't know... start serving poison nuts on accident—"

Thwack! Yule's hand struck out, sudden as a viper, and *smacked* the bowl of nuts clean off the bar. The poor dented thing clattered on the floor some ten feet away.

Deja watched the bowl *wobble-wobble-wobble* its way beneath a table, then stared at Yule, mouth open, single almond still held lamely before him—

Thwack! A second viper of a hand struck out and snatched that too, and over to its fallen nutty brethren it went.

Deja opened and closed his mouth a few times. "Yule, sweetie?" he managed. "The nuts are not poison."

Yule stared at him with eyes like a Labrador who'd just been caught eating Good's second augur and felt just *awful* about it. "The nuts aren't poison?"

"No," Deja assured him. "See, this conversation we're having here? This is what we call a *hypothetical.* It hasn't happened. It's something that might happen or might never happen. But we think about what *could* happen if it did."

This did not clear up Yule's confusion one nut.

"The nuts aren't poison," Deja repeated, "and you are doing a great job. My hypothetical question is: In the very *unlikely* event you *stopped* doing a good job, what would happen to you?"

Yule's confusion reached critical levels. "But I was chosen," he mumbled lamely. "And the nuts aren't poison."

"That's right." Deja reached forward to pat Yule's hand and echoed, "The nuts aren't poison."

Misreading this completely, Yule offered, "Brandy?"

"No, but thanks, babe," Deja said wearily. "How 'bout this: What do you suppose happens to *me* if *I* stop doing a good job? If *I* stop being useful? Or even become a liability? A danger, I mean. You know... to *nuts* or whatever."

Tortured silence. Then, "Were you chosen?" Yule asked.

Deja nodded. "Yeah. I was." He laughed. "Maybe I could take *your* job—oh—oh, no—Yule, honey... *please* calm down. I am *not taking your job.* Hey, hey—Yule? Sweetie-pops? Could you get me some more nuts, please?"

Yule pushed through the swelling panic and provided Deja with another (not dented) bowl of (not poisoned) nuts.

"See?" Deja said, gesturing to the bowl. "You are *so good* at this. *Irreplaceable.*"

Yule's relief at that last statement betrayed the shape of his fear. But was *Deja Vale* replaceable? *That* was his question. And if he assumed *yes,* what happened to him if he *were* replaced? It was a question Yule couldn't answer any more than Marion could. From the back of his mind whispered another question: *Where do the rabbits go each night?*

Deja sighed and stared into the bowl of nuts, sifting through them with a finger like he might find a pistachio or something.

"Did you do a bad job?"

Deja looked up. Yule was staring at him with what passed for a thoughtful expression in his pretty little world. "Sorry?" he asked.

"Did you do a bad job?" Yule repeated. Probably on the verge of asking Deja if he'd poisoned Omega's nuts.

"Uh..." Deja didn't actually *know* if he'd figuratively poisoned the nuts. His gut told him he was a liability, but then his gut told him all sorts of shit all the time. He'd protected Stephanie's baby from Bruno. He'd protected the Potential from the afflicted on the RV. He'd gotten Good back onto the train when they didn't rebound. He'd, *somehow*, helped purge that animal hospital of ghosts and saved Wren. And if Wren could be believed, he'd helped her and Lear escape their original teammate's grim fates at that last mission in a high school he couldn't remember.

And why would Wren lie?

"No," Deja told Yule at last, surprised to find himself almost believing it. "I did a good job."

"Then you don't need to hippo ethical," Yule said simply and Deja couldn't bring himself to correct his precious phraseology. "Maybe *you* were chosen, too."

"Yeah," Deja agreed with a fleeting twitch of a smile. "Maybe I was." Maybe he'd even done a *great* job. But he couldn't shake the feeling that he'd just been *lucky*. Lucky in the ways that Omen, Hart, Marion, Thrall, and Sygil hadn't been.

Blissfully unaware of this darker turn of thought, Yule gave Deja a satisfied smile. Then, he reached for a nonsensical bottle and offered, "Brandy?"

"Good Reapers, no." Deja craned in his seat and called toward the backroom. "Darling? I'm non-dying of thirst out here and these nuts are *not helping!*" At the flicker of worry on Yule's face, he hurriedly added, "Not because they're poison or anything. They're great"—to Yule—"*you're* great"—to the absent owner—"but they're also... *nuts...* and nuts are salty and dry, so...."

Again, no response.

"Darling?" Deja called again, a tad desperately this time. "Darling Dear?"

Still no response.

"She's not here," Yule said.

What might've withered to worry if given the chance never did. Surprised excitement stole the limelight as Jamais, present and intact, took a seat on the stool beside Deja.

"Yule, dear?" Jamais said, not paying the agent to his left a single mind. "Reach down beneath the bar—no, six inches to your left—good. Two shelves down, you'll find a carved crystal carafe. And when you touch it, you'll smell faint smoke on the air from burning leaves. That smoke will feel chill on your cheeks and ears... nip at your fingertips."

Yule's hand did reach beneath the bar, eyes transfixed on Jamais. He listened more closely than he'd probably had reason to listen to a damned thing in his short, immaculate existence.

"Now, grasp it around the narrow neck," Jamais continued, "and taste the coming winter. Hear the crows flying north and the geese fleeing south. The crackle of dried leaves on the wind. Hear them drag across the street like paper wings caressing stone. Do you hear it, Yule?"

Yule nodded.

It was only when Jamais's eyes shifted to Deja that Deja realized he'd been nodding, too.

Like a magician polishing off a trick, Jamais tapped the bar and said, "Then pick up that carafe and put it here."

THUNK. What Yule placed on the counter wasn't the plain, glass bottles he usually served, but a large, cut crystal carafe of glittering amber cider. Deja stared at it. In what must have been a momentary trick of the light, he could've sworn the crystal had been carved with a pattern of *bones*. When Yule poured, it was gray, not amber, that splashed within two glasses of matching, carved crystal.

Deja took his and held it up, inspecting it. No ribs or skulls. Just lines and diamonds.

"Yule?" Jamais asked kindly.

Yule leaned forward. "Yes?"

"Why don't you go into the back and check on things."

"All right. I'm going to go into the back and check on things."

Jamais watched him leave with a pleasant smile. Only once the backroom door closed behind the handsome bartender did he chance a sip. He grimaced and began inspecting the glass just as Deja had. Only, Deja expected they hadn't been looking for the same thing. "So close," he lamented. He gave Deja a sweeping look. "That is some lifeburn you've got."

Deja rubbed a hand over his throat. He didn't think it was still visible. He'd been wrong, apparently. Shocker.

"I didn't mean *there*." Jamais nodded, indicating higher—maybe as high as the forehead. Only, Deja didn't have any lifeburn on his face. "What happened to you?"

Deja blew out a loud breath. "I didn't mind the ritual circle."

"Ah," Jamais said, nodding. "That makes no sense to me, but you may want to get that looked at."

Deja snorted and took a sip of his drink. His tongue coiled against the sharpness until the flavor relaxed into something warm and comforting. Old. "I don't think Osiris can help with whatever it is I've got," he said grimly.

"I never said they could." Jamais eyed Deja the way a sculptor eyes raw marble. "Have you thought about donning something with a tad more coverage? A hat, perhaps?" He gave Deja a subtle smirk. "I think a fedora could be quite fetching on you."

"A fedora is never fetching," Deja deadpanned. "The only thing that would be fetching is *me* while I go chasing after it each time a ghost knocks it off my head."

A half-shrug. "I'm all right with that."

"Oh, well then," Deja said archly. "Let me just go ahead and put my douchey headwear order in with Darling Dear, just for you."

Jamais's eyes crinkled in a smile and, for as long as they did, they looked brown. Deja wondered what color his own eyes took on when he smiled back, if any. As Jamais's delicate-fingered hand gently swirled his drink, back and forth... back and forth... the cut diamonds really might've morphed into a crystal ribcage. "You'll have to wait, I'm afraid," Jamais said. "She's not in."

Deja turned in his seat to look at the door Yule'd disappeared through—the one Darling Dear usually *appeared* through. "You know where she is?"

"Above my pay grade."

"She's somewhere above your pay grade?" Deja asked him. "Or knowing where she'd be is above your pay grade."

Jamais's face said *take your pick.* That look felt as familiar as the cider tasted. Of course, if that feeling of familiarity went both ways, Jamais would trust him enough to answer a simple fucking question.

"Never mind." Deja took a sip and let it linger. It twined across his palate like smoke in the air. He swallowed then took another. Really was the only thing that could wash away the stink of Osiris.

"I expect she's fine," Jamais said. "If you're worried."

"*Thanks.* Good to know."

"Why don't you ever order alcohol?"

Deja shrugged. "Above my pay grade."

An interested hum. "How far above your pay grade?"

"At least as high up as 'Where the fuck did Darling and all the other rabbits go,' I'm guessing."

Jamais nodded solemnly. "Pretty high, then."

"You know, I'm really starting to feel like I should just tell you to fuck yourself. *Again.*"

"Again?" Jamais asked with interest.

"Yeah. *Again.*"

"So why don't you?"

"Fuck if I know," Deja grumbled. "Fuck if I know *anything* anymore." He cradled his glass and stared into the glinting gray.

"The rabbits are wherever they've been ordered to be, as they are wont to do. And Darling, well..." Jamais trailed off before finishing delicately, "is expecting family."

Deja looked up at that. "Expecting family?" he echoed. "Who the hells has *family* around here?"

"Well, Darling Dear, for one."

Deja gave a small snort. "Yeah, well, if anyone would, it'd be her, I guess."

Jamais hummed absently and sipped his drink. He placed the glass on the counter with a sound like stone hitting stone and stood. "Any exciting plans tonight?"

"Well, I *was* going to go tell Janis down in the Warren just how delightfully ridiculous the decor at the vet was before some ghosts ruined it with metaphysically confused fire, but I guess all rabbits but you are *busy*." Deja eyed Jamais consideringly. "Don't suppose *you'd* care to hear about the beach tchotchkes? No? Fine, suit yourself. Fuck off."

The look Jamais gave Deja was unreadable, but as long and binding as an attentive cat's. It was some time before Jamais cut through the silence his stare demanded. "Why did you ask Yule those questions?"

Deja shrugged this off—or tried to. His attempt at an indifferent scoff sounded artificial to his own ears. "Just making conversation," he said.

Jamais clearly didn't buy this, and why should he? Even *Yule* wouldn't have bought that. Deja stared at a knot in the wood beside his gloved hands. Omen, Hart, Thrall, and more had been lost. Marion was in an Osiris recovery bed with little-to-no hope of stepping out of it. Odds were dropping like flies and it wasn't a coincidence. For whatever reason, Oddities were betraying their Odds. Maybe they'd *always* been ticking bombs and it was only now that they'd been confronted with the incontrovertible evidence of that precariously ticking fact. Vex was certainly treating Deja like he was rigged to blow. The man told him again and again that he "wasn't being punished," and maybe he wasn't. But you didn't assign babysitter detail to agents you could rely upon and trust. Omega agents were already spread thin. Was Deja Vale truly valuable enough to justify ordering one of Omega's top agents to chase him around like an overqualified nanny? For how long? Maybe Deja was useful enough to keep around despite the risk. Only, that wasn't exactly a choice *Vex* was making, was it? Because Deja'd told Vex he wasn't having anymore hallucinations. So far as Vex knew, Deja's time bomb wasn't ticking.

Truth was, it ticked every time Deja went out there.

Tick, when he'd collapse from exhaustion and see his dead comrades.

Tock, when he'd catch a glimpse of red that shouldn't—*couldn't* exist.

Tick, when he heard whispers warning him not to take the medicine that would shut those whispers up and *listened.*

Tock, when he saw messages that nobody but him could see and *heeded them.*

Deja's Oddity was a ticking time bomb, all right. And for reasons he couldn't quite explain, it seemed he was hell-bent on making it tick *faster.* But he didn't voice any of this. Instead, he tugged on the question dangling from the edge of those far heavier ones like a loose thread. "You work in the Warren," he began; Jamais nodded. "But... did you *always?*"

Jamais stared at him. "What are you asking me?"

Deja swallowed hard. He was asking if there was a place in this world for agents who couldn't be relied upon in the field anymore. If there was a place in this world for an Odd whose Oddity couldn't be trusted. If he could go to Vex right now and tell the man he was hallucinating worse than ever and to not let him anywhere near the Desert again and have it *all be okay.* He desperately needed to hear that it could all be okay. But he couldn't bring himself to tell anyone *why.*

He felt like a child.

Deja took a shallow breath and asked, "Were you an Omega agent?"

Jamais gave him an almost challenging look. "Isn't it enough for me to be a rabbit?"

"You know the rap code," Deja pressed, just on the edge of desperation.

"Do I?"

"Don't you?"

All of Deja's hopes were tied up in the question. As Jamais held his gaze, those hopes and questions unfurled: *Because if you had been an agent, and you had known the rap code, if you had somehow found a way to send OWLs outside a tether field, then maybe I wasn't hallucinating after all.*

But even if I had been hallucinating: If you were an agent, and now you're not, and you're still here—you still have a place in this world—maybe I can, too.

Maybe it really will be okay?

Jamais's mouth tightened. Sharp eyes drifted to the empty glass beside him. The longer he stared, the higher Deja's hopes got.

And then they went nowhere.

"I already told you," Jamais said at last. "I'm nobody." Deja watched in crushed silence as Jamais stood up. His casual tone was like a canister of turpentine erasing every word that came before it. "Well, give the hat a thought. At least wrap yourself up in a bit of linen." When Deja scoffed, Jamais added, "What could it hurt?"

Deja was surprised to hear his own voice sounding as casual as Jamais's had. "Linen, huh? What, you want me to wrap myself up like a *mummy* or something? I'd look ridiculous."

"Bold of you to assume you don't already. But those linens aren't shielding like the masks and gloves. They're healing. Might be worth a shot." Jamais straightened his gray cap and tie. "At least put up your hood on occasion. You'll catch your death out there," he said as he made his exit.

Deja craned in his seat to watch the "rabbit" go. And as he did, cold bit his cheeks. The smoke of burning leaves peppered the air. The geese called. The crows cawed. One cry sounded like a warning. The other like *welcome home.*

Deja's jaw tightened. Maybe Jamais was never an agent, but there was no way he was really just a rabbit.

And he sure as hells wasn't *nobody.*

DEJA WAITED TWO nights and one day for marching orders that never came. Vex never contacted him for a debrief. No one did. He'd expected Oathe to call him into headquarters, at the very least. Maybe she just couldn't stomach looking any of them in the eye knowing just how badly the Augury had fucked that particular mission up. *Level one and level two demented...* Somebody had to be on the coals for that one. They'd almost lost Wren. He gathered it wasn't him being dragged, as his augur hadn't chirped to summon him to any official coal-dragging.

And Omega sure did love calling up Deja Vale for a good coal-dragging.

Just to make sure, Deja'd even gone back to HQ. One step in the place told him that whatever had held up the trains and brought The Twelve Who Are Thirteen there had yet to dissipate. Constables and agents alike still cluttered up the atrium, collecting outside the elevator banks like wet leaves clogging a storm drain. Deja stared at the numbers above the elevators himself, debating. Should he only ask Vex to sign off on his field damage report so he could requisition a new pair of gloves?

Or should he tell Vex all the things he'd seen on that last mission that no one else had?

Deja was spared from deciding. AI Oathe emerged from the elevator, spotted Deja through the crowd, and pushed her way agitatedly through the hapless bystanders waiting to get wherever they were going. "Vale?" she demanded as she shoved aside a constable. "What is it? You haven't been summoned for a debrief, have you?" Her eyes narrowed. "Or *brief*?"

Deja stepped back before she could shake him. "No, but my gloves were damaged in the field and I need an AI to sign—"

"Vale," Oathe snapped peevishly. "The Twelve Who Are Thirteen are here for a review. The Warren is flooded and Omega is dealing with a crisis. We cannot spare time for your petty needs. Just—just—just *be less reckless next time!*"

Deja didn't point out that in the time it took Oathe to berate him, she could have easily approved *two* field damage reports and *two* requisition request forms. He deserved a medal. What he got was a huff and a prime view of Oathe's agitatedly retreating backside.

So, Deja went back to his apartment. He slept. He dreamt he was bickering with Thorne in a locker-lined hallway about which AI was the biggest pain in the ass to report to, then that he was watching Wren and Ivy debate tether strategy on the train, and then that he was pleading with a chalkboard to give him better news.

He woke up. He drank tea that sometimes tasted like coffee. Still not a chirp from his augur. He'd even taken to keeping it at his bedside in the hopes it might wake him from any dreams that might be memories. That, or nightmares too immersive, too memorable to distinguish from them.

The moon was bright that night. Deja sat sideways on his couch and stared up at it through the small window. He took a sip of strong tea from a chipped mug and cradled it between his chest and bent knees. Steam tickled his throat. He touched a hand to it and winced. The lifeburn had faded enough to escape notice by the time they'd stepped off the train. Jamais had seen it though.

Unless he hadn't. In which case, he'd have to have known it was there.

The thought made Deja want to hope. He choked that hope back with a large gulp of scalding tea.

Commotion on the street. He craned his neck to look out. A pair of constables were speaking to a rabbit. Deja clicked his tongue, glad to see they'd been let out of the Warren marathon meeting from hell or wherever the fuck they'd been. The rabbit held out his arms, and the Constables began to pat him down; the search came up empty. One jerked his thumb over his shoulder, and the rabbit bowed his head, scurrying off toward the Warren (presumably). Deja didn't actually know where the Warren was apart from *down*.

"Dicks," Deja muttered before taking a long, slow sip of tea.

Three sharp knocks at the door.

Deja deigned to pivot his head toward said door, not getting up.

Three more knocks. *Sharper.*

Deja took full stock of just how comfortable he was in his current position, how soft his sweatpants and T-shirt were compared to his uniform, and—

"Vale!" came Good's unmistakable, pissy voice from the other side. "Get off your Odd ass and open the door before I do it for you!"

"Yeah, yeah, all right, I'm coming... *yeesh.*" Deja stood with a dramatic groan and took his sweet time walking to the door. "All right, hold your headless horses," he said and unlocked it. He didn't bother to open it—just returned to his couch, hoping to recapture some of his previous comfort. His sweatpants were plaid pajamas now, and the mug white and smiling as it let off coffee-scented steam. He just managed one last peaceful sip before Good showed himself in.

Good gave the apartment a quick look around. It looked like he was giving thought to taking a seat, but he just crossed his arms and stared at Deja's bottom half instead. "What the hells are you wearing?"he demanded in what doubtlessly constituted a greeting in his world.

Deja shrugged.

"Right. Anybody contact you about the mission?"

Deja bypassed this and asked between sips of coffee, "You checking up on all my neighbors? Or just me."

Good's face contorted. "Neighbors? The fuck are you talking about?" He didn't wait for an answer and Deja didn't have one anyway. "Well? *Have* you?"

"Why would *I* be checking on my neighbors?"

A glare.

"Oh, right. Missions." Deja took a slow sip of coffee—no, it was tea again—and beheld Good's fraying patience over the *chipped* mug. He swallowed. "Previous or upcoming?"

"Either."

"Nope." Another sip of tea. "What is it, dude? Why are you looking at me like that?"

"What are you drinking?" Good asked, sounding almost offended.

Deja blew out a loud breath and shrugged before taking another sip of whatever his breakfast beverage had decided to be in that moment. He licked his lips and offered, "I wanna say... English breakfast?"

Silence. Then, "*Why?*"

Deja shrugged again.

Good's eyes narrowed. "Right. So you haven't heard from Vex."

Another sip of tea—no, coffee. Coffee? No, tea. Both? Neither?

"Vale?"

"Hm?"

"I said," Good gritted, "*so you haven't heard from Vex?*"

"Nope. Went over to get his sign off for replacement gloves, but I couldn't even get up the elevator. You?"

Good shook his head.

Deja paused halfway to a sip, steaming mug hovering before his pursed lips. "I thought you'd taken care of the debrief."

"I did." Good said. "With *Oathe*. I haven't seen *Vex*. So far as I can tell, nobody has."

"That's—oh," was all Deja managed to say.

Good found this about as useless a response as Deja himself did. "*Oh*? That's it?"

"Well, *no*, I'm just wondering why the fuck you're telling *me* this." A pointed, slurping sip. "*Here.*"

Even if Good were reporting on Deja to Hiero, there really wasn't much to report. Unless all she was looking for were signs the Odd was breaking down—that the cost of his Oddity was catching up with him. Deja frowned into his indecisive mug. Had that been what the patched-through communique in Toronto had been about? *Asking about the freak's condition?*

Should've figured that out sooner.

Good stared at him. "Why am I here? Because you were compromised on a mission I was leading."

"I'm fine. So, you checked on Wren, then?"

"There was no reason to check on Wren, because *Wren* is an adult who actually goes in for treatment when she requires treatment."

"Oh... yeah, actually, that checks out." Deja wasn't being fair to Good, really. Whatever issues they might have, Good was a good head agent. He cared about his team. It was perfectly in character for him to follow up with his teammates after a mission—*without* having been ordered by Hiero or anybody else to do it.

With a muttered, "Never mind," Good turned on his heel—

"Hey, Good. Are *you* okay?"

Good turned back, flummoxed. Deja tried very hard to see his mortified face as anything but absolutely fucking precious and failed miserably. "*What?*" Good demanded tartly.

"I mean, that mission. It just... it was a whole lot of not-exactly textbook stuff, and that's never really been your, uh...." Deja coughed a bit. "Have you been *okay?*"

Good narrowed his eyes. He did that a lot. *Could he see okay?* "What do you mean?" Good took a step closer, and Deja leaned back on sheer reflex. "Are you saying you're *not* okay?"

"No! *I'm* fine!" Deja said far too quickly to be believable.

Apparently.

Resented or not, Good took his duties very seriously. *Too* seriously. Had he been ordered to clean the Omega Square Reaper, he'd be out there with a toothbrush right now, silent glare *daring* anybody to tell him he'd missed a spot. With a long-suffering sigh, he tugged off his gloves and kicked Deja's bare (for now) legs to the side to make room for himself on the couch. "I'm not going to bother asking if you went to Osiris," he said, grabbing Deja's chin and lifting it to examine his throat.

"I did," Deja said truthfully, *technically.*

"*Looks* better..." Good said skeptically as he tilted Deja's chin to the side to examine his cheeks.

"That's because"—Good forced his head the other way, and Deja rolled his eyes—"it *is* better."

As Good continued his unqualified inspection, he muttered, "Yeah, I've heard that before."

That was fair. Deja's lips twitched into a one-sided grin as he was reminded of a past mission. "Remember that comic shop in Boston?"

"I remember Boston. Details like 'comic shop' really only matter to you."

"Yeah, okay. The one with the twin level-two ghosts who only ever spoke in sync then?"

Good scoffed. "Not as fondly as you, I'm guessing."

"Oh, c'mon," Deja said. "It was only, like, our third time in the field. We went in there expecting possessed toys and feral cats and afflicted cosplayers, and all we got was two *Shining* rip-offs."

"I still don't get that reference and you know that." Good grabbed Deja's right wrist, and Deja shifted his mug to his left hand to let Good do whatever it was Good felt the need to do—which was turn Deja's hand over to examine his palm. The blossom-like scar had been there for months, but now it had been joined by a newer, shinier scar: parrot bite. It glinted with a subtle sheen where Desert heat had crept through the beak-shaped hole in his glove. Good looked up at him, unimpressed. "You never thought to go to Osiris for something like this?" he asked, raising Deja's hand up like Deja hadn't been applying Q-salve to it three times a day himself.

"Well," Deja said neatly, "people usually *order* me to go to Osiris for things like this."

Good shook his head in disgust and stood. "Do you even have enough sense these days to keep Q on hand?"

Deja scrunched his nose. "Don't you think you're taking this babysitter shtick a *little* too—*yes, yes,* I've got some, yeesh. Stop looking at me like that."

Good didn't need to be told where to go. Before Good's (first) promotion to head agent, he'd been Deja's only other visitor apart from Thorne (brief as their visits were). Deja watched him disappear beyond a door and waited for the comment he knew was coming. He nodded along to it like a familiar piece of music.

"What in thirteen hells happened to your bathroom, Vale?"

When Good returned with salves, a roll of linen bandages, and an expectant look, Deja said, "I dunno... I'm guessing... somebody redecorated while I was gone?"

"Where's the M-balm?"

The truth was: *the trash*. What Deja *said* was: "Rationing, huh... what a bitch."

Good scoffed and resumed his seat beside Deja. After Deja placed the chipped mug of tea on the table, Good cast it another suspicious look. "You're on your last roll of linen. Get more." He unscrewed the salve and held out his own hand. "Hand," he ordered. "No, Vale, your *injured* hand, you absolute fucking—*thanks.*" Good shook his head, muttering, "You never use enough. It's a wonder you're still *any-where*, let alone the field."

Deja watched Good apply salve with incongruous care. The man kept his sharp eyes down, singularly focused on his task. It wouldn't have been accurate to call the experience *gentle* so much as a lack of the opposite.

"What if I weren't?" Deja asked quietly. Good didn't look up, but his hands did freeze a moment before carrying on. When Good seemed determined to ignore the question, Deja asked a more direct one: "Good? What happened to Hart?"

Good's hands went still again. He didn't look up from Deja's injured hand, but he didn't pretend he hadn't heard the question, either. "Why would you ask me that," he said, less a question than an admonition.

"Contrary to popular belief, I am aware of some of what goes on around here. And when it concerns other Odds, information has a way of reaching us. But nothing on her."

For a while, Good didn't move, apart from the tightening of his jaw. Then he said, "She was lost on a mission. An accident."

"I know that, but *how*—"

"What are you really asking me?"

Judging from Good's slightly widening eyes, what Deja said next had not been what Good was expecting. "Do you think I'm a liability in the field?"

Good stared at him. Then, he fixated on applying more salve. Just when Deja figured he'd get no answer at all, Good said quietly but firmly, "You were there when I told Hiero and Vex you were an asset to the mission. That without your Oddity, we'd have likely failed." He glanced up at Deja. "Do you think I was blowing smoke up your ass? Is that typical *me* behavior?"

"Well, no, but—"

"I don't know what happened on that last mission, But I *do* know that if it weren't for you, Wren might not have come back. And if she had, it might've been missing way more than two fingers. I don't know if that's because of your Oddity or just *you making terrible choices* so I won't claim to. But it *was you*."

"Okay, but—"

"But *what*?"

"But what if my Oddity wasn't just useful sometimes?" Deja pressed. "What if it became a liability? If *I* became a li—"

"That's not going to happen," Good cut him off, eyes falling back to his previous task.

Deja watched Good apply salve to his injured hand with obsessive thoroughness. "It happened to a lot of the others," he said. "I don't know how many. Thrall, Marion, Sygil, maybe Omen, maybe...." He left Hart's name unspoken, but Good heard it in the silence. The tension in Good's face and shoulders gave it away.

It was a wonder the man could speak at all, his voice was so tight. "I just told you," Good said. "That's not going to happen." A long silence followed. Good applied a third, then fourth unneeded coat of Q to Deja's hand. His tension didn't ease a moment. He was waiting for Deja to ask what he was about to ask.

And Deja did. "But what if it did happen? What would—"

Good repeated himself. *Slowly.* "It's not. Going. To *happen*." He looked up. "Understand me?" Deja said nothing and Good gave him a challenging look. Deja nodded and Good resumed his first aid.

So Deja sat, silent and staring in wonder at just how gentle Good's hands could be when not *dragging* him someplace. They sat in that suffocating silence until Good broke it: "What about Boston?"

"Huh?"

Good looked up from Deja's hand and so did Deja. "Boston," Good repeated. "What was so special about Boston that you just had to natter at me about it?"

"Oh, right." As Good resumed the work of anal-retentive healing, Deja explained, "I was just thinking about it is all. Probably because of the whole demented-level mix-up thing." Good began wrapping a linen bandage around Deja's hand and Deja cleared his throat. "Do you remember what level they told us the twins were?"

"Four," Good said. "Possession-grade." He shrugged. "Better to have an overestimation than an underestimation."

"Yeah, well," Deja grumbled, "I probably wouldn't have wasted my best Jesus impression on that janitor if I'd known they weren't strong enough to possess a marshmallow." Good screwed the lid back on the jar of salve. "None of that stuff bothers you, huh? Not even M-balm?"

Good wiped his hands clean. "No. Because I'm an adult. And it wasn't an Augury mix-up," he reminded him. "It was an intentional threat inflation for training purposes. A needed one."

"True," Deja said with a fond smile. "I remember Thorne went in, training mortifier blazing like it could *do anything*. Didn't she shoot Vyne in the ass?"

"No. She shot *me* in the ass."

Deja said, "Oh, right," already feeling much more cheerful now.

"As I recall, it was because you told her that's where the ghost was."

"I didn't tell her the ghost was in your ass, Good," Deja said reasonably. "Your ass just so happened to be in the way of where I said the ghost might be." Good's glower glowered harder, and Deja defended, "What? It was *dark*. Thorne apologized, didn't she?"

"*No*." Good's face might just have softened a little as he said, "She snapped at me for getting in the way of her shot. Ghost wasn't even in the room." He gave a small shrug. "After that, everything seemed less... I don't know."

"Intimidating?"

Good hummed in absent agreement.

"Well, that's Thorne for you," Deja said. "Always calming every-body else down in the chaos."

"Was," Good corrected. "*Was* Thorne."

"I know that," Deja whispered. He stared into his mug. "We didn't hear from Vex for four days after that, was my other point."

"Yeah. I remember." Good stood up. "You put this stuff away yourself, I'm not doing it for you. Pick up more bandages and get that checked while you're at it. *Properly*. Since Vex isn't around to order you to do it, I am. *Again*."

"Right. I'm sure your orders will be just as effective as—*yes*, all right, I'll go. Pinky-promise. Leave."

Once alone in the small apartment once more, Deja sank back into the couch and stared out at the green-streaked sky. He really, *really* could've sworn Thorne was still there. He took a sip of lukewarm tea and sighed his disappointment into the ghost of steam, tired of grief.

The third of the surviving letters composed by Ursula during the Saratoga Period. The letter is not dated, but it is estimated to have been composed between October 22, 1877 and January 1, 1878. The handwriting is noticeably less refined than in previous letters. This may not be reflective of Ursula's state of mind, so much as environment. Photographs of the estate show the writing desk described in diaries and earlier correspondence as residing in Ursula's private sitting room, and later bedroom, had been relocated to the downstairs parlor. The removal of a woman's writing implements would not be unheard of during this time period, particularly given the diagnosis of hysteria and the prescribed confinement following the birth of her (ostensibly) second child (see McCleary, 1964). In which case, it is possible a trusted servant secreted paper and pen to their mistress. It has been postulated that Delia Butler, however, was already deceased at this point: A fact potentially corroborated by the tone of lament and isolation permeating the following correspondence.

Cat—

That veiled woman still comes and goes. The walls feel thinner when she's here. Jackson tells me she's gone in a carriage, but I can feel her eyes on me. Despite the cold, I've had him close the flue in my bedroom permanently.

I think there's something in the fireplace.

I am so, so alone. A heart can only withstand so much cruelty before it becomes cruel in turn, and I do not wish to be cruel. You always told me it didn't suit me, and I loved you so for that. I hate to disappoint you now, but I fear the…

The letter continues, but an unknown number of pages are missing. Given the creases of the envelope suggesting voluminous contents, there may well be several pages unaccounted for. The final and only other surviving page is reproduced here:

…could do such a thing? God help me, but I believe I am with child.

Please tell no one, my dear heart.

Please tell me you'll come for me.

An empty envelope from your address is all the comfort I need—just so long as it is your hand that wrote it.

Your devoted slave in eternity and beyond,

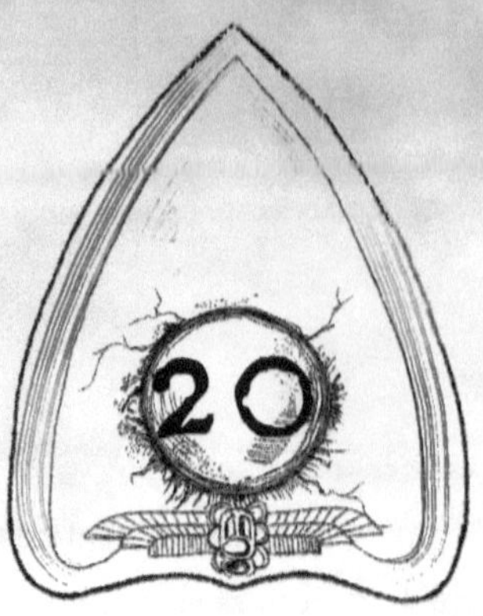

Again, Deja dreamt of his old team. Again, they were just as he remembered them. Again, they were on their way to a mission he couldn't remember leaving for. Maybe they never had, and his mind was only constructing likely scenarios from broken bits of memory and his knowledge of what his team *would* say. An author with mastery of his characters—ones that lived in his mind alone. And as he lie in his bed and stared at his augur, willing it to distract him with *anything*, he regretted tossing the M–balm. He never dreamt with the M–balm. No, that wasn't true. He only wished he regretted it: how any sane, trustworthy agent would. One last stretch and he got out of bed. Washed. Dressed. Changed the bandage on his hand. Had a cup of tea and/or coffee and headed out for Omega HQ to try again.

The fog was thicker that morning, rolling in great, green sheets along the streets. Deja passed through the shadow of the Tower that stood at the center of the Hex. An imaginary chill nipped at him until his feet reached the stones lit up by moonlight once more. A few agents and constables dotted Omega Square, but not many. They moved quickly through the green fog blanketing the place like planes through cloud: quick, sure, and straight. Deja climbed up the stairs and out of the mist. Headquarters was still busy, but not quite as frantic. Given the state of things last time he'd been there, that was a low bar. He did manage to catch an elevator this time, though.

Deja crossed the chessboard hallway that housed the agent inquisitors, carried by habit to Vex's door. He knocked. No answer. He knocked again. A neighboring door opened.

"Vale?" AI Oathe demanded. "What is it?"

"Field damage," Deja said. "I need a new pair of gloves."

Oathe stared at him, the film reel of her past whirring behind her eyes. Then, she jerked her chin, beckoning him into her office. Deja wasn't offered a seat so he didn't take one. He hadn't been in there before; he got the impression that if not for the relative chaos, Oathe's desk would be far neater than it was. Even her usually neatly pressed hair looked a bit of a mess (relatively speaking). A single lock of hair had managed to break formation before getting recaptured by her bun. She shoved a paper at his chest.

Deja blinked and looked down at it.

"Will that be all?" Oathe asked.

"Yes, sir," Deja said, already on his way out.

Again, the wait for the elevator was longer than usual. Again, it came eventually. It was a long descent to the Warren. After he passed the metaphysical boundary of Omega HQ, the lights began to buzz and flicker overhead. Deja ignored them and looked down at his form. Oathe hadn't filled out "gloves." She'd gone with "Whatever Vale needs." The unwritten, "Just do your jobs and take care of it, I've got more important shit to deal with" was evident in the agitated dash of a period.

Deja stepped onto the plain concrete of the Warren and dragged his feet to the first gate. It opened with a touch of his augur. He spared the four constables flanking the gate a quick glance, then kept walking. Then slowed.

Half the rabbits were missing.

More than half, even. Deja passed the desk of the rabbit he'd bumped into on his last visit. Empty. A scant glimpse through the next gate told him there were just as many empty desks in the next area. There could be a hundred reasons why, none of which had anything to do with their being *gone.* He couldn't see all the way to *Otherworldly Letters – Dispatch* and Desk 0044, but worry nagged at him all the same.

Unfortunately for his building anxiety, Deja didn't have a form for the Augury Requisitions Department. But then, he *did* have a form demanding he be given "whatever Vale needs."

"Yes?"

Deja jumped at the unfamiliar, harsh, *male* voice greeting him from Janis's desk. It wasn't a rabbit overseer, but a constable glaring down at him. "Where's Janis?" he asked.

"Who?" the constable demanded.

"Never mind," Deja muttered and passed up the form. "I need to requisition a new pair of gloves and see a rabbit about my augur."

The constable took the form with a *snap* of paper. He eyed it, mouth twisting. He looked around like he was debating asking some- body for their opinion on the matter.

"Do you not have the clearance for that?" Deja asked. "Should I see someone higher up?"

The constable scoffed at him. "I have the clearance," he said before adding an *"Agent,"* so disdainful you'd think it was a slur. Then he stamped the paper like he was flipping Deja off—twice— and thrust it back.

"Great. Thanks."

The gate opened and Deja headed straight for Otherworldly Letters - Dispatch. His feet knew exactly where to take him, but there was no time to marvel at the fact that his internal map of the place operated less like an agent's than a rabbit's. By the time he reached the tunnel leading to Jamais' department, he was nearly at a run. And when he turned inside to see the place at a fifth of its usual rabbit capacity, he really did run—failing to mind a drip-catching teacup in the process.

Deja stared at Desk 0044.

Empty.

The constable at Desk 0000 sounded cautious when she asked, "Agent?"

Deja realized what his face must have looked like to make one of those people *concerned* and forced his features to settle. "Yes, Constable?"

"What are you looking for?"

Still staring off toward the desk, Deja said, "Nobody."

"Can I help you find something, Agent?"

Deja held up his form and said, "Uniform acquisitions. Field damage."

"This way, Agent."

Deja followed. He wasn't much aware of what came after, but as he made his way back up the elevator to Omega HQ, he did it wearing new gloves. His feet carried him to the Floating District without his input, then ran him all the way to Ukiyo. He pushed through the curtains in the doorway and found only Yule, sporting a new bowtie and standing behind the bar with a welcoming smile like he'd been waiting for Deja to show up ever since he'd left.

"Brandy?" Yule asked, just as Deja demanded, "Where's Jamais?"

Yule's smile didn't flicker a moment. "Darling Dear's not here," he said. "She's expecting—"

"Family," Deja finished flatly. "I know." He looked toward the corner where he usually found the rabbit. There was nobody in the bar but him and Yule. A little glimmer of hope made him pull out his augur. He turned it to face the corner, hoping he might spot the rabbit reflected in silver. The surface reflected nothing but distorted lights and shadows. When he shoved his augur back into his pocket and called out to Yule, "Tell him I'm looking for him," he was already on his way out the door.

Somehow he doubted Jamais was expecting family, too.

Like the rabbit had told him: *he was nobody.*

Deja went home. He made a cup of coffee and drank a cup of tea. He got into bed. He stared at the augur on his nightstand and waited for it to tell him to do it all over again—anything to distract from the fact his dreams felt more real, more *believable* than anything else.

"MY ONLY POINT IS," Thorne said, "if the salve helps with the *symptoms* of your being a deeply weird little boy"—Deja scoffed but Thorne carried on roasting him; across the aisle, Lear and Vyne had only minimal success at hiding their amusement—"why wouldn't the salve work as a prophylactic, too?"

Deja stared at her. The shadows of several mountains passed over Thorne's expression of feigned curiosity before he demanded, "A *prophylactic?*"

A shrug from Thorne.

Without bothering to turn around, Ivy helpfully called back from a few seats ahead, "It means—"

"I know what *prophylactic* means! And *no!*"

"I think it merits testing," Thorne said, reasonably. This was met with a reluctant nod of agreement from Lear. She jerked her thumb over her shoulder toward the back of the train and offered, "I can go get you some right now."

Deja opened and closed his mouth helplessly a few times before managing, "*No.* What if it makes me slippery? I can't fight ghosts *slippery!*"

"That's what the *testing* is for," Thorne said with a tone of careful patience. Deja didn't dignify this with a response beyond a half-hearted glare, so Thorne turned to face the seats behind them for another opinion. "What do you reckon, Wren?"

Wren was staring down at her gloved hands. At the second call of her name. she looked up with a questioning hum. Thorne repeated the question; Wren considered a few moments before answering, "Wouldn't that make him slippery?"

Deja gestured at Wren. "*Thank you.*"

Wren clicked her tongue thoughtfully. "Though, I'm not sure it actually *matters* if he's slippery or not—"

"You can all go to hell," Deja grumbled.

Lear snorted from his seat. "We're going to a high school during class hours, Vale. Pretty sure we're already—"

Chirp.

Deja groaned into his pillow and reached out blindly for the augur kicking up a fuss on his nightstand. He rubbed a hand over his eyes and opened it with the other. "Agent Vale," he croaked.

The unmistakable voice of *Agent Thorne* jolted him awake. "*Come on, Vale! Time to get up! The ghosts are calling!*"

Deja levered up, breathless. "What?"

It was Good's tart voice that replied, "*I said, get up and get ready. We have an urgent briefing. Crescent Arcade.*"

Deja didn't respond.

"*Vale? You there?*"

"Yeah," Deja said, rubbing a hand over his face. "I'm here." He frowned. "I've never even *heard* of a Crescent Arcade."

"*Central Hex. Right of the Tower,*" Good said like this was information any agent should be expected to know. It wasn't. Deja had never been to the Tower. He'd never had any reason to get any closer to the Tower than walking through its considerable shadow on the way to someplace else.

After Good said, "*One hour,*" the augur's green light faded.

Deja stared blankly for a while before doing as instructed. But as he made to pull on his shirt, he noticed something odd. The shifting colors and furniture of his apartment were no longer a surprise, but the small pyramid of rolled linen bandages on the coffee table sure was. He stared down at the neatly stacked rolls, listening to his surroundings. No sounds that didn't belong. With a scoff of disbelief, Deja plucked up one of the rolls and examined it. It hadn't been there yesterday. He was sure of it.

There was no hallucinating that.

Even though somebody had clearly broken into his apartment, something like relief washed over his shoulders. That relief chased after the hope that a certain rabbit had left those there. *Jamais wasn't gone.* Deja raised a roll in ironic cheers. "Thanks, *nobody*," he said, then bit the loose end of the linen and tugged the roll down.

The job he was about to do wouldn't be nearly as neat as Good's, but when was it ever?

IF THE TOWER'S mile-long shadow couldn't lead Deja to it, the lack of constables might have. He walked the solitary paths made just a little more chill for lack of light. A trick of the mind. The temperature never really changed because, really, there wasn't one. A hexagonal arcade enclosed the area with graceful arches of white stone. The same stone surrounding the Tower like a moat made up the building, as if it had armored itself with the very world around it. Unlike the sterile white of Osiris, these stones looked too soft to support such massive heights. They were so pale as to appear incandescent. Oddest of all, they didn't even reflect the moonlight or the green of the ever-present fog.

They absorbed it.

Deja craned his neck to look up at the tower. The top was concealed by a spiral of green and gray cloud. Maybe the Tower didn't have a top. He reeled in his gaze and went toward the right. As he got closer to the gap in the arches, he could make out the series of carved crescent moons in the frieze, orbiting between big-eared jackals and crocodiles. In the arcade, his footsteps made no sound. He looked to the left. Nothing but columns. Same to the right. Ahead, though, was a passage as narrow as a tomb's.

Eventually, that passageway opened up to a small courtyard with a hexagonal pond. Though the water was black and still, it didn't reflect the light of the moon. Six white marble benches surrounded the pond, each empty.

Standing amidst them was AI Vex. "This way, Agent," he said, already leading the way to a doorway that Deja doubted he'd have ever found without help. Vex held it open and Deja stepped inside.

It was a large room, dimly lit. The space was elegant but confused, like it didn't know if it was meant to be a parlor or a meeting room. Half was filled with white leather couches and a hearth with crackling green fire. A long, polished white table surrounded by thirteen white chairs took up the other half. Just as Deja began taking note of the other agents present, something chimed from his elbow.

Deja looked down and jumped. It was a someone—or a *something*—presenting a glittering tray of crystal flutes filled to the brim with rich green aether. Their head hardly reached Deja's navel. With the vest and neat shirt tied with a bow, their uniform looked almost like a rabbit's except for the color: pure white. As was the mask. Like the ones worn by the Eyes and Governors, that mask was porcelain, giving only the barest impression of a face. As they passed Deja a drink, their stiff posture and stiffer movements gave the uncanny impression of a mechanical doll.

Deja accepted the glass—and nearly de-accepted it. The hands were porcelain, too.

Maybe it *was* a doll.

Vex said, "Excuse me a moment," and strode back out the door where he held a brief, hushed conversation before returning to the even-more-motley-than-usual group.

Deja stared down at his subtly glowing green aether. Had he actually woken up yet?

"Vale," Ever said, giving Deja a subtly amused smile. The gaslight of the sconces rippled over her pale hair and gloves. "Care to join us?"

Deja continued to stand there, staring at the scene. Four agents were already seated around the table. In the chair beside Ever was Crane. Across from her and looking surly was Good. Wren was fussing with a loose thread in her jacket button beside him with her non-dominant hand. Her right hand was hidden beneath the table.

"Agents," Vex said as he resumed his place at the head of the table; he didn't sit down.

Deja only managed to move again when a throat cleared behind him. He stepped aside and Lear moved to take a seat, followed by AI Oathe. Jolted from his shock by Oathe's pointed look, Deja claimed a seat beside Wren while Oathe sat by Vex. He leaned back and folded his arms across his chest, debating if he shouldn't close his eyes and get some sleep so he could wake up again.

No case file in sight.

Vex stared at the door, waiting for someone and looking as anxious as he ever did. Deja did his level best not to look at the porcelain figure now serving Lear and stared down into his flute of aether. So much for rationing. Eyes nagged at his awareness. The source was Good's pointed look: *Drink your aether.* Deja did. While lazily sipping his flavorless drink, the door opened. A tall masked and hooded agent held the door open for another. The second was short for an agent—even shorter than Wren. But then, they were clearly too tall to serve aether in weird flutes, so who was he to say what their role should be? The short agent stepped inside; they wore the same mask and hood as the first, but their movements were small and unsure. A rookie, maybe. Not Izik, though. Nowhere near tall enough.

The tall agent closed the door, and the mask came off to reveal Ashe. The shorter agent, meanwhile, struggled to locate the bottom hem of their mask. Definitely a rookie. And very, *very green.* The mask came off at last to reveal a pale person with delicate features and hair as white as the ethereal stone of the tower, short and neatly coiffed. Deja still hesitated to assign a pronoun as he watched them take a seat in the chair Ashe pulled out for them. Eyes moved to Deja, freezing him a moment; the left eye was as pale as the rest of them, but their right was piercing and dark. Both eyes looked unsure once Ashe left them behind to take her own place by Oathe at the other end of the table.

Vex cleared his throat. "Lights," he said, and the sconces on the wall dimmed to six tiny glows clinging to life like tired fireflies. He pulled out his silver augur, unchained it, gave it a quick polish then placed it carefully on the table, *Omega* facing up. Three taps of his fingers, and it opened, spilling green light onto the table and casting its glow upon the ceiling.

Wren leaned toward Deja and whispered, "Do ours do that?"

Deja shrugged.

"As Omega agents, you have all been chosen," Vex said. "Now, you have been chosen twice. Each of you has encountered ghosts beyond the scope of your training and returned to us intact." The deepening of the creases beneath his eyes revealed the unspoken addendum: *many did not.* "This mission is crucial not only for Omega North security, but for the very success of our dictate. Everything discussed in this room is of the utmost secrecy."

Subtle movement rippled across the table, every twitch anticipating an answer to the question long forming in their minds, consciously or not:

Are these stronger, smarter, more intentional ghosts part of a pattern?

And if so, what's behind it?

Good shifted in his chair, eyes focused on the glowing augur as its green light swirled and formed itself into an elderly woman's face. Her heavily lined skin was as pale as her wisping, white hair.

Not a what, then. A *who.*

"This," Vex explained, "is the target."

Carefully, Crane ventured, "That's not a ghost... is it."

"Indeed not. She is alive."

Oathe added gravely, "For the moment."

Deja shared an uneasy glance with Wren. Retrieving released souls was Eye work. Agents protected Potentials from ghosts, and Agent Inquisitors aimed their scythes. The Augury were the eyes who determined what souls needed to go where. There was no overlap. There was *never meant to be any overlap.* What could be so important about this woman—this *living* woman—that it merited breaking the Separation of Reaper Powers?

With that rather heavy thought came a brief ping of optimism that he might actually be getting his mortifier back. The whole world had just gone topsy-turvy. May as well benefit from it.

"This is Dr. Rhonda I. Pierce," Vex said as the woman continued to loom above them, "retired Philosophy and Religious Studies pro-fessor, and resident of Skye Chase Senior Living Community. She is expected to pass of natural causes on her ninety-ninth birthday in precisely six weeks. However, we have reason to believe she intends to pass of *unnatural* causes some time before that. *Imminently*, in fact. Your mission is to locate her before that happens, contain her, and maintain your presence *while* it happens."

Crane leaned forward, looking as confused as Deja felt. "How long will that take?"

"Our best estimate is *tonight*," Vex said. "You will be separated into two teams and move in waves. One will wait on the train while the other's in the field. As ever, you will shift the tether field as necessary." He nodded to the short stranger. "Agents Talin and Wren will manage the fields, alternating shifts. Head Agents Crane and Ashe will lead. Crane, your team will take the first wave."

Ashe was silent, but Crane had been pushed to the edge of her seat by a hundred questions. "And on my team, sir?"

"Agents Wren, Good, and Vale," Vex said. He reached below the table for a black case. It opened to reveal nine shining silver augurs.

Without Omega symbols.

Vex said, "Each of you will be issued a specially secured augur so you may remain on full augur contact. The *very moment* you locate Dr. Pierce, you are to alert the rest of your team. And"—he reached into his jacket for a large, black vial capped with a silver screw-top and held it up—"when you see signs of soul fade, *all* agents are to move in and be ready to assist in containment."

Ashe looked grave but unsurprised; she'd already been briefed.

For the first time, Crane looked aghast. "But *why?*" Crane asked. She glanced between Vex and Oathe. "I'm sorry, sir, but head agents were told many times that multiple teams couldn't be sent out at once because the—"

Oathe cut her off. "For your information, the security measures do not prohibit two *teams* from being dispatched, but two *trains.*"

"That has not changed and will not change," Vex assured her.

Just why that assurance was necessary was a maddening mystery. Clearly, the head agents had been apprised on something the rest of them hadn't and *wouldn't* be. Crane was not comforted, and Deja's surprise edged out his curiosity. He had never heard her question one AI, let alone *two.* "But why are we being brought in and not Eyes?" Crane pressed. "We aren't qualified in the use of—"

"Because, Agent," Vex said heavily, "Eyes are not *combat trained.*"

The silence that followed could have smothered a flame.

Wren asked, "Sir, how are we meant to *find* this person? We're not *Eyes.* We can't detect—"

"The professor is nearing the end of her life," Oathe reminded her. "As such, she will be more apparent to you than most of the living." Her eyes drifted to Deja in the unstated second half of her answer: *And even if she's not visible to* you, *she will be visible to Agent Sarcasm over here.*

Vex said, "And you may well find, Agent, that she will be even *more* apparent than most meeting their end." Grimly, he added, "When not concealing herself, that is."

Deja didn't like the sound of that. Judging from the subtle ripples of shifting shoulders and cautiously shared glances, he wasn't alone. The stranger, Talin, reached a hand to their right then rapidly retracted it. No clue what they might've found there that was so shocking. Gum, maybe.

Vex's mustache twitched. "Question, Agent Good?"

"Yes, sir," Good said tightly. His eyes shifted to Ever and back. "Bringing two Odds seems like an unnecessary risk. With agents spread thin as we are, Vale could be put to better use elsewhere."

Deja bit his tongue. He'd as good as *told* Good about his fears of becoming useless—of being dragged down by his own Oddity and taking the rest of his team down with him. Good, it seemed, had taken that barely spoken confidence as proof that Deja's concerns for his own Oddity were *founded.* Hells, maybe that *was* what had happened to Hart, and Good wasn't keen to watch a second Odd self-destruct on his watch. Deja'd really almost believed Good when he'd said it wouldn't happen to Deja. A foolish hope grown from nothing but his own fraying nerve and desperation.

If Good really believed he and Ever could manage to track down a still-living person on their own, he was more than welcome to try.

"I am familiar with your concerns, Agent," Vex said, "but they are unfounded."

Good narrowed his eyes. "That so, sir?"

Before Deja's anger could shift to shock at Good's insubordination, Vex raised the bar for what qualified as shocking up several notches.

"Yes, Agent. Because *I* will be accompanying you."

THEIR TRAIN COMPARTMENT maintained its dignified brass, polished wood, soft gaslight, and velvet cushions for the entire four-hour journey to Skye Chase. The lack of change was unsettling. But then, that might have just been the lingering uncertainty over everything left unsaid at the brief. A hundred questions remained: Like, what sort of soul was so important they had to be retrieved personally?

And was so *dangerous* they had to be retrieved by battle-hardened *agents* instead of Eyes?

Deja ran his thumb over the black vial stashed in his pocket. An identical vial had been given to each of them. Whenever he touched it, the questions nagged at him all over again.

What sort of living person could be so dangerous that Vex had to warn them on six separate occasions to maintain their highest level of alertness in an utterly un-haunted upstate New York rest home?

Now that the warnings had worn themselves out, Vex's eyes were closed, his expression focused. He sat perfectly still, as if reading something only he could see. Intently.

Deja's attention shifted to the only agent he didn't know. Dichromatic eyes fixated on something hidden in their gloved hand. They'd flip it over on occasion and give it a quick glance before concealing it against their thigh—where no mortifier was holstered. From time to time, whatever they saw there drew out a brief, flickering smile. A quick sideways glance told Deja that Wren had clocked the odd behavior too. Ashe, who was seated right beside the newcomer, looked utterly unconcerned by this.

Not that Deja'd ever *seen* Ashe look concerned.

A few seats down, Lear spoke to Ever. Good of him to play nice with his new teammates. "So, uh... what sort messed up ghosts did you run into?"

"One-armed bride with a thing for needles and poetry," Ever said. "You?"

"Rhyming clown. Lot of knives."

"Huh. Weird."

"Yeah."

Beneath Deja's feet, the train vibrated. Its thrum traveled upward, shaking his shoulders before morphing into a deep groan that shook against his back. Once that groan erupted into a soft whistle overhead, Vex's eyes opened and he stood. "We are here. Before Crane's team moves in, Wren and Talin will install the tether field—together. Thirteen nails. And remember, split up if you must, but no agent is to be *alone.* That is an *order.*"

Wren shared a glance with Deja before tugging on her mask. She nodded to Talin and they followed her to the door. The pair shared a few whispers, nodded in some unheard agreement, and the door opened. Deja watched them leave. The situation felt too unreal for him to be scared for her. Personally, he'd never heard of such a thing as dual tether fields, but Wren must have over the course of her more specialized training. She'd just given a single nod when Vex suggested it.

"She'll be all right," Ever said. She was giving Deja a careful look. Like Talin (and Deja himself), she didn't have a mortifier, either. Probably a matter of personal choice and practicality rather than restriction, given her Oddity. He'd never gotten clear on that. Deja could ask her more about it when he didn't have one of Vex's weary stares waiting in the wings along with one of his sighed platitudes: *You aren't being punished, Agent Vale....*

As if he had Deja's snark on speed dial, Vex looked at straight at him. "Agent, I am counting on you."

Deja's brow furrowed. "Yes, sir."

They waited.

Nearly an hour later, the train purred beneath their feet, and the door opened. Wren and Talin stepped inside, looking tired but satisfied with their work.

"It's ready," Wren said. "We got the whole compound of buildings and a fair chunk of the grounds into the field."

Talin only nodded once, silent as ever.

"Well done, Agents," Vex said, standing. "Crane, move in. One hour. And remember, contact me at the first sign of soul-slip. No suspicion or wary feeling is unfounded. You all have your augurs at full chime-capability. Use them."

Crane nodded. "Will do, sir."

Deja pushed past Good to follow Crane down the steps first. A faint scoff followed him, but he didn't spare Good a glance—just stepped down into the parking lot. The life didn't burn there like it did in so many places. Maybe it was the overcast, late autumn sky. Maybe it was the fog that lingered well into the afternoon. Maybe it was the only half-there feel to the occasional silhouettes of life moving around them in passing cars in the parking lot.

But maybe it was the linen bandages wrapped around his hands, wrists, and neck beneath his gloves and jacket. Deja did his best to adjust them through the leather.

Team One stood outside the main entrance of the two-story compound. Crane's right leg filtered through a metal trashcan as she stood and waited for Deja to gather his first impressions of the place. He took a deep breath and did just that—glasses on, first. Skye Chase really was in the middle of nowhere. It was as if some aliens had taken the four-winged compound (parking lot and all) up in their tractor beam then flown over the forests of upstate New York until they found a stretch of meadow big enough to contain it and *plop!* The wrought iron fence surrounding the property seemed like the only thing keeping the parking lot from dropping off the edge of the world and into a mass of thick fog. Deja lowered his glasses and saw dried cattails bent in a small pond, their tips trapped in a paper-thin layer of ice.

Beyond that was dark forest. The urge to look away, to run toward it, to go anywhere else, to bury himself there forever, told him it was vast. *Old.*

He could still feel that forest watching him after he turned away.

Until they stepped through the main double doors, he kept his glasses lowered. The lobby was so aggressively festive that Deja wanted to throw up. Foil glittered in red, gold, and green. *Every-fucking-where.* A fake, thirteen-foot tree stood in the corner. Shielded by plastic boughs were a dozen boxes, each wrapped in cheerful paper as garish as the garland and bobbles adorning every inch of the place. A woman sat behind a desk, subtly flickering with life. Her focus was rapt on whatever it was in her lap, be it book or phone or knitting project. A menorah stood like an afterthought to her right.

Deja side-stepped to the left to avoid her. "Place isn't exactly hopping."

"Good," Crane said. "Keep moving."

They passed the entrance to a large dining room filled with white-linen-draped tables and deep green carpet. A waiter hurriedly jogged from one end to the other—the brief flash of life hit Deja like a half-hearted slap. There was no one else. Deja searched out a clock and found one above the host's podium stationed outside next to the chalkboard advertising tonight's special: *chicken parmesan and pasta puttanesca.*

"It's three o'clock in the afternoon," Deja said. "There should be more people here." He pulled off his glasses entirely and wandered to the large cork board filled with announcements and reminders. He squinted at a pink warning that outside visitors were not allowed until further notice. Beside that was a green sign-up sheet for a bus tour of holiday lights. Two posters heralded the coming of another poster, promising a time when sign-ups for booster shots would be available. Standing out amidst the patronizing serif was a bright poster with bubbly font advertising an event with a *medium* in the Harrington-Davis Ballroom at 2:30.

The date meant nothing to him.

"If this is today," Deja said, nodding to a poster only he could see, "I think I found the old people. So, relax. I know everybody was real worried about the grandmas and grandpas."

Good said, "No one knows what you're talking about." A pause.

"No one *ever* knows what you're talking about."

Deja ignored this all too common complaint and translated, "There's some sort of event here. You know, like elderly enrichment or whatever? I'm guessing it's now. In the Harrington-Davis Ballroom... wherever that is."

"Hm. Target could be there," Crane said. "Worth checking out. We'll split up: Wren and Vale, you—"

"No," Good interrupted.

Crane stared at him. "No?" she echoed sharply.

Good corrected, "I would not advise that," tone far more politic.

"Noted," Crane said, tone far *less* politic.

Good stepped toward her and lowered his voice. "Vex—"

"Appointed *me* head agent, Good. Not you. Take it up with *Hiero* when we get back." Crane turned to Wren and repeated, "Wren and Vale, you take the second floor. Good and I will take the ground level. One sweep and we rendezvous here. And remember what Vex said: Do not hesitate to use intraworldly communications."

"You got it," Deja said as Wren said, "Understood."

He made his way toward the stairs and cast a last look over his shoulder to confirm what he already knew.

Good was watching him.

"Anything?" Wren asked.

For the tenth time.

She ran a hand along the wall while they walked, entirely missing the wallpaper vines that would have welcomed such a gesture. So, Deja did it himself. Gloved fingers followed the vines for a while before breaking off. He was only half aware of his hand's movements as he wrote in looping letters: *Rhonda I. Pierce.* A reminder, maybe.

"Vale? Anything?"

"Sorry," Deja said. "Not really, no." The compound was labyrinthine in its layout. Poor choice for a senior living community, really. According to the maps stationed outside each elevator and staircase, four wings jutted out from the main building that housed most of the community areas, but the wings weren't simple and straight. They coiled and unfurled themselves like they'd been expanded—decades between each addition—and every connection between them was the scrambled result of the horror-struck realization that they'd been building in the wrong place the whole time.

Deja stopped to squint at the fourth such map he'd found. The ballroom—or what he hoped was the ballroom—should be on this floor… *somewhere.* Maybe you had to be pushing ninety to find it like some sort of reverse-Narnia. "How much time we got?"

"We've still got a little over half an hour," Wren said. "Thirty-eight minutes, if you want to get precise about it."

Deja gave her an impressed look. "How do you do that?"

"I don't know, Vale," Wren countered neatly. "How do you *read maps in the Desert*?"

"Touché." Deja scrunched his nose at the map. "We'd probably be better off if it was *you* who could see it."

"You said it," Wren murmured, "not me."

"Wow. Go off, I guess," Deja grumbled. "Come on. Pretty sure it's down here."

"Wonderful."

Red carpet turned purple. Deja stopped, turned around, and walked into the opposite direction—no less confidently, but far more accurately. He flashed Wren an apologetic look and picked up the pace. They reached a hall with a banister overlooking the first floor that they hadn't walked before. A glance over the railing confirmed their location: They were right above the comfy seating area with the grand piano and huge Christmas tree they'd passed on the way up.

"Yes," Deja said, "this is right," and kept moving.

They walked in silence a while before Wren cleared her throat delicately. "So... did you, um, notice anything weird about—"

"*Yes*," Deja said gratefully. "Do *you* know what Talin's deal is?"

Wren shrugged.

"I mean, I'd thought maybe they—*they?*"—another shrug from Wren—"were a rookie, but rookies don't get sent out on tether duty, do they."

Wren scoffed. "Absolutely not, no. Maybe they're just a little *odd*."

Deja stopped.

Wren moved a few steps before she noticed and turned back. "I didn't mean *that* sort of Odd," she said. "But... maybe?"

Talin being a fellow Odd would explain one or two things about their whole, well, *odd vibe*. But that only begged the question of what sort of threat merited an unheard-of *three Odds*—essentially *all* of them—on a single mission. Another question came nipping at its heels: If Talin were an Odd, they were new to Deja. Which meant either they were new *period*, or, they'd been kept secret for some reason. And like he'd said: *Rookies don't get tether duty.*

Unless Talin's Oddity somehow *involved* tethers—

The meandering journey of those thoughts was cut off by closed doors at the end of the hall. Deja could just make out the brass plaque above them: HARRINGTON-DAVIS BALLROOM. He slowed his pace with a relieved sigh and said, "That's it, up there."

They came upon an alcove on their left. Nestled within, a pair of soft chairs flanked a table crowned with a potted poinsettia that may or may not have been alive. In the shade of that plant rested a crystal bowl of red and green M&M's. A man sat there—a lone sentry guarding the ballroom. He was so old, his olive skin looked like the tissue paper stuffed into so many fake presents. Tubing connected his long nose to the oxygen tank he cradled in his lap like a teddy bear. Gnarled hands shakily reached out to the bowl of M&Ms; he discarded each green one he plucked out before managing to get hold of two reds. His hand went still. Clear eyes followed Deja's as the agents moved past.

It was only Wren's whispered, "Vale," that pulled Deja's focus away. That man's soul was slipping; she'd have been able to see him watching them, too. But *she'd* had enough sense not to *look.*

After they finally passed the alcove, Deja caught a faintly rasped, "Merry Christmas." He wanted to answer, but Wren tugged his arm, all but *dragging* him away.

He slipped his glasses into a pocket and searched the area for anything helpful. Beside the doors hung a pair of large framed prints, stacked one atop the other. He edged closer. On top was an antique print of a large, stately home surrounded by dense trees labeled the *Davis Holmes Estate*, built 1833 and burnt to the ground in 1879. Beneath was a similarly old-looking map of the grounds marked with gates, forests, streams, and roads. Marker lines drawn on the glass itself denoted the parcel now containing the Skye Chase Senior Living Community.

"Anything useful?" Wren asked.

"Let's hope not," Deja said grimly. At Wren's blank look, he explained, "It's just a bunch of local history about the building, that type deal."

"Ah," Wren said. She didn't need more explanation than that. It was never a good sign when historical information shifted from Snapple-cap status to actual relevance.

Deja touched his gloved hands to the ballroom doors, letting them hover within the wood. He listened... then frowned. "There's something weird going on in there."

"If the target's in there, we can't just go flying in. Vex seems to think she'll try to give us the slip."

Deja murmured, "Which is intensely weird, but we can all just keep glossing over that, sure." He clicked his tongue and considered their options. There weren't many. "Well, Wren," he said, placing his hands on his hips. "it's a good thing Crane paired me with you—"

"I don't like the way you're saying that—"

"Because I'm about to do something Good would not approve of—"

"A-a-a-and there it is," Wren said. And when Deja turned away from the door to head back to that festively depressing alcove, Wren sighed. "Of course, you are." She folded her arms across her chest and pointedly waited *there*.

The old man in the chair didn't look terribly *mobile*, but he did seem to be waiting for something. The moment he spotted Deja, he brightened. Clear, brown eyes glittered to life beneath folds of skin and bushy white brows. Even so close, even without the glasses on, that feeble life hardly registered as a tickle on Deja's cheeks.

"Hey there, young man!" Deja said cheerfully. He hesitated, then did his best to sit in the other chair without falling through it. It took a few tries (and he just *knew* his ass was being penetrated by that reindeer pillow) but he managed it. Almost. "How are you?"

The man pulled the tubing from his nose and struggled to take a shallow breath, determined to answer. "*Tired*," he said, sounding relieved to be saying it.

"I'm sorry to hear that."

"Everything hurts."

Deja didn't know if Wren was listening from around the corner, or how much of the man's words she could hear. But he did hear her scoff of disbelief loud and clear when he asked, "What's your name, sir?"

A shallow, wet breath. "Thomas... Franklin... Fantauzzi... Jr." His lower lip shifted into a frown so cartoonishly *frown*-shaped, Deja didn't think it'd be possible for someone with more teeth. He blinked rapidly. "Didn't you know?"

Deja gave him an apologetic smile. "Sorry. I'm terrible with names." When this didn't stop the blinking, he added hurriedly, "I mean, it's such a good name. You should be proud to say it."

The blinking stopped. "Thank you. It was my father's."

Deja took a moment to slide on his glasses and confirm what he already knew. This guy was far more visible than he should have been. Only the oxygen tubes around his neck disappeared. He pulled his glasses off and hooked them on his collar. "So," he began cautiously, "Mr. Fantauzzi—Thomas. Do you mind if I call you Thomas?"

A head shake.

"Thanks. Would you mind if I asked you a few questions?"

Another head shake.

"Great. You know a lot of the people who live here?"

A nod.

"Perfect! Do you know, or would you recognize a woman named Dr. Rhonda Pierce? Retired professor?"

Thomas considered this hard. Then his eyes began blinking again, lip not trembling now so much as shaking outright. His whisper was small in every sense of the word when he asked, "You're not here for *me*?"

Deja went stiff. He nearly fell through the chair and onto the floor before catching himself. "I—no," he said. "No, I'm not."

Two fat, cloudy tears leaked from each wrinkle-buried eye. Thomas took a deep, gurgling breath; his next question sounded like it came from underwater: "*Why not?*"

That pleading, pain-stricken face wasn't why Good or Wren or Vex had misgivings about Deja's current tactic.

But it should have been.

"It's not time," Deja said. That had been the precisely *wrong* thing to say. Thomas choked out a sob and Deja tried a little more honesty. With a small, helpless shrug, he admitted, "That's... that's just not what I *do*, Thomas."

Thomas began to cry in earnest—the silent, shoulder-shaking sobs of a heart-broken child. "Tell me where I'll go," he whimpered. "Tell me there's somewhere I'll go! Tell me someone will take me there!" Thomas reached out a hand with shocking speed to clasp Deja's—and clasp it he *did*. It was a violation among violations, but Deja couldn't bring himself to pull his own hand away. "Tell me," Thomas begged, "tell me you'll *come back for me*."

A pair of M&Ms fell to the floor in a flash of red far brighter than anything else.

Deja stared at Thomas, mortified. Because he knew that no one, *no one* was coming for this man. Not if he died well. Not if he passed on in peace.

"Vale!" came Wren's quiet, warning whisper from around the corner.

With a gasp, Deja tried to pull his hand away from the shaking one, but Thomas's grip was strong—likely stronger than it'd been able to be for some time. It was then that Deja realized. It was his own hand that was shaking. "I'm sorry, Thomas," he managed. "I have to go."

Thomas released him.

Deja stood. He stared down at the oxygen tank and the swollen, trembling hand hugging it for dear death. What did he say to this man? *Bye? Good luck with the imminent dying? Enjoy your red M&M's?*

In the end, all he could think to say before leaving Thomas behind was, "Merry Christmas."

WREN WAS WAITING for Deja in front of the ballroom doors. "Any-thing?" she asked, carefully watching Deja's hands as he slipped on his glasses. They were still shaking.

Deja flexed his fingers and rolled his neck. "Nothing useful. So we're assuming this freaky professor lady can see us somehow, right?"

"Right." Wren followed the path of his eyes and suggested, "Think there's a window or something a little more discreet we could check through? See if we spot her?"

"Yeah, I was just wondering that...." Deja twisted his mouth and leaned to the side. "We're on the corner. Don't think we'll be able to reach a window, but I'm betting there's a side room or something. A vent, maybe. Let's check down there."

It didn't take long to find a vent, but it was too small to get more than a hand through. Wren murmured, "Times like these, makes you wish you were a ghost, huh?"

Deja hummed distantly, far more focused on finding an alternate route. He turned a corner, expecting to find a staircase, but found three doors instead. A quick glance over his glasses told him it was a pair of bathrooms and something unmarked that (hopefully) led inside the ballroom. "This one," he said.

Wren followed him through the door and into a storage room lined with boxes, each stuffed to the brim with decorations for all seasons except for this one. An empty box cheerfully labeled *MERRY CHRISTMAS!* in black marker sat open in the middle of the floor. Bits of tinsel and stray bits of red and green glitter lined the bottom with festive detritus. There was only one other door. Wren and Deja shared a look.

"You check," Wren said.

"All right. Let's hope we're in the back...."

Turned out they weren't quite in the back, but they were close. The last row of the audience might have been able to see him if they'd been looking, but no one was, and none looked like the target anyway. Of course, that presented its own problems—he couldn't make out anyone else's faces. When he pulled back and told Wren so, she pulled out her augur.

Deja rolled his eyes at himself. He'd gotten so used to not being able to do anything with it, he'd forgotten it was an option. Not that he was known for checking back with base regardless. He pulled out his.

"Crane? It's Wren." Wren's voice echoed from Deja's palm.

Crane answered immediately. "*Updates?*"

"Yes. Vale and I found that event and there *are* a lot of residents in there." She asked Deja, "How many?"

Deja said, "About a hundred."

"Could be she's in there," Wren explained, "but if we go check there's a chance that if she *can* see us, she *will* see us. Do we go in?"

Silence a few moments. "*Is it possible to reduce the chance of exposure in some way?*"

Deja gave a small snort and murmured quietly, "What does she want me to do, shimmy around on the floor and crawl through a bunch of living legs?"

"*Sounds like a plan to me,*" was the stiff reply.

Deja couldn't see Wren's grimace but he knew it was there. He just shrugged and waved his hand in a silent *whatever*, shooing away the last of his already meager dignity.

"Understood," Wren said. "We've got twenty-four minutes before we're due back on the train, but we'll sweep as much as we can before then."

Deja let out a single, high-pitched laugh at the word 'we,' then closed his augur with a quiet *click* and replaced it.

"Sorry," Wren said, putting her own augur away.

"Well, I'm not gonna be able to do what I said. Even if all these people are on death's door, there's too many of them. I'll have to go around the perimeter. Won't be able to see about a third of the audience."

"No," Wren said, brightening a bit, "but you *might* see if somebody gets up to leave."

"But then she might give us the slip. Isn't that, like, the whole issue?"

"Oh, right. Just...." Wren shrugged and finished lamely, "Do your best." When Deja only stared at her, she gave him an encouraging shoulder pat.

"*Right.*" Deja pulled off his glasses and passed them over to her. "Hold on to these for me, would you?"

Wren stiffened in alarm. "What?"

"I'm not gonna be able to find her with them *on*, and I don't want to risk getting them crushed or lost while I'm *rolling around on the carpet,* Wren."

"Oh," Wren said, relaxing. "Right. Well... be quick."

"Tall order, but I'll do my fucking best."

Deja stepped into the ballroom and retreated to the back corner to surveil the space. High ceilings, plush carpet, and a dozen rows of folding chairs gave the impression of a cheap church. The woman walking back and forth across the stage in a white pantsuit with a mic hooked over her ear just reinforced it. So did the closed, heavily shadowed eyes, and the dyed-blonde hair coiffed so high it doubled the volume of her head. The way she was wandering around the stage with hands outstretched like she was playing Marco Polo with Jesus was just the cheap plastic bow on the holier-than-thou present.

"I'm getting something," she said, tilting her head to adjust her imaginary radio frequency. "It's quiet... so, *so* quiet...."

The elderly audience went totally still. Sweaters stopped shuffling. Whispered gossip stopped gossiping. Cough drop wrappers stopped crinkling.

The woman gasped and whispered, "What was that, dear? You're so quiet, you need to speak louder for me, honey. Can you do that?"

If it weren't for the mission, Deja'd have shouted his own name just to watch her *not say it.*

"Don't be shy, now," the woman said. "We're all friends here. My name is Melody Grave"—Deja snorted and muttered to himself, "*Of course, it is*"—"and I'm here to listen. To help."

Deja shook his head in unseen disappointment at everyone present.

"Frank?" Melody asked, pencil-thin brows arching into the saddest, most determined little rainbows.

In the fifth row, an old woman in a Christmas cat sweater let loose a tremulous whimper.

"Frank, who are you looking for, honey? Speak louder, now, that's a good boy...." Melody tilted her massive head like a puppy hearing the phone ring for the first time. "Your wife? Is that it, Frank? You're looking for your wife? Is she here, Frank? *She is?* Where, Frank, tell me where!"

The whimpering woman pulled out a tissue and dabbed at her eyes. Meanwhile, the game of spiritual Marco Polo resumed, and Melody's hand rose, sweeping back-and-forth over the audience. The sniveling woman blew her nose—

The hand pointed.

"I'm here, Frank!" the crying woman squeaked out. "It's Edith! Your Edith! I'm here!"

Awed whispers heralded impressed applause. A few in the back row reached for tissues themselves. Deja shook his head, mouth hanging open. People sitting next to Edith began to comfort and congratulate her while Melody opened her eyes and raised her hands to the heavens. She was crying every bit as hard as Edith was. Pale blue rivulets of mascara streamed down her face just in case anybody doubted her tears.

Under his breath, Deja mumbled, "The fuck just happened...?" He gave serious thought to returning to the supply room to tell Wren *exactly* what the fuck had just happened so he wouldn't have to be alone in this horrible knowledge anymore. Instead, he threw up his hands, got on his knees, and crawled a line down the left side of the audience while Melanie Grief or whoever-the-fuck bullshitted her way through half a conversation.

Again, he shook his head to himself. "*I hate it here.*"

From what Deja could make out from the back five rows, Rhonda wasn't there. Of course, now he'd seen just what a performance from a medium actually *was*, he sincerely doubted if a philosophy and religious studies scholar would've shown up—unless for sadistic research purposes. All the same, Deja kept crawling, doing his level best to keep the sarcastic muttering and disdainful scoffing to a minimum. Once he reached the front row and found no one Rhonda-I.-Pierce-shaped, he decided Wren's plan wasn't such a bad idea after all.

With a groaned, "Fuck it," Deja stood. Brushing nonexistent dirt from his hands and knees, he studied the room. Nothing happened. Not a one reacted to an Omega agent standing twelve feet from the psychic.

Certainly not the psychic.

Apparently, mediums translated silence into bullshit for a living. *Who knew.* "He says not to worry," she said, voluminous head bobbing and swaying as she jived on posthumous beats.

"About what, Melody?" Edith asked wetly.

Melody. That was it. Deja began walking up the center aisle, scanning the rows as he moved. Behind him, Melody continued, "He says not to worry about... what's that, Frank? Oh, is she worried about that Frank? All right, all right, honey. I'll tell her, but you have got to give me a moment, silly."

Deja scrunched his nose and said, "Thinks she needs a little more than a *moment*, Frank," as he counted the old people who weren't Rhonda I. Pierce. He was at forty-three Not-Rhonda-I.-Pierces already. "Forty-four Not-Rhonda-I.-Pierces... forty-five Not-Rhonda-I.-Pierces...." He counted aloud because he was dead certain at this point that this ballroom of suckers was bereft any Rhonda I. Pierces.

"Frank says," Melody declared with the choked tone of people delivering news that the war was finally over, "not to worry about the *money!*" Edith gasped a sound of pure catharsis while Melody cried out, "Thank you, Jesus!" to yet more applause.

Deja stopped and stood in the second-to-last row with hands on hips. To his right, a small, wrinkled man in a reindeer sweater sat with an empty chair on either side of him, alone. Beady eyes glistened with such sad hope that Deja's amused disdain quickly peeled away. The shaking lip and oxygen tank between his feet ripped that disdain clean off to reveal the anger beneath. With a deep breath, Deja rolled his shoulders, assessing his own condition. For a crowd this size, the lifeburn wasn't bad. He felt remarkably *fine*. These people weren't all on death's door. *Most* of them weren't. The linen bandages must have actually been helping.

Even so, things would get a hell of a lot worse once he got up close and personal to Soulless Dolly Parton over there. He rubbed at the sudden stab of pain in his palm. His hand was shaking. He did not care. He strode up to the front, up the steps, and across the stage.

Melody's eyes were closed again. Her hands wove slowly through the air, a charmer's snake sniffing out fresh prey. The force of her aliveness prickled against Deja's cheeks like an open oven once he got close enough to touch. He placed a hand over his augur for some meager protection and leaned close to whisper in her ear, "Melody...."

"I'm hearing a... an E," Melody said. "Or maybe a—no, it's definitely an E. You gotta speak louder, honey, I can't hear you."

"*Melody.*"

"Melody," Melody echoed. Painted eyes snapped open. She looked from side-to-side then gave a self-effacing little laugh. "Sorry, y'all," she said, closing her eyes again. "Sometimes I forget they're talking through *me*." Soft, understanding laughter rippled across the room, and Melody cleared her throat, composure regained. "It is an E, though," she assured the audience, "I'm sure of that... a woman's voice, very soft, very kind—"

"*Is it*, though, Melody?" Deja scrunched his nose skeptically. "Is it *really* a soft woman's voice you're hearing right now?"

Melody turned her head sharply toward Deja, eyes opening. "Who's there?" she whispered.

"Who's *here* is the very real, very pissed off ghost you summoned with your selfish, greedy little carnival act, sweetheart."

Melody laughed and looked out at the audience. "Sorry again, y'all, I just—I'm just having a hard time getting my rope around this one!"

"Is death a joke to you, Melody? Is *grief* a joke to you?"

Melody wheeled on him and hissed, "You don't know me! You don't know what's in my heart! I am *helping* these people! They can move on because of *me*! They can let go of their regrets because of *me*!"

A hush fell over the audience.

Melody turned back to them with her best, winning smile. "Don't think this one's in the mood to chat, y'all, so let's see if we can't—"

"Find another one?" Deja suggested. "Want me to go get some? Because I can, Melody. I can get as *many as you need.* For *forever*, if you like." He leaned closer. "Because we have *nothing… else… to do.*"

A choked-off *shriek* erupted from Melody's magenta mouth. She stumbled back, just barely catching herself. Her arms stayed stuck out ahead of her like another quake could come at any moment.

Deja began moving toward her when his augur chirped at his chest. He pulled it out. "Yeah?" he asked over the angry and confused chatter rising from the audience.

Wren told him, "*Time's nearly up.*"

"Room's clear anyway," Deja said, glancing at the woman frantically slapping at her own ears on the corner of the stage. "Meet me at the front door?"

"*On my way.*"

Deja walked over to the cowering woman and bent over to say, "This is your last show, Mel. Let me hear you say it."

Melody clenched her eyes shut, shaking her head.

"*Say it!*" Deja yelled. Offstage, a few people jumped.

"This is my last show!" Melody cried out in a completely different accent. Then, she dissolved into eminently un-Southern sobs.

Deja straightened and nodded once in satisfaction before heading off the stage. Wren was walking toward the front door, oblivious to the fact she was about to walk through a long table stacked with books and pamphlets. Deja hummed in interest and walked over to it, ignoring Wren's questioning, "Vale?" The books, naturally, were all emblazoned with Melody Grave's face set amidst heavenly clouds. But to the right of those was a red clipboard, Skye Chase letterhead at the top.

"Vale?" Wren said again. "Maybe you should take your glasses back? You look a little—"

"Just a sec," Deja said, bending over the clipboard. It was a sign-up sheet for this event. Emphatically first on the list in big looping letters was *Edith Cleary, Room D-113*. One line beneath that was *Rhonda Pierce, Ph.D.*, written in about a third the size of the names that followed (and one fifth the size of poor, grieving Edith's). Unlike the majority of the other names, Rhonda's had not been crossed out. She'd never shown up. Beside that unsullied name was part of a room number: D-2—something. The last two digits had been blocked out by the first two letters of two words scrawled in the same impossibly fine print:

MEMENTO MORIEBARIS.

And she'd written it in *red*.

"Vale?" When Deja didn't respond, Wren repeated more loudly, "*Vale.*" Deja looked up. "Anything?" she asked, passing him his glasses.

Deja quickly slipped them on. When he glanced back down at the clipboard, it was gone. So were the red words. They'd been written there by the very living and very *near* Rhonda I. Pierce. Deja felt heat prickling his cheeks like life while he stared at them, wondering what else she'd written—what other impossible messages she'd managed to send him and *why*.

Why him?

Wren asked, "Find anything?"

Deja pulled himself away and shook his head. "No," he lied. "Nothing useful."

Crane and Good were already waiting beside the train by the time Deja and Wren arrived. The second wave were already masked up outside. Ever stood at the ready along with the rest of her team, easily the tallest and largest among them. Even Lear just reached her chin. Talin stood a little ways off, neck craned back, staring up at the sky as if they could see stars, but Deja saw nothing but clouds. Ashe had to pull the agent back to earth with a light touch on the arm.

Wren did the same with her own weirdo, urging Deja up the train steps.

The gaslight still cast flickering, soft shapes against the polished wood of the compartment. Vex was still seated in the same place, hands upon his knees. He gave a single nod to Ashe through the door, and the second wave moved in. The door closed. Vex pulled out his Omega-less augur, discerned something from it, and returned it to his chest pocket. "Agents," he said. "Take this time to compose yourselves. You may well need it." He began passing out vials of glowing green aether. "Two vials each. Drink them quickly."

Deja flopped onto a seat and accepted his vials with a grumbled thanks. Wren took the seat beside him and stretched out her legs, staring at her feet. It was only when Deja didn't need to focus so hard on staying vertical that he realized that the vials weren't smaller or only partially filled. They were proper vials, filled to the stopper with green, dense and dark—like what they'd been served by the creepy attendant during their brief. This abundance of aether wasn't meant to serve the restorative function the way it always used to.

It was a prophylactic.

"Sir," Crane began, "we conducted a search of the main building and found nothing. There was a gathering of some hundred residents which Vale checked. No sign of the target."

Deja felt Vex's eyes move to him—a suspicion confirmed by the "That so, Agent Vale?" that followed.

Deja nodded.

"Tend to any lifeburn now, Agent. While you have time."

Deja said, "You got it, sir," and downed the last of his vials. The last several hours had been filled with uncertainty, but that aether granted him with the same cooling relief which stepping down from the train and into the rolling green fog of Styx station always did: The relief of being home, safe and intact. He got up with a groan to retrieve supplies from the cabinet at the end of the train.

When Wren moved to stand, he waved a hand at her. "I got it, thanks," he said and went to the black wooden cabinet himself. Carvings completely adorned its surface. Apart from the pair of winged and legged eyes, some birds, and some unfortunate beetles getting poked by little dudes with sticks, most of the carvings were too tiny to make out. The cabinet opened with a sound and smell like a massive old tome falling open to the center page. He scanned the various jars, noting the unusual and disconcertingly generous supply of M–balm stocked before passing it by in favor of its less offensive cousin.

Vex said, "Use the M–balm. It's the best thing."

Deja stared ahead a few moments, jaw gritted. "Uh-huh," he said. The black jar opened with a cloud of acrid stink. He dabbed a linen pad into the *tiniest* amount of M–balm he could get away with. Keeping his back turned, he rubbed the balm along his inner jacket collar. Put some Q on there too: More in the hopes it might mask the sweet tar smell of M–balm than anything else. He twisted to look over his shoulder for the closest agent. Unfortunately, it was Good. "Hey," Deja called back to Wren instead, gesturing to his untouched cheeks. "Can you still see this shit on my face?"

"I can *smell* that shit on your face," Good said.

Deja ignored him and gave Wren an expectant look.

She squinted. "Not from here, no."

More quietly, Good said, "I can't see it either."

Deja tossed Good an insincere, "Thanks," and closed the cabinet. "Vale."

"*Yes*, Agent Good?"

Good's mouth tightened. When he just shook his head and looked away to check his mortifier, Deja reclaimed his seat.

"So," Deja asked Crane, "what did you guys find? Anything?"

"No."

"The target is most likely in her apartment," Vex said. "Presently, the second wave is searching the northern and eastern wings. If they find nothing, you will be searching the southern and western wings."

Deja subdued his unexpected jolt of excitement. The western wing was D-wing—the second floor of which housed one Dr. Rhonda I. Pierce. "And if we don't find anything either?"

Patiently, Vex said, "Then we converge back here and move in at once to cover as much ground as possible." His mustache twitched, less patiently. "Yes, Agent?"

"I wanna know just who this person is and what she's capable of," Deja said. "I mean, all we know is she's *dangerous*, but we don't know how, or why, or in what way. What are we? Cannon fodder before the Eyes sweep in?"—he ignored Crane's hissed warning and pressed on—"Do they even *know* we're here? What if we actually find her? She's not afflicted. We can't exactly mortify her, so what *do* we do?"

"You, Agent, will not be doing anything with her. *I* will. *Your* only job is to locate her, notify me, and stay unharmed in the process."

Deja stared at him. He felt the black vial pressing into his leg through his pocket. "That's it."

"That is indeed it," Vex said, holding Deja's gaze like a statue challenged to a staring contest—a statue accustomed to winning.

Good posed the question for him. "And the vials?"

"Last resort," Vex said. "One you will not need when I am there."

"But that's—" Deja cut himself off with a frustrated sound. "Who is this person? If she'd hurt *us*, what makes you think she won't hurt *you*?"

"Nothing." Then quietly, almost reverently, Vex added, "But I have *hope*." He sighed at Deja's mounting discontent. "That is all I can tell you, Agent—any of you. For now. In the event you *need* to know more, you will know more." Then, Vex turned back to Deja, his face more worn than he'd ever seen it.

And in that face, Deja heard what had become the man's tired refrain: *How many times must I tell you you're not being punished before you believe me?*

Deja only wished he knew.

THE SUN HAD SET long before the second wave returned with no sign of the target, not that it mattered much to anyone but Deja. The other team had pushed past their time limit by twenty minutes. Even so, the only way they'd managed to cover two floors of two wings was by contacting Vex for permission to split into four. Vex's mustache had twitched while he stared down at his augur. He'd relented in the end—reluctantly—but only once each agent assured him they would contact him at the first suspicion of anything amiss.

Personally.

Again, Wren whispered to Deja, "Can ours do that?"

Deja hadn't taken notice of the fact that Vex's augur was able to broadcast sound the way it had project the image of the target during the brief. He'd never been in the field with an agent inquisitor before, but was too fixated on the man himself to wonder about any unique capabilities they might have. Each, "*Understood, sir,*" and, "*I will, sir,*" echoing from Vex's augur looked like another stone piled upon the A.I.'s chest. Their collective ignorance weighed heavily. But as Deja took in Vex's lined face and tense shoulders, he suspected that ignorance was far, far lighter than the alternative.

Once Deja and his team made their own personal assurances that they would contact Vex at the first sign of the target, they moved out. It was snowing now. The sky had dimmed to a muted violet-gray bleeding black on the horizon. In the distance, the forest was nothing more than faint stripes of gray beyond a sheer, white curtain—one that fluttered in each new gust of wind.

Deja shivered. Not at the cold. At the being-watched chill kissing its way down his neck.

"We've got two hours this time," Crane said, leading the way to the entrance. "Let's make the best of it."

"Shouldn't we stick to pairs?" Wren asked. "Our chances of finding the target is higher than theirs was now."

Was it? Math was so weird.

"So's the chance she's onto us," Good pointed out. "Separating is our best option." Deja was surprised Good wasn't the one suggesting they stay in pairs and Deja be attached to him so he could keep an eye on the unraveling freak.

"Vale?" Crane asked. "Thoughts?"

Deja shrugged. "They're both right," he said, truthfully but also unhelpfully.

Crane said, "We break into four. Wren and I in the south, Good and Vale in the west." She paused. "After Vale tells us which is which."

Deja jerked his chin past the lobby. "This way." In the end, he needed to escort Crane and Wren to the C-wing before he could do anything else. Good followed him back toward D, surly and silent as ever. They passed the grand piano that served as the nexus of the residential wings. Good seemed suspicious Deja'd taken it upon himself to go the long-way-round before they finally caught sight of a long hall lined with doors—doors Good could see.

"That's it." Deja said. "I'll be up those stairs. Unless *you* want the second floor."

Good shook his head, eyeing him carefully before turning toward his hall. Then, he turned back to Deja with a sharp, "Vale."

Deja (rather diplomatically, in his opinion), suppressed his short sigh. "Yes, Agent Good?"

Good stared at him in silence.

"Great talk," Deja said, turning away—

"Wait."

Deja turned back again.

"Do we have a problem?"

"Yes," Deja said. "And her name is Rhonda I. Pierce."

"Do *we* have a problem," Good clarified. His tone made it clear he knew it hadn't been necessary. When Deja just shrugged, Good said, "Vale, have you ever considered *not* taking every hint of concern for your wellbeing as a personal attack on you and your competence as an agent?"

"*Concern?*" Deja echoed through a laugh of disbelief. "Yeah. *Sure.*"

"What's *that* supposed to mean?"

"It means I don't buy that *concerned*-schtick for a moment. At least, not concern for *me*. For everyone else? Maybe. For you? *Definitely.* And probably for whoever the fuck it is you cozied up with to get that"—Deja jerked his chin at the silver sickle pinned to Good's lapel—"back."

"Vale," Good said levelly, "you have *no* idea what you're talking about."

"No?" Deja countered, folding his arms across his chest. "Then where's Otherworldly Letters Dispatch Department Desk 0101, Good? Because it ain't in the Otherworldly Letters Dispatch Department." Deja returned Good's perplexed silence with an expectant look, like he was waiting for Good to fess up to stealing his aethereal yogurt from the break-room fridge instead of fessing up to some grand machination to grass on Odds to (probably) Hiero. The insult to his intelligence was worse than anything else.

No, actually, it was all pretty bad.

"I have no idea what you're talking about."

"Oh, I'm sorry," Deja said, pressing an ironic hand to his heart, "did you not *know* the special-secret desk number behind your special-secret messages with whatever special-secret friend dug you out of whatever demotion-hole you dug yourself into?"

Good spluttered, "What are—"

Deja took a step closer. "You *lied* to me, that's what." The response was a blank stare. "My first mission back? With Bruno the Rhyming Wonder? You contacted the Augury"—Good tried to stop him with a warning whisper of his name, but Deja plowed over it—"and told *me* that you couldn't get through. Thing is, that message was awfully long just for a rebuff. Even by Warren standards. Especially *these glory days* of open and transparent communication between worlds."

"Vale," Good warned again.

Again, Deja ignored him. "So, maybe he who lives in a glass house should worry about the stick in his *own* eye, Agent *Good*." Good's posture went from defensive rigidity to abject confusion. Deja snapped, "You know what I mean!"

"Promise I don't," Good countered neatly.

Deja growled his frustration. "I *mean* you've got no business acting like *I'm* the one who can't be trusted when *you're* the one—"

"When did I ever act like you couldn't be trusted?" Good demanded, pitch rising along with his indignation.

Deja scoffed in disbelief and thrust an arm in the train's general direction. "You *told Vex* that I couldn't be trusted on this mission—"

"That is *not what I said!*"

"It's what everyone heard!" Deja yelled.

"It's what *you* heard!" Good corrected, taking a step closer. He was close enough to hit now, temptingly enough. "Vex knows better."

Deja huffed a hollow laugh. "*Does* he, now."

"Yeah. *He does.*" Good threw up a hand. "And now here you are. For better or worse."

"Worse for you though, right?" Deja shook his head. "I don't know why I thought I could talk to you about—about *anything!*"

"You're being—"

"I'm being what?" Deja demanded. Good stood there in simmering silence, and Deja said far more quietly, "I'm sorry you lost Agent Hart, Good. I am. But I am not her. I may be an Odd, but I can take care of myself fine without you and have been for years now."

Good said, "And look how that turned out."

Deja's eyes went wide then narrowed. "Fuck you, Good," he whispered. As he turned back toward his own search area, he heard Good do the same.

Good's footsteps couldn't make a sound in the Desert, but they still felt loud. Angry. When Deja chanced a glance over his shoulder, Good had already disappeared into the hall of doors. Deja headed for the staircase to begin his own search for the woman too dangerous for Eyes.

Until he was forced to dart to the side.

Three employees in matching burgundy polos thundered down the stairs, life sparking frantically in their path. Deja pressed himself against the wall. He didn't slide up his glasses, but he did turn away to watch out of the corner of his eye.

"—just found his oxygen tank outside the ballroom, but he's not in his room!"

"Mr. Fantauzzi can't go far on his own," another said with the tone of a statement, but the desperate look of a question.

"Not for long," the first said. "And that's what we're afraid of."

A third said, "We need to call his family," but the first just shook her head.

Mr. Fantauzzi didn't have any family.

The employees disappeared around a corner and Deja glanced up the stairs—the stairs he and he alone knew for a fact led to Dr. Rhonda I. Pierce's apartment. The glass door between him and the outdoors rattled in a sudden gust of wind. He could hardly see anything in the flurry of snow illuminated by the lamp outside. A sudden flash of red drew his eyes down. In front of that door, wedged innocuously within the rubber transition strip, were two red **M&Ms**. He stepped closer and looked out at the quickening, early winter snow. Footsteps dotted the walkway, crooked and fitful. They'd be gone soon enough. There wasn't much time.

Without a second glance at the stairs he wasn't taking, Deja stepped into the night.

DEJA FOCUSED ON the snowy ground, following in the stumbling path laid by a single set of footprints that would remain a single set of footprints. The lonely trail led beyond the bordering wrought iron fence and into the forest because *of course Thomas went into the fucking forest.*

Deja didn't even know if he could pass through that fence. The snow was too thick to see the tether field properly from there. But if Thomas had passed through, Deja would try. By the time the manicured lawn became tall, dead grass and dried wildflowers that could barely peek above their fresh coat of snow, the footsteps had disappeared. He paused to catch his bearings. It was hard to see with the tall lamps behind him; they managed to make it even harder to see through the snow by cloaking what might otherwise have been a clear night with opaque mauve. Still, the forest was close now. The warning tightness in his chest—where a quickened heartbeat might have been if he'd had one—told him so. Wind whistled toward him and it whistled *from* that forest. He wished he could raise his hood and still see and hear.

It was cold. Somehow.

Deja shouldn't be here.

He bit out a quiet curse and turned around. Skye Chase was a distant lantern of dim lights: Each light a window, each window a life. Maybe the target's. Maybe Thomas had even left his own light on. "Fuck me," he bit out, turning back to the forest. "Mr. Fantauzzi?" he yelled.

Another brush of wind, stronger this time. It pressed against Deja's knees like a begging cat, pushing him back even as it urged him forward. "Thomas!" he tried again. The wind cut sharply from behind him, carving a north-western slash in fine powder. He reluctantly followed it to a gate. It was open.

And it led to the forest.

"Of course it does," he muttered. He was able to walk through it, but each step beyond that gate got harder. His rational side knew that was just because he was reaching the edge of the tether field, but it felt like it was the snow and roots slowing him down. There was no transition of thin to dense trees. The compound might just have been carved out from the deepest parts of the forest.

Deja sensed the edge of the tether field and froze. Weird that Wren had placed it this far beyond the fence. "Thomas!" he called. "It's—" He stopped short. He'd never told the man his own name. He regretted that now. "It's me!" he tried instead. "I'm here, Thomas; please come to me, I can't—I can't go further!"

A chirp at his chest. He pulled out his augur and opened it, hoping it wasn't Good demanding to know where the fuck he'd run off to. Instead, it was Wren's quiet, harried voice that spoke over the wind. *"We've got a problem."*

Crane was the first to reply: *"Talk to me."*

"Two ghosts," Wren whispered, clearly trying not to be overheard. *"Wing C."*

Deja mouthed a silent, *"Shit,"* and squinted into the forest he couldn't reach. He glanced over his shoulder; Skye Chase wasn't a distinct shape anymore so much as a paler shade of night.

Good spoke up. *"Demented level?"*

"At least a four."

A crackling hiss followed: Someone—possibly more than one someones—cursing under their breath.

Good asked, *"Where's Vale?"*

"Here," Deja said. "Wing D. Want me to assist in C?"

"No," Crane said. *"I've nearly cleared C-1 and I'm on my way."*

It was Good who voiced what Deja himself suspected: *"What if it's the target doing this? As a distraction? We don't know what she's capable of."*

The fact that Wren wasn't chiming in anymore worried him. Instead, it was Crane who pointed out, "*Anything's possible. Question is, are we being flooded out of C? Or distracted away from somewhere else. I'm contacting Vex. Good? Vale? Keep your augurs close and stay in contact. We may need you.*"

"Got it," Deja said, mingling with Good's, "*Understood.*" He closed his augur and let out a long sigh. It bloomed in front of him in a cloud of white breath. Like it was warm.

Like he was *alive.*

Deja gasped and stepped back, just in case that white plume could burn like so many living things did. Pine needles rustled overhead and he looked up. The wind made a sound like quiet laughter above him. It wasn't the sinister giggle he'd heard from ghosts in the past, but something light. *Curious.* Then, he heard heavy, plodding footsteps. A hand-muffled cough.

Well-honed instincts warned Deja to be ready. Not because he was approaching life.

Because he was approaching a ghost.

"Thomas!" Deja yelled. No response. "*Shit.*" He looked back at the distant mauve sky beyond the trees. Holding fast to the augur in his chest pocket, he stepped deeper into the forest. The snow felt a foot deep, not that he was walking in it. Another step. "Thomas!" He stopped to listen. More of that laughing wind dancing in the treetops, but no more crunching steps. No struggling lungs.

Without understanding just why he did it, Deja put on his glasses, whispered, "Hello?" and stood still, listening.

The wind laughed louder, then—*whooosh!* It *swept* across the tops of the trees before rolling downward to the right. Its winding path lit up a faint, vein-like glow within the snow. A glass votive catching the light cast from the soil beneath it.

Louder, Deja called, "Hello? Where's Thomas?"

Footsteps again—quick ones. Nimble. *Small.*

Deja shifted to face them only to become convinced they were retreating into the opposite direction entirely. In the wake of the pitter-pattering, glittering lights flickered then died. It was behind him now. He turned again. "Please!" he said. "*Please*, take me to Thomas!"

A wheeze. Deja struggled to lift his feet to follow the sound. He only made it four steps before the weight became too much, but that was all it took to reach the crumpled, gray shape in the snow. Over his glasses, he saw Thomas on the ground, eyes clenched shut, clinging to a thick oak tree like a child to his mother's skirt. Both legs splayed out beside him at awkward angles, useless now anyway.

Thomas was alive.

Deja pulled off his glasses and slipped them into his pocket. Now, he could see the frozen tear streaks shimmering in the crevices of Thomas's face. "Thomas?" he whispered.

Thomas didn't open his eyes. He let out a small whimper and shook his head, lips floundering for a word or sound that could capture what his hunched shoulders and clinging fingers already screamed at anybody willing to look.

Deja hesitated, then knelt beside him. He reached out and placed a hand on Thomas's shoulder—really *on* it. The moment he registered what he'd done, the cold snow made itself known against his shins and knees. And when he next spoke, his words erupted in a plume of white before him. "Thomas," he said. "Can you hear me?"

Nothing for a while. Then, the weakest little nod.

"Good," Deja said, smiling in spite of himself. "You know, you'll catch your death out here, young man."

Thomas opened his eyes, barely. "You came back."

"Yeah. I was worried about you, buddy." Deja forced some humor into his voice. "You sure look like you could use a drink, Thomas."

"Tommy," Tommy corrected. He took a deep, wet breath. Deja could see the struggle behind the words and listened closely. "Growing up... my mom and... and pop... and sisters and... and friends all... they all called me 'Tommy.'" He nuzzled his cheek against the bark. "Don't know why... why they *stopped*."

"I'll call you Tommy," Deja said. There weren't protocols written up for this. It was such a departure from anything anyone thought an agent might conceivably do. Even so, he had the sense that this was a violation—a taboo he was about to stomp on and grind into the snow with his boot heel. He did it anyway with one deceptively simple phrase. "My name is Deja."

"I'll... have... a beer, Deja," Tommy said with the ghost of a smile. "Or... maybe... hot cocoa."

"With marshmallows?"

A small nod. Then, a frown. "Deja," Thomas echoed. "*Déja vu...* doesn't suit you."

"No? What would *you* suggest?"

Tommy smiled at him with his eyes, humming thoughtfully. The pain seemed to be less now. More bearable. "Maybe..." he wheezed, "maybe... something... Jewish."

Deja breathed out a laugh. "Something *Jewish?*"

"My wife was Jewish. You remind me of her." Speech came far more easily to the man now—he was slipping. The words were still wheezing, still weak, but they flowed like they came from an antique woodwind instead of a scarred throat. They *weren't* just coming from a throat. Not anymore.

"How so?" Deja asked.

"You're funny... and dark like her. And you care. But you don't want people to know how much. You think they'll use it to hurt you... but not everybody does."

Deja smiled sadly. "Not you."

"No," Tommy agreed, reaching out a gnarled hand. "And not you."

Deja took that hand in his and held it fast. Its twin laid mirrored in the snow, unmoving.

Dead.

Gone.

No, not gone. And not just an echo—demented or otherwise. Even if Tommy were just an echo, Deja was not deaf to the sound that had given birth to it. But that didn't matter. Because Tommy was here. *Right here.*

Deja squeezed Tommy's hand in his.

"My boy," Tommy whispered. "He'd have looked just like you."

Deja did his best not to react to that and asked instead, "When did she die? Your wife."

"Hannah died ten years ago. I was supposed to go first."

"And was that your idea? Or Hannah's?" Deja laughed when Tommy did.

"Hannah's," Tommy said. "She had all the best ideas." He held Deja's hand tighter as he got stronger. "Had three kids: Thomas, Isaac, and Suzanne. Such *good kids*."

Deja's smile faded. He reached for his glasses and looked through them a moment. He'd expected Tommy to look younger for some reason, but he didn't. "When did they die?" he asked.

"We lost Isaac when he was just a small thing," Tommy said. "Not even three." A drowning breath. "Tom died overseas. Suzanne died just two years after her mother. Cancer." His lip wobbled. "Did anyone come for them?"

Something about that moment—that face, that forest—wouldn't let Deja lie. He watched Tommy struggle to breathe and took a deep, shaking breath of his own. "Came for *you*, didn't I?"

Thomas relaxed at that, eyes smiling with every wrinkle he had. "You sure did, Isaac. We always knew you would." A wheeze. "We always prayed you'd be the one to come for us."

The fat tears rolling down Tommy's face warmed Deja's own cheeks. "Of course I did, Pop," he whispered. It didn't feel like a lie. It wasn't true. But it wasn't a lie.

Wind rustled overhead, shifting the snow beside them.

"My boy," Tommy said, voice already fading into that laughing wind. "My beautiful, kind boy...."

Snow drifted beside them in a whisper.

Thomas Franklin Fantauzzi Jr. was gone.

Deja stared down at his own hand, empty of all but a few snowflakes. Then they, too, fell through his glove. They joined the snow that had already gathered on Tommy's waxen hand, unmelting. Beneath the snow, soft light danced across the forest floor like it was tracing a dozen trees' roots. Soon that was gone, too.

Deja looked at the empty shell of a man for a long time. The cold wasn't aching his knees anymore. He stood. It was even darker now. All that guided him out of the forest was the echo of a child's laughter tickling his back. At the gate, he lowered his glasses to search out the distant, lantern lights of the windows.

He smelled the chalk before he spotted it.

Hundreds of white symbols spiraled up each iron bar like coils in a rope. The smell brought with it a deep, visceral *fear* and he stepped back—then stumbled. There was something by his foot. Something not of the living world. He bent down and picked it up. It was a shard of black slate the size and shape of his palm. Written in delicate chalk lines was one word:

Goodbye.

Another quiet laugh echoed from the forest. Deja slipped the slate into his pocket and kept moving. The walk back got harder and harder even as his steps came easier. Tommy's final footsteps had been erased by then; Deja had to retrace their memory back to the D-wing. It may be some time before anyone found Tommy out there in the forest beneath the snow. He tried to calculate just how long it would take as he made his way back to where he was meant to have been but wasn't. Because he'd been watching a child who'd never meant to *grow up* let alone *grow old* die alone in a forest.

Halfway there, Deja stopped in the snow and looked up. According to the maps, there were fourteen apartments on each floor of D-wing, seven on either side. Good must have been nearly done with his sweep and close to wondering where Deja'd gone. Suspicious, probably. Right to be, honestly.

Deja could always claim to be taking more time because he was able to be more thorough. Of course, that should also make him quicker; a glance at a piece of mail should tell him if he was in the right place. His augur chirped furiously against his chest.

A window lit up in the night.

Deja tightened his hand around the chirping augur like it might've opened itself if he didn't keep it closed tight. He looked up. In the last apartment, D-213, a curtain had been drawn back. Staring down at him was Dr. Rhonda I. Pierce. Only, she wasn't hiding from him.

She was *beckoning* to him.

ONCE INSIDE, Deja pulled out his augur. "Yeah?" he responded on his way up the stairs of D-wing.

"*Vale!*" Crane said. "*Where in hells have you been?*"

Deja winced. "Sorry. Technical issues." He didn't give the apartment doors on either side of him so much as a glance and shot straight toward the last door on the right. He opened his mouth to ask for an update but was cut off by Wren's urgent, "*Tether field's just inside the fence. Should I close it in?*"

Vex responded to that, but Deja couldn't hear it.

Tether field's just inside *the fence.*

"*You still there, Vale?*"

"I'm here." Deja slowed his pace as he approached D-213. "I'm still on the second floor of D, what's going on?"

Ever said, "*Five ghosts just came out of nowhere, is what's going on.*"

Deja stopped. If the other team had been called in, the situation had gotten serious. He continued walking. "And the target?"

"*Not here,*" Lear said.

Deja stopped outside the door to D-213. The little plaque glinting in an almost welcoming brass confirmed it as the Pierce residence. "And Good?" he asked.

"Here."

Only, the response hadn't come from his augur. It had come from the other end of the hall.

Deja slid his glasses down, keeping them perched halfway on his nose. Good was striding toward him. Deja snapped his augur shut and returned it to his pocket. "Everything all right?"

"Where the *fuck* have you been?" Good demanded.

"Locating the target...?" Deja said, rather proud of himself for saying something true. If he was going to get out of this with his augur, he was going to have to share his intel. "She's in here," he said, jerking his head at the door to D-213.

Good was silent a few moments. "You're sure?" he asked. When Deja nodded, Good took three quick steps forward, just within reaching distance. "And why am I only hearing this now?"

"*Lower your voice, Agent Fuck-face,*" Deja hissed. He dared a tinge of satisfaction when Good looked chagrined—even nodding agreement. "I just found it, all right?" he whispered. "And like I said, I've been having technical issues since I came up here. I'm lucky I got as much communication as I just did. If I had to guess"—he nodded pointedly to the door—"it has something to do with whatever's in there."

Good couldn't argue with that. Especially not after he opened his own augur only to find it as unremarkable as a pocket watch.

Lucky that.

"You get a range on the interference?" Good asked, voice quiet.

"No. I figured the interference could be intentional, so I didn't want to leave the floor unsupervised. Figured my babysitter would turn up eventually. Surprise surprise, I was right."

Good didn't respond to that. He eyed the door. "Look weird to you?"

Deja looked over his glasses to see what Good saw: The door was only glowing along the bottom. As if it wasn't the first time he'd noticed, he said, "Sure does."

Good slowly reached out a hand, hesitating a moment before placing just two fingertips to the door. They didn't pass through. He made a frustrated sound and stepped back. Then, he stared down at his augur, opening and closing it five times. Once he closed it with a sixth and final *click,* he said, "I'm going to the end of the hall to see if communication's restored. *You*"—he pointed a stern finger at Deja—"stay here."

"*Fine*," Deja said. When Good didn't leave to do as he'd just so resolutely declared, Deja raised an eyebrow. "You want me to go instead, sweetheart?"

Good's only answer was to turn on his heel and jog down the hall.

Deja rolled his eyes and turned back to the door. It didn't look less weird *over* his glasses. Hundreds of iron heads from hundreds of iron nails lined the border.

Hell of a way to lose your security deposit.

He pushed up his glasses and placed a hand to it, just beneath the small brass plaque. It didn't feel like paneled wood. It felt like a *wall*. That is until he whispered, "*Memento moriebaris.*" After that, it felt like nothing at all.

He stepped through.

Good's panicked shouts were hardly more than a whisper on the edge of his consciousness before the sound was choked off entirely: "Vale, Stop! No! *Deja*—"

Then, there was only music.

Bells chimed. Deja looked at the door he'd just stepped through. First over, then through his glasses. Both showed hundreds of white-chalk symbols radiating outward in a spiral from a single hexagram in the center—each one as neat and cramped as those he'd found on the iron gate bordering the forest. Inside the hexagram were larger drawings. A pair of eyes, one closed, and one open. The open eye had been covered in a twelve-pointed star. Beside those were six small sickles. He reached out to one—

"Leave it."

Though quiet, that hoarse voice echoed with a hundred million lectures, shouts, arguments, pleas, cries, and whispers.

So, Deja left it. He retracted his hand. Good was still calling out variations on *Deja Vale* between bangs on the door, both sounds as feeble as a moth's wings.

"He can't get in here," the voice continued over the fading names. "None of them can."

Deja pulled off his glasses, wondering if he hadn't stepped through some portal and into another building entirely. Gone were the ubiquitous white walls and beige carpets. Instead, the floor was solid wood, and the walls a fine indigo paper emblazoned with golden vines, flowers, and beetles. The ceiling was higher than it ought to have been, but maybe that was just an illusion, a trick played on the eye with black paint and dangling, brass astronomical instruments. He reached up and touched one. It teetered gently in its orbit as hollow planets shifted from one season to another.

Old bat was *definitely* losing that security deposit.

A brittle cough. "Are you done? Hurry on in, then. I'm not paying to ward the whole wing."

The voice came from a high-backed, green velvet chair, nestled amongst a dozen tall, wooden shelves packed to overflowing with books. The chair faced a crackling stone fireplace which Deja was pretty sure nobody else had. All he could see of the chair's occupant were a pair of fuzzy bunny-slippered feet resting on an ottoman, and three taut strings connected to the three balls of yarn rolling perilously close to the fire: one black, one white, one red.

"Give me a minute, boy. I need to get this finished by Christmas. The baby will be wanting it soon."

Deja made his way deeper inside, warily eyeing the carved wooden masks that covered the entire wall above the sideboard to his right. Most were young women, their small features painted white, and crowned with fine, black hair. They changed with the light as he moved—coy smiles shifting to menacing laughs and back again. Some were yellowed old men with wisps of white beard. Others were gar-ishly painted, horned, and wild-haired. He eyed a red one on the top row. There was something naggingly familiar about the bright paint, gold leaf, and cartoonish features. Only one mask looked to represent a child, and it was the most unsettling of all. As Deja held its empty gaze, he thought he might just hear laughter. Not light like the laugh-ter in the woods, but something smirking. Something predatory.

Without even intending to, Deja's hand reached for it.

The laughter got *louder*—

"I wouldn't touch that," the voice warned. "Lucy gets tetchy. Only listens to her papa."

Deja forced himself to step back and took in the blank spaces on the wall. Assuming Rhonda kept things as neat as her handwriting, six of thirty masks were missing. He wandered over to the large table cluttered with open books (with as many handwritten notes as typed words), twin microscopes, glass-encased specimens... a dozen petri dishes filled with dirt. He eyed the black leather-bound notebook stamped with peeling silver initials:

R.I.P.

Resting atop was some sort of dried plant. Brown and velvety with fan-shaped paper petals edged in variegated stripes of purple, deep brown, and white.

"*Trametes versicolor.* Turkey tail fungus."

Deja nodded an acknowledgment nobody could see and continued surveilling the table's more literary contents. Two peeling brown volumes from The Complete Works of Charles Dickens were being used to flatten some newspaper; *The Collected Papers of Joseph Lister* prevented him from seeing which works those volumes contained. Six identical books were stacked with neat, glossy black covers facedown. The binding read:

THE SARATOGA SPIRITUALIST SOCIETY:
AN ANTHOLOGY OF PRIMARY SOURCES
by RHONDA I. PIERCE, PH.D.

Deja's brows went up as he read the back cover copy where other scholars lauded the ambition of the work, and thirsted over what a breakthrough it was for a dozen different fields. The blurb noted that the author was a direct descendent of the founder of the Saratoga Spiritualist Society himself, Professor Abraham Jude Davis Holmes.

Davis Holmes... Where had he heard that name before?

Framed pictures hung from every wall in clusters like lichen on a rock face. One smacked him upside the memory when he recognized it— the same one hung outside the ballroom. This print of the Davis Holmes estate might just have been original. Beneath it was a technical drawing: A patent for some sort of agricultural equipment. He had to squint to make out the tight cursive:

WHEAT GIN. JOSIAH M. DAVIS. 1793.

His eyes were drawn to the thing like a horrible accident. There was something grotesque about all those tiny decapitated scythes, trapped within a mess of metal bolts and gears.

A dry cough from the chair. Then, "Damned thing never worked right."

Deja straightened. He gave the incongruous cat doll dressed in an elaborate Victorian dress a passing, wary glance. "Dr. Pierce, I presume?"

"I don't have office hours anymore, boy."

Deja took cautious steps until he could finally see the woman cradled within the chair, *knitting.* She was small, pale, and wrinkled as a well-explored map. Her hair was so thin and white it looked more like a trick of the light than anything else. Four needles pinned it behind her head in a careless bun; when a few strands managed to escape, she blew at them, too engrossed in her knitting to use her hands.

Deja bit back a scoff at this *utmost threat.* A scarf halfway to creation wriggled in her lap: white and black rabbits on a field of red.

"I can't do sweaters," Rhonda warned as if the disembodied Omega agent had been about to request one. "Too finicky. Me, I like a rectangle."

Deja spotted a pouf stacked with books, crowned with an atlas of the Amazon rainforest. He almost reached out to move them, then rolled his eyes at himself. He, being incorporeal, took a seat inside them. "Seems pretty finicky to me."

"I can do *patterns* just fine," Rhonda said. "It's tubes I don't like. People've got their own tubes, see, and they're all different lengths and sizes."

"Sounds like a real pain in your tubes."

Rhonda snorted and looked up with clouded blue eyes that might have been another color entirely decades ago. She returned to her knitting. Needles *clicked* and *clacked* in an ensemble with the crackling logs and the tower of a grandfather clock in the corner.

Crickle crack.

Tick tock.

Click clack.

Deja stared into the fire, listening.

Crickle crack.

Tick tock.

Click clack.

Something *jabbed* Deja in the ribs, and he stood, turning rapidly. Rhonda warned, "Mind the books."

Deja stared down at them. "Yeah," he said. "I'll do that." He abandoned his seat and approached the fire. A row of statues lined the mantelpiece. Five footless terracotta people with matching painted smiles and closed eyes stood there, each holding a different object: a basket of fruit, a basket of wheat, a hammer, a basket of coins, and an urn. The one carrying the coins had a neatly braided ring of red yarn around her neck; the end dangled down to her fused legs. The absence of a sixth statue was betrayed by the gap and dust-free circle it had left behind.

Crickle crack.

Tick tock.

Click clack.

Sputtering flames disrupted the rhythm of the room. Inside the fireplace, shards of terracotta were scattered among the wood and ash. Deja could just make out a painted smile through the fire.

It had been carrying a lamb.

"What are these things?" he asked.

"Shabti dolls," Rhonda said, taking on the tone of a teacher tired of answering the same question for the hundredth time (a tone Deja knew well). "The ancient Egyptians believed they'd provide their servitude in paradise. Lighten their burdens in the Field of Reeds."

Deja muttered, "Hardly seems fair."

Crickle crack.

Tick tock.

No *click clack.*

Rhonda stared up at him, brow pinching into a dozen new creases. "Why not?"

Deja's brow pinched, too. "Why not?" he echoed. "Where's *their* paradise?"

"Perhaps their idea of paradise isn't like yours," Rhonda countered neatly. "Spend more than an hour around here, and I think you'll find most people will happily sacrifice reeds, milk, and honey so long as they know *they will be.*"

Deja scoffed and turned back to the statues. They smiled back at him. "Yeah, well... ask them again after a year or two of *being slaves.*"

"It'll be the same," Rhonda said simply.

Deja glanced over his shoulder. "You seem awfully confident."

"Of course I am." Rhonda jerked her head at the mantel. "They all watched me throw *that* one into the fire." Deja stared at her. Rhonda stared back. "You hear me, boy?" she said, her voice a low quake beyond the reach of the *ticks* and *tocks.* "They *watched.*"

Deja returned to the relative sanctuary of terra cotta smiles. The Shabti had seemed so happy before. He wanted to look away but didn't. The flicker of flames made those smiles seem so, *so real.*

And *scared.*

It was only the distant but decidedly heavy *thuds* against the door that pulled Deja's eyes from the painted smiles and terrified eyes. Two of them. Good had found back-up. But if the others were shouting Deja's name, it was only Good's muffled '*Vale!*' that he could hear—and barely.

Rhonda shook her head to herself as she knitted and pearled a black rabbit's tail. "They won't be getting in here," she said. "Eyes tried... got close. *Agents,* though... *agents* have about as much chance as Anne's toy poodle next door." She tutted and added, "Blasted menace... scratching up my door. Shouldn't let the thing get out, but does she listen? No. That's the problem with children these days: They *never listen to sense.*"

"Right...." Deja leaned against the mantel. "Missed you at the psychic shit-show, by the way."

"I'll bet," Rhonda muttered. "There is nothing the living cherish more than the dead, boy. It's an unrequited love, of course." A few more stitches. "Whose bones did the vulture pick on?"

"Edith. Told her not to worry about the money."

"Don't worry about the money—of all the—" Rhonda shook her head, tutting. "Woman's living off her husband's pension. Tanked a few months back. Well's gone dry. She's got another month before they kick her out of this place, at most." Her head kept shaking, keeping time with the *tick-tock* and *click-clack*. "Vultures."

"Why do you stay here, then?"

"It's defensible enough and the food's all right," Rhonda said. "Besides, it was here or the coast. Can't stand the smell of the ocean." After another few stitches, she muttered, "Like salty piss."

"*Defensible*. How so?"

"Find it hard to believe you don't know," Rhonda said, looking up at him. She dropped her knitting into a basket and stretched out her bunny-slippered feet.

"Believe what you want," Deja said with a one-sided shrug. "Still don't know."

Rhonda squinted, scanning his face like it held as many symbols as her front door. "Why did you say those words at my door?"

"I read them by your name," Deja said. "On the clipboard."

"I'm certain you did, that's not what I asked." Rhonda stood with a groan. The top of her white head barely reached Deja's chest. "What do those words mean to you?"

"I was just about to ask you the same question."

"Hmm...." Rhonda's eyes were no less suspicious but became far more knowing. "They did a real number on you, boy."

"Excuse you?"

Rhonda lifted herself onto her toes, peering up at him. Deja fought against his reflex to lean away. "Yes, sir," she grumbled. "A *real* number."

And with that, she shuffled her way to the table and shifted the stacked books to reveal a kettle and a cutting board bearing four large mushrooms, long-stemmed and white. Each had a fluttering white collar near the top of their stems that reminded Deja of the little capes Osiris attendants wore. Half of one mushroom went into a gold-veined (and possibly broken) black teapot along with something that might've been *dirt.*

"Tell me," Deja said, following Rhonda to the small kitchenette. "What does 'memento moriebaris' mean? Why do I keep seeing it?"

Rhonda hummed in interest as she filled the kettle. "*Do* you now," she said ironically. "Well how about that."

"Please. Is it—you're the first person I've met who sees it too, and this whole time I just thought—"

"You were going insane?" A laughing cough. "Of course, you're insane. You're insane because they *made* you insane."

"What does—what does that even *mean?*" Deja demanded, throwing his hands in the air. "Why is it I'm the only agent who sees it?"

"Because they're not like you, and you're not like them," Rhonda said like she'd been asked to explain to a toddler why they couldn't have ice cream for breakfast every day. "And yet, you're really all the same in the end. Pass me that jar of—never mind. You people are useless." After she set the kettle on the stove, she mused, "I suppose the trains change around you. Elevators, too."

"Yeah...? They do that around everybody."

"And the people? Have *they* started changing yet?"

"What? I—"

Rhonda sliced through his confusion. Her voice bore all the certainty of a guillotine. "Tell me, boy—who's that man outside the door? The one calling two of your names? The one you can *hear?*"

The instinct to shield that name was strong—far stronger than Deja's knowledge that he was probably trapped here. But when he only gritted his jaw, Rhonda took that as her answer. Moreover, it was an answer that made her nod like a cynic pleased to see the world burning according to her predicted schedule.

Deja's defensiveness didn't have time to take root before Rhonda asked, "Do you *dream?*"

"Everyone dreams."

Rhonda gave a patronizing little hum. "Mhmm...."

"*The fuck!*" Deja recoiled from the knitting needle she'd just jabbed into his hip.

"Hurts, doesn't it!" Rhonda said, slipping the needle back into her bun. "Do you drink much, then? Eat much?"

Deja's face scrunched in confusion as he rubbed at his hip. "The fuck does that have to do with—"

"You do, don't you?" Rhonda pressed. "You age, I can see that, and I won't be the only one." She stepped closer. "What else do you do, eh?" The loudest "*Deja!*" yet sounded from the hallway outside. Clouded eyes ghosted to the door then back again, returning with a curling, satisfied look. "Tell me, *Deja...* what other *hungers* do you chase in that broken shadow world?"

Deja stared at her, silent. Something like shame washed over his shoulders as Good called his name again. The voice came less from the door than the knowledge that Good had called out for him. So did the two muffled mortifier shots.

Rhonda didn't so much as flinch at the weapons firing; she just kept casually preparing her forest-floor tea. "Yes, sir... you're really all the same in the end." The statement had the feel of an oft-sung refrain. The extra creases on her mouth, though, hinted otherwise.

With a sniff, Rhonda set her tea aside to steep. "Why did you go into those woods?"

"I don't know, Rhon-Rhon," Deja replied smoothly, "why did you graffiti up that gate?"

Rhonda grabbed a small aluminum can and placed a gnarled finger on the pull-tab, threatening to pull the trigger. "Answer me, boy."

Deja scoffed.

Rhonda opened the can with a metallic *rip.*

Deja opened his mouth to retort but stopped short. *Paralyzed.*

A black cat hopped onto the counter and stared at Deja. A series of meows from his feet told him at least three more cats had come into the kitchen. His eyes followed the cat to the floor. He had no choice but to watch Rhonda spoon cat food into six mismatched bowls, kicking himself for not smelling the signs before.

Unless she'd cloaked them somehow.

Once the cats became singularly focused on their dinner, Deja stumbled, freed from their gazes. His breaths came in gasps and he backed against the wall.

Rhonda held up a foil bag of treats featuring a cartoon mouse and threatened, "Don't test me, boy. I *will* shake these." Then, she sighed down at the chubby white cat with brown patches; it sat in the corner, staring at the cabinet wall. "That one didn't take from the off," she said, ruefully eyeing the cat. She nudged it with her slipper, and it began eating dust bunnies off the floor, purring like mad all the while. "Between you and me, Mr. Buffins has never been *all there.*"

Deja struggled to swallow. "*How* many agents were sent after you last time?" he asked, counting six cats.

"Six," Rhonda answered, smirking. "Or *three*, depending on who taught you to count." She held up the bag of treats again. "Well?"

Deja's jaw clenched. "What was the question?" he gritted.

"Good lad." Rhonda placed the treats on the counter and poured herself a cup of tea. It smelled how it looked—like dirt. "Chaga... among other things," she said as if *that* was what had Deja in a querying mood. "Foraged it myself."

Deja stared at her.

"I asked," Rhonda repeated, "why you went into those woods?"

Deja took a deep breath and said, "I was looking for Thomas."

"Figured that. Why the hell would you do that? You trying to earn your wings or something?" When Deja rolled his eyes, her mouth curled into a satisfied smile. "You got that reference... didn't you?"

Deja didn't answer.

Rhonda bobbed her head and continued, "Don't get me wrong, it made for an interesting experiment. But what *compelled you*?"

Somebody fired their mortifier at the door, and two cats glanced over their shoulders. One froze Deja in place for a moment before it lost interest and resumed eating.

"I don't know," Deja admitted.

"*You don't know.*" Rhonda hacked a dry cough into her shoulder and took a slow sip of tea. The steam cradling her chin looked more solid than her thin hair. She smacked her lips, cloudy eyes narrowing at him. "What happened out there?"

That earlier shame crept back, warming Deja's cheeks. He couldn't say why. "Nothing," he said. "We just talked."

"Do that often, do you?" Rhonda asked. "Talk to the living? Bet they just *love* that." At Deja's pointed look, she barked a laugh that summoned a coughing fit. Between wheezes, she managed, "Don't know that I count."

Deja closed his eyes and sighed. "What does it *matter?*"

"Funny, I keep asking myself the same thing. You can't go back again, you know. Whatever any bright-eyed, sentimental revolutionary idiot says... you can't go back again."

"This is pointless," Deja said, walking away. "I'm leaving."

"No, you're not. But you're certainly welcome to try, *lover boy.*"

Deja shot her a last glare before striding to the door. The moment he got within six inches, the chalk symbols glowed. *Red.* He closed his eyes and groaned, "*Please. Please,* just tell me what *Memento Moriebaris* means."

"What, they don't teach you lot Latin over there?" Rhonda asked, clearly amused. "*Quelle surprise!*"

"No," Deja gritted. "They mostly teach us how to fight."

Another pair of *thuds.* The mortifiers hadn't worked (apparently), and it was back to incorporeal–body ramming.

"Oh, yes," Rhonda said. "And *so effectively,* too."

Deja stared at the door. The central sigils, the two eyes and six sickles, had stopped glowing. He blinked. "I think you need to touch up your freaky artwork over here," he said, pointing.

Rhonda scoffed and walked over to him. The humor and disdain drained from her face along with the blood. She spun on him; her words came out in an accusatory hiss. "*You didn't tell me you brought an inquisitor.*"

A voice sounded from beyond the door, as distant as though the entire compound separated them. But it *sounded.* "Reve!" Vex ordered. "Release that agent. *Now.*"

Rhonda's—*Reve's*—jaw clenched. She looked up at Deja. Disgust burnt through the cloudiness of her eyes.

Deja shrugged. "You didn't *ask*."

"*Move*," Reve growled.

Deja bowed ironically and stepped aside.

Reve drew two pieces of sharpened chalk from her pocket like they were knives and began scribbling furiously with both hands, muttering to herself, "*I am not going back, you hear me?*" The words rang like a prayer made order. A pair of scales came into being. Then, a pointy-headed, big-eared dog. Soon enough, they began to glow with the others.

Deja took another step back and watched her retrace symbols. She chased the ones that began to fade before their eyes. Whatever was happening on the other side of that door, it was making Reve sweat.

At the top of the door, out of her diminutive reach, symbols began to fade. They didn't disappear. They were rewriting themselves. The first letters that made any sense to Deja emerged:

Mind her advice.

Deja's brow pinched. He hadn't gotten any advice... *had he?*

Scratch, skritch, scratch. Reve's withered hands flew with remark-able speed across the door. The moment a symbol began to fade, she redrew it in a fury, muttering under her breath all the while. After drawing a pentagram and filling it with a web of gibberish, she let out a short sigh of exertion and stepped back to eye her handiwork. Once she noted the cats were still eating their dinner, she turned back to the door. Absently, she said, "The family reunion will just have to wait," while foggy blue eyes combed every inch of nail-pierced wood.

Then, they reached the top where the message had appeared. She frowned.

Deja followed her line of sight. The words had changed. They were bigger now, written in slashing capitals like a warning.

A threat.

LET HIM GO.

Before their eyes, more words appeared—larger.

NOW, REVE.

Reve stared at it. It was the second such message to appear on the door, but only then did it hit him. Reve had written *Memento Moriebaris* on that sign-up sheet. She could write words in front of her with her creased-paper hands and *only* words in front of her. She hadn't ever been the one sending him those impossible messages. But she could read them. She was reading one now. Because those messages weren't the hallucinations of a fractured mind.

They were real.

Just when it seemed like Reve was about to argue with her door, she let out a resigned breath instead. One wrinkled hand covered a symbol Deja hadn't noted before and couldn't see now. She was panting, arm trembling with strain. "Once I wipe this," she said carefully, not looking at him. "You will have eight seconds to leave. Understand?"

Deja held up his hands. "Wait—"

"I haven't the *time,* boy!" Reve bit back.

"Please," Deja begged. "Tell me what it means. Tell me something. *Anything.*"

Reve eyed him, face flickering with something almost like pity—affection, even. With a heavy sigh, she reached out with her other hand and pointed the chalk at Deja's abdomen. She hesitated, then pressed harder—

Deja gasped. He could've sworn that cold chalk was piercing his skin. Just as soon as the sensation had come, it disappeared once Reve dropped the chalk to the ground where it broke apart without a sound.

"Fine," Reve whispered. In a flurry, she wiped away the chalk symbol beneath her hand, hissed, "Stay out of Osiris. Never give in to forgetting. Trust *no one*. Least of all yourself," grabbed Deja and *shoved* him through the door—

Deja fell against Good and Lear, taking them both to the floor with him.

The world no longer looked like the Desert of the Living. It bore the colorless pallor of the Hereafter. Standing before the closed door with arms folded across their chest was a figure in a long, black jacket that hung more like robes. Their face was nothing but a suggestion formed by shadows beneath a massive, black hood. One black-gloved hand held a lantern the like of which Deja'd never seen before: It glowed the same black light as the Hereafter's moon. The figure's other hand rose to push back the hood.

It was Vex.

And he *wasn't wearing a mask.*

Deja stared at him. In that moment, nothing in his universe mattered more than the fact that he wasn't the only one barefaced in that Desert hallway.

Vex was oblivious to the agent's inner turmoil. He just hummed absently, one hand tracing his beard as he considered the door.

Deja scrambled for the first of his hundred questions, but when Good pushed Deja off of him, *pain* pierced his abdomen—just where Reve had jabbed him with chalk. Deja'd hardly managed a grimace before Good was frantically inspecting his gloves, then his face.

"Did she do something to you?" Good demanded while Lear got to his feet behind them with an indignant grumble. "Are you injured?"

Deja ignored this and asked Vex, "What's going on? Where's everybody el—?"

Good gripped Deja by the front of his jacket and *yanked* him back around to demand, "What the *fuck were you thinking*, Vale?"

"Agent Good," Vex warned, "time and place." He glanced at Deja, then returned his focus to the door. "Agents Wren and Talin are closing in the tether field. Agents Crane and Ever are dealing with the ghost infestation in the south. Agent Ashe is outside, keeping watch on the window to this apartment." He gave Deja a pointed look and added, "And Agents Good and Lear are escorting you back to the train."

Good spluttered in protest. "But, sir, we can't just leave you here with no backup!"

"Sir," Deja said hurriedly, "I can tell you what I saw in there! Don't you want to—"

"No," Vex said. "I want you back on the train. Now." He shifted his eyes to Good and gave him a single, firm nod. Then, strong arms hoisted Deja up.

Deja shot a glare over his shoulder at Good. "I can *walk.*"

"Then do it *faster*," Good said, shepherding Deja toward the stairs like a pissy border collie. Deja allowed himself to be pushed onward. He looked over his shoulder. Vex was reaching into his jacket for something. Deja didn't see what, though, because once they'd reached the top of the stairs, they'd also reached some sort of border. Now Vex was gone from sight, and color had returned to the world... everywhere except for the large circle where all was gray, just outside Reve's door.

He'd seen that before—

Three augurs chirped.

Good gave Deja a push. "Keep moving," he said and pulled his augur out; Deja and Lear did the same, listening. "Good here," he said, his own tinny voice backing him up from Deja's augur.

"*Oh, thank Reapers, finally—*"

"Ever?" Good hurried down the stairs. "What's happening? Crane?"

"*We cleared C,*" Crane answered between panting breaths, "*but now we've got another ghost blocking us from the rendezvous. We can't reach Vex and it's not looking good. We could use an assist.*"

Good shared a glance with Lear. "Lear and me have got orders to get Vale back to the train—"

Ever said, "*You got him out?*"

"We did," Good said, shooting Deja a look which strongly suggested he regretted doing so.

Under his breath, Deja pointed out, "We're going to be passing through the lobby to get there. Hard to avoid helping."

Crane made much the same point. *"That'll take you right to us."*

"All right," Good said. "Hold tight. We're on our way." He closed his augur and told Lear, "Get ready." Then to Deja, "And you—*stay out of it.*"

"What?" Deja demanded. *"Why?"*

"Because—just *do it.*"

Deja glared at Good and muttered, "Fine," and followed.

The distant shriek of an undead child beckoned them. Every echo of it broke apart into a dozen fits of giggling laughter that rolled through the halls like dandelion seeds on the wind: A hundred wishes blown in their direction, every one of them cruel. Deja tensed. He'd heard that menacing laughter before—just minutes ago.

He'd bet his augur that now, *seven* of thirty masks were missing from Reve's wall.

Lucy had come out to play.

Ghostly giggles lured them to the high-ceilinged seating area with the grand piano and massive Christmas tree. Huddled behind the largest couch were Ever and Crane. Ever's hands clutched her own throat. Crane's hands were empty. When she spotted the other three agents, she beckoned frantically.

They darted over to crouch beside them. Good and Lear pulled out their mortifiers, but Crane said, "Don't bother," nodding up at the balcony. "Whatever's going on with the tethers and the rest of this madness, it's neutralized our weapons, too."

Good examined his mortifier, aimed it (unwittingly) at a golden present, and fired a low-powered test shot. Nothing happened— more than usual. "*Damn it.*"

Crane said, "Welcome to our world, Good."

Lear grunted and murmured, "Worked fine in the hallway."

"Yeah," Good agreed. "Because Vex was there with that lantern."

Deja would have very much liked to get more details on said lantern, but Ever cut in with a raspy, "Shh!"

They obeyed.

Swish...tap.

Swish...tap.

Swish...tap.

Good whispered, "What is that?"

"Jump rope." Crane jerked her head at Ever, adding, "And it can get pretty creative with it," while Ever nodded grimly.

The piano began to play, but not a song. Random notes tip-toed from right to left, high to low. Just like a child might do. The jump rope skipped closer.

Swish...tap.

Swish...tap.

A voice joined the dissonant band now, small and girlish. It rhymed to the rhythm of the jump rope. "*Miss Lulu had a baby, she named him Tiny Tim. She put him in the bathtub, to see if he could swim!*"

Swish...tap.

Swish...tap.

A sharp ache panged in Deja's abdomen; he gripped at his stomach. When he pulled his hand away, he smelled chalk. Tasted it.

Under his breath, Good demanded, "Vale? What is it?" while the ghost continued jump-roping and sing-songing.

Swish...tap.

Swish...tap.

"*The nanny called her papa to tattle on Lulu, and when she did her Papa took her to a padded room!*"

Swish...tap.

Swish...tap.

"*They zapped her on the tummy, they zapped her on the head. They zapped her 'til her hair fell out and then they zapped her dead—!*"

BUMMM! All the piano keys pounded at once.

From *above* them.

Crane yelled, "Move!" but she didn't need to. The agents had already begun scrambling away. All except one.

Deja stared in confusion at the chalkboard, overturned desks, and examination table on the other side of the room. A beak-masked technician pulled a small but powerful flashlight from his coat and pointed it at him. Blinding white light gave way to snow. The technician, chalkboard, and table were gone. A small child bundled up in wool darted past the agents, laughing. Deja followed him with his eyes to find a dark-haired woman kneeling in the snow beside a girl, showing her how to pack a snowball in red mittens. She looked up at Deja and grinned. That smiling family was replaced by a Christmas tree, marking hollow presents like a gravestone.

Good shouted, "Vale!"

Arms slipped around Deja's waist and dragged him away, just before the grand piano *crashed* in a mess of splintered black wood where they'd been. Good hauled Deja back toward the hall where the others had already retreated. The other agents were doing their best to conceal themselves behind the narrow bit of wall surrounding the doorframe.

Crane asked, "You good, Vale?"

"He's fine," Good said like he wasn't still holding Deja up.

Deja pulled himself away from the hand supporting his back. Even as he looked around to assure himself that he wasn't halluci-nating—wasn't *still* hallucinating—he said, "I'm fine."

Lear pointed to the balcony with a weapon that wasn't good for much else. "We need to get up there."

"Can't," Crane said. "They just closed in the tether field, and the only stairs to that area are outside it."

"Well," Deja said, rubbing his eyes, "there is an elevator over there and... that doesn't help us, never mind."

Your team needs you, Vale. Get your shit together.

Between rasping breaths, Ever managed, "Where's Vex?"

Good answered. "With the target. Ashe is assisting. Any word from Wren or Talin?"

"None," Crane said. "But the tether field feels weaker—"

"Yeah," Lear said, gesturing to his now-useless mortifier. "We'd noticed."

"*Meaning* we don't have much time," Crane continued. "This whole situation is full of unknowns."

"Should we just leave it here?" Lear suggested. "Neutralizing that ghost's not our mission, and this place isn't likely to have much in the way of Potential life showing up."

Crane shook her head. "We can't know that."

"A notice over there said outside visitors aren't allowed," Deja pointed out. "But if Psycholocks over there is throwing pianos? We shouldn't just leave it skipping around a fully-stocked old people home."

"I'm with Lear," Good said. "That's not our prerogative. Right now, *our* prerogative is getting Vale back on that train."

Deja scoffed. "But we can't just—"

"Does it look like it's interested in these people, Vale?" Good snapped.

"No," Deja said, "but I'm guessing the sound of that *fucking piano explosion* is gonna draw one or two people here!"

"Employees, you think?" Crane asked.

"It's night now," Deja said. "Maybe a few hang around, but a resident or two or *ten* is gonna come nosing around any second now. They may be on the old side, but they're not all *that fucking deaf.*"

"Well," Ever croaked, "we can't get up to it and we can't *shoot* at it. What are we meant to do exactly?"

They all looked at one another, silent.

Then, Deja asked, "Why hasn't it followed us over here? Doesn't strike me as *shy.*"

Crane perked up a bit. "You're right," she said. "Ever, have *you* seen it leave the piano room"—she plowed past Lear's murmured *ex-piano room* and continued—"because *I haven't.*"

Ever thought hard, head bowing. "No," she said, raising her head. "I haven't."

"So," Lear said, "you're saying it's almost like it's got its own tether field?"

"Maybe," Deja said. "If not that, something else restricting its movements. Three guesses *who.*" He took a bracing breath and straightened. "All right. I'm going to go over there and try someth—"

Good dragged Deja back down and growled, "The *fuck you are!*" just as Crane sighed, "I do hate it when you say that."

Deja yanked his arm free of Good's grip. "That ghost isn't a haunting. It's a *chess move*. We don't need to take it out if we can make it move where we need it—away from *here*."

Ever asked drily, "And what happened to protecting the non-deaf old people from flying pianos?"

"I don't think we need to worry about that," Deja said, ignoring Lear's grumbled, *I really wasn't*. "*Look*. Just give me one minute to try something, and if it doesn't work, it can't be any worse than hiding here until we either get lost to oblivion or rebound onto the train. Right?"

Silence.

All faces turned toward Crane. "Fine," she said over Good's spluttered protest. "One minute."

"Thanks, Crane," Deja said, straightening from his hiding place—again. Good's hand was still on his back. One sharp look, and that hand retreated like it had been burned.

Deja cleared his throat and stepped into the (aptly named) ex-piano room, adjusting his glasses. From above him came the *swish... tap... swish...tap* of the jumping rope. A nearby vase exploded in a burst of porcelain, water, and lilies.

Lucy was getting tetchy, all right. *But she listens to her papa.*

Deja made straight for the center of the room, carefully avoiding the broken bits of spirit-charged piano and shattered vase. He placed his hands on his hips and looked up at the balcony where Lucy was skipping rope.

Every inch of that ghost looked like an antique doll brought to life, from its plump cheeks and bouncing braids to its puffed-sleeve dress. But when it turned to skip rope in the other direction, there was no more cherubic face. Only charred flesh peeling back from shining, white bone. Little Lucy was utterly unfazed by the man standing on the floor beneath her. And why wouldn't it be? All it'd seen of Omega agents was how frustrated they got when they couldn't shoot something.

And how vulnerable they were to flying pianos.

It just kept singing its little rhyme to itself: "*Miss Lulu had a mommy, as pretty as can be. And when she yelled at Lulu, she hanged her from a tree!*"

Deja muttered, "The fuck is it with ghosts and *rhyming* these days?" while he braced himself to do something characteristically idiotic. The deep breath *in* he took felt like his own. The "*LUCY MARIE HILL!*" he shouted *out* did not.

The jump rope stopped *swish-tapping.*

"Get down from there, Lucy!" Deja pointed to the ground beside him. "*Now!*"

Lucy leaned over the balcony, braids and jump rope dangling over the rail. "Papa?"

"Papa means it, young lady!" Deja said. "Get down from there, and go back to your room this instant, or I will tie your jump rope into *knots*. You hear me?"

Lucy's bottom lip quivered tremulously. When Deja's brows went up, she whined, "But I—"

"Now!" Deja thrust a finger toward the D-wing. "Or no bedtime story!"

"But—"

Deja roared, "*NOW!*" It was probably just his imagination—or something worse—but he could have sworn he heard the rattle of shattered porcelain at his feet when he'd shouted that.

Lucy deflated. "Yes, papa." She huffed before bowing her head and marching herself back toward D-wing.

Deja watched her disappear into a vent and listened for the *swish-tap* of jump rope or a tell-tale giggle. Silence.

"*Papa.*"

Deja only just managed to not jump out of his uniform. Lucy was beside him, tugging at his sleeve. One of her eyes was nothing but a black hollow carved into skull. The other was green, round and pleading. Her little hand made a tiny, fretful gesture: *closer.* Something about the fear on her face made Deja lean closer. Lucy beckoned him again. Deja leaned even closer. He smelled buttercups.

And burning hair.

"*Papa*," Lucy warned, her whisper a crackle of static on his cheek. "These woods *eat men like you.*"

Before Deja could say anything, Lucy had skipped away and slipped into a vent behind the Christmas tree. Once she was gone—*really* gone—her absence wrought a change as palpable as a shift in air pressure after a storm.

Slowly, the other agents filtered into the room. Good kicked aside a bit of piano and moved beside him. "What the fuck was that, Vale?"

"*Effective*," Crane answered for Deja. Her voice sounded assured, but there was a definite wariness to her bearing—and the distance she kept from the Odd. She wasn't the only one. "All right, Good, you've got your orders. Take Ever with you. Lear, you're with me. I'm going to try and make contact with Wren and Talin. We may need you, Good, so once you've got these two back on the train, meet—"

"*Frank?*" a small voice called out from above them. One only Deja could hear.

Deja pulled off his glasses. He didn't learn more about the rendezvous. His attention was fixed squarely on the balcony. Little Edith, clad in a fluffy pink robe, stood on a chair behind the railing, smile wet and wide.

A thick red cord dangled from her neck.

"It's me, Frank!" Edith said, almost cheerful. "It's me! Your Edith!"

Then, she *jumped*.

Deja lunged forward but was soon pulled back by two pairs of hands.

Edith's instant death *cracked* like a bullwhip, splitting the air in two with the sound of it. The very heart of the building broke for her, and Deja fell, too—

"He's—!"

"*—I don't know.*"

"*What of the other one?*"

"*I don't know—*"

"—Vale!"

Deja was on his knees. He couldn't see anything but blinding white, but he could feel the cold press of tile through his pant legs. No, carpet. He shouldn't be feeling that. A hand squeezed his shoulder, another touched his chest. Then carefully, if a bit awkwardly, that hand replaced his glasses. Somebody pushed his hood up over his head, and the world no longer felt quite so broken. The floor no longer felt so real. Blinding white gave way to darkness.

"Can you stand?" Vex asked, voice soft and solid as a pearl in that comforting nothing.

Deja tried to speak and failed. He shook his head.

Vex barked out, "Ever!"

"I've got him, sir." Strong hands slipped beneath Deja's arms and lifted him up. Her augur burned white-hot against his back even through two layers of leather. Ever felt it too and she nearly dropped him. "No, I got him, sir," Ever insisted, lifting him into her arms like a hapless groom.

Deja felt himself rising higher and higher—

"—*there is only one place he can be.*"

"*Impossible.*"

"*No—*"

Deja jerked himself upward to brace against the long, nonexistent fall. Everything was blurry, but he knew it was Ever above him. She'd just laid him down upon the bench. They were on the train now and Vex was speaking.

"Wait for me here, all of you. I will retrieve the others."

Several agents responded at once with protests before cutting themselves off. And when Deja finally looked up at the agent inquisitor, he wondered if the real reason Ever had dropped him onto the bench hadn't been *shock.*

Vex stared them all down with his one remaining eye and said, "That is an *order*."

The last thing Deja saw was Vex disappearing beneath his hood before he, too, sank back into blackness.

THE SICKLY SWEET stench of resin and herbs.

Light, brighter than bright.

A voice as sharp as its beak demands, "What happened here?"

Another voice. Softer. Hurried. *Scared.* "I don't know."

Rustling fabric. That sharp voice returns. "What of the other one?"

The soft voice takes on a hard edge, but only just. "I *don't know*."

"What do you mean you *don't know*?"

A third voice is steady and calm but it cleaves the air into silence. "She means what she says, technician. Leave her be."

A quiet, high-pitched whisper. Distant chirping birds muffled by dense leaves. A pair of voices emerge from the flock in the brush. "If he was not left behind," they say in perfect sync, "and he was not retrieved, there is only one place he *can* be."

Silence, thick and still. The third voice is a stone. It drops into that pooling silence. "Impossible."

A bare palm on his forehead. A mother checking for fever.

"No," it says. "Not impossible. Not for him."

He tries to open his eyes to see a familiar face, but there is nothing but a shape eclipsing burning light. The shape retreats, and he wants to call out to it but he can't move.

Six gray figures move in pairs, always in pairs. They form a wall around him. He wants to leave. To run. But he can't.

He can't walk through walls.

"Is he going to be all right?" the soft voice asks.

"Yes," another voice says, also soft. "He's been through worse."

Polyester scratched against Deja's cheek, and reality bled back into focus. He cracked one eye open.

Crane sat across from him, watching him carefully in turn as she swayed with the gentle motion of the train. "He's up."

Deja only noticed the hand on his shoulder when it pulled away.

"Vale?" Wren asked from above him. "You with us?"

Deja took in a deep breath. He winced at the invisible fist clenching his throat, and just managed a barely there nod. He pushed himself onto his elbows.

Wren sighed her relief. "See? Told you he's been through worse."

Deja looked around, blinking blearily. Good was seated at his feet, Wren at his head. Lear was at the other end of the car, exchanging hushed words with Ever as he helped apply Q-salve to her strangled throat.

The train groaned around them. Shadows shifted beyond the windows. They were moving... and no one else was there.

Deja went stiff. He just got out a rasping, "Where's Vex?" before his throat sprang back like an overextended rubber band.

"He went back for Ashe and Talin," Crane said. "Said another train was coming for him."

Deja stared at her, silent.

"We know," Wren said. "But there's nothing we can do now but get you and Ever to Osiris and—"

"No," Deja said past the strain. "I'm fine. Just exhausted. I'd rather just go home." He turned away from Crane's perplexed face to find Good staring at him, eyes narrowed.

Wren said, "But Vale, we don't know what happened to you in—"

Good cut in, "Vex left Vale to me. I'll get him where he needs to go." The train passed through a mountain, and they fell into darkness before emerging amidst clean steel and neat plastic leather. A mechanical bird chirped overhead.

"All right, Good," Crane said. "You take care of Vale. I'll... I'll wait at the station for Vex. Wren? Can you—"

"Yes," Wren said. "I'll see to the rest." Her hand pressed against Deja's forehead, gently guiding him back down against the now-smooth cushion.

Deja closed his eyes. Veins of light pulsed in the darkness. He smelled chalk. He tasted medicine—no, marshmallows melting into hot cocoa. A child laughed. He read the writing on the wall and knew it was the last time he ever would. He was too broken, too tired to say goodbye, when one voice asked, *"Are you there?"* just as another voice answered, *"Not for him."*

"IF YOU CAN'T WALK," Good said, "I am carrying you to Osiris."

Deja managed to push himself to a sit. The compartment had emptied of all but his own pathetic, frail self, and Good's impatient sighs. "I just need a minute," he whispered, wincing at the glare of Good's unmasked and resplendent resting bitch face.

"Train won't wait forever," Good said.

The traitorous thing agreed with low groan that rumbled against Deja's back.

"I *know*." Deja took a deep breath and stood. A cautious step... then another... and another. "See?" he said with only the afterimage of humor. "One foot in front of the other. Just how I remember it."

"Right," Good said flatly. "Now see how you do down stairs."

"Stairs. No problem."

Stairs were a problem, but not one that couldn't be remedied with Crane's quick reflexes steadying his fall. She stood on the platform and held Deja's arm as he walked down. "You good?"

Above him, Good answered, "Doubtful."

"You're sure you've got it?" Crane asked, and not of Deja.

"I've got it covered." Good gripped Deja by the upper arm and guided him forward only to jerk him back when he stopped walking—which was fine by Deja. The wash of green steam rolling over his feet made him feel worlds more stable on them. "You'll let me know when he gets back?" Good asked Crane quietly.

Crane nodded. "I will."

"Thanks," Good said and proceeded to march Deja onward.

The staircase to the massive atrium of headquarters had never looked so grand, but Deja made it to the top. More out of spite for gravity and Good than anything else. His shins wobbled on the last ten, but he climbed them with as much dignity as he could muster (given another agent was gripping his arm like a pissy parent escorting him to his *other* parent so he could tell them just what horrible thing he'd done in person).

As they moved, Deja looked up at the ceiling where silver-painted constellations glinted beyond the haze of the steam constantly circulated by trains. They passed through the stone archway with its carved *MORS AEQUAT*, and the ceiling became polished marble. His stomach somersaulted—he'd nearly missed a step. The hand on his arm tightened. Amazing how his arm hadn't broken off as a defensive measure like a newt's tail, really.

Good guided Deja past a flock of constables. Again, his grip tightened. Whether the numbness of Deja's arm was from the vise on his bicep or something else, he didn't care to suss out. He glanced over his shoulder at the mountain of steps he'd just scaled on the off-chance he'd catch a billowing gray coat or twitching mustache. Nothing. Just the empty maw opening up to the trains below.

Deja stopped. He had to wait. They, all of them, had to wait. Vex had lost an eye. That shouldn't be possible. Not impossible in the way a ball falling up the stairs was, but in the way the sundering of an anchoring, beloved landmark shouldn't be possible. It shouldn't be *allowed*.

Good kept Deja moving. It wasn't until he dragged him through the atrium to the front doors, down the spilling black steps, past the Reaper statue, and through the archway beyond that Deja realized they weren't heading to Osiris at all. Before Deja could even open his mouth, Good answered the question. "I told you if you couldn't walk, I'd take you to Osiris."

A surprised, "Oh," was all Deja managed.

Good shot him a sidelong look. "You wanted to go to your apartment, yes?"

"Yes," Deja said with something like confidence. "I do." An awkward pause. "Thanks."

Good didn't respond beyond a shake of his head and an almost silently murmured, "Such a pain in the ass." Suddenly, his head perked like a dog who'd heard a delivery truck pull into the driveway. He released Deja's arm and snapped to attention.

Chief Inquisitor Hiero was striding through the crowd of constables, straight for them. Her movements were so sharp and sure, Deja was compelled to check for ice skates. He did.

No ice, no skates.

"Agents," Hiero said.

Good inclined his head. "Chief Inquisitor."

Keen eyes drifted to Deja and he cleared his throat to offer a reasonably dignified, "Chief Inquisitor."

Hiero's attention shifted back and forth before settling on Good. "Back from a mission?"

"Not as such, no," Good explained with just a hint of world-weariness. "Field test."

"Field test?" Hiero echoed, one brow rising in a silent order.

Out of the corner of his eye, Deja just caught the slightest glance from Good in his own direction. But what Good said was, "Just keeping on top of the mortifier issue." And he said this with the tone of a person lying in front of an uncooperative dog about going to the park when *really* they were going to the vet.

And Good was speaking to the vet.

"I see," Hiero said, straightening. "I trust you will be sharing any results from this field test."

"Of course, sir," Good assured her. "I'll be sure to forward you a copy of my report once it's completed."

"Very good, Agent." With a last sharp look Deja's way, Hiero turned on her heel and strode off. Four of the constables who'd just been awkwardly milling about followed her in something like formation.

Deja stared after them until he was yanked away by Good yet again.

"Move," Good ordered in a low voice.

Deja did. He moved all the way back to the border between smooth pavement and cobbled stone that marked the entrance to his building.

When Deja hesitated at the door, Good demanded, "What?"

"Will you chime me when he gets back?"

Good countered, "If I do, will you get some *actual fucking rest?*"

Deja nodded.

"Do that then." And with that, Good turned on his heel and strode off toward headquarters.

Deja called out, "So you'll—"

Good didn't bother to turn around or slow his pace as he called back, "*Yes!*"

"*Great,*" Deja mouthed. Something moved in the alley to the Floating District.

It was Jamais. He stood in the alleyway, barely visible through the fog-filtered gaslight. A sharp pain stabbed Deja's navel, and he stumbled sideways into the brick wall. Jamais's expression wasn't clear, but Deja could see him nodding his head up toward Deja's apartment. Deja opened and closed his mouth a few times. His mind settled on a word, but the rest of him was too tired to share it with the class.

Then, Jamais jerked his chin again. *This* time, indicating the direction Good had gone off to.

Deja startled when Jamais's voice came from behind him. "Good *Reaper,* you are an absolute disaster," Jamais grumbled as he grabbed Deja by the shoulder.

Deja blinked away his surprise and blinked *Jamais* away, too. It was *Good* grumbling at him now. *Good* steering Deja away from the wall and into the building. *Good* pushing him up the stairs and into his apartment. *Good* force-marching him to his bed.

The mattress creaked when Deja plopped onto the edge. Good began bustling around the place, muttering to himself about "Insane fucking idiot," and "too fucking qualified for this shit," and "just restocked those fucking bandages, how the hells have you already used half of them," and "swallow a fucking mortifier blast, I swear," but Deja wasn't paying attention. His focus was entirely on the small window beside his bed and the rabbit standing on the street below, looking up at him.

Jamais waved.

Deja managed a feeble wave back.

"What in seven hells are you waving at?" Good demanded, already nudging Deja aside to look. Before Deja could attempt to explain the rabbit outside his building, Good grumbled, "Great. Like I wasn't already regretting not dumping your ass at Osiris." He shoved an uncorked bottle of aether at Deja and ordered, "Drink that. *Now.*" Deja sighed took a small sip as he watched Good pull out his own chiming augur. Once open, green light rippled over Good's hardening face. The augur snapped shut and Good's eyes drifted to Deja's. "You. Stay. *Rest.* That is an order. Got it?"

Deja nodded again. He realized Good wasn't moving and looked up to see a grimace meeting him.

"This is usually about when you'd start making stupid puns," Good said.

Deja didn't respond.

"Vale?"

Still no response.

Good hesitated, then left Deja to his rest.

Once Good reached the door, Deja called out to him in a rasping voice, "Hey, Good?"

Good turned.

"Thanks. For saving me from the flying piano." With a ghosting smile, Deja added, "I know music's not your *forte.*"

Good stared at him. "Was that a pun? Your face looks like it made a pun."

Deja shrugged. Not his best, but yes, puns were made.

"Stay here. Rest," Good said. The door clicked shut after him.

Deja turned back to the window. Nothing there but rolling green fog. He didn't rest. He stood and stumbled his dream–like way to the bathroom, shrugging out of his jacket and dropping it behind him.

It landed with a sound it shouldn't have made. He picked it back up, bunching it in his hands until he felt something in each pocket. In the left, was the vial Vex had given them. He'd never used it. He'd never even thought to use it. In the right pocket was the broken slate he'd found by the gate that led to the forest. The chalk *Goodbye* was just as clear as it had been when he'd first found it beneath the snow. He left both where he'd found them and let his uniform fall again. The mirror got only a fleeting glance while he tugged off his gloves and tossed them to the floor with a whisper of silk. There went his shirt, too.

The earlier shame burnt into him by Reve's questioning returned, prickling along his shoulders. He was afraid to look himself in the eye. A child caught in a lie by a parent. But in keeping his gaze downward, he spotted something odd. He placed a hand to the skin beneath his own navel. The black sigil that had always been there had expanded, and not for the first time. He'd woken up in Osiris months ago with an added ring of unintelligible markings interweaving with the one he'd always known. His eyes followed the marks up. It didn't just ring his navel anymore. Now, the sigil stretched up his abdomen toward his sternum, like a tree limb just beginning to branch out. Or a skeletal arm with only the barest notion of a hand.

A hand trying and failing to reach for *him*.

Deja placed his own hand over the highest point of the sigil, just where Reve had stabbed him with the chalk. He stared at the body that no longer felt like his own. *What did she do to me?* asked a mind that no longer felt like his own.

In a way, it never really had.

An incoming train sent a fresh wave of green steam rolling over the platform. Deja leaned against the wall, arms folded across his chest as he awaited orders to get on a train himself. Head Agent Ivy and Lear were some distance away, speaking in hushed tones. Without trying to, Deja caught the odd snip of conversation.

"—irregular, is my point—"

"—mix-up is all—"

"—theirs? Or *ours*?"

A metallic *snap*. Thorne rocked back on her heels while opening and closing her augur. The impatient groan didn't quite make it out but was very much evident.

"You're gonna break that thing," Deja warned.

Thorne's face pivoted toward him. She stared him down and closed her augur with a pointed *snap*. "So sorry, *Agent Good*," she said and Deja rolled his eyes. "How *is* Mr. Fancy-Pants Head Agent doing, by the way?"

Deja gave her a puzzled look. "Why would *I* know?"

"Know what?" Vyne asked, smoothing out her uniform as she approached. Once she reached them, she began untying and retying her long, black hair.

Thorne told her, "How Good's doing as head agent."

Vyne made a silent *ah* of understanding. "And how is he doing?" she asked, very much directed to Deja.

Deja looked between his teammates and demanded, "Why does everybody think I would know?" This garnered little response beyond a shared look between Thorne and Vyne. "I don't know," he said tartly. "He's Hart's problem now."

"So that's his team's Odd, then?" Vyne asked. "Wonder whose idea that was."

"See?" Thorne said, bumping her shoulder against Deja's. "You *do* know things."

Deja stared at her, mouth pressed to a thin line.

Vyne looked up at the ceiling, eyeing the silver inlaid constellations thoughtfully. "It's an interesting choice. I bet it could work well. He is a very good shot and has always been very calculating with his tactics. Hart's Oddity is well suited to that, I should think."

"What's she do again?" Thorne asked. Again, this was very much directed to Deja.

Deja gestured to Vyne and said, "Why are you asking *me*? She clearly knows!"

"Because you're the expert? *Obviously?*"

Vyne shook her head in reluctant amusement and told her, "She lures in ghosts. Makes herself an irresistible target and draws them out."

"Really," Thorne said, voice going quiet. "So, if a bunch of ghosts are hiding in the air ducts or something she can just..." she trailed off with an impressed laugh. "Wow. That is *way* more useful than some people I could mention." When Deja glared sideways at her, she only added, "Bet she actually follows orders, too."

Deja deadpanned, "Funny."

"Oh, come now," Vyne soothed. "Vale is plenty useful." Thorne hummed in mock-interest, and Vyne elaborated, "He sees things. He is... *observant.* He can also *hear* things. And... *listen* to them," she finished delicately.

Deja bit back a laugh. He began to slouch against the wall but straightened once he spotted Head Agent Ivy approaching. Her pale eyes skipped over Lear who was checking his mortifier a few yards away, then narrowed when they landed on the other three agents. "Where's Wren?" she asked.

"Where *is* Wren?" Deja echoed. He ignored Thorne's snort and her muttered, "Oh, yes, *very observant,*" and pushed away from the wall to look around the station.

Past the green steam and occasional conductor, he spotted the team of agents clustered on the opposite platform. Odd. He didn't think they'd resumed deploying multiple teams at once. There were a few agents he recognized and one he knew well: his fellow Odd, Omen. One of Omen's hands was running over his closely cropped black hair, the other was in his pocket. Deja couldn't see it, but he knew Omen was fiddling with the piece of chalk he always carried. Omen noticed the gaze and gave Deja a small smile that lit up his dark gray face before turning back to his conversation with his own head agent.

Wren wasn't there either.

A *tap, tap* on his arm.

Ivy nodded to Wren, who was tapping Deja's shoulder. "We're all here," she barked. "Let's move out!"

Tap.

Deja's eyes blinked open only a moment before closing again.

Tap.

"Go away..." he groaned, burying his face back into the pillow in the hopes he might accomplish the same depth of unconsciousness if he could only be quick enough. His body sank and—

Tap.

Deja levered up and blew out a breath to budge the hair from his face. It didn't work.

Tap tap.

Bleary eyes shifted toward the source of the sound. The window. But on the way there, they landed on the augur on his nightstand. Their last mission dropped upon his consciousness in one heavy load and he scrambled to the window. An agent was down there. Even masked, Deja instantly recognized Wren. He opened the window and stuck his head outside—

A pebble hit him in the forehead with another little *tap.* "Ow."

"Hey!" Wren stage-whispered.

"I have a door, Wren! The fuck are you doing out there?"

Wren took a quick step back. "What are *you* doing in *there?*"

"I was in my bed, *sleeping.*"

Wren stared up at him a while. "What, really? *Why?*"

"Because I—I don't know," Deja said quickly. "What is it?" Orders of ultimate secrecy kept him from calling out the question he really needed answered: *Have you heard from Vex?*

Wren didn't answer anyway.

"Just get up here."

Wren took a step back. "Or, you could come down here."

"You can manage stairs better than me right now," Deja said and closed the window. A glance at his augur told him he hadn't missed any chimes. *Still?* For a while now, they'd believed interworldly communications to have been potentially compromised. Then Desert intraworldly communications. Had intraworldly communication within the *Hereafter itself* become suspect, too? He didn't know. He didn't like not knowing.

But not enough to put on actual pants. Not when every step he took felt like daring his knees not to buckle, or his vision not to black out. That unsteadiness was only marginally better than yesterday. Deja had been at home for three days, as Good had ordered. Rested, as ordered. He'd sleep. He'd wake. He'd drink his coffee-turned-tea until the tea turned back to coffee. He'd look out the window and watch the moon. He'd think about an old man peeling back to reveal a helpless child in the snowy night. Of Edith's kind face and blank eyes. The *snap* of noose and neck. The whisper of a murderous child. The black hole where Vex's eye had been. The warning Reve had sent him off with after receiving a warning of her own from letters that shouldn't have *been.* The empty desks in the Warren. And then he'd just sit. Not even waiting anymore.

The possibility that Deja might be finally about to learn of Vex's fate wasn't enough to stop his morning dance. This time, though, it didn't sweep him up. He *took* it up. Some people laughed to keep from crying. Deja was lighting the burner beneath his kettle and washing the dark ring from yesterday's mug to keep from screaming. He scrubbed at a stain that had never come out before and wouldn't start now, counting the steps Wren may or may not be taking from the street to his apartment. *Seven steps to the stairs: one, two, three, four, five, six, seven.* Made himself a cup of coffee fated to become tea. *Thirteen stairs to the first landing: one, two, three*—his mind followed her up the stairs as his body sat on the couch to look out the window. Clouds began swirling away from the moon like a great ball of yarn coming unwound, and something occurred to him for the first time. Maybe it had been Wren's interruption that did it.

The impossible OWL on Reve's door had warned Deja to mind her advice.

And Vex had never warned him *not* to.

Why not? Vex knew Reve had spoken to Deja at length. Did the man just trust Deja that implicitly? If he did, why was Agent Good still tasked with Deja's supervision? Surely, it couldn't be *Reve* that Vex trusted. During the brief, when Deja had demanded to know just why Vex seemed to think Reve wouldn't hurt *him* if she were such a danger to agents, Vex's answer had hardly inspired confidence:

"Nothing," he'd said. *"But I have hope."*

At the time, Deja'd been too involved to appreciate just how *deeply* unsettling that response had been. But now he could—as well as the reason for his disquiet. It was because when Vex had said it, the look on his face was not that of an Omega commander, confident in his own abilities and that of his team.

It was the face of a terrified, vulnerable woman surrendering herself to prayer in the face of a ghost.

A widow desperate to believe the lie that her dead husband was still there for her.

An old man reaching for his lost loves, his lost youth in a snowy forest.

A child.

It was a face Deja only ever saw on the *living.*

Three quiet knocks on the door. Deja took a sip of his tea before leaving it behind to open the door to someone who'd never been there before.

Wren didn't come in.

"Wren...?"

Wren took a deep, bracing breath... and stepped inside.

Deja closed the door, asking "How many doors did you have to knock on before you found mine?"

Wren blinked at him. "None...?" Once inside, she had eyes for anything but Deja. She stared at the couch first—for a long time, too. Then her eyes shifted to the half-drunk mug on the table. It smiled at her.

"Well? Have you heard anything about Vex?"

"No," Wren said. "Sorry."

"Oh." Deja hesitated. "Is, um... is everything all right?" *Stupid question.* "Did you need me for something?"

Wren managed to tear her attention away from the drink. "No," she said, only for her eyes to drift away once more. They skipped over the kitchen like a stone over a calm lake before landing back in that mug. Deja imagined the splashing sound her heavy gaze might make in a world governed by different metaphysics than theirs.

"Did you *want* a cup?" Deja asked, and Wren turned sharply toward him.

"What?"

"A cup of coffee. Did you want one? Are you *sure* you're all right?"

"I... yes," Wren said, unconvincingly.

"*Yes,* you're all right, or *yes* to the coffee?"

"Um..." Wren glanced back toward the mug. It was still smiling.

"Let's start with the latter and work back from there?"

Deja gave her a single nod and moved to the kitchen. "You got it."

Five minutes later, Wren was seated on his couch, staring into her very own mug of black coffee. Or possibly black tea. Deja could make no promises in that department. He sipped his own now-lukewarm drink, debating if he ought to leave Wren to her beverage-induced existential crisis and nuke it in the microwave. Seeing as he only had a microwave half the time these days, he just took another middling sip.

The steam twirling from Wren's chipped mug was fading fast, too. She looked up at Deja, watching him drink a few moments like a stray dog unsure if the food she was being offered was really safe. He didn't think asking just what had Wren so nervous—or *here*—would get him answers any faster. So, he said nothing, only waited for Wren to finally pick up her coffee and—

"Wren?" Deja asked.

Wren was frozen, staring down into her mug with wide eyes, their fear reflected in rippling black.

Deja's brow pinched. "Is it okay?"

"Fine," Wren said, sounding anything but.

Deja relaxed a bit when she placed her lips to the mug. They sat in silence a while. Every now and again, Wren would shake her head in discomfort or disbelief or both. Outside the window, the clouds rolled across the black light of the moon, as usual.

Once Deja's own drink hit bottom, he ventured, "Did something happen?"

Wren's mouth twisted. "Not sure myself. Not sure why I'm here either, really. Guess I was just curious."

"Right." Everybody was curious about him these days. "You've never been here before, have you?"

"No. Has anyone else?" When Deja nodded, Wren prompted softly, "Thorne?" and mirrored Deja's answering nod.

"And Good." Deja'd expected a surprised look, but what he got was another *that makes sense* sort of nod. He put down his mug. "Look, Wren. Not like this isn't fun and all, but I'm not exactly fit for company right now."

There was no wryness or humor on Wren's face when she looked at him, gaze steady. "I wanted to know what you remember."

Deja gave her an odd look. "About what?"

"The last mission. When we—when we lost—"

"I told you," Deja whispered. "It's not much."

"Try. *Please*, try."

"I don't think that's how it works, Wren."

"But you can do *so many things*!" Wren said, gesturing to her mug. "So many things that shouldn't be possible—things that don't work that way, but you *make* them work that way."

"Yeah, well," Deja said, slumping back into his seat. "Sometimes I wonder if that's not *why* I can't remember."

Wren looked taken aback at that. "What does that mean?"

"I don't know," Deja said with a weak shrug. "Just a feeling more than anything. I don't have much in the way of cogent theories, just, well, *feelings*. Moods, maybe."

"Then what's your feeling?"

Wren looked so sincere when she asked that Deja didn't know if he'd be able to forgive himself if he didn't try. He looked at her gloved hand resting against the back of the couch. "How's the hand?"

Wren's eyes shifted to her hand, too. She raised it, turning it this way and that like she was grading a diamond in the light. "These two fingers"—she wiggled her pinky and ring finger—"are gone. They fixed me up with a prosthetic, which is nice. Having to stuff the gloves was a bit annoying."

Except, they shouldn't have had to. Osiris technicians had regrown lost limbs plenty of times, though some took longer than others. Why was this any different? Deja cloaked his unease with a one-sided smile and said, "Probably less annoying than having empty-glove-fingers flapping around, though."

"You're not wrong," Wren said wryly. She gave Deja's shoulder a poke with a real finger then replaced her hand on the back of the couch.

Deja sighed his surrender. "Okay, just... promise me you won't think I'm losing my mind." He snorted a laugh and muttered, "I can only handle so many people waltzing out of this apartment thinking I'm absolutely nuts."

"I promise not to think you're any crazier than usual," Wren assured him.

"Gee, thanks." Deja took a deep breath. "I remember being summoned for a mission... I remember waking up in Osiris after. And I remember—or, I think I might remember—scattered pieces between those two things, but only after the fact. I remember remembering it."

"I don't understand."

Deja gave her a pointed look and raised his mug. *Join the club.* When Wren's expectant silence only persisted, Deja tried, "Okay, well, you know how you remember yesterday?"

"Sure."

"And if you think real hard about how you remember yesterday *today*, then *tomorrow* you can remember remembering yesterday. Or remember *remembering* the day before yesterday, I guess."

Wren stared at him, brow furrowed as she tried to follow along. "Okay...."

"But maybe something happens. Like, I don't know, you hit your head. So you forget the day before yesterday. But you remember *yesterday*. And *yesterday*, you remembered the day *before* yesterday."

"So I'd remember remembering it? I suppose I don't understand the difference."

"Feeling," Deja said. "Detail. The emotion of it. The smells. Sensations. Anything you didn't think to consciously note yesterday. Like, say yesterday you only thought to yourself, 'I went to Omega Headquarters for a mission.'"

"Then that would be all I remember," Wren said, nodding slowly.

"The fact that I went. *In theory*."

"Right. You wouldn't remember how the clouds looked, or who you might've run into in the elevator, or what the mission was even for. But you'd know you had one."

"So, you remember remembering?" Wren asked. "You remember remembering you, what, had a mission?"

"Well, yeah. But it's less that than..." Deja trailed off and looked at his own hand and the scar on his palm. The shiny patches of life-burn had since faded, but the scar might never. Like Wren's missing digits, it should have been something Osiris technicians could fix. But they didn't.

Wren was staring at it too. When she realized Deja'd noticed, she cleared her throat and gentled him back. "What is it you remember remembering?"

"The pain," Deja said. "The grief. I remember remembering the pain and the grief."

Wren's face flickered. "But you don't remember what *caused* the pain. You don't remember anyone dying or seeing—" A shaky breath. "Seeing them die."

"No. There's just the pain. Everything else is... *gray*." Deja scoffed and murmured, "Nothing I'm not used to," before taking a sip of tepid tea.

"The pain? Or the gray?"

"Both, I guess. Suppose I meant the gray, though." Deja huffed a hollow laugh. "You know, it's funny? I was talking to Izik a little while back about training. How we got sent out into the Gray to prepare us for the Desert. Only, I never really had a problem with it the way Good and everybody else did." A small shrug. "Guess it didn't really occur to me just why that was until now."

It sounded like Wren didn't really want to know, even as she said, "Tell me why."

"Well, the Gray is where they send us to prepare for that feeling the Desert gives us, right? The feeling we don't belong— that the world doesn't want us there." Deja gave Wren a wan smile and admitted, "Thing is, I never really needed the practice, did I? Being, well, *me* and everything. Only now it's *all* the time that I feel that way. Pretty sure I didn't before, but... maybe I did and just didn't realize it? Either way, everything now's just..." he hesitated before finishing weakly, "gray."

Wren sank back into the couch with a quiet, "Oh." They sat like that a while, the black light of the moon glinting off Wren's pale hair. At last, she placed her mug down on the table and said, "I'm sorry."

Deja frowned. "For what?"

"For saying you were lucky before," Wren said. "For not remembering."

Deja smiled half-heartedly at her. "Funny you should say that, because *I don't think I disagree anymore.*"

"I see...." Wren stood and straightened her jacket. "Thank you for this." She made to leave but stopped halfway to the door and turned back. "You know what? Maybe everything *is* pain and gray. But that's all right. Because you're *you*. And you're not like the rest of us. *You* can bear it."

"Yeah?" Deja asked grimly. "And why's that?"

Wren opened the door and gifted him a brief, flickering smile. "Because, Vale, you're just *odd* like that." A quick farewell nod. "See you."

"See you," Deja said to the closing door. He placed his mug back on the table. Wren's cup was completely full. Probably hadn't taken a single sip. When picked up, the coffee's black surface trembled with distant accusations. Each one felt far warmer, far realer than the untouched, tepid drink cradled in his hands. *What other hungers do you chase in that broken shadow world?* Deja turned back to his little window, alone again. He reached out to the glass and traced over the condensation–blurred face he found there: two dots for eyes and a mouth that couldn't be bothered to frown. He stared at it. It stared back. He let out a sigh that expanded the fog canvas, then choked it off, unfinished.

That breath had revealed a clumsy but distinct word, probably traced by a finger: *Mind*. Deja took another deep breath and let it out slowly to reveal the rest of the message. As he read the impossible words for the second time, he could have sworn he felt another breath ghosting along his cheek, warm with the whisper of shame:

MIND HER ADVICE.

Impossible words had just bled through the Hereafter's walls. That is, if they were even there at all.

Stay out of Osiris.

Never give in to forgetting.

Trust no one.

Least of all yourself.

THE SARATOGA SPIRITUALIST SOCIETY

AN ANTHOLOGY OF PRIMARY SOURCES

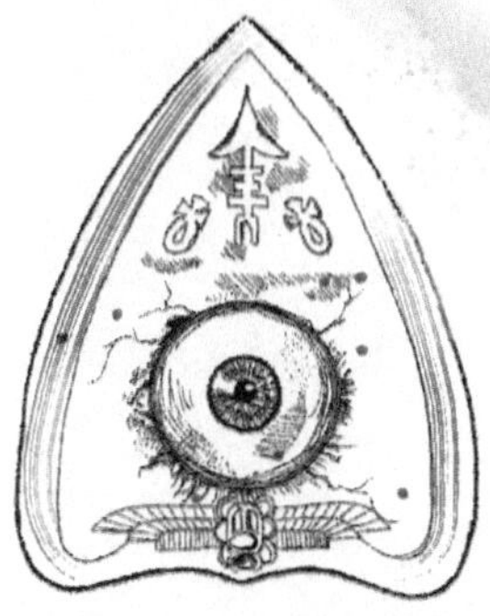

MORS AEQUAT

The last of several fragments composed by Ursula during the Davis Holmes' Saratoga Period. Like the others, it is impossible to distinguish whether this was part of a letter or mere reflection meant for Ursula's eyes alone. Given its contents, it can reasonably be placed between October 23rd 1877 and October 1st 1878, the date of Ursula's confinement.

... that woman's horrible, clouded eyes watch me from the fireplaces...

A NOTE FROM THE AUTHOR

If you enjoyed this book, please consider
tossing the author a bone (ha) by reviewing it online—maybe even find some
opportunities to harrass people in your immediate vicinity about it (e.g. elevators,
busses, coffee shops, work, phone solicitations for donations, ambulance rides,
waiting rooms, funerals, etc.).

R.I.P. (Read In Peace)

P.S. But for Reapers' sake, harrass them *gently*, please.

P.P.S. And maybe wait for the END of the funeral...?

P.P.P.S. Like, after the *body's* not there anymore, but the *snacks* still
are.

P.P.P.P.S. To reiterate: Snacks? Yes. Corpses? No. Cremains? Um...
maybe...?

P.P.P.P.P.S. *READ THE ROOM* is what I'm saying.

P.P.P.P.P.P.S. WAKE! *That's* what that's called! Harrass people at the
wake.

P.P.P.P.P.P.P.S. But *gently*, please.

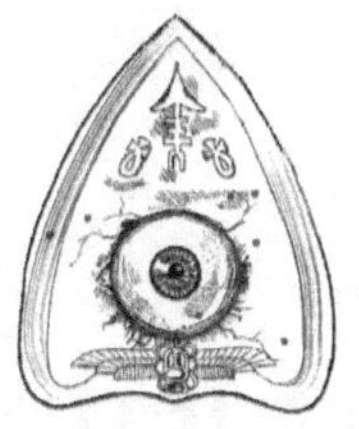

ABOUT THE AUTHOR

ELIJAH B. WILDER writes things—mostly stuff like this. Otherwise, he's wandering around cemeteries at the crack of dawn in search of mushrooms and answering awkward questions from concerned locals. Then he's asking the caffeine-deprived officer 'what he looks so *grave* for,' and digging himself deeper until he awkwardly blurts out, "I'm conducting an ecological survey of residual arsenic from 19th-century burial sites!" which, while not wholly *un*true, is also a lie, and this not-wholly-untrue lie lands him in a city planning meeting in a capacity he is in no way qualified for: professionally or spiritually. As you may have gathered, he's got a great deal of all-too-specific knowledge on Victorian death practices and mycology, and makes it everybody else's problem. His parents would like him to let you know that he has a Ph.D. in philosophy, but the truth is he spends very little time philosophizing, and way more time begging his dog to please, *please* just come inside, and trying to remember what the hell he came downstairs for anyway.

If *you* know what the hell he came downstairs for, please contact him at ElijahBWilder.com.

Acknowledgments

IT TOOK A GREAT DEAL of support (i.e., loving goading) to convince me that I had any business *writing* let alone publishing my stories—I mean, the NERVE of me.

My first readers were those distinguished few whose taste, judgment, and friendship I had enough faith in to entrust them with my naked heart in prose form: Mel and Jessica. Thank you, Mel, for supporting my work at every angle—from the encouragement to begin, to the laptop with which that final period was typed (or was it an ellipsis...). Jessica, my favorite sister, gets the bonus epithet of "first fan"—thank you.

Many thanks to my parents, Sean and Nancy, for raising me into the sort of person who ponders obsessively over puns and death (and for supporting me despite having raised me into the sort of person who ponders obsessively over puns and death).

Grātiās vōbīs agō to Alissa Corsi—my friend, copyeditor, and emotional-support grammarian—for being genuinely so damned good at her work (even if she is biased against italics—allegedly); Sophie, my one-bird Greek chorus *slash* parrot sensitivity reader; the kind staff of Mrs. London's who kept me supplied in dark roast coffee with oat milk, and treehugger cookies. I loved the unliving fuck out of every one of those cute little doilies. So did Sophie.

A final, resting thanks to my Nanabooboo
for looking *so proud*—**R.I.P.**